THE ALCHEMY OF MOONLIGHT

DAVID FERRARO

THE
ALCHEMY OF
MOONLIGHT

PAGE STREET YA

PAGE STREET
PUBLISHING CO.

First published in 2023 by
Page Street Publishing Co.
27 Congress Street, Suite 1511
Salem, MA 01970
www.pagestreetpublishing.com

Distributed by Macmillan, sales in Canada by The Canadian Manda Group.

27   26   25   24   23   1   2   3   4   5

ISBN-13: 978-1-64567-972-1
ISBN-10: 1-64567-972-1
Library of Congress Control Number: 2022949684

Cover and book design by Rosie Stewart for Page Street Publishing Co.
Cover Illustration © C.J. Merwild

Printed and bound in the United States

For Patrick.

Part
One

ONE

I'd never seen a dead body before. Or rather, I'd never seen *part* of a dead body. I was staring at a severed hand. It lay just off the footpath like an apparition. It didn't belong on the sunny grass, a perversion of the peace of the otherwise tranquil summer afternoon. Birds were chirping overhead, unperturbed by the sickening sight, as the sun warmed my skin.

Digging my kerchief out of my pocket, I dabbed at the beads of sweat dotting my forehead. It had already been a long day, and this discovery was sure to pose additional obstacles. It was bad enough that I was new to this whole servant thing. I was used to being waited on hand and foot, not being the one *doing* the waiting. I didn't need anything mucking up my day, not with how slow I was at performing menial tasks normally. But I figured I might as well resign myself to this unpleasant task. Then I could get back to finishing my actual chores. I groaned internally as I imagined how late into the evening I may have to work to catch up.

I glanced up the path toward the stables. The forest blocked most of the view of Château le Blanc, but I caught a glimpse of a chimney through the dense branches. It was reassuring that I was nearly there.

I turned my eyes back toward the unnerving sight of the severed hand. It wasn't so much severed as torn. There was no clean cut but instead jagged, loose flaps of skin clinging to a bluish wrist, two bones jutting out, as if snapped like matchsticks.

I swallowed past the bile rising in my throat. There was little blood, thankfully, just a small pool, long since cooled and congealed beneath the wrist.

Someone would have to see this. It would be unpleasant, but it would be easier if I brought it to the house, and a message was dispatched to the gendarmerie in town. I looked down at my kerchief, grimacing as I decided I would have to carry the limb wrapped in the cloth to transport it. The kerchief would be ruined, of course, but it couldn't be helped.

Bending over, I held my breath as I drew closer to the hand, its fingers lifted and curled into the air, as if reaching for something in death before rigor mortis had petrified it in place. I paused as I noted a trail of ants crawling along its side, venturing into the exposed wrist.

With a grunt, I bunched my kerchief and nudged the hand tentatively. Half a dozen flies scattered, buzzing indignantly as I lifted the hand by two fingers and wrapped it quickly in the cloth. I turned away at the waft of rot exuding from the limb, doing my utmost to banish images of maggots feasting as I hurried up the footpath, holding the offending item as far from my body as I could.

The stablemaster watched as I approached, removing his hat

and giving it a good dusting off across his knee before replacing it. Amusement pulled at his lips as he lifted a leg to lean against the fence. A horse nickered in the stables behind him, but he didn't mind the sound, more interested in what I was doing holding a kerchief out as if it contained a rattlesnake.

"What do you have there?" The man asked, tilting his head curiously.

I hesitated as I came to a stop. "It's . . . well, it's a hand."

"A hand?" the man's eyebrows knit together. "You don't mean a person's hand?"

"I do. I found it along the path. I expect the count will want the gendarmerie informed."

The stablemaster pursed his lips. "The master doesn't like trouble. No, sir. I can't see him wanting the gendarmerie fussing about the grounds."

I blinked at him. "Are you suggesting that I ignore it?"

"No, no. Nothing of the sort. I would pass it off to Grimes if I were you. He'll know how to handle it. No need to bother the count."

"Right, then." I inclined my head slightly as I continued up the path.

Château le Blanc was growing clearer now, rising like a refuge from the dark forest. Just the sight loosened some of the dread coiled in my chest. I stepped into the clearing, surveying the hedge maze briefly before returning to the house, a white three-story château, sprawling and elegant. Ivy climbed up the side of the building, clinging to the stone and threatening to crowd in on the windows. It reminded me briefly of La Vallée, my ancestral home, and a pang of sadness tugged at my chest before I banished the thought and refocused on the task at hand.

I strode purposely toward the servants' entrance before hesitating on the doorstep, wondering how appropriate it was to bring such a vile thing indoors. I reached out for the bell, pausing as I heard footsteps approach from behind. Glancing back, I saw the stablemaster had followed me. He nodded, sidestepping me and opening the door. "I'll do you the favor of fetching Grimes."

"I appreciate it," I said, and nodded back, surprised by his thoughtfulness, if not outright relieved. It spared me the undesirable task of surprising the butler. Given that Grimes held my employment in his hands, I did *not* want to get on his bad side or cause him any unnecessary grief that would look unfavorably on me. Esteem was everything for a servant.

A disturbance from the drive caught my attention. A cloud of dust bloomed into the air on the tail of a small carriage pulled by a single horse, its head lifted proudly as it clopped along the gravel. Not visitors to the château. This carriage was far too simple for nobility. Plus, the servants' hall would have been abuzz with the impending arrival of any guests.

"Dupont."

I blinked at the name before realizing it was the last name I'd adopted to conceal my true surname. I scrambled to attention as Grimes stepped out from the servants' entrance, the stablemaster at his heels. Grimes's eyes immediately sought the offending article in my hand, and he grimaced before holding a kerchief to his face, as if the mere thought of the hand was revolting to him. The butler's eyes darted up as the carriage grew nearer, and he nodded to the stablemaster. "That's the doctor now. Intercept him as he's coming out of his carriage and be discreet about it."

The stablemaster bowed his head slightly before taking off around the front of the château.

"The doctor?" I asked. "Is someone ill?"

Grimes waved a dismissive hand. "Mrs. Blake is having one of her pains again. You know how fragile women are."

I fought the urge to roll my eyes. "Ah. So the masters of the house are in good health," I said. Mrs. Blake was the cook. "Good to hear."

"I should think so," Grimes agreed, standing taller. "The family would hardly be seen by a country doctor, much less an apprentice, when they have their own personal doctor who comes up from the monastery. That's the sort of efficiency I can get behind, Mr. Dupont. Medical needs and spiritual needs all rolled into one individual, caring for the body *and* the soul."

"As you say," I said, not knowing how else to respond. I'd seen a monk in the house previously, so this must have been the family's doctor he spoke of. He'd seemed cold and off-putting, to be honest, but then again, I'd never been one for religion. I'd gone to church with my family and attended with the servants now, but I would hardly say I was devout. I only went to keep up appearances.

In another minute, the stablemaster had returned, slightly out of breath, with a man behind him carrying a doctor's bag.

"Mr. Valancourt," Grimes greeted the doctor. "So good of you to come."

"The pleasure is all mine," Valancourt assured him, flashing a mouthful of pearly white teeth as he tilted his head at the butler.

I stared at the doctor openly. Rather rude, I knew, but he was probably the most beautiful man I'd ever laid eyes on. I recalled that Grimes had referred to him as an apprentice, which led me to believe that he was only a year or two older than me.

Handsome *and* smart, I thought, drinking him in. That was a winning combination in my opinion.

Valancourt had a dark complexion, his hair shaved close along the sides, but with a crown of obsidian curls. I wondered briefly if his family was from Africa or the Caribbean islands. His smile was roguish, with dimples appearing at the corners of his mouth that sent pangs through my chest. I followed the stubble along his jawline until I lifted my gaze to his eyes, dark pools of warmth I could feel myself sinking into, like gravity wells. I leaned toward him instinctively, wanting to be nearer to him, as his eyes found me. I noted the long lashes surrounding his eyes, the way his lips parted slightly. He had very nice lips.

"And who is this?" Valancourt asked, eyes running over me briefly. I felt heat in my cheeks and knew that I was blushing, but it couldn't be helped. I was prone to blushing and easily flustered. My father had always teased me about it, good-naturedly.

"This is our Second Man, Mr. Dupont. He's only been with us a week now." Grimes sighed. "A week and he's already brought trouble to our doorstep."

I ducked my head. "Apologies, Mr. Grimes."

"Nothing to be done for it. But perhaps the good doctor could help save us some grief."

"I'll do what I can," Valancourt agreed, looking confused. "But I was under the impression that I was here to see to Mrs. Blake?"

"Yes, yes," Grimes agreed. "The more pressing matter is that Dupont found a . . . *hand* on his way back to the house. If you could secrete it away to the gendarmerie and spare the family any unnecessary distress, I'm sure they would appreciate it."

Valancourt frowned. "I see." He squinted at Grimes before

turning to me. "I'll need to take Mr. Dupont with me, of course. He'll need to make a statement at the very least. But otherwise, I'm sure we can keep this quiet so we don't ruffle any more feathers."

"We are in your debt," Grimes acknowledged. He met my eyes and pursed his lips. "Since you likely won't be back in time to serve dinner, Dupont, I'll expect you to make up the time by assisting Fournier with his valet duties tonight."

"Of course, Mr. Grimes," I agreed, bowing as the butler strode back inside. The stablemaster, who'd been listening the entire time, slunk away back to the stables as well.

When the door to the servants' entrance closed with a solid thud, I let out a breath and turned to find Valancourt watching me. I blinked and turned away from those penetrating eyes. "I'm sorry for the trouble."

"It's no trouble," Valancourt assured me. He gestured to the kerchief. "May I?"

"Oh, yes. Please." I handed it to him, nausea sweeping through my stomach briefly as I caught sight of the red blossoming along the bottom of the cloth.

Our fingers brushed against one another's and my heart fluttered, causing me to momentarily forget what we were doing. I wanted to hold on to his warmth for a little longer, even for another precious second, but it wasn't to be. Valancourt pulled away from me, eyes never lifting from the kerchief. He was clearly not affected by the contact as I had been.

Disappointment doused my excitement. What had I expected to happen? What I felt toward men wasn't an acceptable feeling. At least that was what my aunt professed. I didn't understand how something like love, something that felt so right, could be so wrong.

Valancourt unwrapped the hand and examined it briefly, dropping a barrage of one-syllable reactions like "ah" and "hmph" and "my." I hadn't the stomach to watch, turning away until the doctor refastened the kerchief and folded it into some parchment. He knelt down to secure it somewhere in his doctor's bag, and when he looked back up at me, his eyes were shining, and I felt like I was falling under some inexplicable enchantment once more. He had one of those faces that was warm and inviting.

"I apologize. I get carried away sometimes and this is fascinating. Usually they're attached to people."

I stared at him until I realized that he'd told a joke. A weak joke, but a joke nonetheless. I humored him with a chuckle.

The doctor winced imperceptibly at my reaction but recovered with a wide smile. "I don't think I properly introduced myself. I am Valancourt. Bram Valancourt." He stood and reached out a hand.

I shook his hand, his attention flustering me. "Emile St. Aubert."

Valancourt blinked, then watched me thoughtfully as he dropped my hand. "I thought your name was Dupont."

My eyes widened, and I cursed my slip of the tongue. A pretty face and I'd completely forgotten my cover story. "I . . . yes. Please call me Dupont. It's more a nickname. Or better yet, just call me Emile."

"Very well, Emile. And I suppose you'd like me to believe that you're used to a life of servitude with not a single callus on your hands?"

My heart stuttered with panic. I opened my mouth, then closed it as anything intelligible fell directly out of my mind to gather at my feet. Valancourt was observant. I wasn't used to people giving a servant a second glance.

"Whatever the reason for the subterfuge, it's none of my business," Valancourt assured me, no doubt noting the distress on my face. "I was curious, is all. But I won't press you."

"Thank you." I bowed my head as the tension melted in my chest. "I appreciate it."

Valancourt's eyes lingered on me for a moment, as if trying to decide something, but he shook his head in the end and gestured toward the servants' entrance. "Why don't you wash up and meet me at my carriage? I'll be done seeing to Mrs. Blake in short order."

"Thank you," I repeated, catching his eye.

"Don't mention it, Emile."

And with that, Valancourt swept back along the house to the front entrance, leaving me to watch him go.

It was a nice view.

TWO

I'd always been a romantic at heart. I supposed it stemmed from growing up with two parents who doted on one another, love in every glance. I wanted that for myself, that easy devotion, wherein every step was taken in consideration of the other, a dance meant to only make each other happy. I didn't think that was too much to ask, but society had other ideas. My life would certainly have been much easier if I'd given in, taken a wife, even if the marriage was devoid of love. I could have probably even been happy with that sort of life. After all, many matches were made due to title, feelings of the heart a passing consideration. But I didn't want that for myself. I wanted to feel every day, to burst at the seams with happiness over spending my life with that one person who was the center of my gravity. Like my parents had. And so, I refused to compromise. That was also how I found myself in such perilous circumstances. For my ideals. Because my heart demanded that I have what I deserved.

I tilted my head, listening to the beats of the horse's hooves upon the packed dirt road on our way into town. The sound made for a pleasant backdrop to the sunny wooded scene that passed by leisurely. I hated to intrude on the peace, but the silence was growing too much for me in my agitated state. I didn't want to think about the gendarmerie. If they deemed me a person of interest, they could check into who I was, and that would not do. This would all have been for naught. "Why don't you see to the Montoni family, if you don't mind my asking?"

Valancourt pursed his lips beside me, a quirk that I found very distracting. "Let's just say that some families aren't ready to face advancements in technologies. They would rather stick to traditional practices of medicine."

"And you are averse to these traditions?"

"When it comes to health, yes. Which is why the servants of that house receive better care than their masters. Rather backward from the usual way of things, wouldn't you agree?"

I chuckled. "I'm sure they have their reasons, Valancourt."

"Bram."

I blinked.

"If I am to call you Emile, you must call me Bram," Valancourt insisted.

"Of course. Bram."

Bram smiled lazily at me, and I felt my cheeks warm. I shifted uncomfortably and cleared my throat, searching for a distraction from my flustered state. "How long have you been studying medicine? You're a doctor's apprentice?"

Bram considered for a moment, and I watched the light play over his features as we progressed along the road. "My father is a doctor. It's a family business. I've been helping him since I was very young. As his apprentice, he trusts me to carry out simple matters around town. He wants me to take over the practice eventually."

"I'm sure you'll make him proud."

Bram raised an eyebrow. "You don't know the first thing about me, Emile."

"I know that you're a man of integrity." I shrugged. "You can keep secrets."

"And don't ask many questions?"

I stared into my lap. "I'm sure you've seen your share of severed hands as a doctor?"

Bram smiled at the pitiful deflection. "Severed hands, no. Not many. But this profession is always full of surprises. Some can be pleasant, of course. It's not all disease and death."

"Oh?"

"Certainly. Watching medicine I've administered take effect, and seeing a sick man return to his family. Knowing that by treating a common ailment, a child will grow to play, and love, and start a family of their own one day . . . it's very rewarding. And I get to be a part of that."

"That does sound rewarding," I agreed.

Bram nodded. "It doesn't leave much time to build a life for myself, I'm afraid. It's very demanding. Friends are hard to come by when you have to dash off at a moment's notice."

"That sounds like it could get lonely."

"It's worth the sacrifice," Bram assured me. He met my eyes, and I held my breath as he watched me for a moment, tilting his head as he considered something. "You're very thoughtful, Emile. And articulate. Especially for a servant."

I ignored the dubious note in his voice. "Thank you. I do my utmost to be diverting."

"*Mmm*," Bram returned, leaning back in his seat. He clearly saw right through me, that I wasn't a servant any more than he was. But he was polite enough to move on and allow me my secrets.

For now.

"And how far from the château did you find it?" the tall gendarme with the bushy mustache asked, scribbling in a notepad hurriedly. His partner, a short, squat man with an upturned nose, squinted at the hand lying on the table before them. With only the indirect light of the room, the bluish-white hue of the hand made it look like stone. Something about it lying there, naked and exposed, made me uneasy, like I was observing something perverse. But nobody else in the room seemed to share the sentiment.

I held myself still, as I had throughout the interview. As if by moving I might draw unnecessary attention to myself. I felt a bead of sweat drip down the nape of my neck, but I ignored it. "It wasn't far. Maybe a five-minute walk from the stables."

"And it was just off the footpath?"

"Yes, sir."

The tall gendarme exchanged a look with his partner, and I tensed, waiting for them to dive into questions aimed at me: What I was doing there, who my last employer was, where my parents lived. But those questions never materialized. The tall gendarme closed his notepad and nodded his thanks to me. "Very good, Mr. Dupont. If we have any further questions, I assume we can find you at Château le Blanc?"

"Of course." Relief swept through me and my shoulders relaxed.

Bram frowned. "You will want me to examine the hand, I'm sure?"

"No need." The short gendarme tossed a cloth over the hand and swept it into a box. "He was clearly the victim of a wild animal. No one from town has been reported missing, and unless they are, I expect this will remain the case of an unfortunate stranger passing through who encountered some bad luck."

"Bad luck?" I echoed, swallowing hard. "What sort of animal wrenches a man's hand from his arm?"

"A bear, most likely. Although it could have been any number of animals. The woods aren't safe to wander alone at night. You'd be wise to remember that, Mr. Dupont."

I shuddered as my imagination conjured a bear surprising me in the woods, its muzzle opening wide, dripping saliva. What a horrible way to meet one's end.

"I could perhaps narrow down the offending creature for you with a proper examination," Bram persisted.

The gendarmes shared another look. The tall man straightened. "We won't waste your time any more than we have already, Monsieur Valancourt. If we have any further need of your services, we'll contact you. But this is a clear case that need go no further."

"Good day, and thank you for bringing this to us." The short man tipped his hat before disappearing into a back room with the box. The tall gendarme sat down at his desk and began to rifle through some paperwork, making it clear that we'd been dismissed.

I left the room feeling uneasy. I was relieved, of course, that they hadn't asked any personal questions, but the lack of any questions was odd.

When Bram closed the door behind me, I noted the tight set of his jaw and knew he felt the same. We'd been humored.

The gendarmerie had never had any intention of investigating the matter. Whether it was a lack of thoroughness on their part or something more sinister, perhaps a crime they were already aware of and were looking the other way . . .

"Come along, Emile." Bram placed a hand on the small of my back and guided me forward. "There's nothing more to be done here."

My legs obeyed, and I felt an electricity hum through my body at his touch, although he could have hardly felt the same. When I looked up at him, it was to find him clearly distracted. His hand on my back had been an automatic reaction, not some form of intimacy. Of course. It would have been silly to imagine otherwise.

We left the station and headed back to his carriage, but Bram paused as we reached it, and seeming to remember himself, withdrew his hand from my back and straightened. He considered me for a moment. "I don't suppose you have to go back right away?"

I licked my lips. "Grimes did say that he was covering for me today."

A smile broke out over Bram's face. "Then you simply must accompany me to dinner. I haven't been to my club in ages, and I do hate going alone. You can be my excuse. It's just in Saint-Baldolph."

My stomach flipped at the thought. I hadn't eaten in a club in ages. To be waited on, to go out and enjoy someone's company . . . it was so tempting. But it would take an hour, at least, to reach Saint-Baldolph. "I . . . I'm sorry, Bram, but I don't think I would be back in time. I still have to assist with valet duties tonight."

The smile on Bram's face never faltered for an instant. "Your next day off then. Come, promise me."

"I . . . yes. I would love to," I agreed, returning the smile.

"It's settled then. In the meantime, we can get a bite to eat at a pub."

"That would be perfect."

Satisfied, Bram clapped a hand on my shoulder and led me away from his carriage and up the avenue in the opposite direction. I tried not to glow from the attention, but it was hard to keep from beaming. Here I was about to have dinner with a handsome doctor's apprentice. Perhaps I hadn't completely ruined my life, after all.

I was still high from my time with Valancourt when I returned to Château le Blanc.

Bram, I reminded myself, as I was let into the servants' entrance. He wants you to call him Bram.

The meal at the pub had been overcooked and the room noisy, but Bram was so charming and funny that it was easily one of the best dinners I'd ever had. I marveled at how just one acquaintance held the power to change my perspective. I'd been depressed and lonely for the past week, but my mood was quite the opposite after a short afternoon out.

The kitchen and workrooms were cramped and dark, but they were organized and kept free of clutter. I was amazed that so much of the upkeep of the château came from this small area. The servants slept on the third floor, in rooms hardly bigger than closets, giving ample space to the parts of the château reserved for Count Montoni and his family. Those rooms were open and ornately decorated, although I'd seen very little of them thus far. From what I could tell, it looked expensive but was dark and drab. Windows were fitted with heavy drapes, the furniture stiff and a blue so deep they may as well have been black. It certainly wasn't to my taste but suited the gloomy disposition of Montoni. The tableaux were the worst part of the château. I knew many grand houses decorated with taxidermy animals to portray moments of gruesome confrontation, but they were not to my taste. There seemed no rhyme or reason for where they were positioned. I would turn to a corner of a room, and there would be a patch of tall grass, or a pheasant bursting from the reeds to escape a fox, as if frozen in time. It was hard to tear my eyes from such morbid scenes, but they also left me more than a little unsettled.

As I continued up the narrow hallway, I paused at a side table, having noted a spider sitting in the middle of a web. It was a brown and black thing with visible dark pools of eyes and long, thick legs covered in fine hair. I'd come across several similar arachnids in the previous week, and cobwebs seemed to appear out of nowhere. I wondered if there was an infestation somewhere. They weren't exactly small spiders, either, but could fit comfortably in the palm of my hand. Not that I was going to hold one.

I grabbed an empty vase and scooped the spider inside, careful to cover it with a cloth as I carried it to the door and let the spider outside. I hated to kill anything unnecessarily, even a creepy little spider that had way too much hair for its own good.

"There you go," I said, dusting off my hands as I watched the spider scamper into the grass. "You'll be very happy out here."

That done, I replaced the vase and cloth on the side table when my eyes drifted to the spiderweb left behind. I supposed I had better clean that up as well.

"You must be Dupont." A man well into his fifties with a thin mustache hurried over to me. "Grimes said you would be helping with my valet duties tonight."

I pivoted to face him. "Good to meet you. You must be Fournier."

"I am, but we can exchange pleasantries later. There's much to do. If you haven't had supper, don't expect any until after we've seen to the young master."

I inclined my head, not letting on to the fact that I had, indeed, already eaten.

"Can you sew?"

I wrinkled my nose. "Sew? No, I—"

"Well, I don't have time to teach you. You'll be cleaning the boots then. Come along. I'll show you what to do."

I gave one last regretful look back at the spider's empty web before following.

The next few hours were busier than I'd expected. I hadn't realized all that went into a valet's duties. I'd assumed they just helped their master get dressed, arranged things for them, and accompanied them on their travels. Of course, I'd never studied their daily chores in any detail. Nor had I ever pondered what they consisted of. Coming to Château le Blanc as Second Man had been enough of a lesson. I'd thought I could get by with what I'd seen around La Vallée growing up, but I'd needed a tour from Grimes to truly educate me on the tasks I was to perform.

Count Morano was nephew to the master of the house, Count Montoni. Morano had been away for the past fortnight, so I hadn't yet met him, or his sister, who'd also been traveling. I'd only seen Count Montoni this past week, a middle-aged man who spoke in a clipped way to the servants. I didn't particularly like him, but I couldn't exactly afford to be picky. I could only hope that his wards were more amiable.

There was plenty to do upon the young count and lady's

return. It didn't help matters that Morano rang for us early, which meant that he was turning in well before the other members of the family.

"Just let me do all the talking," Fournier told me. "Follow my lead."

Which was all I really could do, given that I had no other experience to draw from.

After a quick knock on a door on the second floor, and a muffled reply, we entered Count Morano's bedroom. He lay on his bed with an arm thrown over his eyes. He was lean, with corded muscles along his arms.

"What an exhausting trip," Morano said, and sighed. "Fournier, remind me to never visit Monsieur Pierre de la Motte again. He's so tiresome."

"Of course, my Lord," Fournier agreed. He stepped forward and helped Morano into a sitting position, where I was able to get my first proper look at him. He was very handsome, and close to my age, with a chiseled jawline and defined cheekbones. His hair was just a little long, walnut brown with a curl that fell into his eyes before he pushed it away.

As I watched silently, Fournier pried off Morano's boots and stockings, and as the count lifted his arms, slipped off his shirt to reveal a powerful chest and defined muscles along his stomach. A patch of dark hair spread over his chest, drawing my eyes along his body appreciatively.

"And who's this then?" Morano's voice drew me up to his green eyes, crinkled in amusement. I bowed, hoping the count hadn't caught me staring.

"Second Man," Fournier said dismissively. "He was hired while we were gone."

"Ah, yes. To replace . . . what was his name?"

"Hargrove."

"Ah, yes. Hargrove. I hope he's getting along wherever he moved off to."

"I'm sure that is the case, my lord."

I looked up after another moment to find myself gazing after Morano's naked backside as he crossed the room to wash his face with the water basin. I was mesmerized by the knots of muscles along his back, and the mounds of flesh that led to his legs. I flushed a deep crimson and found myself unable to form coherent thoughts for a moment as Morano ran a damp towel over his broad shoulders.

"I'll be wanting a bath tomorrow night," Morano announced.

"Of course, my Lord," Fournier replied, glancing back at me. He gestured to the discarded clothing on the floor and I blinked, remembering myself. I scrambled to gather the garments and with another look from Fournier, hurried from the room and down to the servants' hall, where the rest of Morano's travel attire had ended up for washing.

I was still burning from what I'd seen, but I busied myself with cleaning Morano's boots until Fournier returned.

Being a valet was so . . . intimate. I'd had my own valet at La Vallée, but he'd been my grandfather's age and I'd known him all my life. It was nothing to disrobe in front of him. But seeing Morano in such a way, I wasn't sure I would be able to meet his eyes without blushing from the memory of his beautiful body.

"I hope you're free to help tomorrow night," Fournier said, stalking into the room with the air of someone who was busy. "It's a two-person job to haul the bath into his lordship's chamber, and keeping the water warm can be a challenge."

I blinked, trying to push away thoughts of that body sprawled out in a bathtub. "But I have my duties."

"Can't be helped. His lordship requested you specifically. I'll clear your evening with Grimes."

"Of course," I agreed, although my mind was racing. Whenever I'd taken a bath, it had been behind a screen, and my valet had merely handed me my clothing, although I knew that some men preferred their valets to be more attentive. For my sake, I hoped that Morano was modest. I wasn't sure I would get through such an experience without blushing furiously, and perhaps giving myself away. Liking men had completely ruined my old way of life. I couldn't afford for it to happen again, or where else would I go?

THREE

As the hour of apprehension approached the next evening, I braced myself to help serve the family dinner. I hadn't had much to do when it had only been Count Montoni, standing at attention and filling his wine every so often. Now that his nephew and niece were back, and some neighbors had been invited over, I couldn't coast by as a wallflower.

Donning white gloves and willing myself to be steady, I followed Grimes through the hall to the dining room. A row of suits of armor led to intimidating, oversized doors boasting metal rings as door handles. Very medieval. It made me feel as if I were going to face the Inquisition in a dark dungeon. I swallowed hard as the sun lowered in the sky through the windows, the weak light reflecting off the metal armor once worn by honored knights, clawlike gauntlets holding on to swords and morning stars as if ready to fight from beyond the grave. The helmets were closed, but even without seeing that empty darkness within, they felt ominous, the protruding faceplate giving them the appearance of birds of prey, watchful and waiting.

I'd been served meals all my life, so I knew what was expected of me at supper, but it was still easier said than done. Leaning over with a serving dish at just the right angle and height, ensuring the utensils were facing who I was serving, were little things to many, but to a servant, they were what lay between employment and begging on the streets. I noted Grimes watching me with an extra careful eye as I offered the first dish to Montoni, who took a good portion of onion sauce with his broiled duck.

I managed not to drop the tray on him, so I counted that as a point in my favor.

I made sure the serving spoon was secure, my finger lingering on it for a moment. Another noteworthy quirk of the Montoni household was that all of the cutlery was gold. And I believed it to be *real* gold. It was a bold way to brag about one's wealth. After all, any visitors would be a captive audience to the splendor at mealtimes.

As I approached Lady Morano, I noted her lustrous blonde hair, a contrast to her brother and uncle's dark hair. She was very pretty, and when she smiled, her whole face lit up, features lightening in a way that put those around her at ease. Just now, she seemed dreadfully bored of the conversation coming from Count de Villeforte to her right. As I drew nearer, I heard him speaking about parliament and sympathized with her. Upon seeing me, she brightened. "Oh. A new face in the château?"

I bowed courteously as Grimes straightened and answered for me. "He is the new Second Man, my ladyship. He was hired last week."

"Ah. And does he speak? And have a name?"

I suppressed a smile. "Yes, my lady. I am Dupont."

"Wonderful," Lady Morano tilted her head to look me over. "It's good to have someone so young and handsome to ring for."

"He will not be replying to any of your calls, Blanche," Count Montoni said, his nasally voice haughty. "You know better. No corrupting or cavorting with the servants."

"I was merely making an observation." Blanche winked at me. "I wouldn't dream of corrupting him. But he is handsome. Wouldn't you agree, Henri?"

I looked up to find Count Morano watching me. "As you say, sister."

"And where are you from . . . Dupont, was it?"

Montoni cleared his throat. "Enough chatting with the help, Blanche. You have perfectly good conversationalists on either side of you with much more fascinating things to say, I'm sure."

I bit back a retort and had to fight to school my features into indifference as I carried on with my duties, offering the serving tray to Blanche. To her credit, she offered me an apologetic smile on behalf of her uncle but said no more to me.

"Oh, I claim the bath tonight," Blanche said as I strode over to Henri with the duck course.

Henri, I thought, taking in the count's handsome face once more. It somehow suited him. And unlike his sister, who seemed rather carefree, he seemed to be performing for the company, eyes watching everyone around him, calculating, as if waiting to strike.

"Oh, no, sister," Henri teased, his voice surprising me with its levity, given what I'd just been thinking. "I am far dirtier than you. It'll be a right scandal if I don't scrub out what's caked beneath my nails."

"Really, Henri?" Montoni scowled, shaking his head. "That is hardly proper talk for supper." He paused. "And ladies first. If your sister is to find a good match, she must always be ready to receive company."

Henri scooped a good portion of duck out of my tray and smirked up at me as he replaced the spoon. "It seems that you get a reprieve, Dupont."

I opened my mouth but was unsure how to reply, so I didn't say anything. I heard Henri chuckle low in his chest as I walked away, color rising to my cheeks once more.

Deep shadows began to pool around the château by the time I finished with my duties for the day, and even though I would need to be up by six, I was wide awake. It was past midnight when I gave up on trying to sleep and took the servants' stairs down to the second floor, walking along the darkened back hall toward the balcony.

I started when I rounded a corner to find myself face-to-face with a badger, drawing itself up, teeth bared. A taxidermy figure. I chuckled at how easily I'd been frightened and stepped closer to the tableau taking place in a patch of clover and weeds, which I realized had been dried and painted to resemble life. The badger's glass eyes gleamed, almost appearing real, its impressive snarl a work of great skill, no doubt, but I was still left unsettled by the mammal. I sympathized with the reaction of the mouse that cowered before the badger.

I shook my head as I continued to the balcony. As soon as I let myself out into the night's embrace, I sighed with pleasure, a soft breeze caressing my skin. I'd always loved the night: the stars overhead, the buzz of insects, and that feeling of being the only person awake in the universe. For me, night had always been a time of contemplation, reflection, philosophy. I hadn't had that since I'd run away from home, and I missed it terribly. I felt so scattered and harried here. I didn't know how servants did this for a living. With any luck, I would only need to hide away until my eighteenth birthday, whereupon I could claim my inheritance. I still wasn't sure how I was going to do that, given my aunt's interference, but I had six months to find a way.

I leaned against the balcony railing and stared up at the sky until the chill of the evening chased gooseflesh across my arms. I lingered still, reluctant to return to my claustrophobic room, when I looked out over the hedge maze and noticed a peculiar light emanating from beyond the manicured bushes. It was a pale glow that wavered like candlelight from a white-marbled building near the tree line.

A mausoleum.

I shivered. I wasn't one to believe in superstition, but the flickering light made the trees around the mausoleum appear as if they were alive, or dark figures moved about them.

Nonsense, I chided myself, shaking my head. *You're more tired than you realized.*

But then I swore I saw a dark shadow dart out from the cover of the forest to enter the hedge maze from the opposite end. But why would anyone do that at this hour? Then again, why would anyone be at a mausoleum in the middle of the night? Something felt wrong, and I briefly considered rousing Grimes but quickly decided against it. He'd already made a comment about how I was disrupting the peace of the house. This would only add fuel to that fire.

I couldn't dismiss what I was seeing any more than I could have ignored that hand off the footpath. Resolving to uncover the source of the strange phenomenon, I hurried inside and down the servants' stairs before I could change my mind. As much as my mind wanted to jump to thoughts of ghosts and grave robbers, I wasn't expecting to run into anything of the sort. That would be absurd. There was sure to be a perfectly reasonable explanation for the events that were playing out. But I also knew that I wouldn't be able to get a good night's rest at the château ever again if I didn't investigate.

My steps faltered briefly as I stepped out into the night air, where I debated whether I should turn back for a light. But by the time I returned, any sign of whoever had entered the maze might have vanished. In any case, the moon was enough to see by, even if it was still over a week away from being full.

Footfalls muffled by grass, I approached the main entrance to the hedge maze and hesitated. I'd never been in the maze before. It hadn't looked terribly elaborate from the second-floor balcony, and really, it was meant for a leisurely walk rather than some puzzle, so I figured it would be safe enough to enter, even at such a late hour. While servants weren't strictly forbidden from entering the maze, there was an unspoken line between what was for servants and what was for the family of the house and their guests. It would be looked upon unfavorably if I was caught in the hedge maze. And so, I simply needed to avoid being observed. Easy enough under cover of darkness.

Guarding the entrance of the maze, pouring from out of the side of a hedge, was a figure etched in milky white stone, arms positioned to convey the act of escape, as if it had run from something within. Not creepy at all. Its head was angled as if looking about for its pursuer, eyes solid orbs of white. The figure was naked with snakes arranged in a halo around a woman's head. Medusa, clearly. Ironic that she was the one made of stone in this instance.

As I slid past the statue, it seemed to stare at me imploringly, its position of flight causing me to hesitate, as if it were warning me not to enter. But that was silly, of course. It only felt ominous because of the stillness of the night. It made me feel alone, vulnerable, as if I was being watched. But if I gazed upon this statue in the middle of the day, I knew that it would be more amusing and beautiful than portentous.

The path was much darker than I anticipated, the angle of the moon throwing much of the maze into inky blackness, while only slivers of the ground were illuminated to see by. I rounded one corner and then another, choosing my way at random, until I came upon a dead end and was forced to retreat my steps briefly before carrying on. This occurred several times before I began to worry that I would find myself lost within the hedges. But the maze was not limitless, and I eventually stumbled upon a clearing at the center of the maze. Columns lined the wide area, with red flowers overflowing from pots. I was sure they were lovely during a noonday stroll, but in the dead of night, they looked like blood spilling from their containers.

A fountain gurgled at the center of the clearing, a sound calming to my nerves just then. I approached the fountain cautiously. It was elaborate, with three statues standing at the center, back-to-back. These weren't creatures like Medusa; they were goddesses, faces tilted up toward the night sky, as if they could sense the presence of the stars overhead. I had an interest in Greek mythology, so as I slowly circled the three statues, I recognized

Selene with a crescent moon atop her flowing hair like a crown brandishing a torch. Next to her was Artemis, a quiver of arrows dangling from her back as she considered an arrow that she held up to the sky. Finally came Hecate in swirling robes, pressing a large key to her lips. The goddess of the moon, the goddess of the hunt, and the goddess of witchcraft and magic. The white stone seemed to glow with an unearthly radiance, as if they had been conjured by some fairy magic, an impression magnified by the clear sky reflected in the water around them. The scene was ghostly and surreal, making me feel like a trespasser on some sacred land, finding my way there by accident as I stumbled through the maze.

The crack of a twig snapping directly behind me broke the spell, and I whirled around, eyes wide and half expecting a ghost to materialize. The figure that I faced was no spirit, however, but a woman wrapped in a dark hooded cloak. I was sure it was the same figure I'd spied running from the mausoleum. Red hair spilled out from around her neck, and I could make out a spray of freckles across her nose. Her green eyes widened as she took me in and retreated a step.

"Where's Hargrove?" she exclaimed, voice accusing.

My heart pounded as the woman's eyes raked over me, assessing. "I . . . I saw a light in the mausoleum. I'm Hargrove's replacement."

The woman drew back, as if I'd struck her. She paled, those freckles standing out even starker against her nose. "No." She put a hand to her head and turned away. I watched her awkwardly, feeling like I'd walked in on some sort of secret rendezvous between two lovers.

Of course, I realized, closing my eyes. The candle at the

mausoleum had been a signal for Hargrove to meet his sweet-heart in the maze. It all made sense now.

The woman suddenly faced me again and took a step nearer, threateningly. "You never saw me."

"What?" I blinked at her curiously before it dawned on me that finding her in this compromising situation could be ruinous to her virtue.

She scoffed. "Just promise me."

"I don't even know you. What could I possibly have to say?"

"I think it would be in both of our interests if—"

Her voice broke off as the sound of voices spooled out to meet us. I couldn't hear what was being said, but they were drawing nearer. Someone else was in the maze. Someone might find me there, where I definitely should not be.

Before I even had a chance to consider my options, the woman fled, her cloak billowing out behind her as she darted out of the clearing in the direction of the mausoleum entrance. I stared after her silently until the voices came to me again, this time even closer. They were clearly headed this way. I had to leave *now*.

I sprang toward the exit the girl had disappeared through, but before I reached it, the voices cleared, and I saw two fig-ures rounding the hedges at the opposite end. I dropped quickly behind a stone bench and tried to steady my breathing as I heard a girl sigh.

Was I really about to be caught in the middle of another lov-er's rendezvous? Was this *the* spot for couples to court each other unchaperoned? It was scandalous. I couldn't imagine why any woman found a man's attentions worth the risk of her reputation.

But then again, I had risked everything for a chance at love as well, hadn't I?

"He's going to ruin us," the girl said. "I cannot believe how careless he is." A pause. "Oh, don't give me that look. Uncle's spies won't overhear us out here."

"Very well. I think he's driven by rage," a man answered. Henri. I would recognize his voice anywhere.

I chanced a peek over the back of the bench and saw the pair pause before the fountain, confirming that he was with Blanche. His sister.

I felt a moment's relief that it was only the two siblings and not a couple bent on their own self-destruction, before realizing that this was terrible. If I was caught by *them*, of all people, I would be cast out of the château before I even stepped foot out of the hedge maze.

"Rage," Blanche scoffed. "A woman has no outlet to channel her rage. I've managed to keep mine in check all these years. You'd think someone as old as Montoni could manage."

"Blanche . . ."

"No." She wheeled on her brother and poked him in the chest. "Don't defend him. He is on the verge of destroying everything. And I'm not just being a foolish *girl*. You know it's true. He's gone too far, and he's going to cross that line again. We cannot wait for that to happen."

"What do you suggest? That we kill him?"

I waited for a laugh from Blanche, or some retort, but she only looked at her brother coolly. "That would cause its own problems. We need him, for the moment, but that doesn't mean we let him get away with anything he pleases. He has to be curbed."

"And, pray tell, how do we manage that?"

Blanche tilted her head up to the sky and was silent for a moment. "I don't know. A retreat to Udolpho to rein in his behavior would be ideal, but I don't see him agreeing to that isolation voluntarily."

"Then any further talk of—"

Blanche held up a hand, silencing him. "See? Do you smell that? I told you someone has been visiting the maze at night."

I lowered myself behind the bench, trying to get as close to the ground as possible, as if I could sink into it. I was thankful for the shadows gathered around me, but they wouldn't do much good upon a close inspection of the area.

I heard gentle sniffs, as if they'd turned up their noses to scent the air.

"A woman's perfume," Henri said.

"And it's fresh," Blanche agreed.

I held still, but I heard them rush past my hiding place. I didn't let myself relax, though. I remained curled up in a ball for another five minutes. And then, I tentatively examined the clearing and listened for any sounds the night might carry to me. When I was certain the coast was clear, I left my hiding place and skulked as stealthily as possible back through the maze. It seemed that I'd gotten better at navigating the hedges, for I only met one dead end before I found myself leaving under the watchful gaze of the stone Medusa.

I quietly retraced my steps through the château until I closed my bedroom door behind me with a relieved sigh. That had been close. Too close. And for what? To break some girl's heart?

The conversation between Henri and Blanche had been odd, I recalled as I undressed, but it put an idea into my head. The siblings had been speaking of their uncle's death, certainly to inherit his wealth as much as to do away with whatever ruinous behavior he was involved in. If there was something truly scandalous occurring at the château, and I could uncover what it was, then perhaps I need not worry about my inheritance at all. My inheritance could be well beyond my grasp, but I could possibly secure something to fall back on should that prove to be the case. After all, a few weeks in, I knew that life as a servant was no option for me. I needed freedom and wealth. Independence. I could gain that through the secrets I unearthed here, from this wealthy family. Surely they would do anything to stay in good graces with society.

Was I really thinking about blackmailing my employers? Was I willing to stoop so low?

I put my head in my hands. My circumstances left me little choice but to do the unthinkable to secure a life for myself. The siblings had mentioned a retreat of some sort—Udolpho. Perhaps I could bargain for that isolated place in exchange for my silence.

Of course, I would have to uncover the secrets being harbored by this family first. I did feel dirtied by these thoughts, but this was no matter of the heart, so I felt I could bend my ideals in this case. After all, my integrity was secondary to my survival.

I groaned as I realized how little rest I was going to get and fell back onto my bed, willing sleep to claim me. My thoughts swirled with new machinations that I feared had the power to corrupt me. I would have to do some soul-searching to discern if I was able to carry out a plan as disdainful as the one I was entertaining. But entertain it, I would.

FOUR

I rearranged the wood in the fireplace for the fifth time, then stopped to stare at my work before turning to my flint and scrap of steel. "Just work already," I murmured, rubbing the flint and steel together awkwardly. I watched several sparks fly, pleading with them to catch. But they wouldn't cooperate. I cursed as every last spark died upon impact. I didn't know what I was doing wrong. I'd certainly seen many fires in my day, but I'd never bothered to watch their construction. I'd assumed it was an easy task. Simply use a flint, right? But it turned out this was one of many things a servant did that seemed easier than it actually was.

Once I left this servant role behind, I was never going to do anything so difficult and asinine again.

"Problems?"

I started and glanced back to find a young woman behind me, outfitted in a black gown. She peered over my shoulder at my work and snorted.

"What?" I frowned up at her.

"Where's the kindling? You can't expect to start a fire without kindling, not with those huge logs."

"I . . ." I squinted at the girl. She was in her early to mid-twenties, with copper skin and shoulder-length hair. I knew I'd seen her around the château assisting Lady Morano, but I wasn't sure we'd ever formally been introduced.

"Am hopeless?" she helped, grinning.

"That's not what I was going to say."

"*Hmmm*," the girl paced, tapping her lower lip. "Clueless, maybe? Or perhaps ineffective? Wait! I have it—incompetent. Yes, that's most certainly it."

"I am *not* incompetent," I protested, rising to my feet and the bait. "I'm just . . ."

She leered at me and I sighed, gesturing to the fireplace. "Alright. If you know so much, why don't you show me how it's done?"

"And get my dress filthy with soot?" She sent me a mock-horrified expression before winking and leaving me staring after her, incredulous. Had that really happened? Had she just insulted me and left me to fail?

I turned back to the fireplace and sighed, regarding my flint with disdain. "You're not even trying," I accused it. The flint gleamed, as if mocking me in response.

As I dropped down to one knee before the infernal hole in the wall once more, a boy strode in and stopped behind me. I glanced up and he nodded politely. "Annette said I was to assist in starting a fire?"

Annette. That was her name. At least she hadn't completely abandoned me. I supposed I should be grateful, even if she *had* been poking fun at me.

"Your help would be most welcome," I told him, watching carefully as he got to work, so I would never find myself in such a pitiful situation again.

Incompetent. The nerve of the girl. If she'd known who she was really addressing, she would have begged for forgiveness. But as it was, I supposed I couldn't blame her. I must have looked pretty pathetic crouching down into the fireplace begging for sparks to catch.

I still wasn't sure if I should thank Annette for her intervention the next time I saw her, or outright ignore her. I had some time to decide.

Once the fire was lit, Grimes and another boy set up tea on a side table before I was roped into helping serve the family and their guests. Thankfully, I wasn't required to do much more than stand at the table, observing as Grimes himself saw to Montoni and a brooding fellow named Count Magnus, who was a friend from a neighboring town. The two women in his company were equally dour, making me wonder how he could sustain a friendship with such joyless people. I certainly would have made my excuses to distance myself from their society. Upon further reflection, the scowling Montoni would likely fit in with them just fine. Just what sort of secrets could he be hiding behind that brooding visage? And how advantageous would it be for me to find them out? And how could I possibly ferret out what his niece and nephew had only hinted at in the hedge maze?

My eyes found a taxidermy owl, legs outstretched, talons grasping for a rabbit on the run, length stretched out to mimic an all-out sprint from death. The owl's eyes were focused intently on its prey, its beak open as if letting out a battle cry. I found myself nodding. It really was a work of art. The expressions of the animals, the positions of their bodies . . . it was incredibly masterful. I blinked, realizing that the tableaux were growing on me. That was worrisome. As was the fact that I somehow found the dead and stuffed animals more interesting than the count and his guests. But as I watched an insipid interaction between Count Magnus and Montoni, I decided it was the truth.

When the siblings finally arrived, a good twenty minutes had gone by. They likely wished to limit their time with the dowdy guests, and I couldn't blame them for their tardiness. Blanche wore a canary yellow dress trimmed with fine lace that was gorgeous when paired with a stylish white bonnet. Pastel flowers crowded the crown. Henri was dressed to impress in a double-breasted tailcoat in a striking velvety green. I caught myself staring and turned away, cursing his roguish good looks. But I couldn't ignore him in an outfit that emphasized his broad shoulders and slender waist, conjuring up images of his naked backside. I tried to distract myself by straightening the teacups set out as Blanche approached the table.

"Good afternoon, Mr. Dupont," she greeted with a flirtatious smile. "I hear we have you to thank for the roaring fire. I believe you've saved us from a chill in this drafty old room." She met my eyes and quirked an eyebrow in amusement. Clearly, Annette had informed her of my blunderings. They'd probably had a good laugh over it.

"No trouble at all, my lady," I said with an easy smile, unwilling to show her that she could get under my skin. I poured a cup of tea for her with a sure hand and offered her a tray of sugar cubes, of which she took three. She had a sweet tooth, then.

"Should we go through to the parlor?" Montoni asked, getting to his feet and indicating the adjoining door to his guests.

"Perhaps Lady Morano will grace us with a song on the pianoforte."

"I'll join you in a moment," Blanche promised. "I'll wait for Henri to get his cup."

Montoni nodded but was clearly distracted by his guests, speaking in low tones as they made for the other room. I watched him go, pondering how Blanche and Henri had spoken of his anger. He was an unpleasant fellow, certainly, but I didn't see any hint of rage in his actions. He came across as arrogant and snobbish but also in control and possessed of good manners, at least toward his own class.

"Ugh." Blanche scowled as soon as the door had closed on Montoni, "They're worse than the de Villefortes. Why can't he have any amusing acquaintances? And now I'm apparently to be the entertainment for the evening."

I blinked, studying Blanche more closely. I'd been thinking the same thing. Perhaps, under different circumstances, we could have been friends.

"Oh?" Henri smirked, sidling up to her. "You know it's only going to be worse at supper. Uncle will likely plop you down right between Magnus and one of his dullard daughters. You won't be able to escape them."

"Unless you talk of how filthy you are again," Blanche brightened. "That was brilliant. The de Villefortes couldn't leave fast enough."

Henri chuckled and gave her a mock bow. "It was my pleasure."

I watched them with amusement, and as Henri was about to rise, he lifted his eyes and met mine. He had such beautiful green eyes, standing out like emeralds made even more brilliant by that coat. I looked away, straightening, a flush climbing my cheeks.

Blanche sipped at her tea and strode over to the fireplace, gaze lifting to regard the portrait of a woman with striking features and a mysterious smile. Her eyes were the same blazing green as Henri's, but her hair was wild and golden like Blanche's. The woman had to be a relation.

"Our mother," Henri said softly as he followed my stare, and my thoughts. "There never was a more fearsome, charming woman who walked this earth."

"What happened to her?" I asked, before realizing I'd spoken out of turn. I was Henri's servant, not his friend. Posing such questions to an employer was impertinent.

But Henri didn't seem to notice. A memory tugged his lips into the ghost of a smile as he examined the portrait across the room. "She was always so curious about everything. Enchanted by life, nature. She made it a habit to go exploring where no woman had a right to, never mind the danger. If she hadn't fallen from that cliff, I'm sure she would have found a different way to meet her doom."

I winced, sorry that I'd brought up such a sensitive topic. "I'm sorry for your loss."

Henri remembered himself and an easy smile slid into place, hiding his grief. He gestured to the tea. "Pour me a cup?"

Wordlessly, I obeyed. When I offered him the sugar, he waved it away.

"Henri," Blanche said his name softly and looked back over her shoulder at him, eyes tinged with sadness. "I don't feel much like company right now."

"I know, sister." Henri strode over to her and slipped an arm over her shoulder. They looked up at the portrait of their mother as one. "But you won't be alone. Just pretend it's only you and me. Together always, right?"

"Together always," she agreed, leaning her head against his shoulder.

I looked away, feeling like an intruder in an intimate moment.

A bout of laughter echoed from the next room, and it was as if a spell had broken.

"Could it be?" Blanche lifted her head and put a hand to her chest in mock surprise. "Could they be . . . having fun?"

Henri snorted. "It didn't look to me as if that bunch knew how to have fun."

"I guess we'll just have to go and see then." Blanche hooked an arm through her brother's and strode toward the closed door, leaving me behind, all but forgotten.

It was getting late in the day, and my mind raced as the hours bled one into another, toward the time when I would be forced to confront Henri's bath. It was a stupid thing to be worried about, but I couldn't help but feel like I would do something to give myself away. In such an intimate environment, at such a moment, how could one not? Particularly with Henri, who seemed to notice all with those piercing eyes of his. Then this ruse would collapse in upon itself and I would be even worse off. I couldn't go back home. Not yet, anyway. And I didn't know how I would find work again. I had called in a favor with a classmate to secure this position. The timing of the Second Man job opening had been dumb luck, coinciding with my flight into the dead of night. My classmate had thought nothing of it when I'd asked him to produce a glowing reference for a member of my staff whom I claimed we could no longer afford but deserved more than we were sending him off with. I proposed that a second reference would only be fair for the poor soul. He just hadn't known that he would be writing a reference for *me*, under an assumed name. And by the time news reached him of my disappearance, he would have forgotten the small favor I'd begged of him.

But I would not be able to replicate that occurrence, not now that my disappearance was likely widely known. My only choice was to keep my head down for the next six months until I came of age, and circumstances once again favored me. Unless another opportunity presented itself first.

I was lost in such dire contemplation as I dusted the chandeliers in the front hall from the top of a rickety ladder. A spider stared at my feather duster, its dark pools of eyes unblinking each time I inched the duster a little closer in its direction. It had to be seething that I was undoing its hard labor by striking through its cobwebs with an easy flick of my wrist, but it was helpless to do anything about it. I felt a little bad, but I was sure it could rebuild its web in no time, and I would still have done my duty as Second Man with a clear conscience.

Furtive footfalls resounded beneath me, and I ducked my head to find Annette bustling in, holding an arm against her body, as if injured. When she caught my eye, a look of relief washed over her features, and she tried her best smile. It was a good smile, but I knew immediately that it signaled she needed something from me.

"There you are," Annette said, and sighed. "You must come, quick."

I raised an eyebrow, pointedly returning to my dusting. "Oh? Must I?"

"Yes! I . . . you *owe* me."

I snorted and gazed down at her with a cool, even stare. "I don't agree with that assessment. If anything, you owe *me* an apology."

"An *apology?* For sending you help to get that fire going?"

"For laughing about it with her ladyship."

Annette scowled. "Don't be so sensitive."

I bristled. Sensitive. Incompetent. I was growing weary of being labeled in such terms by someone who didn't know the first thing about me. But that was how it was with the working class. Everyone assumed things about servants based on their first impressions and didn't care to uncover more. They were of passing interest, and then they were wallpaper, meant to blend in. It was perfect for what I needed just then, to hide from the public, to become invisible, but it was infuriating to be taken for granted in such a manner. I would be interacting with my household very differently once I returned to La Vallée.

"Okay, okay," Annette held up a hand in surrender, wincing and leaning into the arm cradled against her side. "I'm sorry. It wasn't meant maliciously."

"Then I accept your apology." I started down the ladder, eyes drifting to her arm. "What happened?"

"I strained it or something," Annette shrugged. "All I know is it's worthless at the moment, and I need another pair of hands."

"And you immediately thought of my hands? Struggling to light that fire with a flint?"

"See! Sensitive."

I set down the feather duster and contemplated Annette. "Alright. You did come to my aid. I suppose I can return the favor."

"Thank you," Annette said, although her expression was less than amused. "You're too kind."

"I do pride myself on my kindness," I agreed with a sigh, following her out of the hall and enjoying the annoyed silence emanating from her.

We climbed the staircase to the second floor and through halls I recognized as leading to Henri's bedroom. I hesitated as Annette approached Henri's door, but then she swept past it, relieving any accumulating dread.

At the end of the hallway, Annette knocked sharply on a door and entered a room decked out with butter-yellow silk curtains and periwinkle bed sheets, a contrast to the rest of the drab château. It was like walking into a corner of sunshine in the darkness. And sitting at a vanity was Lady Morano in a voluminous blue gown, a deep ultramarine that looked stunning against her blonde curls, although her hair looked bereft of life at the moment.

Blanche met my eyes in the mirror before her and smiled. Without turning, she chuckled. "Really, Annette? You brought a boy to my room? My uncle would have you hanged."

"My apologies, mademoiselle," Annette bowed as she closed the door. "The maids seem to have been given the evening off. It was him or Mrs. Blake, and she's a clumsy old bat with the fattest fingers you've ever seen."

"He'll do, I'm sure. He can follow instructions, surely."

I frowned, stiff and uncomfortable to find myself in Lady Morano's room. "I'm sorry, but I have no idea what I'm doing here."

Annette patted my shoulder. "Well, I can't make the lady up with a useless arm. You're here to help."

"Unless this is too shocking for you," Blanche added.

"Because you're too sensitive," Annette whispered at my back, causing me to bristle.

"Fine, fine." I stomped over to where Blanche sat. "What's the occasion? You look ready to welcome royalty."

"Lady de Gondelaurier is throwing a ball," Blanche informed me as I stepped up behind her and felt the weight of her hair. "It's only the second of the season. I simply have to be the most desirable woman there."

"I'm sure there's little doubt of that."

"Why, Mr. Dupont, you shameless flirt. I should have you thrown out this instant." But she said it with a gleeful smile, drinking in the attention.

"Here," Annette pushed her way in beside me. "What you need to do is——"

"I've got this," I insisted, hip-checking her before snatching up a brush and running it through Blanche's already silky hair. I gazed at Blanche's face in the mirror, but I wasn't really seeing the girl. I was gauging the overall look of her face and how her hair complemented it. After a moment's consideration, I glanced at Annette. "Do you have any extra fabric from this dress? I just need a strip, maybe a foot long."

Annette blinked. "I . . . I think so."

"Get it."

The girl was so startled by the command that she didn't even argue as she raced from the room.

"Now," I said, stroking Blanche's hair. "What we need to do here is get the hair off your shoulders."

"Off my shoulders?" Blanche echoed, eyes wide as she watched me comb my fingers through her tresses.

I nodded, pulling her hair back from her shoulders. My fingertips grazed her skin and she blushed, but I paid her no mind. "We need to show off that beautiful neck of yours. Meanwhile, we're going to pull your hair up in an elegant chignon. If Annette does her part, we'll have that fabric threaded through your hair, and you'll be the height of fashion."

I dropped her hair, and she turned in her chair to face me. "Who are you?"

I grinned. "Someone who knows what he's doing. Now, where's your rouge?"

Forty minutes later and I'd accomplished what I'd set out to. I doubted Lady Morano had ever looked better. She was a vision in her dress, with her hair swept up. She didn't need much makeup, but I knew how to use it sparingly in her favor. The result left her looking fresh-faced and youthful.

"I'm speechless," Annette admitted, staring at Blanche in the mirror as we all admired her.

"That must be saying something," I teased, and the lady's maid laughed.

Blanche touched her hair as if she couldn't believe it was real. "How did you learn to do this?"

I shrugged. "My mother. I enjoyed helping her get ready for parties and dinners. When I took an interest, she let me do her makeup and hair, and then corrected me until I got things right. Before I knew it, I had an instinct for what to do." I gestured to Blanche. "But it's easy when the subject is already so beautiful. If you have a necklace with a blue sapphire, it will really complete the look, but earrings will do too."

"I have just the thing," Blanche told me, grinning as she opened a vanity drawer, searching. "I'm not completely clueless,

I'll have you know."

I returned her smile and then noticed the time. "Is your brother going to the ball as well?"

Annette smiled knowingly. "Fournier was looking for you when I went to fetch that extra cloth. The count was going to take his bath ahead of the ball. I'm afraid they got on without you."

"They . . ." I felt the stress in my chest unfurl like a flower greeting the sun. "Perfect."

"Your mother wasn't a servant then?" Blanche asked all of a sudden.

I blinked. "I'm sorry, my lady?"

"You said that she attended parties and dinners."

"Oh, yes," I licked my lips. That had been a stupid thing to say in an unguarded moment. I scrambled for an excuse. "She was . . . she worked at a restaurant in Paris. She always had to dress up for the occasion, you know. Loads of dinner parties."

Blanche nodded slowly, but I noted the small pinch between her eyebrows that led me to believe she didn't buy it. I was a servant, though, so she wouldn't puzzle over it for long. I enjoyed the attention, however. It made me feel like myself.

"Well, you came to my rescue tonight," she told me, producing an expensive-looking necklace with a large blue sapphire at the center. As I'd expected, it set off the entire outfit. "I owe you, Dupont."

"It was my pleasure."

There was a soft knock at the door and then Henri was standing there, gazing in at us with surprise. "Are you getting started without me? I was hoping Annette would give me the first dance."

"Oh, you." Annette blushed and ducked her head.

"And this is where you've been hiding," the count chastised

me. "You managed to avoid me again, it would seem."

"But look at his handiwork." Blanche twirled for her brother. "Don't I look marvelous?"

"You are a vision, dear sister. All of the eligible men will fall madly in love with you tonight if they aren't blind."

"Naturally."

"And you did this?" he turned to look me over.

"Well, just the hair," I murmured.

"And the makeup," Blanche added. "Annette's arm is . . . oh, do make sure you see Monsieur Valancourt, Annette."

"I will first thing in the morning, my lady," Annette assured her. "Don't worry about me. Have fun tonight."

"Speaking of which, we should be going." Henri held out an arm for his sister and together they strode from the room, but not without one more hasty thank-you from Blanche and a lingering backward glance from her brother.

As soon as they were out of sight, Annette grabbed my arm and sighed. "Come along, Dupont. I am in desperate need of a drink."

FIVE

I had the following day off, and the first thing I did was visit a public bathhouse to wash away the grime of the past week. Soap and water could do wonders with a washcloth, but I never felt completely clean until I was wholly submerged and covered in bubbles.

That done, I decided to pop in on Bram. If he hadn't only been being polite, I would very much like to take him up on dinner.

After some inquiries, I found his house. As I approached, I noticed him walking up the street toward me from the opposite direction, as if returning from an errand. He smiled when he spotted me, his dimples making my knees turn to jelly. "Emile! I was just talking about you, isn't that funny?"

"Good things, I hope." I scratched the back of my neck shyly as he reached me.

"Always. I hear you were the hero last night, saving Lady Morano from a fashion disaster."

"It was nothing."

"Not from what I hear." Bram clapped me on the back. "Annette was going on and on about it. Like she'd witnessed some magic trick."

Ah. Annette. Of course. She would have seen Bram that morning for her arm.

"Will she be alright?" I asked.

Bram nodded. "I gave her some laudanum for the pain. In a few days, she'll be back to her old self."

"Good to hear."

A short silence descended over us as the doctor tilted his head. "Is there something I can do for you, Mr. St. Aubert?"

"Emile," I said automatically, scanning the area to make sure no one had overheard him. "Emile, please."

Bram nodded, then watched me expectantly.

"It's my day off," I said, finding I was unable to meet his eyes. "I was thinking that if . . . I mean, if you can get away this evening—"

"Yes," Bram cut me off, and I looked up, surprised by the delight in his voice. "This is perfect, actually. I have tickets to the opera. We could have dinner beforehand."

"Are you sure? I mean, if you have other plans . . ."

"I assure you, I do not. I was to go with my father, but he was called away to tend to one of his patients and will be out all day, so he won't be able to make it. This is an elegant solution."

His smile was so dazzling that I stared at him for a moment. I probably had a stupid grin on my face, but I was so glad this was working out.

Bram glanced down at his watch. "I'll be finished with my appointments by four. Shall I fetch you at the château then?"

"Please."

"Perfect. It's been too long since I've had a night out."

"I look forward to it," I said, stepping back and attempting to temper my excitement. I didn't want to seem overeager and make this outing weird. It wasn't as if there was anything romantic about it. We were new acquaintances hoping to enjoy one another's company. I may have felt something stirring inside me for Bram, but it was a feeling I was used to suppressing: unrequited infatuation.

Bram offered me a final wave before turning up the walk to his house. I stood on the sidewalk watching him for another moment before I retreated to the château, feeling light and energized.

Stepping into the role of a servant was much more tedious than I'd expected. A distraction, an actual social activity, would be precisely what I needed to forget my troubles for the day.

I hadn't eaten food with such obvious delight in a long time, even longer than I'd been away from La Vallée. I hadn't appreciated what I'd had then, and the sophisticated food, paired with champagne, was a reminder of what waited for me in six months' time. I only had to hold out until then, and I could return to this luxury.

Unless I uncovered the Montoni family secret, I reminded myself. Then I may not have to wait such an interminable amount of time to return to a lifestyle more befitting me. I still wasn't sure I was capable of blackmail, but if Montoni had compromised himself in such a way that he *could* be blackmailed, then it wasn't as if I would be putting the screws to an innocent undeserving of it.

By the time we left the club, the day had already progressed significantly, and it was a long carriage ride from Saint-Baldolph to the opera house in Voiron. We talked about Bram's business and his family, while I spoke about working for Montoni and his family, and the servants I interacted with. I tried to press Bram for information on Montoni, but all I was able to discern from his vague responses was that he wasn't fond of the family, although he didn't disclose why. I deflected any conversation of my own family by mentioning that they were deceased, a clear signal to Bram that the subject was to be tabled for now.

Near to Voiron, the roads darkened quickly, and we wordlessly watched the sun set from the carriage. Bram scooted nearer to me to get a better view from our window, and I stilled at his closeness, inhaling the scent of soap and something herbal and clean, like basil. "There's nothing quite like a sunset in the countryside," Bram said. He leaned over me, eyes focused on the sun, bleeding brilliant magentas and streams of marmalade over the darkening landscape.

I tried to watch the sunset, to observe the beauty he found outside our window, but my eyes kept sliding to Bram, his strong jaw, his Adam's apple bobbing as he swallowed. He was so beautiful in his clear delight that I wanted to lean forward and kiss him. Or maybe run my hands through the curls of his hair. Something. But then his eyes slid to mine, and I ducked my head, embarrassed.

"It's a . . . fine sunset," I told him, offering a smile. I cleared my throat and scrambled for something to say before the silence became awkward. "So, this opera we're going to see. Do you know anything about it?"

Bram's eyes sparkled. "Oh, yes. It's *Faust*. Do you know it?"

"I've heard of it. A man makes a deal with the devil?"

"That's the one." Bram turned in his seat to face me better, as if he couldn't contain his excitement. "In Paris, at the Palais Garnier Opera House, a ghost is dictating who will perform in the lead soprano role. It's a sensation, and now all of the opera houses are playing *Faust* because of it."

"Rather morbid, isn't it?"

Bram chuckled. "But you have to admit that it makes for a compelling story. What marketing genius."

I shook my head in amusement. "People will believe anything these days. There are no such things as ghosts."

"No? Are you sure about that? Mediums are everywhere now. They hold séances to contact the dead. People swear by them, that they say things they could not have known."

I shrugged. "People hear what they want to hear." Of course, it had only been a few nights prior that I had seen a candle in the mausoleum at the château and had briefly conjured up thoughts of ghosts. But it hadn't been a ghost in the end. Just a woman whom I'd had the unfortunate task of delivering bad news to. "I don't believe in ghosts any more than I believe in unicorns or fairies."

Bram sat back in his seat. "Well, you know that I'm a man of science. I believe in facts myself. But that doesn't mean there's nothing to it. The natural world is full of all sorts of strange phenomena. Not all of it can be explained away."

"Not yet."

"Not yet," Bram acknowledged with a grin. "I suppose this means that you won't be frightened of the opera. It won't keep you up all night, at least."

"I should think not."

At least I hoped it wouldn't. I did have to return to work early tomorrow. It would be a late night, but I couldn't have passed this up. I needed this. And if the consequence was that I had to suffer through a tiring day, so be it.

"I'm glad we're doing this," Bram said, watching me.

"Me too," I told him. His eyes were so warm and intoxicating that I had to look away. I glanced out of the carriage to find that the sun had slipped completely past the horizon. The warm colors lingering over the land were cooling even as I watched. "And then it was night."

"The night's not so scary. But consider yourself under my protection. I promised you a good time, and that involves getting you home in one piece."

"But not too early."

"Oh, no. You can bet it won't be too early."

In another hour, we were at the opera house, and just in time, since most of the chairs were already filled as we were escorted to our seats on the main floor. I looked up longingly at the private boxes, where I was used to taking in the symphony or plays, but I was lucky to find myself here at all tonight.

As the lights dimmed, excitement simmered inside me. I did enjoy a good opera, and while this wasn't going to be the glory of the opera houses of Paris, it was sure to be a spectacle. And I'd always been curious about *Faust*.

I was amazed at the talent as the opera commenced. The voices soared and the drama unfolded against shockingly elaborate set designs. I loved the lead soprano and decided that the Opera Ghost would have likely demanded her play on his stage had he heard this voice. I was so engrossed with the performance that I was startled when an intermission was announced.

"Are you enjoying it?" Bram asked as several people stood to stretch their legs before the next act.

"I love it." I beamed, and Bram rewarded me with a bright smile of his own. "Thank you. I'm having a lot of fun."

"Think nothing of it. It was my pleasure."

Bram excused himself to find a room to relieve himself, leaving me to observe the people around me. I looked up and found myself drawn to a figure in one of the private boxes.

I paled and turned my head away quickly. *Had he seen me?* No. He couldn't have noticed me. He probably never bothered to gaze down at the general populace. I didn't dare look back up to make sure. Alexander Westenra was the oldest brother of the closest neighboring family to La Vallée. I didn't know what he could have been doing so far from Nemours, near Paris. It wasn't as if Voiron was a city of note. He couldn't be looking for *me*, could he? My aunt wouldn't have sent him. Surely not.

I considered leaving, but that would likely draw Alexander's eyes right to me. Even if he wasn't looking for me, he must have heard about my disappearance. He was a neighbor, after all, and news carried far.

For the moment, I was one among a crowd. If I kept my face turned away, he would never know I was here. At the end of the opera, I would blend with the masses as we left together, Alexander never the wiser.

I produced my kerchief and dabbed at my forehead. I never imagined I could run into anyone I knew this far off the beaten path. I hoped this was a chance encounter and not something more organized. I thought of myself as safe, tucked away in the servants' quarters of a faraway château. There was nothing to direct people my way, so their net would have to be cast wide to come this far, if that was even what this was. And yet, they would still never find me among Montoni and his family. This would have to serve as a reminder that I needed to lie low. I couldn't go out and about, announcing my presence, even in obscure places such as this.

I could *not* get caught.

"Is anything the matter?" Bram asked as he returned to his seat beside me. I tucked my kerchief away and forced a smile into place. Now that there was a body beside me, blocking me even more from prying eyes, I felt much better. There was no way Alexander would spy me here. I was fine. I just had to relax.

"Everything is perfect," I lied as the lights dimmed once more, shadows racing to offer the cover I needed to let my guard down.

Bram patted my hand reassuringly, and I reveled in the momentary warmth it provided before he pulled away. It was all I needed to forget about Alexander and to merely be there with Bram. And I lost myself, once more, in the music.

SIX

espite a diverting evening in the company of a handsome doctor, I had to resign myself to returning to my chores the next morning. I didn't regret the late night; it had been past two in the morning when I'd arrived back at the château. I was feeling the lack of sleep as I trudged through my day in a daze.

I'd fallen asleep on the way back, but a carriage swaying gently to the sound of clip-clopping hoofbeats was a recipe for sleep. I'd awakened at the doors of the château with Bram's cloak thrown over me like a blanket. Very chivalrous. I hadn't wanted to say good night, but I'd also desperately wanted to slip into my bed.

"Thank you for such a pleasant evening," I'd told him as I'd stepped down from the carriage.

"I'm glad you enjoyed yourself," Bram had said, looking dead tired himself. "We'll have to do it again."

"We will."

I smiled to myself as I walked down the hall reminiscing, and hummed under my breath as I recalled music from *Faust*.

I stopped and pretended to tip an imaginary hat to a taxidermy lynx, ready to pounce upon an invisible intruder. Its eyes stared back at me without amusement, mouth yawning wide to showcase deadly teeth. "And would you like to dance, monsieur?" I asked it playfully. I reached out an arm to compare my hand to the feline's massive paw and shuddered, imagining the damage its exposed nails could do.

"I'll have to refuse a dance," I told it, bemused. "I'll be happy to reconsider once you've had those nails trimmed, but not a minute sooner."

A shadow fell across the door, and I stiffened, pretending to dust the top of the lynx's head. It likely came across like I was petting a dead cat.

"Was that the doctor's apprentice who dropped you off last night?"

I swallowed, glancing up to find Henri watching me, arms crossed. I immediately scrambled into a bow. "My lord. Good morning."

Henri raised an eyebrow. "So?"

I lifted my eyes to meet his. "Yes, sir. We went to see *Faust*."

"*Faust*. Interesting. And did you enjoy it?"

"Yes, my lord."

Henri's gaze lingered on me for another moment. "You look terrible. Tell Grimes I ordered you to take a nap before dinner tonight. We can't have you serving like that."

I swallowed hard. "I'm sorry, sir."

He waved the apology away as he swept from the room before I straightened and stared after him. That had been odd. He'd seemed upset. Or perhaps jealous that I'd seen *Faust?* I tried to sort out what could have put him in such a mood, but then I figured that sometimes people merely woke up with a foul disposition. I doubted he actually concerned himself with me at all but was taking something out on me.

But I did take him up on his offer of a nap, to Grimes's annoyance. An order was an order.

It was as I was tugging on my gloves in the kitchen, waiting to bring up the trays for dinner, that I considered perhaps Henri didn't care for Bram. The family had their own doctor, after all, who dealt in traditional medicine. Maybe Henri felt threatened by Bram. Bram had hinted at a dislike for the family on his end just last night, so perhaps the feeling was mutual.

I didn't have long to ponder the matter, however, as I was handed a tray of food to bring up to the dining room. My mouth watered as I smelled pheasant, recalling my dinner with Bram the previous evening. And then I recalled his dimples. And his smile. Those eyes that I felt pulled toward.

You need to get ahold of yourself, I chastised myself, lifting my chin and trying to focus on the task at hand. I pushed Bram from my mind, although I knew that he wouldn't be banished for long. I liked Bram. A lot. Even if that meant that he was a companion, a friend, I wanted to be in his circle. When he'd spoken animatedly about the opera, or when he laughed, he was like a flame, burning so bright one couldn't look away. I wanted that in my life, someone with so much passion and charm and . . .

I let out a breath, trying to clear my head again. Dinner. I was serving dinner. Daydreaming could wait.

The family was not hosting any guests this evening, so it was an easy enough dinner to navigate, even if they did still demand perfection from their servants.

Blanche smiled at me like an old friend as I served her but didn't dare speak to me before her uncle, who seemed distracted this evening, poring over some documents in a reprieve from his usual good manners when in company. I tried to catch a glimpse of what interested him so, but he foiled my attempts at every turn, covering the papers with a sleeve, or turning to another page just as I approached. It was frustrating, but I had to appear uninterested so as not to arouse suspicion. Just when I'd resigned myself to failure, I managed to spy some articles pertaining to livestock, and I realized that it would have been too good to be true to find Montoni reading incriminating letters in the company of others. He wouldn't be so careless.

"Uncle," Henri said after I'd served him and had gone to the side table to wait silently to refill glasses, "have I mentioned how tedious Fournier was while we were gone? He was downright incompetent. Did you know he even ruined my favorite dinner jacket?"

"And what would you have me do about it?" was Montoni's reply, not bothering to look up from his paperwork.

Henri exchanged a look with Blanche and winked at her, his eyes finding me briefly before straightening and clearing his throat. "I was thinking. Fournier is getting on in years, and I think it would be more appropriate to have someone who can keep up with me in his valet duties, someone closer to my age."

"Oh?"

"Yes. I propose I take the new servant, Dupont, on as valet. He seems smart enough on his feet. I'm sure I could train him easily."

"Annette could help," Blanche agreed, sneaking me a sly look.

I blinked at the proposal. *Valet?* I couldn't be valet. I could hardly handle my duties as Second Man, and being a valet required much more skill. I stood frozen as I watched the proceedings. Were they going to even ask *my* opinion on the matter?

I swallowed hard, feeling Grimes's eyes on me.

The butler cleared his throat then and addressed the family. "I hadn't realized that Fournier had been found lacking. I'm sure a replacement can be procured, but if this is a first offense, may I suggest that he was just out of sorts on this one occasion?"

"It's been a gradual decline," Henri declared with a regretful sigh.

"Then I can take out an advertisement in the papers for a replacement. You see, we need a Second Man. Dupont was hired specifically for the role, and I'm afraid we can't leave it vacant for long."

"That's why my solution is so ingenious," Henri beamed. "They will simply trade roles. That way, poor Fournier will still be employed and looked after by the family for his many years of service. I'm sure he could handle the duties of Second Man, just as I'm sure Dupont could meet the challenge of valet with little effort."

Grimes had gone pale, and his mouth kept opening and closing like a fish, as if completely flabbergasted. I couldn't blame him. I felt rather the same.

"What do you say, Uncle?" Henri asked Montoni.

"Fine, fine," Montoni said, and waved his hand as if to dismiss the topic. "See that it's taken care of, Grimes."

Grimes bowed stiffly. "Yes, my lord." When he straightened, he sent me a murderous look, and my eyes widened. He approached me and stopped to stand beside me as we watched the family dine. "Was this your design?" he demanded in a whisper.

"No," I said in a low voice. "I swear it. I had no idea. I don't even want to be valet." Truthfully, I was terrified at the prospect of being valet. My incompetence could reveal my true station. And I already found it difficult to spend time around Henri without getting flustered. To spend many more hours at his side could be downright disastrous.

Grimes sighed. "Well, there's no way around it. Congratulations on your promotion, Dupont." He stepped forward to fill Montoni's wine glass as I met Henri's level gaze. There seemed to be a promise in his eyes. I wasn't sure I liked the look. But it was done. I would be spending more time with Count Morano, whether I wanted to or not.

I stood awkwardly in the doorway of Henri's bedchamber after a timid knock.

Henri smiled up at me from where he'd been lounging on his bed with a book. *The Count of Monte Cristo*, a book I rather enjoyed. So, we had something in common at least. "Ah. You're here."

"I am here," I agreed, unsure as I stepped inside and closed the door behind me. "I'm not sure what I'm supposed to be doing, to be honest."

Henri tossed aside his book and sat up, eyes drifting over me, as if wondering what to make of me. "You cut a handsome figure in your new uniform. As I imagined you would."

"Thank you, my lord," I said, self-conscious as I looked down at my simple black suit. It was actually a little small and dug into my waist, but it was the best that could be done on such short notice. New clothes had been ordered but wouldn't likely arrive for a fortnight. Until then, I would have to suffer through it.

"Are you happy with your promotion?"

"I . . . I was happy in my old position."

Henri laughed and bounded to his feet, striding over to me quickly. He looked down at me with a mischievous grin. "That wasn't an answer. See? That's why I think we'll get along very well. That, and how you managed to save my sister from catastrophe. She was the talk of the ball, you know, thanks in no small part to your skills."

"Thank you, sir."

Henri placed a finger under my chin and lifted my face until I was looking into his fiery green eyes. "If you can manage to make a girl look that stunning, taking care of me should be simple enough. Men are much more straightforward when it comes to dress and hair. You needn't worry."

I swallowed hard as he removed his finger but held my gaze. I didn't know what to say, so I awaited his direction.

"Typically, my valet will choose my outfits for me. You will help me in and out of my clothes. Will that be a problem?"

I felt blood rushing to my face. "I . . . no, sir. No problem."

Henri smiled knowingly. "See. The evidence is right on that adorable face." He leaned forward until our faces were mere inches apart. "But I'll be polite and disclose my secret first."

My eyes widened. He . . . he couldn't know who I was. Unless Alexander had been in the neighboring town the previous night to flush me out, after all. My nails dug into my palms as I clenched them, trying to come up with something clever to say in my defense, or to refute the claims. But my mind came up blank, and I doubted I would be able to deflect what was coming.

"I like men," Henri announced, watching me with a level gaze, as if waiting to gauge my reaction.

I blinked. Oh. Did he mean *that* secret? Could he possibly have inferred that I liked men as well? Apparently, I had so many secrets that it was hard to keep track.

"Sir, it's an honor to have your confidence. I'm not sure what that has to do with me, but I swear I will—"

"Will the fact that I like men get in the way of your duties?" he cut me off.

I paused, my mind whirring. Too much was happening at once, leaving me dazed. How could I regain control of the conversation when I was thrown so off-balance? "I don't follow, sir."

Henri smirked. "See? That wouldn't be the reaction of someone who didn't have their own secret to hide. A man who does not like men would be uncomfortable with the very idea of helping me in and out of my clothes. It didn't even occur to you."

I blinked. "But you're a count, sir. I couldn't—"

"There's no point in denying it, Dupont. Now let's drop this charade, shall we? I believe you're like me." He bit his lower lip. "Are you? You can be honest with me, Dupont. I've been honest with you."

I felt my mouth grow dry. He wanted me to . . . say that I liked men? Out loud? I'd never been able to say that about myself, not directly. It was so taboo and . . . and did Henri merely want to humiliate me? Was this whole valet promotion some elaborate machination to reproach me before I was dismissed? But then, why would he admit that he himself liked men? To make the dismissal more palatable?

"My lord, I . . . I need this job." I felt tears pricking behind my eyes as desperation gripped my chest. But I refused to let them be produced. "I don't know what you think you know, but I assure you that I can carry out my duties. Like you said, what I managed with your sister—"

"Of course, you can carry out your duties," Henri said, looking a little confused. "I just want to know that I can rely on you, Dupont. I want to be able to trust you, but that goes both ways." He took a deep breath. "Now, can you trust *me*?"

I stared at him a moment, but I realized that he wouldn't be put off. What would be the point of delaying the inevitable? Yet, I couldn't meet his eyes as I said it.

"I like men."

It felt so strange to say it aloud, as if I was listening to the confession from someone else entirely. My cheeks burned with shame.

Henri let out a deep sigh. "That wasn't so hard, was it?"

Tears bloomed in my eyes despite myself, and I swiped them away angrily. "Do you want me to pack my things?"

Henri snorted. "Of course not. Would you have me pack my bags as well?" He patted my shoulder, then strode over to his bed as I composed myself. I took a few deep breaths to calm my racing heart. I couldn't believe that had happened.

"Sorry," Henri said as he perched at the edge of his bed and regarded me. "I thought that we needed to clear the air. Doesn't that feel much better, having it out in the open?" He grinned at me, and I couldn't help but smile back. I was still rattled by the fact that this man, whom I'd only known for a matter of days, a man who was contemplating murdering his own uncle, knew my dark secret. How could I possibly feel safe with such personal information in his hands? And yet, I knew a secret of his as well. It was strangely intimate, like some barrier between us had fallen away. Yet, the trust that he'd spoken of wasn't so easily gained. It was one thing to share in a secret, and yet another to let my guard down around a man capable of considering diabolical deeds. "And please call me Henri. At least when we're alone together."

"Thank you, Henri. I . . . I don't understand how you . . . knew."

Henri pursed his lips. "I've been watching you, Dupont. I can see myself in you. Your struggle to find your place in a society that shames you for who you are. I know how it feels. But I also see a determined young man, pushing through his uncertainty. You're strong. Stronger than you give yourself credit for. You can do this job. You'll be a marvelous valet."

I swelled at his praise, but my doubts crept in at the corners. This did present me with an opportunity to get closer to the family and its secrets. But my own secret was also on the line, and Henri was already coming far too close to exposing it. My fledgling plan to uncover what the family was hiding could be dashed before it even began if I didn't tread very carefully. "Thank you, sir. I'll do my best."

Henri nodded slowly. "I also . . . I mean, I find you terribly fascinating. You're handsome and quick, and . . ." He looked away, swallowing hard. "Look, I'll be honest. I like you, Dupont. I thought that if you could step into this role, maybe it would make things easier . . . and maybe we could . . . get to know each other better. As a valet, you would travel with me, be my companion. It's the perfect cover for . . ."

He let his voice trail off as he caught my horrified look. I hadn't meant to let it show, the discomfort at his words. I found that I liked Henri. I even found him attractive. But I couldn't see myself in some sort of secret relationship with him, especially as I was plotting to blackmail his uncle.

"What is it?" Henri asked, straightening.

I licked my lips. "Sir, I couldn't possibly . . . I mean, you're my employer and it wouldn't be appropriate."

"Appropriate?" Henri snorted. "By the narrow minds of this society? Of course not. That's why we are forced to the shadows. That's why one gesture in public could be ruinous. It's absolutely ridiculous. But that's why this has to remain a secret. We can find comfort in one another, but it stays here, behind these walls."

I took a step back. My mind was racing. My heart thumped furiously. I couldn't. A secret relationship? Stealing kisses in corridors and sending longing glances across crowded rooms? That would make it seem like there was something wrong with two men being together. I didn't want to feel like that, like I was a dirty secret. And where could this take us, in the end? In the best-case scenario, I would be returning to my old life, and come into my inheritance when I turned eighteen. Anything with Henri would only make that more difficult. And worst case? I would blackmail his uncle. I wasn't sure I could be in a relationship with someone I was lying to. "I don't want to sound ungrateful, Henri, but it would be one-sided. I would be serving you out there, in public. There wouldn't be any hope of us being true equals. No relationship can be founded on that."

"One-sided? You just told me that you like men. I'll take care of you. I'll make sure you have a good life. It will be equal in that we'll both be looking out for each other. What's so wrong with that?"

Bram's face swam through my mind. His kindness, his laughter, his gentle nature. Henri was . . . *arrogant*. This was arrogance personified. How could he assume that I would go along with this? That I should be *honored* to find myself at the receiving end of this proposal.

I lifted my chin, steeling my resolve. "I'm sorry, sir, but I can't be a part of this. I would be at your mercy, and I cannot compromise myself in that way."

"You can't, or you won't?"

"I won't. I . . ." I hesitated before forcing myself to look him in the face. "I like you, Henri. Quite a bit. I think we could be good friends. But I don't want anything more than that."

Henri's face darkened. "Is that so? After everything I did to get you this promotion, now you don't want it? I can't just tell my uncle that I was wrong about Fournier and have everything return to the way it was." He shook his head. "No, we're stuck together, Dupont, unless I come up with a way to undo this."

I swallowed hard. "Sir, please—"

"Think long and hard about this. I just want us to act on what we're feeling. Our impulses. Our desires. I don't care what society says about love between two men, we deserve to experience it."

A flash of anger boiled over inside me. He spoke of love and twisted it to suit his needs, and I couldn't take his hypocrisy any longer. I set my jaw as I met his eyes. "What feelings? I don't know you and I'm not sure I even want to."

"Get out of my sight," Henri growled. "I don't know why you're denying this for us. And do me a favor and keep this between us. You are a servant, after all, and I wouldn't want word to get around that could be detrimental to you."

I stared at him, reading into his words, until he lifted a finger and pointed at the door. "Think it over. And get out."

I didn't even bother to bow in my haste to leave his bedroom. I shut the door behind me hard and leaned against it, shaking with indignation. Did he really think he could just . . . *order* me to fall in love with him? Did he really expect a *command* could thaw a heart? It was shocking. It was *unthinkable*.

This was the whole reason for the promotion, I realized with dawning horror. Fournier hadn't been inept. Henri had merely wanted me to be his secret companion. What had I gotten myself into here? What were my options? Where would I go if I had to leave? Henri was just as callous and volatile as his uncle. I couldn't care for a man who would try to manipulate me. Frankly, I would be justified in relieving these arrogant men of their wealth. After a proposal like that, I was *owed* some recompense.

I stumbled back to my room in a daze. As I sank onto my bed, I tried to see it from Henri's perspective. He had to feel trapped. Society wouldn't allow him to follow his heart. I knew how that felt perfectly well. He was desperate and . . . lashing out. Perhaps once he'd had some time to calm down, he would realize he was being unreasonable. But could I take that chance? Could I just *hope* that he would change his mind? He was my employer, and he had all the power here.

My plan, it seemed, had backfired on me spectacularly.

SEVEN

I splashed cold water on my face and rubbed the crust from my eyes the next morning. I looked above my water basin to the mirror, at the face of a boy who was in way over his head. I wasn't sure what to do, and I had no one to talk to about this. I just wished that Henri would recognize that he couldn't *force* me into a relationship. Maybe after sleeping on it, he would have come to that conclusion and would give me some space.

There was quite a bustle in the château as I made my way to Henri's bedroom. I sidestepped a troop of boys marching flowers through the hall, wondering what could be going on, when I recalled someone mentioning the ball. I just hadn't realized it was today. Montoni would be hosting, of course, thus the bedlam as orders could be heard ringing throughout the great house.

When I stood outside of Henri's room, I stared at the door for a moment, hesitant to venture inside. Dreading it. But there was no point in putting off the inevitable. I gave two sharp knocks before I opened the door and stepped inside, bracing myself for an angry count.

"Ah, there you are. How do I look?"

I paused in the doorway before slowly closing it behind me. Henri was already dressed in a gray coat and riding boots. I was surprised, but also relieved. He seemed much more rational at the moment. "You look dashing, my lord. Are you going riding?"

Henri glanced at me briefly as he adjusted his collar in a mirror. "Yes, with my sister. All of this . . . *chaos* is unsettling. I would rather be away until the ball this evening. We're going to ride into town and have lunch at a pub. We won't be back until after four to change."

"Very good," I said, watching his reflection. Our eyes met. "You didn't wait for me to help you change this morning. Am I to . . . help you this evening?"

Henri sighed and put a hand to his head. He turned toward me, eyes closed for a moment before he regarded me. "I don't want to make you uncomfortable, Dupont. I know that dressing me makes you uneasy, so I'm trying to assuage some of that until we get to know one another better. I realize that I came across as . . . aggressive last night. And harsh. I'm actually rather embarrassed by my actions. I'm not used to being turned down."

His words came out in a rush and by the time I'd processed them, Henri was standing before me, clasping my hands. "Please forgive me," he said. "I don't want to start on the wrong foot with you."

I blinked stupidly for a moment before nodding. "Of course, my lord."

"Henri," he corrected.

"Henri. I'm glad you feel that way."

Henri smiled, a charming smile that made my heart flutter briefly. "Look. I'm not giving up on you. I just came to the realization that I have to win you over. I want you to *want* to be with me. And that won't happen if I force it. Please . . . give me a chance, Dupont. That's all I ask. Take your time. Observe. You'll see that I'm worthy of your affection."

Henri was still holding my hands, and I gently pried mine away from him, a smile glued to my face. I wasn't sure how to take this earnest entreaty. Was he trying to manipulate me? Or did he mean what he said? My initial impressions of Henri were of a shrewd, calculating man. Warm and handsome, but cunning. I wasn't sure I could trust him, and last night had nearly convinced me of that. Now I wasn't sure. But I could do as he asked and observe, even if I didn't think anything would come of it. After all, this could be the opportunity I'd been waiting for. If I went along with this, I could gain Henri's confidence and be in a better position to uncover Montoni's secrets. I just had to play my cards right.

"Okay," I said, "but I can't promise that I will warm to this."

"You will," Henri said confidently, winking at me and patting my shoulder. My heart stuttered again, like a traitor. "Take the afternoon off. Do whatever you like, so long as you're back by four."

"Thank you," I said, genuinely pleased by his generosity.

Henri grinned as he swept past, leaving me standing in the middle of his room, gazing after him dumbly.

Since I had leave, I decided to go into town. I wanted to thank Monsieur Valancourt for the opera, and I felt like I'd been too tired to properly thank him when he'd dropped me off. I figured that I could offer to buy him lunch to show my appreciation.

Plus, it would give me an excuse to see him again.

I felt apprehensive as I approached his house, just off the main street. I wasn't sure why I was nervous, but butterflies gathered in my stomach. What if he hadn't cared for our time together and politely put me off? I wasn't sure I could bear it.

I paused at the corner to gather my courage to face Bram, when I noticed a man gazing at me from across the street. I started as I realized it was Count Montoni. Straightening, I began to lift my arm in a wave, before realizing that the count was not looking at me at all, but rather at a shop ahead of me.

Of course he wouldn't notice you, I chastised myself, shaking my head. *You're merely a servant, beneath his notice.*

But why was he observing the shop? I craned my neck to see that it was an apothecary. An advertisement for a medium was in the window as well. Some sort of occult shop then. What was Montoni's interest in such a curious place?

I flicked my eyes back toward Montoni to see him step back into the shadows of an alley, yet he remained watching the storefront. Perhaps he had followed someone there and was waiting for them to reappear? Either way, it unsettled me, and I moved along before he noticed me lingering.

Another minute and I was standing at Bram's doorstep. Before I could talk myself out of it, I lifted the heavy door knocker and announced myself. I was debating knocking again when I heard the lock being unfastened, and a woman pushed the door open to regard me.

"Can I help you?" she asked, looking me over. "I'm afraid the doctor is out on a house call at the moment, but if it's urgent—"

"Oh, no," I apologized, stepping back. "I was looking for Bram, er, Monsieur Valancourt. I didn't mean to disturb him."

"Not at all. He should be in his study. Please, come in."

"Thank you." I sent her a grateful smile and followed her inside and down a short hall.

"Bram doesn't have many visitors," the woman prattled on. "He's always so busy with his work, doing this and that. I think he's trying to prove to his father that he's ready to take on more responsibility, but I think he needs to get out more. Anyways, he should be right through here. I'm Sybille, if you need anything." She pushed open a door that was slightly ajar and glanced around briefly. "A visitor for you, monsieur." She slipped out of the study as I entered a small room lined with books.

Bram was sitting at a desk but pushed back his chair and stood when he realized it was me. "Emile. What a pleasant surprise."

I rubbed the back of my neck shyly. "Hello, Bram. I didn't mean to interrupt your day. I came to offer to buy you lunch. As a thank-you."

Bram waved the gesture away. "No need. That is to say, I'll let you buy me lunch one day, but not as payback." He pulled a chair out for me, across the desk from him as he returned to his seat. "I already ate today, I'm sorry to say."

"That's okay. Another time then."

Bram grinned. "I hope that's a promise. I had a wonderful time the other night."

"Me too."

Bram watched me for a moment and then frowned. "Are you sleeping well? You have circles under your eyes."

"Oh," I straightened and rubbed at my eyes, as if that would help. "I . . . not really, to be honest. We had the late night at the opera, and then something unexpected happened that kept me tossing and turning last night."

"What was it?"

I opened my mouth, then closed it. "It's nothing."

Bram leaned forward. "Emile. You can tell me anything. Maybe talking about it will help."

I swallowed hard, meeting his eyes. Those beautiful dark eyes rimmed by those long lashes. I wondered how they would regard me if he knew the truth about me. Henri had reacted in an unexpected way when he'd ferreted out the truth about me. Not everyone would react the same, but it made me hesitate nonetheless. Especially since Alexander had nearly seen me at the opera, and being so nearly discovered had been a close enough call. I didn't need to invite more trouble to my doorstep. Revealing truths about myself would do nothing but make me more conspicuous.

"What is your opinion of Count Morano?"

"Count Morano," Bram's mouth turned downward imperceptibly. "I would watch myself around that one."

I sat up. "Why's that?"

Bram hesitated. "Count Morano used to come around often, if you must know. He seemed to enjoy my company and would invite me to dine with him and his sister. Once after supping with them at a pub, I'd forgotten my hat and went back in to retrieve it, when I overheard him talking about me to several men at the bar. He said that he felt sorry for me apprenticing to a man who had such backward ways of conducting medicine, that the townsfolk were *experiments* for him in his attempt to advance the field. These were some of my father's customers, mind you, his livelihood. *Our* livelihood. He said he wouldn't trust us with his horse, let alone his family, and they should reconsider who they had seeing to their health."

I winced. "That's awful."

Bram fidgeted, as if embarrassed by relating this encounter to me. "When the most powerful family in town talks about you like that, word gets around. We lost the confidence of several patients. We still haven't recovered some of them. Morano, at least, had the decency to look chagrined when he realized I'd overheard, but then said, 'I don't suppose we'll be seeing you for dinner tomorrow then.' Like this wasn't my profession he was calling into question." Bram shook his head. "That boy is thoughtless and doesn't care about the difficulties he causes to those around him."

My stomach twisted. This account served to confirm my opinion of Henri's character. He could spin pretty words to cover ugly lies, but I would remain wary around him. If that was how he treated his friends, I could only imagine how he would treat his servants in the end.

Bram sat up. "Emile? Did something happen with Count Morano?"

I gazed around the study, searching for something to change the subject, but my mind was spinning, and I couldn't focus.

"Hey," Bram was suddenly at my side, a hand on my shoulder. "What is it?"

"I'm worried about my job," I blurted, embarrassed to find that I was crying.

Bram handed me a kerchief from his pocket, and I ran it over my eyes, blinking back more tears. "It's silly, really."

"Hey, it's not silly. Please. I'm here to listen."

I held his kerchief out to him, but he waved it away. "You keep it."

My mouth felt dry as I opened it. I didn't know why I felt compelled to tell him the truth, but he wasn't like Henri. Bram had been another victim of Henri's selfishness, and he hadn't been obligated to relate what was clearly a troubling exchange from his past to a relative stranger. He'd told me because he trusted me, and I should be able to return that trust. Maybe Bram would understand. He seemed so empathetic, the very opposite of Henri. On the other hand, Bram might find me revolting, turn his back on me, and I would never see him again, but was it really a friendship to begin with if he rejected me in such a way? All I knew was that I really, *really* wanted to be able to talk to somebody about this.

"I became Count Morano's valet. I didn't want the position, but I couldn't really refuse either. And then I found out it was because he likes me." I licked my lips and watched Bram to gauge his reaction, but he looked more confused than anything.

"Of course he likes you. I'm sure everyone likes you."

I blinked at him for a moment before shaking my head slowly. "No, I mean . . . he prefers the company of men. And he likes *me*."

Bram looked startled but didn't flinch. "Did he force himself on you?"

I stiffened. "What? No. He didn't do anything. He said he wants to win my heart or something like that." I reached out and touched Bram's arm. "But you can't tell anyone. Please."

"Of course not," Bram agreed, seating himself on the edge of his desk as he appeared to turn my predicament over. "How does that make you feel?"

I sighed. "Confused. Frustrated. I already told him no, but he wants me to think about it."

"Well, you can't let him coerce you."

"I know, I know. I . . . I mean, I do find him attractive. I also like . . . men." I winced as I said the words out loud, that I'd admitted such a startling truth. But Bram only nodded, as if he'd already known. "But I just . . . I don't think I can be with him in the way he wants me to be." I shrugged helplessly.

"Thank you for telling me that, Emile. That was very brave of you. And for now, if he seems content on trying to win you over, maybe you allow that while you look for employment elsewhere."

I shook my head slowly. "No, that's . . . that won't work. The letter of recommendation I procured was a fake. Or rather, it was real, but it was written as a favor, and I can't replicate that again. I don't think I'll be able to find other work."

Bram frowned. "Emile. You gave them the name Dupont, didn't you? St. Aubert is your true surname."

"Yes." I let out a shaky breath. "Yes. I'm in hiding."

"From whom?"

I stood, unable to remain idle while confessing. It felt good to have this out, but it also made me nervous to admit these things. Trusting someone was hard. Though I wanted desperately to trust Bram. "My aunt. When my father died, I inherited every-thing as his sole heir."

Bram squinted at me. "And that wasn't a good thing?"

I began to pace. "No. Well, yes and no. I'm sorry, Bram. I wanted to tell you from the beginning. I just couldn't. I had to keep my head down and bide my time until I come of age in six months. Then my aunt won't be in charge of my finances.

They'll be mine and I can collect them and . . . I don't even know. Somehow, I'll be able to escape her clutches."

Bram held up his hands. "Whoa, slow down. Who is your aunt?"

I hesitated. "Madame Cheron. She was my father's sister. She's just . . . she's terrible, Bram. I think she resents that my father left everything to me, even though she has her own money."

Bram walked around his desk and sank back into his chair, assessing me over his steepled fingers. The scrutiny made me shift uneasily. "Why are you so afraid of your aunt, Emile? I feel like I'm missing something. What's the worst she could do? Withhold your inheritance?"

I released a loud sigh as I returned to my chair. "Worse. She threatened to have me committed to an asylum."

His eyebrows shot up. "On what grounds?"

I looked back at him glumly. "Deviancy. She found out that I like men. And if I don't renounce my ways and marry before I turn eighteen, she will see her threat through."

"Then she will inherit your father's estate in your stead." Bram shook his head. "Devious."

"So, I ran away. I figured that if I hid until I came of age, I could return to claim my inheritance and be gone before she has a chance to challenge it." I winced. "It's not the most solid plan, but it's all I have. I can't just pretend that I don't have these feelings. How fair would it be to marry a woman when I couldn't love her? No one deserves an empty marriage."

"Many people marry for titles, especially the nobility. That being said, your aunt is a monster. You should have the right to love whomever you want."

"But if I don't marry, the line will end with me. That is my aunt's main complaint."

Bram nodded and stroked his chin. "She does have a point. If only there was a way to satisfy her without resorting to turning your back on who you are."

"There's not. And now that I think of it, that's probably what Henri wants: to wed a woman and have me as his lover. Appearances would be satisfied, as would his own desires. It's rather brilliant, really, especially if he can pull it off with someone as close as his valet." I couldn't help the venom from leaking into my voice and put a hand to my head. "I'm sorry, Bram. You didn't deserve to be lied to, and you didn't need to shoulder this burden. It was of my own making."

"I'm happy to be in your confidence," Bram assured me. "It means that you trust me. I wanted your trust very much."

I smiled. "Thank you."

"Of course."

"And I don't regret running away. If I hadn't, I would never have gotten to know you."

Bram watched me for a moment, and then straightened a document on his desk. "Well, I can assure you that this will be our little secret."

My heart sank. I'd been hoping for more of an enthusiastic response. It kind of hurt, but he had said that he'd wanted my trust. At least he didn't hate me, which could have very well been the case. Yet it did make me wonder if he would feel comfortable alone in a carriage with me again. Was I making this situation worse? Was I scaring away my one friend in this corner of the country?

Bram cleared his throat. "If Count Morano tries anything to force you to obey his . . . *wishes*, come to me. I'll help if I can."

"I appreciate that. More than you know."

Bram nodded, then sighed as he regarded his watch. "I have to make a house call shortly. I'm sorry."

I shook my head. "No, it's quite alright. Thank you for listening. And not hating me."

"Emile," Bram sighed. "I could never, ever hate you."

I walked away from Bram with a little heartache, but I knew I could rely on him should I need someone. I wasn't completely and utterly alone.

EIGHT

I turned my back as Henri began to disrobe. I distracted myself by smoothing out the wrinkles of his coat, a brown tweed that I thought would go well with his complexion. Annette had helped me press his dress shirt earlier, one of many lessons I was sure to receive from her. But she hadn't made a big deal out of it. She'd had her own duties to perform and was efficient in showing me what had to be done.

"I'm afraid my sister is jealous she couldn't borrow you tonight," Henri said, suddenly beside me. "I think poor Annette seems second-rate now, by comparison."

He was shirtless. My eyes drank in his broad shoulders and corded arms, zeroing in on his naked chest, dark hair spread across it in the most enticing ways. Of course he noticed my stare, and smiled knowingly as I handed him his dress shirt. I kept my gaze trained across the room as he slipped into it. I wouldn't give him any encouragement if I could help it. But that body of his made it very hard.

"Help me?"

I turned to find him buttoned into his dress shirt and holding the tweed coat out to me. Stepping up behind him, I slid his arms into the sleeves. I walked around to face him, trying not to notice the glimpse of hair at his collarbone before I fastened the last button at the top and helped him with his cravat. He watched me all the while, even as I tried to ignore him.

"Thank you," he said softly, and his eyes were so tender that I found myself fussing over his coat, running my hands over it to smooth it out, and . . . lingering.

I forced myself to step away and cleared my throat. "You look stunning, my lord. The girls will be swooning over you."

"As if I care," he said, and snorted, turning to a mirror to give himself one last look. "You do good work, Dupont."

I nodded and we stared at each other for a moment before Henri swallowed and turned away. "I should get down there," he said. "Can't be late to my own ball."

"Couldn't have that," I agreed.

Henri chuckled. "And if you don't mind, maybe duck in to see how my sister is faring? She gets anxious at these things."

I watched him leave before sitting on the edge of his bed. What had that been? Dressing him had been so intimate, almost too much. My heart still hadn't slowed from the closeness of him, and what that had stirred within me. Perhaps I was thawing toward him?

I shook my head, reminding myself that I was his *employee*. Even if I did find him attractive, I couldn't act on it. I wouldn't have that sort of existence. And anyway, in six months' time, I would be leaving Château le Blanc behind, and Henri with it. If not sooner.

Blanche was putting the finishing touches on her hair when I arrived at her door.

"Oh, great," Annette sighed. "Here to show me up again, are you?"

"Annette, be nice," Blanche reproached with a frown. She walked over to me and twirled in place. "What do you think?"

She wore a pink dress gleaming with beads and trimmed with fringe. The neckline plunged a little more than was probably proper for society, but I wasn't going to point that out. In all honesty, I didn't think the color did her many favors, but she was such a beautiful creature that I doubted it would make any difference.

"I think you'll be the belle of the ball once more," I said, inclining my head. "Good work, Annette."

Annette met my eyes and gave me a begrudging nod, even deigning to smile.

Blanche's eyes shone. "It's so exciting, isn't it? So many handsome young men begging to dance with me. And oh, how I love to dance." She demonstrated by waltzing across the room, laughing as she fell onto her bed. She held up her feet and Annette obliged by slipping her shoes on. "And how does my brother look?"

"Perfect, of course," I replied dryly. "*I* dressed him."

Annette snorted, and Blanche rolled her eyes.

"I'll be damned if I let that smug prig outshine me." Blanche grinned, standing and fussing over her hair for a moment. "Well, wish me luck, darlings."

"You hardly need any," I told her.

Blanche blew me a kiss and shimmied from the room.

Annette and I remained staring after her for a moment. "She can be exhausting."

I laughed. "She is full of energy."

"Spirited."

We exchanged amused looks.

"Do you like working here?" I ventured to ask.

Annette raised an eyebrow. "Why? Having second thoughts now that you've secured your big promotion?"

"I wasn't gunning for a promotion. But the Montoni family is intense, wouldn't you agree?"

"Well, Count Montoni is," Annette acknowledged. "But Blanche and Henri are good kids." She cocked her head. "I can't speak for being a valet, but being a lady's maid is a good job. You get to see the world. It's probably the best either of us will ever get, given our lot."

"I didn't mean to sound ungrateful. I was curious how you found it here."

Annette pursed her lips. "There are some oddities."

"The gold cutlery."

"The gold cutlery," Annette agreed, an impish smile flashing over her lips. "But more than that. You'll find out later this week, I'm sure. The staff will be given the evening off, but we'll remain on to wait on Henri and Blanche. And the doctor will see to Montoni."

"That's rather generous." I paused, eyes narrowing. "The doctor will be here? You mean the monk?"

"Yes. The family gets sick, you see. The doctor comes around and . . . my, he makes my spine tingle."

"They get sick?"

"Yes. I think it's something the doctor gives them. It's supposed to be cleansing, I think, and they sweat it out all night." She waved a hand. "It's an odd quirk; puts me on edge."

I frowned. "Yes. I'd imagine it does." Perhaps there was more to this than it seemed. Perhaps the leverage I sought would be found during one of these nights. With the château all but empty, it would give me the perfect opportunity to poke around without prying eyes.

"And of course, there's Udolpho Castle. It's never fun to venture to that infernal place."

I perked up. "Udolpho Castle?" I echoed. I tried not to seem too interested, even if my hopes were tied up in the retreat. "What's that?"

"You'll find out eventually. The family makes at least one trip out to that dreary pile of stones each year." She glanced up at the open door briefly before leaning into me. "The place is haunted, you know. I've heard it myself. The walls themselves moan."

I shuddered, trying to discern whether Annette was teasing me or not.

She looked serious.

But haunted or not, Udolpho might be my best chance at independence. Good thing I didn't believe in ghosts. After all, it clearly hadn't hurt the Montoni family over the years. A drafty castle was bound to be better than a padded cell.

A figure was suddenly standing in the doorway, and we both looked up expectantly. A woman was holding a bouquet of flowers. "Is this Lady Morano's room? I'm to arrange these for her." She smiled and stepped into the room. "Perhaps you could fetch a vase for me?"

I blinked. Her red hair was a stark contrast to her plain black uniform, and those freckles spread across the bridge of her nose . . . She clearly wasn't a member of the household staff. Had she been sent to the château with this delivery? I narrowed my eyes as I suddenly placed where I'd seen her before.

I straightened. "What are you doing here?"

The woman tensed and then scowled as she recognized me from the hedge maze. "No need to cause a scene." She tossed the bouquet of flowers aside, dropping the pleasant tone of her voice. "Give me a moment alone in her room and you'll never see me again."

Never see her again? I didn't understand her need for subterfuge unless it was for a sinister reason. Did she plan on doing something untoward to the room? An act of vandalism? Or was she looking to steal items of value? I felt uneasy as I noted the dangerous gleam in the girl's eyes, as if she wouldn't balk at doing me harm to have her way.

I met Annette's startled gaze and nodded to her. Annette frowned, but walked to the door, giving the mystery woman a wide berth. As soon as she crossed the threshold, I said "Get Grimes. Quick."

The girl growled and spun toward Annette, but the maid had already scampered up the hallway. When she turned back to me, I was brandishing the only thing I could find within reach that could fend off a dangerous person: a fireplace poker. I held it up threateningly.

"You can just leave now, before he gets here," I said.

The woman eyed the poker in my hands, before searching the vanity behind me. She gave a frustrated grunt before whirling away and fleeing into the hall.

I held my ground for another minute before peeking into the hallway. The mysterious woman had vanished, but Montoni hustled up the hall toward me, Annette at his heels.

"Where is she?" Montoni demanded when he reached me, his eyes finding the poker in my hand.

"Gone, my lord. She fled."

"And you didn't go after her?" Montoni roared and slapped me. My head snapped to the side, and I gasped. The blow had been vicious, and my cheek stung fiercely. I held a hand up to it, shocked by the actions of this man. If only he knew who he had attacked so ruthlessly.

When I looked back up, Montoni was heaving, his face red. Suddenly I understood Blanche and Henri's fear.

"You," he growled. "You're the one who found the hand off the footpath." He sneered at my surprised look as I wondered how he had uncovered that detail. Hadn't Grimes wanted that kept secret?

"The gendarmerie warned me about you," he said, as if hearing my thoughts. "Trouble has a tendency to follow you, doesn't it?" He leaned into me, and I shrank back, bracing myself in case he should strike me once more. "I'm watching you, *valet*. If anything else goes awry around here, I know who to seek out."

I gaped at him. Was he threatening me? *Me?* Because I had innocently stumbled upon a severed hand and had the audacity to report it, as was my duty? He must have realized that I had just stopped an intruder from accessing his niece's room, and yet he blamed me for this? And now I was under Montoni's scrutiny. It would make it harder to uncover anything of consequence that he might be hiding.

Aside from that ugly temper.

"Uncle?"

Montoni's head turned back up the hallway as Henri appeared. When Count Morano saw me cradling my cheek, his face hardened. "What happened?"

"A woman tried to enter your sister's bedchambers," Montoni declared, scowling. "These two deterred her."

"And that earned him a beating?"

Montoni grunted and turned to me. "What did she look like?"

Annette stepped forward. "Red hair, sir. In her early twenties, I'd say."

"Let me guess: freckles across her nose."

I blinked and met Annette's eyes. "Yes, sir."

Montoni stomped away in a huff. Clearly, he knew who the mysterious woman was. That was curious. Perhaps she knew the very secret I was hoping to discover. People didn't go to the lengths that woman had for no reason. But then why target Blanche's room? Was the whole family involved in covering something up? Just what was going on here?

"Are you alright?" Henri was suddenly in front of me. He gingerly lifted my chin and turned my stinging cheek toward him. He winced. "You should apply a poultice to that." His fingers on my chin drifted toward my lips before he seemed to remember himself and stepped back. "Annette, I trust you can see to him?"

"Of course, my lord," Annette curtsied and hurried to my side. "I'll bring him down to the kitchens at once."

"Very good."

I allowed Annette to lead me away, glancing back once to find Henri watching our progress with concern. I felt the phantom touch of his fingers on my skin and shuddered, but I knew not if it was out of fear or pleasure.

NINE

A nnette unearthed a salve from the kitchen, and I stepped out
into the cool night air to soothe my stinging cheek. I leaned
into the stone of the château, reveling in the numbing cold I
found there. Montoni had been surprisingly strong. And violent.
I hadn't feared him before, but I felt something akin to it now.

The sweet sounds of an orchestra floated out from the ballroom to greet me as I circled the château, stopping at a window
wall that led out onto the patio. I caught glimpses of dancing
through the curtains, and smiled at the gaiety. How I wished
I was in there, enjoying myself. I missed balls and gossip and
good music. If I could be in the middle of the fray, I would be
reacquainted with happiness. Instead, I was left out in the cold,
hoping my cheek didn't swell to twice its size by morning.

I sighed.

"There you are."

I jerked back from the windows, as if I'd been caught peeping, which I supposed I had been. Bram stood before me, grinning. The smile vanished when he caught sight of my cheek. "That doesn't look good."

He approached and ran the back of his fingers lightly down my cheek before pursing his lips. He knelt down suddenly, and I realized that he had his doctor bag with him. After rummaging for a minute, he pulled out a poultice and handed it to me.

I smiled gratefully. "You're a lifesaver."

Bram led me to a low wall to sit, and I held the poultice to my cheek. After a minute, I felt something like a cool caress over my cheek. It was heavenly.

"What are you doing here?" I asked as he watched me.

Bram shrugged. "Oh, you know. I was in the neighborhood . . ." At my dubious expression, he smirked. "Madame Mason fainted. I was summoned. Once she was revived, Annette told me you required a poultice."

"I am lucky you had one."

"I always come prepared."

We smiled at one another for a moment before a shooting star caught our eyes from overhead. We tilted our heads toward the night sky. The stars were dazzling. With the sound of music in the background, it almost felt magical.

"Quite a night. The sky is beautiful," Bram observed.

"Not as exciting as what's going on inside," I countered, pointing a thumb back toward the window wall.

"Do you like that sort of thing? Dances? Preening socialites?"

"I would kill to be a preening socialite right now," I sighed.

Bram snorted. "I couldn't imagine it. You're the most down-to-earth man I've ever met. Practical, smart . . ." He looked away for a moment before brightening. He stood and held a hand out to me.

I cocked an eyebrow. "What?"

"Dance with me."

"What?"

"Come on. Out here on the patio. No one will see."

I considered his hand for a moment and then grinned, setting down the poultice. I took his hand and followed him to the window wall.

"A waltz," I said after listening for a moment. "Do you know it?"

Without a word, Bram led me into a waltz, spinning me slowly and carefully across the stone ground. I laughed as I was twirled, and beamed up at Bram as he held me close, his hands gripping mine confidently.

"You're very good at this," I praised him.

"My partner makes it easy on me."

I raised an eyebrow, less than convinced, and he laughed as he pulled me in closer so that our chests touched. His eyes bore into mine so earnestly that they took my breath away.

And then he kissed me.

I was taken by surprise, so I stood still momentarily as his lips pressed into mine, imploring mine to part and meet his. I melted into Bram's embrace and opened my mouth to him, deepening the kiss, soft and urgent at the same time. By the time the kiss ended, we were both out of breath. I stared up at Bram with wonder. "I didn't think . . . I'd hoped, but . . ."

In response, Bram covered my mouth with his again, lips crushing into one another with more need now. His arms circled my back, pulling my body against his solid form, and I sighed into his mouth.

Bram disentangled himself and gazed down at me, searching. "Was that alright? I didn't mean to surprise you like that. You just looked so handsome, and I got caught up in the moment and . . ."

"It was perfect," I said breathlessly, tentatively reaching up to stroke his cheek. My fingers slid down to his swollen lips. "You're perfect."

Bram swallowed hard. "I've wanted to do that for a while now. It killed me to hear what Morano did to you." He grabbed my hands. "Did he do that to your cheek?"

I blinked. "What? No. Henri wouldn't strike me. It was Montoni."

"Montoni." He scowled. "We need to find a way to get you away from here."

"No, it's . . . I don't think it will happen again. Henri has actually been very kind to me. I think he intends to keep his word. He won't pressure me."

Bram didn't look convinced. "You're sure?"

"I'm sure. I'm safe for now. I'll let you know if that changes."

With a sigh, Bram released my hands. "Very well."

I smiled. "Thank you for your concern though. It means a lot to me. Truly."

"Of course I'm concerned." Bram pulled me to him, arms snaking around me once more. His mouth found mine in a slow, sensual kiss. I felt myself burning for him by the time it ended, and I was left staring into eyes I knew I would never grow tired of observing. "I should go," he said with reluctance. "When I was summoned, I was with my father at a farmhouse where there's a sick brood of children. I should really get back to help him."

I nodded. "Then go. I'll still be here tomorrow."

Bram lifted my hand and kissed it gently. "Sweet dreams."

I chuckled. "Good night. And good luck with the . . . *brood*."

Bram rolled his eyes but was grinning as he left me on the

patio, soft music still wafting from the ballroom behind me. I leaned against the low wall and placed the poultice back against my cheek. I felt as if I were in a dream. Had that really happened? Had Bram just danced with me and kissed me? I hadn't even been sure he liked men and suddenly I was in his arms, more sure of him than anything in the world. If I'd been reluctant to fall for him before, I allowed myself to let my guard down now. Bram was charming, warm, thoughtful . . . I could actually see myself with him. And it didn't hurt that he was an excellent kisser. Perhaps I could continue to see him when the dust settled from my inheritance, or when Udolpho was in my possession.

I sighed, deciding that I should probably return to the servants' hall. When Count Morano turned in, he would ring for me, and I would need to be available. It would likely be hours yet, but I wouldn't turn down a late dinner in the meantime.

I started back toward the servants' entrance when a figure stepped out from around the corner.

I tensed, expecting to find the mystery woman waiting to attack me for interfering earlier. But the figure I found looming over me was no woman. I blinked as I realized that it was Count Morano.

"Henri?" I asked, squinting up at him.

Henri crossed his arms. "The apprentice? Really? Did you have fun dancing with him? Kissing him? Laughing at me behind my back?"

I took a step back, startled. "Henri, it wasn't like that. I never meant to hurt you. What happened back there just . . . happened. It had nothing to do with you."

Henri's jaw tightened and he let out a sound of disgust. "Monsieur Valancourt isn't allowed anywhere near Château le

Blanc any longer. I'm giving the order tomorrow to turn him away should he come. From now on, you can all be seen by Monseigneur Schedoni. Our family physician should be good enough for the rest of you."

I winced. "Henri. He didn't do anything wrong. And I'm not yours to keep. I can do what I like."

Henri frowned down at me. "I mean to keep my word and let you come around, but the one thing I forbid is for you to let that man onto these grounds. Do I make myself clear?"

The count's voice was low and dangerous, as if on the verge of erupting. I felt fear course through my body as I nodded my acquiescence. "Yes, my lord."

Henri's cheek twitched. "Get inside."

I nodded and stumbled toward the servants' entrance, eyes burning with tears. I gasped as I flung myself inside and slammed the door shut behind me.

TEN

I was kept busy with chores over the next few days. Overnight it seemed my workload had tripled, as Henri demanded his whole wardrobe be meticulously sorted and mended where necessary. It was a good learning opportunity, and I spent most of my days in the company of Annette, who taught me to patch holes, strengthen buttons, and sew. I hadn't seen Bram in that time, but I did catch wind of the fact that he'd been to the château and turned away, at the request of Count Morano. As promised.

I suspected that part of the reason I was being kept so busy was so that I wouldn't have the opportunity to go into town to call on Bram myself. It was infuriating, and I chalked it up to jealousy on Henri's part. He was acting out like a child. Hardly the sort of behavior that was going to endear me toward him any time soon.

Henri was down to tea one afternoon, and while sorting through his wardrobe, I came across a locket in one of his coat pockets. I sat down on the edge of his bed and opened the clasp to reveal the portrait of a young woman with blonde hair and a young man with a carefree smile. I studied the two figures briefly before I recognized the woman as the same as the portrait in the library downstairs. Henri and Blanche's mother. Her eyes weren't painted with the same ethereal green in this picture, but I recognized her nonetheless. The man, I presumed, was their father. He was a handsome man with meticulously styled walnut hair and a neatly trimmed mustache.

"They made for a fine couple, didn't they?"

I gasped and dropped the locket, earning a reproving look from Annette. She scooped down to pick it up and smiled at the portraits. "You can really see the resemblance, can you not?"

I stood and peered over her shoulder. Now that I was looking, I could see Henri's jawline in his father, and Blanche's nose. "Did you know either of them?"

Annette tapped the portrait of the man. "I knew Count Victor Morano. Countess Helena Morano had already killed herself by the time I was hired by the family for her ladyship. That must have been, oh, five years ago now."

I blinked. "Wait. Their mother killed herself? I thought it was an accident, that she lost her footing while exploring a cliff."

"It's likely easier to imagine it happening in such a way." Annette sighed, returning the locket to my hand. "But I heard from a reliable source that she threw herself off that cliff. I've even heard that she was running from her husband at the time, but I believe that to be a wild embellishment."

Frowning, I held the locket closer to my face, examining the smiling woman with eyes so like Henri's. It was hard to believe that such a beauty would end her life in such a gruesome way. Or be driven to it. Feeling a little uneasy at the revelation, I closed the locket. "What was their father like?"

Annette smiled. "Oh, he was a kind man. Imagine the polar opposite of Count Montoni. Generous, warm. He always took the time to converse with the staff and treated us exceptionally well. But I'm afraid his wife's death took a toll on him." She shrugged. "Bullet to the head. It was a terrible time, that. And so hard on the children, Henri in particular."

"That's . . . awful," I said quietly, trying to imagine a younger version of Henri experiencing such a tragedy. It had to have been traumatizing. I suddenly felt very sorry for him. No child should have to suffer through such things.

I recalled the hurt, the betrayal, I'd seen mixed in Henri's face the other night. I hadn't recognized it then, but I did now. He'd probably felt like he hadn't been enough of a reason for his father to stay. And now he felt like he wasn't enough for me to like him. I did sympathize with Henri in this new light, but I couldn't let him control me, even if he desperately needed to feel in control of the situation. It wouldn't be fair to either of us, and his self-worth would be even worse off if I left him abruptly in six months.

"But enough gossip," Annette said. "Bring down any other coats you find that need mending, and we'll finish this up today. Then you're going to return the favor and mend some of her ladyship's things."

"I insist upon it." I hesitated as Annette turned to leave. "Say, Annette? Can I beg a favor?"

Annette looked wary. "What is it?"

I licked my lips, unsure of how to secure Annette's aid. I'd come to the realization that if I was to uncover something damning against Montoni, that I would need help. If he was suspicious of me, he could have warned other servants, such as Grimes, to watch me. I needed to tread carefully if I didn't want to find myself tossed out or, even worse, at the mercy of the gendarmerie. Annette was a trusted member of the household staff. She was the perfect candidate to aid me in my search. But how to convince her . . .

"Count Montoni doesn't strike me as a very noble man," I said slowly. "He seems paranoid, like he's hiding something . . . something important. I think we would all be better off if he was convinced to leave this household in the hands of Henri and Blanche."

It wasn't a lie. Not exactly. Part of my negotiation with Montoni, given the temper I'd witnessed, needed to extend to his niece and nephew. I wouldn't feel good about occupying their family retreat if I left them to fend off Montoni's rage, especially given that they seemed willing to go to extreme lengths to curtail whatever trouble he was getting himself into. I only needed to secure an escape for myself to get away from this family. As cruel as Henri was, I didn't need to make an enemy of him while his uncle was the more present threat, especially since this family had seen enough tragedy already.

Annette's eyes narrowed. "What are you saying exactly, Dupont?"

I shrugged. "I'm just asking you to keep your eyes and ears open. Between the two of us, we might uncover whatever it is that Montoni is trying to keep under wraps. That information could be enough to free us all from him. Just imagine how much lighter Blanche would be without her uncle around."

"That, she would," Annette considered. She crossed her arms. "I can tell you have your heart in the right place. I'm not sure what could be so important that it would drive Montoni from the château, but I also saw the way he treated you outside my lady's room. He feels threatened by something, sure enough. No, I don't suppose I mind keeping an eye out, but anything you come across, I want to hear about as well. If I'm doing this, I want to do this as an equal. In this together."

I raised an eyebrow. "Very well, Annette. We share what we uncover."

Annette grinned. "I'll try to convince Ludovico to watch for anything suspicious as well."

"Ludovico?" I echoed, trying to place the name.

"Hardworking, reliable. Does odds and ends. He can keep a secret."

"Very well. But don't speak about it to anyone else. Even your lady. If Montoni catches wind of our plans, there's no telling what he could do."

"I won't breathe a word. But mind you, I'm not sticking my neck out and snooping unnecessarily. I didn't work my way into this position just to find myself out on the street."

"Perfectly understandable."

Annette sent me a conspiratorial wink before shuffling out the door. When I found myself alone once more, I took up the locket and spared one more glance at the couple before replacing it in the pocket where I'd unearthed it.

I came upon Fournier as he was bustling down the hallway on a Friday evening, suitcase in hand.

"Fournier," I strode quickly over to catch up to him. The man paused and looked back at me uncertainly. I tried for a smile as I scratched the back of my neck. "I wanted to make it clear that I didn't seek the valet position."

Fournier grinned. "Ah. Still hung up on that, are you? No need to worry. In truth, I was glad to leave that position behind."

"You were?"

"Of course. My lordship is very particular, and I was always worried about bumbling something or other. Second Man is easier by far." He reached out and shook my hand jovially. "No hard feelings, Dupont."

He turned and headed up the hall once more, and I watched him go as Mrs. Blake also made for the door, suitcase in hand.

"Mrs. Blake? Where is everybody going?"

Mrs. Blake smiled. "Ah, you're one of the unlucky ones who gets to stay behind. The family gives the staff a night off once a month. They even spring for an inn in town for us. Quite generous of them." She shrugged at my surprised look. "There's turkey in the icebox for your dinner. The family ate early tonight, and I'll be back by eight tomorrow to have breakfast ready, although it's usually served late on such days."

"Oh, alright then."

"Alright then," Mrs. Blake echoed, turning once more for the door. I watched her leave before walking to the kitchen. It was dark and small, but once I lit a candle, it was much more inviting. I found the turkey and some rolls for a sandwich and was just sitting down to eat when Annette breezed in.

"Is it to be turkey again?" she grumbled, rummaging about the kitchen. "Mrs. Blake needs to be a little more creative, if you ask me." She started a fire and set a kettle on the stovetop. "Some tea will be nice now, won't it?"

She sat down across from me and assembled a sandwich for herself.

"It's just you and me then?" I asked.

"Just you and me until Father Schedoni arrives."

"And then?"

"And then it's you, me, and Monseigneur Schedoni."

I rolled my eyes. "Thanks for that. I know basic addition."

"It was unclear."

I snorted and we sat in silence for the rest of our meal, Annette offering me a bitter black tea that I added honey to. When the bell rang for the library, we looked at each other.

"Are you prepared for a long night?" she asked as we made our way to the staircase.

"I'm not sure what's expected of me."

"Schedoni will show you. The rest you'll manage." She hesitated. "It's not pretty. You have to be strong. Hargrove was a squeamish man, but he bucked up when he needed to."

I frowned. "Wait. Hargrove attended to Henri on these nights? Not Fournier? I assumed it was the valet's duty."

Annette shook her head. "No. Count Morano chooses who attends to him. He chose you."

"Well, then. Lucky me." I paused. "Tonight would be a good night to procure information."

"If it's to be had," Annette agreed, smiling at me slyly.

Part of me felt a little bad for leaving out the fact that the information we uncovered could buy my way to a life out of my aunt's reach, but after Montoni confronted me about the hand I'd found, I was beginning to realize that some things were better left alone, and unsaid.

We arrived in the library to meet an expectant family. Count Montoni was seated before a roaring fire, wine glass in hand, looking as comfortable as could be. When he noticed me, his lips curved ever so slightly into a sneer. Henri and Blanche sat together on a sofa, looking a little more nervous. Father Schedoni was at the window, watching the sky. He was tall and thin, a coarse brown robe draped over his form. His hood was pushed back, revealing a man in his forties with salt and pepper hair and a neat beard. When he turned to face me, he offered a cold stare, and I had to suppress a shiver.

"It will be sundown shortly," Schedoni announced, turning to the family. "You'd best retreat to your rooms. Annette, I trust you know what to do?"

Annette nodded and accepted a small leather case from the monk before gathering Blanche and leaving the room.

"I will show you what needs to be done," Schedoni told me, all business. "I'll be back for you shortly, Count Montoni."

Montoni waved him off, and Schedoni led me and Henri from the room.

Henri looked pale. When I sent him a questioning look, he only responded with a tight smile.

Once we reached Henri's room, Schedoni set a leather case down on a side table and gestured for Henri to get into bed. Henri took off his coat, revealing a short-sleeved cotton shirt underneath.

"Now," Schedoni said, opening the flaps of the case, "I will give the count his first injection. You will need to give him an additional injection every two hours. However, if he seems to be worsening, particularly if the capillaries of his eyes burst, or you notice blood in his mouth, you may need to give him an injection sooner. So, you must remain vigilant."

I stared in horror as Schedoni revealed a row of large glass syringes with metal plungers. Inside each needle was a black substance that seemed to shimmer in the light with a greenish hue. The monk removed one of the syringes and I retreated a step.

"Injections?" I echoed, my voice rising an octave.

Schedoni eyed me warily. "Yes. In the arm." He tapped the syringe he was holding and squeezed on the plunger enough so that a small amount of liquid emerged. "Begin like this to expunge any air."

I nodded, my eyes wide as he approached Henri and showed me where to feel on his upper arm for the proper injection site. I was sweating as Schedoni pressed on the plunger, emptying the contents into Henri's arm.

"Like so. Very simple," the monk said as he tossed the empty syringe into a rubbish bin. He glanced up at the darkening window. "Now I must see to Count Montoni. I would recommend a water basin and a cloth to attend to the accompanying fever. Try to make him as comfortable as possible. There will be times when the patient will be unable to speak or communicate his wishes."

I watched, incredulous, as Father Schedoni strode from the room, leaving the patient in my care.

I turned to Henri and swallowed hard.

"You'll be a great nurse," he told me with a lopsided smile. "I have faith in you."

I ran a hand back through my hair. "You should have sent for someone more experienced. Like Valancourt."

Henri's face darkened. "I don't think I ever need to see that man again."

I pursed my lips and stepped over to the needles, grazing my fingertips over them. "What is this?"

"Medicine."

"Yes, but what kind of medicine?"

Henri didn't answer but stared up at the ceiling. "I know you must hate me right now. I'm sorry."

I watched him for a moment. I could tell he was trying to be brave, but he was fidgeting.

"I can feel it coming," he said softly.

I approached him cautiously. "What do you feel?"

He grunted, and then his back arched. He huffed and fell back onto the bed panting. I gripped his shoulder, where I could feel the heat of his skin through his shirt.

"Oh my God," I said, drawing back. "I . . . I'm going to get some cold water. You just stay. . ."

I hurried from the room and down to the kitchens to fill a basin. By the time I returned, Henri's shirt was soaked through with sweat. I grabbed a cloth and sat beside him, dabbing at his face and pushing the hair from his forehead.

"I'm sorry you have to . . . see me like this," he managed, gritting his teeth.

"Don't worry about that right now," I told him. "Just rest. I'll be right here."

Henri nodded and laid back, eyes closed against the pain.

I turned to glance at the syringes and wondered what sort of traditional medicine this monk was subjecting this family to.

When I turned back, Henri's eyes were wide open, and the green of his eyes had been completely swallowed by the black. In fact, it seemed that his irises were ringed with a strange gold. I drew back, shaking, as Henri seemed to fight against the pain, face screwed up, eyes squeezed shut once more.

"Henri?" I called tentatively. "What can I do for you, Henri?"

He opened his mouth but then gnashed his teeth together.

I wasn't sure what I could do, so I ran the cool cloth over his face again. Henri seemed to relax slightly under my touch, and when he opened his eyes again, they were the rich green I was used to seeing, if not unfocused and dazed.

"There you go," I cooed. "You're okay."

He grabbed for my free hand and held it tightly, meeting my eyes. I offered him a smile and continued to attend to his fever.

The time came when I would have to give him an injection. I stared at the syringe nervously, getting used to how it felt in my hands.

"You're doing great," Henri encouraged weakly from his bed.

I nodded, unsure.

"Hold up the syringe," Henri told me, "Then tap it. Yes, like that. Now, squeeze the plunger just a little until some of the medicine leaks out. Perfect."

I followed his instructions, but I still wasn't ready when I was faced with his bare arm. His skin was slick with sweat, and I was afraid that I was going to make things worse. He was clearly suffering under the effects of whatever this was, but who was I to interfere? Stopping the process now could prove to be fatal, and for all I knew, this was some sort of lifesaving treatment.

I recalled Schedoni's instructions, prodding Henri's arm and hoping to locate the site of the last injection, but I couldn't find it. Despite being such a large needle, it clearly didn't leave much of a mark behind.

I swallowed hard as I pushed the needle into Henri's arm and before I could think about it, I pressed down gently on the plunger until it was empty.

I let out a ragged breath as I withdrew it, gauging Henri's face. *What would happen if I accidentally killed a count*, I wondered.

But Henri only sent me a weak smile in response and sagged back against his pillow.

I perched nervously at his side, realizing that this was, indeed, going to be a terribly long night.

ELEVEN

After two hours, I gave Henri another injection. His pain seemed to subside a degree, but he remained feverish and mumbled incoherently as I doted on him.

When I next needed to fetch a new basin of water, I decided to look in on Father Schedoni to inquire about this treatment. Just what sort of sickness was this? They'd all seemed fine until I'd given Henri his injection, as if the medicine itself had made him ill. I'd never heard of this practice before, and it seemed both odd and painful. I didn't understand why the family bore it.

As Henri drifted into a fitful sleep, I crept from the room and marched to the east wing, where Count Montoni's room lay. As I walked, I realized that this presented me with an opportunity. Surely, if there was something incriminating to be had on the count, it would be in his bedchamber, locked in a drawer or tucked into a wardrobe, among his personal effects. I would simply need to get Schedoni to leave me alone for a time to search.

I wasn't worried about Montoni, given that he would likely be in a similar state to his nephew, not even lucid.

I could play up how sick Henri was, I devised, like it was life and death for Schedoni to check on him. I would, in turn, offer to watch Montoni in his absence.

I'd only been to this part of the château once, and the heavy candelabras that lined the passage had been lit then. Now, in the dark, I only had the moon to see by. Luckily, it was a full moon, so light spilled into the dark area liberally with each window I passed.

I began to feel apprehensive as I approached Montoni's room. I had to sell this lie, and Father Schedoni cut an intimidating figure. Holy men always made me feel uneasy, even when they were kind. Schedoni did not strike me as such.

A small recessed hallway led to Montoni's bedchamber. Like the dining hall, this was lined with suits of armor, the metal gleaming in the moonlight that managed to bleed into the darkness this far. I eyed a spear held by one of the clawed gauntlets and shivered before my gaze shifted to a morning star. Most of them held swords before them in dignified repose. I found it depressing that these suits once protected knights during battle, and now stood motionless, discarded, in the dark corridors of châteaus such as this. They deserved better.

I was surprised, as I neared, to find that Montoni's bedroom door was ajar. I could make out Schedoni pacing within, his brown robe a blur of movement in the flickering candlelight beyond.

"I've intercepted several of his family's letters," the monk was saying. "They are threatening to send an inspector. It may require a lot of money to make them happy, should it come to that. Too much money, mind you."

"I know, I know!" Montoni moaned, as if in pain. The moan

transformed into a cry of agony. "Father, I can't take it. Give me another injection, please. I beg of you."

"I need you coherent for another moment," Schedoni admonished him. "Push through the pain and focus. This is important. You were very sloppy with Hargrove. Should another incident occur too soon, I'm not sure all the money in the world can keep a reckoning at bay. People are already suspicious. Bribes will not be effective if this blows up."

I backed up from the door slowly, wincing as I collided with one of the suits of armor. I glanced up at the protruding helmet and clenched my jaw as the visor shifted on the helmet, dipping to reveal a gaping, empty darkness within.

I cursed silently and ducked behind the suit of armor as the door to Montoni's room was thrown open, flooding the passage with weak light. I tried to keep my breathing shallow as Schedoni lingered in the doorway, eyes narrowed as he peered into the corridor.

Something brushed against my hand, and I glanced down to find a spider crawling over it, pausing to stare at me with its large black eyes. And then I felt a subtle shift on my shoulder, and I saw another spider perched there, its hairy arms searching along my shirt.

I wanted to shriek and fling the spiders off me, but I didn't dare move. Schedoni momentarily disappeared back into the bedchamber, but he didn't close the door. I took the opportunity to fling the spider from my hand, but before I'd had a chance to dislodge the one on my shoulder, the monk returned, carrying a lantern. I held my breath as he stepped into the hallway.

I realized the implications of what I'd heard. Montoni had murdered Hargrove. I'd replaced a dead man. And I would very

likely find myself following suit if I was discovered to have overheard secrets not meant for my ears.

Schedoni took another tentative step into the hallway, eyes
searching the darkness as his lantern pressed it back. I felt more
movement across my arm and stared in disbelief as several
more spiders crawled along my arm, and then more, skittering
down the side of the suit of armor I clung to for concealment.
I lifted my eyes to see the mouth of the helmet erupting with
furry bodies. In a moment, the entire suit was covered in a
wriggling mass of spiders, many of them scampering over my
skin in their determination to leave what was likely a nest I had
inadvertently disturbed.

I squeezed my eyes shut and closed my mouth as spiders
descended over my face, featherlight touches that made me want
to run from my hiding place, ripping at my hair and clothing. But
I remained still, trying very hard not to think about what was
crawling all over my body.

In another moment, the light retreated from the hallway, and
I squinted to find that Schedoni had moved into the hall beyond.
I carefully extricated myself from the suit of armor I hid behind,
still teeming with a mass of bodies, and slid behind a different
knight's armor. I took several deep breaths to calm myself as I
felt spiders sliding down my pant legs, although I could tell from
the pressure I felt along my body that several still clung to me in
various places, including the back of my neck, where a furry leg
teased at my shirt collar. I didn't dare tempt fate any further by
trying to rid myself of the spiders, for I feared the rustling of my
clothes would alert Schedoni to my presence.

Finding nothing in the hallway beyond, Schedoni returned
to the corridor where I cowered. The spider at my neck had

determined that my shirt would make a warm, cozy place to hide, and I bit the inside of my cheek as I felt it squeeze inside, sliding along my flesh. Another probed at my ear and I found myself holding back a fresh scream as I wondered if spiders could slip into ears and lay eggs within.

Schedoni's lantern lifted suddenly, and I held very still as he pressed it close to the suit of armor that seemed alive with spiders. The monk made a disgusted sound at the back of his throat, one that I agreed with, and scowled down at a cluster of spiders that had managed to find their way to his foot. Schedoni took a step back, looking them over briefly, before lowering his shoe onto them with a wet crunch. A yellow-green liquid oozed out from beneath his shoe as he lifted his foot to reveal the flattened fur matted with green puss. With a sneer, Schedoni wiped the remaining viscera from his shoe across a clean stretch of carpet and returned to Montoni's bedroom, this time closing the door firmly behind him.

The moment the door closed, I stepped out from my hiding place and flung the weight of spiders from my body. I untucked my shirt and fanned the fabric at my back furiously until I felt the spider clinging to me drop to the floor. I batted at my head for good measure and continued to smooth out my clothing as I scurried from the corridor, leaving the nightmarish suit of armor behind and shuddering at the memory of furry legs traversing my skin.

I very much wanted to take a bath, or even roll around on the grass outside, but I'd already left Henri for longer than I'd intended and rushed down to the kitchen to fetch a new basin of water. When I returned to Henri's side, he was sweating profusely and whimpering softly. I wasn't sure if he was asleep, but I squeezed his hand gently and murmured to him as I wiped at his brow. I couldn't bring myself to return to Montoni's room after nearly being caught, and after what I'd overheard, I wasn't sure I was brave enough to rifle through the count's belongings with him in the room, even if he was incoherent. I could only hope for another opportunity.

The rest of the night passed rather tamely by comparison. I continued to administer the injections, and vowed to speak to Henri about what he was putting into his body. If he expected me to do this for him again, he was going to tell me exactly why I was doing it, or I would have no part in the affair henceforth.

Just before sunrise, Henri received his last injection. Exhausted from the sleepless night and constant worry, I allowed myself to fall onto Henri's bed, relieved to have completed my role. I wanted to slip into unconsciousness and not awake for a week. When I closed my eyes, I saw spiders spilling out of Henri's mouth, and I gasped at the vision. But Henri was fine. His breathing was even, he looked almost peaceful now that he'd fallen asleep. I closed my eyes again and hoped for dreamless slumber.

TWELVE

I awakened to sunlight flooding the room. I still felt exhausted, so I closed my eyes again, wishing for sleep to reclaim me. I felt warm and comfortable as I nestled into my pillow, although it wasn't as soft as I was used to. My mind began to recollect the evening's events, and I realized that I must still be in Henri's room. That explained why the room had seemed so bright. My small room on the third floor didn't even have a window. I should probably go to my own room, but maybe a little longer . . .

My eyes shot open as I heard a steady heartbeat beneath my ear. I blinked my sleep away and stared at the chest I was sleeping on, a powerful chest, covered in dark hair. Henri. I was sleeping on Henri's chest. It was warm and . . . and his arm was around me, pressing me against him. I took a deep, shuddering breath because it felt really good. But I had to go.

I lifted my head carefully so as not to wake Henri, but I found that it was unnecessary. Henri's eyes opened and a smile drifted lazily across his face. "Hello," he said.

"Um, hi," I returned, heart skipping a beat. I'd never woken up with another man before. Even if nothing had happened last night between us. I'd never felt a man's arms around me like this either. It was . . . everything I'd imagined and more. I just wished the circumstances were different.

Henri pulled me back down and we faced each other. His eyes looked into mine, and I suddenly found it very hard to breathe. "Thank you for taking care of me last night."

"Of course," I said, sitting up again. I could feel my face turning red. I had to get out of there. My eyes darted past him, where I spied his sweat-soaked shirt crumpled in a ball. He must have slipped it off after I'd fallen asleep.

"No, no, no," Henri protested, dragging me back down. He pulled me flush against him and curled into me, his arms holding me tightly, securely. I closed my eyes, basking in the feeling of warmth radiating through me.

I could have this every day if I wanted it, I realized. Waking up next to Henri, in his arms. He'd offered it to me, and right now, I wanted it more than anything. It felt so right. I relaxed back into him and let myself have this moment.

When I woke up next, I realized that the day had progressed significantly. The room wasn't nearly as bright.

Something had awakened me, so I sat up to find Henri walking toward the bed with a breakfast tray. I blinked. "What's this?"

"Breakfast," Henri stated the obvious. I spied scrambled eggs, toast, and bacon. "Mrs. Blake is used to us sleeping in on these days, so it's breakfast for lunch."

I stared as he set the tray down before me, my stomach

choosing that very moment to announce how hungry I was. To cover up the sound, I cleared my throat. "Shouldn't I be the one fetching us breakfast?"

Henri grinned. "I wanted to let you sleep a little longer. You needed the rest." He procured two small plates, which he filled for each of us. We leaned back against his pillows as we ate, and I was surprised to find that the silence was comfortable between us. Nice, even. Did I like Henri's company?

Henri sighed contentedly as he took a bite of toast, then stared down at his plate. "I know you're upset with me. For Valancourt. It's just that . . . I like you, Emile. I like you even more than I thought I could."

"You can't control me, Henri."

"I know." He raked a hand through his hair. "I just don't know how to be what people need me to be." He glanced at me. "Like you were, for me last night."

"You're there for your sister."

He nodded. "Yes, but that's different. She's family." He shook his head, as if to chase away a thought. "Tell me about your family."

"I . . . I'm an orphan."

"I'm sorry," Henri picked at the comforter. "We have that in common, I suppose."

"I suppose we do," I agreed, suddenly feeling awkward. I stood abruptly, not wanting him to take my lingering as assent to ask follow-up questions. "I should probably clean this up. We'll cause a scandal if we hole up in here any longer."

Henri snorted. "True enough. And don't mind if anyone gives you any sideways glances. I think half the staff believes we throw wild orgy nights when we send them off."

I blinked. "Are you serious?"

"I don't know." Henri laughed. "It's what I would think."

I grabbed a pillow and lobbed it at his face. "Most people don't have such filthy minds, Henri."

"Oh, my mind is very filthy," Henri said gravely, shaking his head.

I turned and walked from the room without a backward glance. "That, I believe."

Since the whole château had been given the previous night off, Annette and I were given leave the following day. We walked into town together but parted at a bank where she claimed to have some business to attend to. Despite my earlier promise to share information with her, I'd kept what I'd overheard between Montoni and Schedoni to myself, given its sensitive nature. I needed to process the information before I did anything with it. I was hoping Bram would have some insight to offer.

I continued up the main street, only pausing when I noted a crowd gathered at the corner where I would normally turn toward Bram's residence. When I realized the gendarmerie were there as well, I picked up my pace, wondering what could have happened. I hoped that the crowd I was seeing wasn't the edge of a larger mass, since Bram's house was so close.

But I needn't have worried. The clump of people congregated in front of a shop. As I drew nearer, I realized that it was the apothecary I'd noticed Montoni observing previously. I paused at the edge of the crowd, craning my neck to see if I could make out what had happened. I saw that the front window had shattered, and it looked as if the door had been forced in, splintered nearly in two.

"All right, all right," a gendarme stepped in front of the shop, holding his hands up imploringly. "Break it up now. Nothing to see here. Break it up."

The crowd murmured in response, dispersing begrudgingly as I walked slowly up the adjacent street to Bram's. This was my first opportunity to check in with Bram since he'd been banished from Château le Blanc. I didn't want to leave him in suspense any longer than was necessary.

When Sybille opened the door for me, she greeted me with a warm smile. "He's back in his study," she told me, leading me along the familiar hallway. "Been spending more and more time in there lately. I hope you can pry him away for a time. It would do him good."

"I'll do my best," I promised, and started as the door to the study opened ahead of us and Bram stepped out, lowering a top hat over his head.

"Monsieur, you have a visitor," Sybille announced as Bram spun toward us with surprise. She nodded once to me and swept past with a wink my way.

Bram beamed. "Emile! You're okay. I was getting worried."

I lifted my eyes to his and found an earnestness there as he searched me. "I'm fine. I've been busy. Intentionally, I'm sure. You must have realized that Count Morano banned you."

"Yes, I'd gathered that."

"He saw us that night." I lowered my voice and glanced up the hallway, as if Sybille might be lurking nearby to uncover our secrets.

Bram frowned. "Did he now? I take it he didn't like what he saw."

I licked my lips. "Clearly."

Bram nodded back toward his study and withdrew his hat.

"I'm interrupting something," I observed as he closed the door behind us.

"I was going to get a bite to eat. You're welcome to join me." He turned to me and pulled me to him.

"I mean, I think I have some time."

He grinned. "Yeah?"

And then his mouth was on mine, and I felt my knees grow weak. He pushed me against the door and pressed his lips to mine like a drowning man, desperate and greedy for air. I ran my hands over his chest and through his hair, finding that I couldn't get enough of him. I wanted to touch him all over and pulled him against me harder.

Bram gasped and pulled back, clearing his throat and straightening his cravat. "I'm . . . I'm sorry."

"It's fine. More than fine."

Bram chuckled, his eyes flicking down to my lips again. "I know. But I'm a gentleman, and as such, should show at least a modicum of restraint."

"Well, as long as it's only a modicum," I teased.

With a knowing smile, Bram opened the door again. "Shall we? If we have time, there's a wonderful little café nearby."

"I'll clear my schedule."

"Have fun, you two," Sybille called out as we slipped outside.

Bram waved to her, and I sent him a curious look when he closed the door behind us.

"Does she know?" I asked.

"About you and me? I can't keep much from Sybille."

"But your father—"

"Doesn't care who I see, so long as I'm happy."

I absorbed that, thinking how much easier my life would be if my aunt had adopted that attitude. "Must be nice."

"Well, it's nice not to have to keep it a secret from my family, but the rest of society is a different beast entirely."

We began walking up the street when Bram paused at the apothecary. "It looks like the crowd is finally gone."

"What happened?" I asked, squinting into the darkened shop now that I didn't have a mass of people obscuring my view. Shelves were knocked to the floor, bowls of herbs smashed to pieces and spilling their contents across the ground. It looked like it had been ransacked.

"I noticed it in that state this morning when I was out on an errand. I'm not sure."

I saw the gendarme who had interviewed me a few weeks back standing inside, gazing down at something covered in a white sheet.

"Is that a body?" I asked, eyes wide.

Bram hesitated. "Let me see if they need my expertise. I'll only be a moment."

I nodded as Bram stepped through the doorway, careful not to disturb the door. I hesitated a second before following. I stared at the door as I slid past it. It seemed to have been broken in half before part of it had been wrenched away and discarded onto the sidewalk. I frowned, realizing how similar that was to a man's hand being wrenched from his arm. Pure brute strength. But a bear couldn't have just wandered into town and attacked this shop, leaving the others unmolested.

I stepped over a yellow powdery substance and carefully made my way to where Bram was conferring with the gendarme. I should have been worried that the gendarme might have new questions for me, but given our last encounter, I doubted he had any interest in me whatsoever. The room smelled of herbs and spices, but also something sickly permeating it all. My eyes wandered to the sheet at their feet, and I wondered if what I was smelling was blood.

Something shifted deeper in the room, a deck of tarot cards tumbling from an overturned case, spilling into the chaos. My eyes swept the walls of the shop, halting at a nearby shelf. I touched a book of medicinal cures, before my fingers wandered to one of lunar goddesses, dusted with plaster. I recalled the intimidating statues in the hedge maze. Interesting to find something on the goddesses here. Perhaps such a book would prove enlightening. Casually, I slipped the book into my pocket before looking up to find four deep claw marks gouged through the wall. Shuddering, I turned to find the gendarme reaching down to pull the sheet aside, revealing a woman's corpse. She stared blankly up at the ceiling, her skin unnaturally pale. It made the freckles across her nose appear much darker. I swallowed hard as I took in her red hair, spilling out around her face, as if framing it with blood. Her throat was missing. The lower half of her body was gone as well, intestines spilling out onto the hardwood.

I turned away and stumbled back outside, holding a kerchief to my mouth. Bile rose in my throat, but I took several deep gulps of air to force it back down.

"Emile? Are you quite alright?"

I nodded, shaken, as I turned to find Bram behind me, the gendarme scowling over his shoulder.

"I'm fine. Thank you," I said as Bram placed a hand on my shoulder. "I just wasn't expecting . . ." *Half her body to be missing.*

"Let's go," Bram insisted. "There's nothing I can do here."

I let him guide me to a carriage. "It's unpleasant to see something like that," Bram said, and I closed my eyes, trying to banish the image of the woman. What a terrible way to die.

"What did that?" I asked.

"I don't know. The gendarmerie think it was a bear, the same bear who attacked the stranger, in fact. Apparently, once a bear gets a taste for human flesh, it continues to seek it out."

"You don't believe it was a bear." It was a statement, not a question.

"No. No, I don't."

We stepped out of the carriage at a café where Bram ordered us sandwiches. He also ordered me a glass of wine, to calm my nerves. I wasn't very hungry, but I made an effort to eat.

"I overheard something at the château," I said after picking at my sandwich.

"Oh?"

I nodded. "It was between Count Montoni and his doctor, Father Schedoni."

"Schedoni," Bram wrinkled his nose. "What was it?"

"I think they killed Hargrove. And I think the gendarmerie are being bribed to cover it up."

Bram was silent, and I looked up to find him watching me. "You heard them say this?"

I frowned, trying to remember Schedoni's exact words. "Yes. Schedoni was chastising Montoni for being so sloppy with Hargrove. Hargrove's family is threatening to send an investigator. They mentioned hush money, and bribes to make questions go away in town."

Bram set down his sandwich and wiped his forehead with the

back of his hand. "Emile, they're dangerous men. I don't want you getting involved, at least not right now. We would need more than your word to make any moves against them anyway."

I swallowed hard. "That isn't all. I . . . I recognized the woman in the shop. The one who's . . . dead."

Bram sat motionless as he waited for me to continue.

I licked my lips and leaned forward, lowering my voice even more than it had already been. "I caught her in the hedge maze. She'd left a candle in the mausoleum window. I think it was a signal for Hargrove to meet her. At the time, I thought it was a romantic rendezvous, but now I think it was more than that. She tried to sneak into Lady Morano's room. When Montoni heard about the intruder, he knew exactly who she was. And I saw him watching the apothecary. He must be involved in this murder too."

The waiter approached our table with the check, and I sat silently as Bram paid before realizing that I'd promised to buy lunch. I frowned. I would have to get it the next time.

Bram set his napkin on the table and crossed his arms, regarding me. "Emile. A man could not have done that."

"Are you sure?" I asked. "Couldn't someone make it look like a wild animal attack?"

Bram leaned back in his seat, contemplating. "Perhaps. They would be going to a lot of trouble. It would be easier to stage it like a robbery gone wrong, wouldn't you agree?"

"I do, but I don't believe a bear wandered into town, attacked a single shop, then left without anybody seeing anything either."

With a sigh, Bram stood and we left the café, walking back to his office this time, rather than hailing a carriage. "Who was this woman? According to the police, she was just the owner of an apothecary. You think she was some assassin on the side?"

"I don't know," I admitted. "I know it's farfetched, but I think they're linked. And I think that hand I found belonged to Hargrove."

"Or it was someone passing through as the gendarmerie suggested."

I sent Bram a dirty look and he held up his hands. "I'm just trying to examine this from all angles. You may be jumping to conclusions here."

"I'm not. That woman was involved with Hargrove, perhaps had him spy on the family for her. Then Montoni had him, and likely her, killed." I glanced at him. "Does Montoni have a reputation?"

"A reputation? For gambling, certainly. He's known quite well for that. But nothing as serious as murder."

Gambling. Murder. Bribery. Montoni was not an innocent man. If Montoni had had no qualms with murdering two people in cold blood, he wouldn't think twice before killing a black-mailer. I would need to be smart about this. I didn't see how I would find proof that Montoni had committed murder, but he had murdered Hargrove and the woman for a reason. I needed to uncover whatever secret was damning enough to justify murder. Then I could use that information in exchange for Udolpho and my silence. But it had to be hard proof. I would need to keep digging. I would also need to be careful that I didn't become another victim.

I glanced up at Bram, imagining him with me at Udolpho, our own private castle where we could perhaps live free of judgment, in isolation. It could be perfect, if all the pieces fell together just right. Perhaps he could begin a practice in whatever neighborhood we found ourselves in. I wondered if he would go with me if I asked him.

"Did you notice anything else suspicious at the château?" Bram asked, breaking through my thoughts.

"Yes."

I told him about the injections Father Schedoni had given the family, who'd fallen ill afterward.

"It is odd," Bram acknowledged, looking perplexed. "It's also rather ironic that Henri framed my father's practice as some medical experiment that would harm people when Schedoni seems to be doing just that to them."

"It's dangerous then?" I asked.

"I don't know. It almost sounds like some sort of debilitating disease in the family bloodline. I wasn't aware of any such history, but maybe that's why they insist on having their own doctor."

"What kind of disease?"

Bram shrugged. "There are a lot of illnesses out there, Emile. Many of them are passed on to subsequent generations. Some diseases are rarer than others. Without more information, I couldn't begin to hazard a guess. The treatment sounds extreme, however, in my opinion."

I nodded slowly. Maybe what I'd seen wasn't as strange as I'd thought it was.

"Look, Emile, you're under a lot of strain right now. Why don't you concentrate on taking care of yourself?"

"What?" I turned to face him. "What are you talking about?"

Bram shifted. "I mean that I don't want you getting in over your head any more than you already are. You have to focus on what's going on with Count Morano and your inheritance. That's enough. The family illness, the murders . . . leave those to the professionals. They have a doctor. We have the gendarmerie. That's what they're there for."

I let out a deep breath. "I suppose you're right. I just don't trust the gendarmerie. Or Father Schedoni. It makes me anxious that these nefarious things might be taking place right under our noses."

"But you need to take care of your own problems. It's okay to let things go. Other people can deal with their own issues, and you don't need to feel guilty about that."

Bram came to a stop, and I realized we were back at his house already. A small crowd had once more gathered at the corner as the body was taken out on a pallet, the remains thankfully covered. We watched for a moment before I felt Bram press my hand.

"Stop worrying about other people," he said softly. "Your life is worth fighting for. And if you have to overlook some things or hurt some people while working toward your own happiness, then maybe that isn't such a bad thing."

I turned to him. "What do you mean?"

Bram squeezed my hand. "Sometimes you have to take what you need from people. You can't count on everybody to have your best interests in mind, and you can't wait for people to save you. The Montoni household isn't going to save you. Whatever they've gotten themselves into doesn't matter. Find a way to get your inheritance, no matter who it hurts. That's what I mean. It's okay to just look out for yourself."

"You're saying that I should be more selfish. Because I've had many selfish thoughts lately."

"Good. Keep having them. Follow through with them. You deserve a happy ending. Don't let anyone tell you otherwise. Do what it takes to get that ending, Emile. Take what you need because everybody is going to try to take from you."

I squeezed his hand back. His encouragement was so sincere. He really did want the best for me. How could I tell him what I wanted for us? That I wanted us to be together, in a life I secured through blackmail? A wave of shame shot through me, but I took Bram's advice and shook it off. I would have to get used to subterfuge if I was to have any hope of happiness.

I opened my mouth to say something to that effect but was cut off by the sound of a loud scoff. "Are you serious?"

I looked up to find Count Morano striding toward us, jaw clenched.

I met Bram's eyes briefly and swallowed hard before turning back to Henri.

"What can I help you with, Count Morano?" Bram asked cheerfully, stepping forward to meet him.

"Don't patronize me." Henri scowled, shoving past him as he stomped over to me. He was breathing hard as he glared at me. "Were you leading me on? When all you really wanted was to return to this country doctor of yours?"

"Keep it down," Bram said, voice low as he drew up next to me. "Or do you want a scandal on your hands?"

Henri snorted. "What do I care of scandal? Did Emile tell you how we spent the night together?"

Bram blinked and met my gaze, but I shook my head. "Not like that," I protested, turning to Henri. "You know very well that it wasn't like that."

Henri smiled dangerously. "Yet you woke up in my arms. You didn't leave."

I hesitated. "You were ill."

Henri shook his head slowly, knowing that he'd caught me in

a lie. He hadn't been ill by then.

Bram's fists clenched and his cheek twitched as I looked on, horrified. "Emile is not a piece of property to own. He can see me if he likes." He took a step closer to Henri, his voice restrained fury. "You know, he just feels sorry for you. You're pathetic. Forcing someone to love you is pa-the-tic. I know you have issues because of what happened to your parents, but that doesn't excuse your behavior now. You're a man. Act like it."

Henri looked to me. "This is your knight in shining armor, then? This is the man who's captured your heart?"

I couldn't meet his eyes.

"Fine." Henri held up his hands, as if giving up. "Have your little doctor friend for today, but remember, you work for *me*, and you have to come home to *me*." He turned and stomped away, and I felt like crying. For Henri *and* for Bram. I wasn't even a part of their world, not really, and look at the chaos I was causing. I would be gone soon, in six months or less. I was being unfair to everyone in this scenario.

"Emile," Bram put a hand on my shoulder.

"I'm okay," I told him. "I just don't see a way where everyone walks away unhurt. It's not fair to him either."

Bram sighed. "Emile. You don't owe anyone anything. Especially not a spoiled count."

I felt tears stinging my eyes as I pulled away from Bram. "He's just another man like us, Bram. A man who can't live how he wants. If I was in his position, I can't say I'd act much better. He's been through enough pain, and I'm likely going to hurt him more before I'm through. I already can't give him what he wants, and I don't need to make it any worse, for either of you."

"What are you saying?"

I took a deep breath. "I'm saying that we need to respect Henri's wishes. Whether you like it or not, I do have to go back to the château tonight, and Montoni is one thing, but I don't want to cause any more damage to Henri and Blanche than has already been done."

"So, you're going to go soothe his bruised ego."

"Yes. And I need you to accept that."

Bram eyed me warily. "So, you're okay with him using you? He's going to take advantage of his position and you're just going to let it happen, then act like the victim."

I glared at him. "That's what you think of me?"

He pursed his lips. "If you can go back to that . . . *predator* who takes what he wants and discards people when he's through with them, then yes, I think you're a fool. You need to get your head on right, Emile, and see that man for what he is." He turned and strode up the walk to his front door. With one last look at me, he stepped inside.

I stared at the closed door for a moment. Now Bram was jealous, too? I understood his animosity toward Henri. Given how Henri had jeopardized his father's practice, I couldn't even blame him, but what he was saying about Henri was fueled by that personal history. In fact, Bram's advice about looking out for oneself had probably been informed by Henri's treatment of him, his betrayal. But that didn't mean that Bram was wrong. In fact, his words resonated with me. Society was not fair. It didn't allow for the passive to thrive. I would have to take what I wanted if I was to have it at all.

I kicked at a rock and grunted my frustration as even the stone refused to cooperate, sticking obstinately to the concrete. My eyes found the crowd gathered around the apothecary, even though the body had been removed. I couldn't let that mystery go like Bram wanted me to. I needed to find out what Montoni was hiding. Bram didn't understand how difficult it was going to be to appease my aunt and win my inheritance. My route to happiness was going to be much more complicated than just taking what I wanted. I was going to coerce it from the hands of my enemy.

I just hoped that Bram understood in the end.

THIRTEEN

Henri avoided me for the rest of the week. When I came to help him change in the morning, it was only to find him already gone. When he rang the bell at night, a pile of clothes waited for me to mend and press, but Henri was always absent, usually down the hall at his sister's door, speaking to her from the doorway and watching me out of the corner of his eyes.

Five days of this, and I finally saw a carriage arrive for teatime, and I knew that Henri would have to be in his room changing. I seized the moment and rushed to his bedchamber, knocking once before stepping inside so that he wouldn't have the opportunity to refuse me entry.

Henri scowled when he saw me. "Yes, Dupont?"

"We need to talk."

"Do we now?" He stood in front of his mirror, adjusting his cravat.

I was surprised by how much his indifference toward me stung. The truth was that Henri *was* a spoiled count, but that didn't mean that he didn't have feelings. I didn't need to add insult to injury by being so adversarial toward him when I was planning to secure Udolpho from his family by underhanded means. I even liked things about Henri. But I needed to remain in his good graces until I had more information on Montoni. And to do that, I had to be kind to him, even if sometimes I wanted to strike him across the face for his obstinate behavior.

I racked my mind for something to say to him to smooth things over between us, but nothing came to me. Instead, I marched over to him and wrapped my arms around his waist. "I miss you." And as the words left my mouth, I realized there was truth in them. I did miss his company, when he was the kind, flirtatious count. But I loathed the jealous one.

Henri stiffened beneath my embrace and turned to face me. "What?"

I pressed my face into his chest, worried that he might see the falsehood in my eyes. I felt bad for the deception, but it was necessary. This was merely an act. An exaggeration of my affections. I had to make Henri believe that I cared for him more than I did, but I had to keep that distance between us. "I miss you. Please don't be like this. I'm so sorry. I know how much you've been hurt in the past, and I don't want to be another source of pain for you. I just . . . I really care about you."

I cringed internally, worried I might have overdone it. Henri couldn't be so self-absorbed that he would believe I would apologize to *him*.

"You do?" Henri relaxed beneath me, and I felt his arms slide around me. I melted into him, burying my face in his neck. Okay, so maybe he *was* that self-absorbed. Perhaps this would be easier than I thought.

"I'm so confused, Henri. I'm being so unfair to you and Bram. I feel like I don't even know what I want anymore." I pulled back and looked up at him, widening my eyes for effect. "But I know I can't stand for you to be upset with me."

Henri's features softened and he cupped my cheek. "Emile. I missed you too."

Our faces were inches apart, and I held my breath as my eyes inadvertently wandered down to his lips. My treacherous mouth wanted to meet his. Part of me thrilled at the idea of kissing him, even as my mind warned me that I was toeing a very dangerous line between convincing Henri that I wanted him and convincing myself of the same.

There was a soft rap at the door and we leaped apart. Henri cleared his throat, eyes still glued to me. "Yes?"

Annette stepped inside, brightening when she saw me. "Ah, there you are." She glanced at Henri. "Forgive me, your lordship, but Dupont has a visitor."

"I do?" I asked, taking a step forward. I thought that Bram had been banished from the château altogether, but perhaps since he'd asked for me specifically, he'd been allowed entry. I was glad, especially since I didn't feel good about how things had ended between us the other day.

Henri's hand shot out and he grabbed my arm. "Emile, no. Just . . . leave. Don't even go for your things. Walk out the servants' door now. Leave and don't look back."

I sent him a confused look. "Henri, you don't have to be so afraid of Monsieur Valancourt, I assure you. Did I not just make that clear?"

Henri swallowed hard and seeming to remember that we had an audience in Annette, he dropped my arm.

As I followed Annette out the door, Henri glided along beside me. "I'm going with you," he said.

I winced. "I'm not sure that would be a good idea."

Henri hesitated. "I'll leave if you want me to. I promise."

I pursed my lips, unsure of why he was acting so strangely. Was I *that* good of an actor? Maybe I *had* overdone it. "Very well. But be nice."

Henri nodded and grabbed my hand, interlacing his fingers with mine. I tried to shake him off, but his grip was firm. Even as we passed a maid, bowing low for the count, he didn't loosen his hold. Did he *want* to cause a scandal?

At the library door, Annette knocked quickly, stepping inside and then aside as she announced me. "Mr. Dupont, sir."

I smiled as I entered the room behind her, Henri finally freeing my hand.

"Ah, here's the man of the hour," Count Montoni greeted me.

I was confused for a moment as I continued to walk into the room. Blanche sat on the sofa, offering me a tight smile, but Bram wasn't in the room at all.

Montoni scanned me, as if seeing me for the first time. "It seems you've worried many people over the past few weeks, *Marquis* St. Aubert."

My steps faltered at his words; at the same moment, I noticed the figure sitting in a chair across from the count. My blood froze as the door slammed shut behind me. Apparently, Alexander Westenra had seen me at the opera, after all.

Aunt Cheron rose from her seat and smiled at me with a mixture of amusement and triumph. "How good to see you again, Emile." She looked me over appraisingly before adding "Nice uniform."

Part
Two

FOURTEEN

"I'm so sorry," Henri said into my ear as he conveyed me to my new room.

I held on to my small pack of things gathered from my old room like a lifeline, feeling numb as I focused on taking one step after another along the hallway. My new room, one of the guest rooms, was positioned between Henri's and Blanche's. I hardly noticed as Henri opened the door, and I found myself in a room every bit as nice as the count's.

As I stood in the doorway, Henri pried my pack from me and set it on the bed. "We'll take care of that later," he promised, trying for a smile. "For now, let's get you dressed for dinner. You're close to my size. I'm sure something will work." He steered me to his room and shut the door firmly behind us, leaning against it for a moment to look at me.

I walked over to his bed and perched on the edge, mind roaring. I couldn't believe that it was over. Aunt Cheron had found me, no thanks to that insufferable Alexander Westenra, and the ruse was at an end. Now what happened to my inheritance would be up to her. What happened to *me* was up to her. Running away and taking on the role of a servant would certainly help her build a case of insanity against me.

Henri knelt in front of me and grabbed my hands in his. "I'm so sorry, Emile. I didn't know it was that bad."

I swallowed hard and nodded, tears threatening me.

"When I saw your likeness at the post office, I felt betrayed, and I was already so angry with you, and . . . I just thought you were rebelling and needed to be put in your place. I didn't know she was so cold and . . . I just didn't know."

I blinked and looked at him. "What?"

"I mean, you're a marquis! You made a fool out of my family and me. And then you chose Bram over me, and . . . I thought I would send you home and that would be that. I didn't think about why you'd left." Henri looked away. "I'm so sorry."

I tore my hands from him and glared at him. "You're *sorry*? Do you have any idea what she's going to do to me? She's going to have me committed. I will spend the rest of my days in a padded cell because I *hurt your feelings*."

"What?" Henri looked shocked as he drew up to his feet. "What are you talking about? No one said anything about an asylum. Whatever reason could she give for doing that to you?"

"Deviancy," I said, spitting the word out. "She knows I like men."

Henri's eyes were saucers. "I . . . I won't let that happen."

"And you think you'll have any say in the matter?" I put a hand to my head. I was shaking I was so frightened. What if I made a run for it right now? Just bolted out the doors, as Henri had suggested. But, of course, I wouldn't have the element of surprise now. They would be on me before long.

Henri's strange behavior made more sense now. He had known. He had *informed* my aunt that I was here. And here I'd been stupid enough to think *I'd* been manipulating *him*.

"You've ruined me," I said flatly. "I hope you're happy."

"No." I felt Henri's weight as he sank onto the bed beside me. "I will do everything in my power to keep that from happening. Do you hear me? I will not see you committed anywhere."

I dragged my hand from my eyes and gazed at him, his earnestness, his clenched jaw. He was determined. But that alone wouldn't be enough. I choked on a sob and Henri's arm wrapped around me. He pulled me against his chest and held me as I cried. I wanted to hit him. I wanted to pound on his chest, but I couldn't find the strength to protest. Many minutes passed before I was exhausted from the display of emotion, but Henri still didn't let go.

"I'm going to fix this," he vowed into my hair. "I will find a way. I promise."

I nodded and pulled away from him, even though I didn't believe he could do anything to change my circumstances. But I needed an ember of hope and him looking out for me was something I could hold on to.

"*Deviancy.*" Henri scowled, crossing his arms. "This world is so cruel."

"I should get dressed for dinner," I reminded him, my voice hoarse. I wiped at my tear-stained cheeks and walked over to his mirror. My eyes were swollen. I looked awful.

Henri pulled a suit from his wardrobe, and when I didn't make a move to change, he helped me out of my clothing and into what he'd chosen. He was careful as he maneuvered my limbs into the clothes, and wiped at my face with a cloth to help freshen me up. I sat passively, letting him do all of this. I was just too tired to fight, or do anything, really.

"Emile."

I blinked and looked down at Henri's hand around mine, and then up into his face. "Henri."

"Can you ever forgive me, Emile?" he asked. His voice broke halfway through the question and his face crumpled. He turned away from me, and I knew he was hiding tears.

I put a hand on his back automatically. The fog that veiled my mind cleared as I rubbed my hand slowly up and down his back. Examining my own situation, I was paralyzed with fear, but once I focused on someone else, it was like my mind reset.

I could still make this work, I realized. I could stick to my alternate plan. Montoni's secret was still out there, waiting to be discovered. Udolpho Castle was still waiting to be seized. My aunt's arrival didn't need to change things. So long as I kept up pretenses and did as she asked until I could gain control of the situation, I might come out of this unscathed. I could sidestep my aunt and blackmail my way into a quiet life. I only needed to put off my aunt from committing me to an asylum. I'd been able to fool Henri easily enough, after all. Aunt Cheron would be shrewd, but I had to try to appease her with deception. It was my only choice.

"You didn't know," I said, sighing heavily. "You couldn't have known because I was keeping things from you. This is just as much my fault."

Henri seemed to calm down, but he shook his head. "No, this is my doing. I should have been a better friend."

"You're being one now."

Henri smiled and nodded. "I will be a good friend to you. I swear it."

"I know." I glanced over at the door, my stomach churning at having to face my aunt again so soon. "Now, let's get this over with."

I walked along the hallway leading to the dining room with a growing fear in my chest. By the time I reached the door, I stopped and turned to Henri, pale. "I'm not sure I can do this."

"You can," Henri promised. "I'll be there with you." He grabbed my hand and offered it a squeeze. I'd needed that reassurance. I might have been playing Henri, but his strength was all that was keeping me going at the moment. "Just look at me if you feel scared or anxious."

I let out a deep breath. My eyes wandered briefly to the suits of armor lining the hall, and I was reminded for a moment of the spiders in the suit in Montoni's hallway. I'd learned some of this family's secrets already. I just needed to press on until I procured enough to secure my freedom. I could do that. I *had* to do that.

Before I could talk myself out of it, I returned to the door and stepped into the dining room.

"Aw, it's about time," Count Montoni said as I strode in, Henri at my heels. "We were about to send up a search party."

Grimes stepped forward and froze when he caught sight of me. He blinked before glancing uncertainly back at Montoni. "My lord?"

"Ah," Montoni grinned, as if savoring my humiliation. "Hadn't you heard, Grimes? Our valet here is actually a marquis in disguise. Like something out of one of those silly novels the ladies read these days. Rather shocking, isn't it?"

Grimes stared at me and seemed to turn an odd shade of green before he bowed.

"Oh, none of that," I said.

"Nonsense," Montoni said, rising from his seat himself. "We should all rise to greet Marquis St. Aubert." He turned to my aunt, who sat beside him. "Except for Madame Cheron, of course."

Aunt Cheron inclined her head as Blanche stood, a tight smile in place. Her eyes bled sympathy as she watched me approach the table and take a seat beside Henri.

"You must have had quite a few adventures," Montoni observed as he seated himself once more and picked from a plate Grimes offered him.

"Quite," Aunt Cheron agreed. "You chose a roundabout way of seeing the world if that's what you intended, nephew."

I lifted my chin. "I've learned quite a bit in my travels, actually. Count Montoni's household has been very generous. I learned to fasten buttons, sew, clean boots, and even light a fire. Do you know how difficult it is to light a fire?"

Cheron frowned at me. "Why on earth would a marquis wish to learn to build a fire?"

I smiled thinly at her. "Sometimes it's nice to know that I'm capable of performing a task a child can execute."

Blanche chuckled, then did her best to cover it up with a cough. It wasn't very convincing. I noted Montoni's fingers digging into the table.

"Is this real gold?" Aunt Cheron asked, picking up a fork and looking it over. "I didn't realize your household was so well off, Count."

"We have our resources," Montoni said, clearly relieved to have the topic changed. "We wish only for the best, should a beautiful woman find herself a guest at Château le Blanc."

"Oh," Cheron blushed and looked away demurely.

I stared at her. Really? She was flirting in front of me now? I was going to have to be subjected to this? Perhaps being institutionalized wasn't such a bad option, after all.

"So," Montoni straightened in his seat. "Emile will inherit the late marquis's fortune when he comes of age. And you oversee it in the meantime?"

Cheron took a sip of her wine. "Indeed. Of course, I have my own household to oversee. I married well, you know."

"Aw, and your husband is . . . ?"

"Passed on. Over ten years ago."

"I am sorry to hear that," Montoni said, although he hardly seemed it. If anything, he looked quite the opposite. I could practically see money signs flashing in his eyes. Once a gambler, always a gambler, I supposed, and a widow was the perfect purse to continue to feed the filthy habit.

Cheron turned to me, and I cut at my food, pretending to be eating, although I had no appetite. "Of course, I had to leave La Vallée empty in the marquis's absence. There was no need to staff the house when it was vacant."

I looked up and blinked. "La Vallée stands empty?"

"Oh, yes. The entire staff has been dismissed."

I let my fork clatter to my plate. "But you can't do that."

"Of *course* I can do that." Aunt Cheron's eyes narrowed. "I am in control of your finances, and I am not going to bleed money while you play servant."

I clenched my jaw and glanced over at Henri. Henri's green eyes were waiting. They conveyed to me that he was with me through this trial. I felt myself calm at his attention, an odd sensation, and continued to stare at him. His hair was falling into his eyes, and I resisted the urge to reach out and push the stray lock back. He was a friendly face in a sea of enemies, I supposed. I needed that right now. Maybe he wasn't so bad after all, I mused. He'd been manipulative and had taken advantage of my position since meeting him, but I was the same, was I not? I actually rather admired his cunning. Perhaps we weren't so different in the end.

Conversation resumed around me as I watched Henri pick at his food. I followed his example, continuing to observe him throughout the meal. I didn't have much else to say, and Aunt Cheron seemed content with the company of Montoni.

By the time dinner was over, I was exhausted again, but I was happy that I'd borne it. Henri had had a big part in that. I couldn't overlook his kindness, even if this situation was partly, if not mostly, his doing.

We left Aunt Cheron and Montoni to themselves. While walking back to our rooms, Blanche took my arm and leaned into me, her head nestling onto my shoulder. "So, you helped your mother get ready for *real* balls and dinner parties."

"Yes," I agreed, sighing. "I apologize for the falsehood."

Blanche snorted. "Surely you're jesting. Having you here is the most excitement I've had in a very long while. Even before your secret life was laid bare. As a marquis, I mean. Not your *other* secret."

I shot Henri a look as he walked along my other side. Henri shrugged. "She knows about me."

"And I knew about you when you didn't fall madly in love with me." Blanche sighed, looking up at me through her lashes. "That would clearly be the only reason you showed no interest."

"Clearly," I agreed, smiling in response.

Henri took my other arm and leaned his head on my shoulder as well. I smirked at him, and he shrugged, lifting his head after a moment. He didn't release my arm, however.

"You know we're on your side, right?" Blanche asked me.

"Oh, you too?"

She nodded. "Of course. I'm here for you. Remember? I still owe you."

"I suppose you do."

The siblings had actually made me feel a little better, but I still felt panicky about my situation. When I returned to my room, I unpacked my small bag of things, mostly toiletries, and sat on my bed. The book I had nabbed from the apothecary stared back at me as well. I hadn't had a chance to page through it yet.

I blinked as something skittered across the sheets, and I realized that it was a spider.

"No, no, no," I told it, rushing to grab a glass. "You are not going to be laying eggs in my ears tonight. I have enough to contend with."

I scooped the arachnid up and brought it downstairs. I nearly took the servants' staircase, but realized that I wouldn't be welcome there anymore. I would be expected to use the main stairs and the family's rooms. It would be an adjustment.

As I sauntered to the front door, a servant straightened beside the doorway. He looked at me curiously. I recognized him, but I didn't think I'd ever exchanged a word with him. I nodded and he stepped into my path. "Sir?" he asked. "If you need something outside, I can retrieve it for you."

I blinked and then realized that he was guarding the door. Of course. So I wouldn't run off in the middle of the night.

I shook my head. "I just want to let this spider outside." I held up the glass, where the figure of the spider could be seen struggling within.

The man hesitated, then nodded, escorting me out the door

as I stooped to let the spider go. I watched the spider scamper off into the grass, lingering, knowing that I would have to return to my room like a good marquis confined to house arrest.

I sighed, feeling ridiculous that I was suddenly jealous of a spider.

Back in my room, I dropped onto my bed and picked up the book from the apothecary. I began to read but couldn't focus on it at all, and it only seemed to be going over myths of the lunar goddesses that I already knew. I tossed it aside as hopelessness clouded my thoughts, wrapping around me like a cocoon.

A light rap at the door made me sit up, and Henri slipped inside. He smiled as he shut the door behind him.

"Is something wrong?" I asked, then snorted. "I mean, something *else*?"

Henri approached me with a candle and set it down on a side table. He turned to watch me for a moment before shrugging. "I wanted to check in on you, see how you're doing."

"Did you know they're guarding the doors?"

Henri ran a hand back through his hair. "I suspected they would."

I lay back on the bed. "I'm okay, all things considered. I'm just waiting for things to get worse. Aunt Cheron is going to bring up my inheritance soon, and my conditions for claiming it."

Henri grabbed my hand and I squeezed it. "Thank you," I told him. "I don't think I could have handled today without your presence."

"We're in this together. I'm not going to let anything bad happen to you."

I wish I'd seen more of this Henri before my subterfuge had begun in earnest. Perhaps things would have progressed differently between us.

"Do you want company tonight?" Henri asked softly.

I opened my mouth to tell him no, but then I realized that I very much wanted company. And I wanted it to be him. Not because I thought I could procure information from him, but because I *wanted* him there.

I nodded.

Henri scooted onto the bed beside me and made to throw an arm around me. I pulled away from him, wincing at the hurt look that flashed across his face. "Sorry," I murmured. "I wasn't expecting . . ."

"No, of course," he agreed. "It was presumptuous of me."

I hesitated. I might end up regretting this, but I liked the feeling of his arms around me. I wasn't sure what that meant, but I could use that comfort right now.

This is bad, I told myself but ignored the voice. I'd needed comfort when my parents had died, and I'd received none from my aunt. Henri had likely needed comfort when his parents had died, but he had been thrust onto the icy brute Montoni. We both likely craved real connection, given our losses. We weren't so different in that way, I supposed. Maybe it wasn't too late.

"Okay, go ahead," I said, trying to ignore the triumphant grin that spread over his face as he pulled me back against him. I felt his warmth all along my body, and relaxed into the embrace. I looked back at him, narrowing my eyes. "Just keep your shirt on this time."

Henri chuckled, deep in his throat, making my heart flutter. "Fine. For tonight."

Satisfied, I smiled and closed my eyes, pulling his arm tighter around me.

FIFTEEN

T he days stretched into a week, and while I wasn't eager for
a confrontation with my aunt, I almost wanted to get it
over with. But instead, she spent her days mooning over Count
Montoni, who seemed genuinely pleased by her attentions.

I hadn't heard from Bram in that time, and I wondered what
he must be thinking, if word had reached him of my aunt's
arrival, or if he'd put me from his mind for the time being, thinking I was angry with him.

"You should really be grateful for the hospitality of Count
Montoni these past few weeks. He is a generous man, keeping
you on even now, despite your subterfuge." Aunt Cheron twirled
her parasol as we slowly walked the hedges of the maze. In the
daylight, the aisles seemed much wider, and everything so green
and luscious that it was like a different environment altogether.
"I'm frankly amazed that he didn't turn you out immediately.
A show of appreciation is in order, I should think."

"Yes, Aunt."

Cheron sent me a quick look of disapproval. "And while we're here, call me Abigail. Referring to me as your aunt conjures up images of aged spinsters. I don't want the count to get the wrong idea about me. I was a married woman, and I still have plenty to offer a man at this stage of life."

I fought from rolling my eyes but inclined my head in acquiescence.

We stepped into the center of the maze, the statues of the three goddesses also less sinister bathed in sunlight. At the bottom of the fountain, silver discs reflected the sun. I narrowed my eyes as I realized that the reflection of the moon in the water was likely the cause of the statues seeming to glow with some supernatural light. It reminded me that I still had the book from the apothecary to pore over. I didn't understand their significance here, but perhaps the book would offer insight.

"There is a ball tomorrow evening. The count went to considerable lengths to secure an invitation for you to attend."

"A ball?" I frowned. "Why would I wish to attend a ball?"

"Because you are looking for a wife. Or have you forgotten our terms already?" Cheron sniffed. "I believe I made myself very clear on the matter. I would think you eager to secure a wife, given the alternative."

I swallowed hard. There it was then.

"I wonder what my late father would think of you committing his only son to an asylum. Do you think he would be proud of your behavior?"

Cheron flinched as if struck, before whirling on me with a sneer. "My brother would have been severely disappointed in you. Your *way of life* would mean the death of our bloodline. I never had children, no matter how I tried. My late husband's fault, of course, because I certainly performed my wifely duty." A muscle twitched in her jaw. "This family will not end with the scandal of one ungrateful brat."

I pursed my lips, holding back a retort I was sure to regret. I glared at my aunt, recognizing my father's chin in her face, and his striking blue eyes. My eyes. I looked away. It didn't seem right that this woman, so cold to me, was a part of my family. But the proof was there, right in her face. I was deeply saddened to realize that she was my only attachment to my old life, to the parents I'd loved.

"I will attend the ball," I found myself saying.

Cheron watched me for a moment, and then nodded. "That's more like it. And don't fret. I didn't marry for love either. That's not the point of bringing two houses together. It's about sustaining and strengthening our families. A good match is an alliance of power. So long as you're discreet, I don't care what else you do, as long as you produce an heir. And I don't find that unreasonable. It's your duty."

I bit down on my lip. I felt tears coming and there was no one I would rather cry in front of less than this woman with my father's eyes. She didn't realize how incredibly unhappy I would be in a life that was a lie. I thought of Bram, of his warmth, how genuine he was, and could see a simple life with the doctor. Simple, but happy, free of judgment and constant paranoia at being found out by a family I was forced into, a family I would only come to resent. I could never be married to another man, of course, but we could still be together, happy in the fact that we were meant for each other. The fact that Bram's father only wanted for his happiness proved that it was possible. Just not for me with Aunt Cheron's threat looming.

Unless I managed to secure Udolpho.

I would play along for now. Perhaps I could satisfy her with a false engagement or become so busy with these useless balls that I could buy the necessary time to uncover Montoni's secrets. But I would not marry. I didn't wish to have a constant reminder of how I'd failed and lived a lie. That might be a worse fate than an asylum.

I just wanted love. Real love. Was that so much to ask?

Trunks of my clothing arrived from La Vallée that afternoon, a party from my aunt's staff deeming to visit my abandoned estate to arrange it. Annette assisted in making my wardrobe present-able, which consisted of a lot of pressing. She seemed agitated as we made idle chitchat with a new servant who worked with us, under Annette's watchful eye. As we neared the end of our work, Annette dismissed the servant, sighing heavily as the door closed behind her.

"She seems like she'll get the hang of things," I observed.

Annette shook her head. "She will. Doesn't have the instincts I would like, but she'll do." She glanced over at me with a small smile. "Excuse me. I should be addressing you as 'my lord' now."

"Enough of that," I scowled. "But thank you for allowing me to do some work. I needed a distraction, and I can't exactly go into the servants' quarters asking for a feather duster."

"Grimes would have a stroke," Annette said, chuckling. She shook her head. "Anyway, I did want to show you something, my . . . er, Emile."

I quirked an eyebrow as she withdrew a butter knife from her uniform. "If you plan to murder me, I confess I have no money to speak of at the moment, and you should probably use a sharper instrument."

Annette rolled her eyes. "Don't worry, my lord. If I was planning on murdering you, I would do it quick in the middle of the night."

"Oh." I blinked. "Good to . . . know."

Annette flashed me a wicked smile before drawing the knife closer to my face. "No, silly. Look closer."

I narrowed my eyes at the knife, noticing that the gold was tarnished. Then I frowned. It wasn't tarnished. It was . . . peeling, revealing silver beneath the gold exterior.

"What is this?" I asked, snatching the knife and scraping a fingernail over it to reveal more silver.

"Gold paint," Annette said as she watched shavings fall into my lap.

"I can see that, but why?" I looked up to meet her eyes.

"Someone is stealing the gold cutlery and replacing it with cheap imitations. They probably get a good amount for it too."

"Did you bring this to Grimes's attention?"

"Not yet. For now, I set the fakes aside, until we decide what to do with them."

I tapped my lip, wondering if perhaps this wasn't the work of a servant at all. What if Montoni was worse off than he let on? Perhaps his gambling debts had gotten the best of him. If he needed more money for bribes, the gold in his house would be a logical place to start. As would a vulnerable widow who had a fortune of her own. Aunt Cheron might be satisfied that the count kept me around out of the goodness of his heart, but I wasn't that naïve.

"Well?" Annette prodded. "What should I do with it?"

"Keep it set aside for now. We'll think on it." I looked up, smiling. "Good work, Annette."

Annette stood and curtsied for me before leaving me to my thoughts.

Blanche was over the moon that I would be attending the ball with her and Henri, and insisted on helping me pick out an outfit.

"We are going to be the only thing anybody is talking about," Blanche said decidedly as she rummaged through my things. "When it's Henri and me, the whispers follow us everywhere we go. We are the most desirable people in the room. But the three of us!" She squealed. "I can just imagine the looks on the other girls' faces when I stride into that room with two of the most handsome men on my arms. No one will be able to ignore us."

I watched her from the edge of my bed with amusement. "So, I'm only a pretty accessory to you?"

Blanche paused and glanced back at me, grin wide. "A very, very pretty one."

I laughed, shaking my head. "You are too much sometimes. I can't imagine any man meeting your rigorous standards for a husband. How do you ever hope to find one?"

Pausing in her rifling, Blanche turned to face me and leaned on the wardrobe, looking thoughtful. "I do have high standards, but it's more than that. I need someone to accept me, who's strong enough to be my equal. It is very hard for a woman. Most men want to keep us locked up, quiet and attentive. I can't have that. I need someone who will let me shine, and not have the pride to keep me under lock and key. Jealousy is the downfall of all men."

I thought of Bram and Henri, and their demonstrations of

jealousy. "I can't argue with you there."

"But I also need a man who understands me, who can . . ." She swallowed and came to sit beside me. "He needs to be able to accept all of me. Even the parts that aren't always apparent. We all have . . . secrets. We have demons that we try to keep at bay. I need a partner who will be able to acknowledge those demons and not be afraid of them."

I nodded, thinking I understood. I certainly had parts of myself that I was ashamed of, and qualities I didn't like, that weren't admirable. Finding a partner who could see those ugly parts and still love you, admire you even . . . that was what made for an honest, lasting love. My life was full of scheming these days, and there was no one so cunning as Henri. He would certainly understand that ugly part of me. Because it was in him as well. He was deceptive, but he was also tender. He'd cared for me at my lowest, as well. I couldn't ignore that kindness. He may have informed my aunt on my whereabouts, but my manipulations were perhaps just as bad, if not worse. Udolpho was likely a part of his inheritance, and I was planning on stealing it out from under his nose.

Likewise, Bram would be able to see past my ugly traits as well. He'd all but encouraged me to abandon playing nice. He was insightful and knew what it was to be human in a society stacked against us.

I grabbed Blanche's hands. "I understand."

"I knew you would, Emile." She patted my cheek and returned to the wardrobe, pulling out a chocolate-brown jacket. "Now, put this on. I simply must see you in it."

I obeyed. And that ended up being the jacket I wore to the ball the next day.

I was nervous as our carriage waited in the queue at the entrance of an elegant mansion. There was a charge in the air, something lively. If I weren't attending the ball under such pretenses, I imagined that I would be looking forward to this, especially given my present company.

"Isn't it a beautiful night?" Blanche asked, leaning over to get a better look at the approaching mansion doors.

"It will look even more beautiful with you out there, sister," Henri said, grinning at her candid excitement. He met my eyes and winked.

I swallowed and looked away. He wore a cobalt blue jacket lined with gold. It was stunning in itself, but cut to fit Henri . . . I could hardly look at him. I kept thinking about him without his shirt on, and how good it felt to be in his arms. Since that first night after my aunt's arrival, we'd slept in our separate rooms, but I would be lying if I said that I hadn't thought of sneaking over to Henri's room in the middle of the night. Just to have somebody next to me. I still hadn't sorted out my messy feelings for him yet, but he was growing on me, despite myself. Trying to manipulate him had backfired as I'd gotten to know him.

"I haven't been to a ball in what seems like ages," I said.

"I wish I could take you across that dance floor," Henri told me, voice low.

I nodded, not trusting myself to look at him. I noticed Blanche tilt her head toward her brother ever so slightly, catching the longing in his voice. It was hard to miss.

"But surely Emile will be my first dance," Blanche said, glancing my way. "Won't you, Emile?"

I grinned at her. "It would be an absolute pleasure." And I meant it.

After we were announced, I did indeed dance with Blanche, but her suitors were eager for the chance to sweep her off her feet, and she was busy with them the rest of the night. She looked breathtaking in a fuchsia gown. I'd done her hair again, so she was, naturally, a vision. But it was her ever-present smile and genuine laughter that really made her shine. She hadn't been bragging when she'd said that all eyes would be following her.

Henri stayed by my side as much as he could, but we were also in demand that evening. I was flustered trying to keep all of the names and faces right in my head as I was introduced to one girl, and then another. I asked several to dance, since I knew that Aunt Cheron was in attendance somewhere and I needed to appease her that I was at least trying to make the acquaintances of women.

After one girl with a seemingly limitless supply of stamina finally allowed me the chance to catch my breath, I found myself sipping on champagne and watching the dancers with a smile on my face. Despite myself, I actually was having a good time.

I stepped over to get a better view of the orchestra when I nearly collided with a girl in an ice-blue dress. Her golden hair was up in a twist like I'd never seen before and I had to stop and admire it, staring to try and decipher how it was done.

"Hello," she said after I'd been looking at her for a moment. She quirked an eyebrow at me.

"I beg your pardon," I said, flushing. "Your hair is just amazing."

"Thank you," the girl said, touching her hair tentatively and grinning with pleasure. "It's the latest fashion out of Paris. I wasn't sure my maid would get it right, but she never disappoints." She gave me a brief once-over before holding out a gloved hand. "Carmilla."

"Emile." I took her hand and lifted it to my lips.

"Charmed." Carmilla looked about the room, eyes settling on the dancers in the middle of the floor. "It certainly is a lively party."

"Yes, it is. I'm having a grand time." I hesitated and gestured to the floor. "Would you like to . . . ?"

I let my voice trail off and Carmilla offered me a dazzling smile before taking my arm. I couldn't help but think that perhaps Blanche had some competition, after all.

As I led Carmilla onto the floor, I caught sight of Aunt Cheron standing with Count Montoni. She was staring directly at me. Pretending not to notice her attention, I swept my partner into a graceful dance. It was a lively number that required us to switch partners more than once, but at the end of it, we were back in each other's orbits. When the music slowed, I put an arm around her, grinning. Dancing truly did make me feel happy.

Carmilla's collar had gone askew, and I adjusted it for her near her shoulder, my fingers grazing over her skin. I winced at how cold she was. I found the room rather stuffy myself, but she could have been outside in winter for how cool her flesh felt.

Carmilla's gaze drifted past me, and as we turned, I found that her attention was focused on Blanche, who was earning the admiration of many of those around her in others' arms. I couldn't blame Carmilla for watching the girl, or perhaps being jealous, but the look in her eyes was nothing of the sort. It was more wistful. It was the sort of look I had spied on Henri's face tonight as we'd passed one another in the sea of dancing bodies. A longing that made me believe that perhaps I had more in common with this girl than I'd at first realized.

"Do you need a moment?" Carmilla asked me after a minute. "Perhaps I've tired you out."

I offered her a smile and led her from the floor, bowing to

her gratefully. "You are a talented dancer. And it was very nice to meet you."

"You as well," she agreed, eyes glittering with something almost wolfish. "Perhaps I will see you around, Emile."

"It would be my pleasure, my lady."

She inclined her head and walked away, glancing back at me once with a knowing smile.

I ran a hand through my hair and stalked to the back of the room to grab a refreshment. Henri found me a moment later. "She was pretty."

I raised an eyebrow. "Oh? Are you spying on me now?"

"Hardly." Henri grinned, taking a sip from a champagne flute. "It's just when I see you out there dancing, it's like everyone else ceases to exist."

"I'm that good, am I? Perhaps I missed my calling."

"I can't help but be jealous of everyone you dance with. I want to be the one holding you in my arms, making you smile like that." His hand briefly grazed mine. "And anyway, that girl seemed like a trollop."

I laughed. "Well, since you're the expert on women, I will accept your counsel."

"As you should."

"Count Morano!" a girl cried out, approaching. She was very pretty with curly black hair that grazed her shoulders in a seductive way. "I almost didn't recognize you."

"Octavia," Henri greeted her. "It's so good to see you."

"Dance with me, Henri. We simply must catch up."

"So bold," Henri waggled his eyebrows. "I like it." He handed me his barely touched champagne glass and allowed Octavia to pull him out onto the floor.

I watched them go, and I felt my heart squeeze a little as they began to dance together. Henri grinned down at her, clearly enjoying himself. I suddenly understood what he meant. I was jealous as well. I wanted to be out there with him.

I drained the rest of the champagne and went in search of a room to relieve myself. Outside the ballroom, I saw handfuls of people clumped together talking, but no one I recognized. I walked in the direction of a servant standing outside of a discreet room, which I assumed would be where a chamber pot lay in wait.

"Emile," a voice called, and I looked around, unable to place where it had come from.

I paused in front of a room I hadn't noticed, the door slightly ajar. I squinted as a figure stuck his head out and gestured me inside. I recoiled, only to blink at the shadowed face. Wait a moment, was that . . . ? "Bram?"

With a quick look around to see if anyone was watching, I ducked into what was clearly a coat closet. As the door closed at my back, I regarded the doctor with surprise and awe. "Bram? What are you doing here?"

"I came to find *you*." He sighed. "I wasn't sure what became of you when I heard that your aunt arrived."

I looked him over in the weak light and smiled. "It is good to see you. I didn't like how we left things."

"Nor I," he said, grabbing my hands. "I'm sorry. I've been so worried."

I swallowed hard. "I'm confined to the house. I couldn't get word to you, or I would have written."

"I know, I know." Bram waved my explanations away. "But how *are* you? Has your aunt made any reference to her earlier demands?"

"Oh, yes. Why do you think I'm here?"

Bram sighed and nodded. "I figured as much." He reached up and touched my cheek. "I missed you."

"I missed you." My heart was beginning to thud in my chest, and I leaned into him, glad when he finally slipped an arm around my waist. I gazed up into his worried face with a touch of sadness. His eyes still called to me, as did his lips. In that moment, I wondered if the only reason I'd been growing so close to Henri lately was because I missed Bram. Henri was always nearby, a convenience. Yes, Henri was beautiful and I enjoyed his company immensely, but I couldn't completely forget his past actions toward me. Meanwhile, Bram was dependable and charming, on top of being incredibly attractive. I felt like I could trust him in a way that I couldn't Henri, even if I had come to see Henri as a sort of protector.

"We're going to find a way out of this," Bram murmured into my hair. "I swear it."

I nodded. "I know. It's just . . . I feel hopeless. Sometimes I think I should give in to my aunt's demands and be miserable."

"Perhaps you should revisit the circumstances around such an arrangement. You might surprise yourself and find a way to satisfy your aunt and get what you want in the end. It may just take some finessing." He pulled back and lifted my chin. "Be strong for me, okay?"

I smiled, although he clearly had no clue how obstinate my aunt could be. "Yes. Okay."

He returned my smile and then leaned in to kiss me. I felt a promise in his kiss. That it wouldn't be our last. That he would find a way for us to be together.

"I'm sorry I lied to you," I blurted out.

Bram blinked at me. "Lied? About what?"

"About who I was." I ran a hand back through my hair. "I wanted to tell you. There were several times where it was on the tip of my tongue, but . . . I didn't want you to treat me differently when you learned about me."

"Learned . . ." Bram tilted his head. "Whatever do you mean?"

My breath caught in my throat. *Oh.* He didn't know.

"Bram . . ." I licked my lips, my mouth suddenly dry. "I . . . I thought you would have heard when my aunt arrived. I'm . . . I'm a marquis."

Bram watched me, a smile twitching at the corner of his lips, as if waiting for me to finish a joke. "And you didn't think I would work that out on my own?"

A sense of relief flooded through me. "I should have figured you'd piece it together. And I'm sorry. I should have told you sooner."

Bram shrugged away my apology. "But something did just occur to me. You're a marquis. And you were literally waiting on a count. When you're his superior." He put a hand to his mouth as if to stifle a laugh.

"It's not funny," I protested, smacking his shoulder.

"It's a little funny," Bram said, snorting.

"Okay. Maybe a little."

We grinned at each other.

"Does this change anything between us . . . ?" I asked tentatively.

"Change anything? Well, it certainly exacerbates the issue. As a marquis, you will have all eyes on you. What can I do to help?"

"Just promise you won't give up," I said. "Please. You're my only real friend and . . . I need you. I'm surrounded by enemies, and I still need to make it to my eighteenth birthday without being shackled to a repugnant life. I must find a way to escape my duty. Then there will at least be options before me."

Bram closed his eyes for a moment and nodded to himself. He let out a breath and his eyes seemed clearer when he reopened them. "Can you leave in the middle of the night if I have a horse waiting?"

I shook my head. "The doors are guarded."

Bram chewed on his lower lip, looking thoughtful. "A distraction will be necessary. I'll have to come up with something. Perhaps I can arrange for food poisoning."

My eyes widened. *"Bram."*

"If it comes to it. Should your aunt decide to whisk you back to La Vallée, I might not know until it's too late."

"I would find a way to send word."

"See that you do. And if I come up with some way to secret you out of that infernal château, I'll find a way to let you know. Just be ready at a moment's notice. Have a bag packed. Can you do that for me?"

I nodded.

"Good man." Bram gazed into my eyes with worry. "Please be careful, Emile."

"I will. And thank you."

Bram nodded, determination set in his jaw. I was asking a lot of him, and I wanted to assure him that it would all work out, but I couldn't make such a promise. Any talk of our future would need to wait for a more opportune time, not during a brief exchange in a broom closet. I would have to be content knowing that conversation was yet to come.

"Promise you won't do anything reckless on my behalf," I said. "It may be too late for me, but I won't let you throw your future away. Your practice needs you. This town needs its doctor."

He squeezed my hand and gestured to the closet door. "I'm glad to see you're alright, and I intend to keep you that way."

I opened the door a crack and looked around before darting out. It was only when I was halfway across the room that I realized he'd never promised not to put himself in danger.

SIXTEEN

"I have a surprise for you."

I looked up from a tattered copy of *The Castle of Otranto* to find Henri grinning at me with mischief.

"Oh?" I set the book aside and waited for him to continue.

"You've been acting strange since the ball, and I thought maybe a change of scenery would do you good."

I raised an eyebrow. It was true that I'd been lost in thought over the past few days, but it was only because I was worried about Bram and what he might be planning. I was also confused about my feelings for Bram and Henri. Sometimes I wondered if marrying into misery would be a relief just so I wouldn't have to hurt either of them by choosing one over the other.

"I don't think my aunt would allow for a trip," I said. "Especially an impromptu one."

"No, but . . . we won't be going far." Henri held out his hand and I took it, allowing him to help me to my feet. I couldn't help but give in when he was acting so mysteriously.

Henri grabbed a sack on the way out of the château and made for the back of the house. When we arrived at the stables, I wondered exactly what he had in mind.

"Two horses, Cyrille," Henri ordered, addressing the stablemaster.

Cyrille blinked at us, then crossed his arms, eyes lingering on me. "I apologize, my lordship, but Count Montoni expressly forbade me from giving the marquis a horse."

Henri's smile faltered briefly before he recovered. "Very well. Give *me* a horse then."

Cyrille shrugged and saddled one of the horses. It was a black stallion that seemed to have a mellow temper. "Old Stormy will do well for you. She might not be the fastest horse, but she's trustworthy and loyal to a fault."

I smiled as I reached out and stroked Stormy's neck. She watched me with dark eyes while Henri secured his sack to the front of the saddle and then lifted himself onto her back. Once seated, he ordered me onto the horse at his back.

Cyrille pursed his lips but said nothing as I mounted the horse.

I was used to riding solo, so I wasn't sure what to do until Henri reached back and grabbed one of my arms, wrapping it around his midsection. "You'll need to hold on," he told me.

I nodded and we started off at a trot. I clung to Henri, something I suspected he rather enjoyed. I leaned into his back, placing the side of my face against his shoulders, and sighed. It was nice to get out of the château, even if it was a short-lived ride into the neighboring hillside.

"We could always try to make a run for it," Henri said, suddenly.

"What?" I asked, startled.

He shrugged. "Just take off on Stormy here. Get as far as we can, make our way across the country, maybe over the border into Italy. We could hide, become other people. We wouldn't have our riches or titles, but maybe we could be happy."

I smiled at the thought. I was almost tempted, but I realized quickly that we couldn't. "And Blanche?"

Henri was silent, and I knew that I'd touched on the biggest flaw of his plan. Blanche enjoyed her life. So long as she could find the right husband, I imagined she would remain very happy. A hard life working the land wouldn't do for her. And Henri couldn't abandon his sister, even for his own happiness.

"It's a nice fantasy," I said to Henri's back. "I think you would be worth giving everything up for."

Henri straightened and glanced back at me. "Do you think so?"

I nodded, and found that I meant it. "We could be free, not have to worry about our obligations and just . . . be who we are. Together."

"And Bram?"

My smile faded and he nodded to himself before turning to watch the path again.

We rode in silence for another twenty minutes before we stopped, and Henri disembarked. He helped me down and I gazed around at rolling hills, wondering where we were. There was a large tree nearby, and after Henri unpacked the sack he'd stowed, we headed toward it. Beyond the tree, there was a steep drop that allowed for a magnificent view of the countryside, boasting fields of lavender. And in the distance, I could make out the town.

"Henri," I said breathlessly, wide-eyed. "It's . . . beautiful." I leaned into him and settled my head onto his chest. We looked out over the town for several minutes before Henri pulled away, leaving me to ogle at the beauty before me. When I'd finally had my fill, I turned back to find Henri watching me from a blanket on the ground. He had a picnic spread out around him.

I blinked. "What is all this?"

"Our getaway," Henri shrugged, patting the blanket beside him. "I figured we deserved a break, or a distraction at the very least."

I obliged, and Henri made a plate for me. It was simple. Cold turkey, rolls, cheese, biscuits with jams, and some croissants. But it was also perfect. To top it off, Henri poured us a sweet strawberry wine.

"I feel so spoiled," I admitted. "You really didn't have to do this."

"But I wanted to."

I glanced up and met his eyes. They were sparkling and intense. He seemed genuinely happy that I was pleased. After a moment, he looked away, blushing. He lifted his glass of wine. "To our futures. May they be bright, and what we want them to be."

I lifted my glass to his and drank deep.

When we finished eating, we lay on the blanket and stared up at the sky drowsily. I wedged into the crook of Henri's arm as I watched clouds lazily drift across the sky.

"Henri," I said after a while.

"Yes?"

"I've been meaning to ask you for a while now. I don't want to spoil the mood, but I have to know—what are those injections for? Why do they make you so sick?"

I studied Henri, noting his throat bob as he swallowed hard. "I don't want to talk about it. Please."

I searched him for another moment, then sighed. "Very well." Henri had never been one to divulge family secrets, no matter how I tried. I wasn't really expecting it to be any different now.

"But I'm not . . . it's just medicine. I have to go through that to stay healthy, but I *am* fine. We all are."

"It's a disorder that runs in your family?"

Henri smiled, a bittersweet smile. "Yeah. It runs in the family alright."

I nodded and patted his hand. He grabbed it and squeezed it tightly. "I've never met anyone like you, Emile. I hope you know how truly special you are."

"You're special too." I turned to face him, and he also turned so that we were looking into each other's eyes. "Once one gets past that wall you've put up to protect yourself, you're really sweet and thoughtful." I reached out and ran a hand back through his hair.

And then I kissed him.

I didn't realize what I was doing until it was done. My lips found his and I felt an electricity thrum through me. It was a slow and sensual kiss that made me want to touch more of him, which I did. My hands found his chest and his arms, his back. We pressed close to one another, unable to get enough until we were both out of breath and panting for air. Even then, I only allowed enough room for breath between us. I stared into his eyes, shining and so tender that they melted my last reserves.

"Henri," I managed.

The next kiss lingered. Time seemed to lose all meaning, coming to that single point where our lips touched. It was a sensation like nothing I'd felt before. Not even with Bram.

When I next pulled away, I swallowed hard, feeling as if I'd made some sort of discovery about the world, or *my* world, at least.

"Emile," Henri said. "I . . . I want you to know how sorry I am for my past behavior. I was a brute and I took advantage of you when we first met." He ran a hand back through his hair. "I've been very lonely for a very long time, and I just wanted something for once in my life. It was wrong of me, and I apologize."

I nodded slowly, absorbing his words, unsure if I could absolve him of his actions so easily.

As if reading my mind, he sighed. "I know that's not enough. I will show you that I've changed. And I . . ." He grabbed my hand, and I gazed down at it briefly before meeting his intense eyes. "You make me want to be a better man, Emile. I'm trying. I think you bring the best out in me, and I want you to know that I will continue to do better."

I was moved by his words, and an aching in my chest made me want to match his words with a confession of my own, yet I couldn't bring myself to admit I'd been manipulating him myself.

"Well," Henri licked his lips and turned away, glancing down at his watch. "It's getting rather late." He sat up and began to gather the remains from our feast. I watched him for a moment, wondering if I could begin anew with Henri. I could see him trying, and I did consider him my friend now. Yet I was still trying to use him for my own ends. Between the two of us, perhaps I was the worst in this scenario, and that made me feel uneasy.

I watched the fog roll in that night, thick and otherworldly, blanketing the grounds around Château le Blanc like floodwaters. It swallowed the grass and the drive so that it looked as if the whole world was being erased.

After our kiss, Henri and I had avoided each other for the rest of the day. He hadn't even been able to meet my eyes at supper. I wondered what it meant. For my part, I was trying to sort through my feelings, my mind spinning in circles as it tended to do when I had to reflect on matters of the heart. With distance, I wondered if it hadn't been the circumstances that had made me feel something more for Henri. Sometimes my heart seemed a fickle thing, for I found myself longing for Bram once more. All this time spent in Henri's company was unfair to Bram, and I wondered if it was because I was unable to see Valancourt that my esteem for him had receded. Because when I was in his presence, I felt a glow in my chest, something radiant. I'd felt something with Henri, but it had been different. Different and similar at the same time. But even as I thought of Bram, I couldn't get that kiss with Henri out of my mind. Weeks in his company and we'd never kissed. Was what I'd felt just the culmination of a month's longing to feel his lips upon mine? My whole body had responded, and I wanted to kiss him again.

I groaned and put a hand to my head. I was hopeless. What did I *want*?

I read from the book I'd liberated from the apothecary as a

diversion from my thoughts. I rather admired the strength of the goddesses, and was drawn especially to Artemis, who was gentle and sensitive but also fierce and tenacious. But I still wasn't learning anything noteworthy, which was frustrating.

Feeling restless, I wandered through the dark halls of the château before stepping out onto the balcony to get some air. I stared over the edge to the ground below to get a better look at the fog, swirling like a living thing. I got the impression that it wanted to swallow me whole.

Looking up, my eyes wandered over the hedge maze, finding the mausoleum where, to my utter astonishment, I spied a candle burning from within. Again.

"What in the world?" I murmured, straightening and squinting into the darkness. If the mystery girl had lit the candle previously, and she was now dead, who could be out there now? Was it someone else? What a coincidence that would be. I'd thought the candle had been a signal for Hargrove to meet with her in the hedge maze. Was a similar system being used for new players? And to what end?

I took the stairs to the first floor, intending to investigate, when I spied a servant standing at the door, looking half-asleep. I cursed silently, then decided to chance the servants' hall to see if a guard was posted there as well. As luck would have it, the door was unmanned. An oversight on the part of Montoni and my aunt, or perhaps sloppy discipline on the part of the servants. Either way, it was fortuitous at the moment, and I tucked the inconsistency away in the back of my head, should I need it to escape my present situation in the near future.

Someone had left a cloak on a hook by the door, and I liberated it, throwing it around myself as I slipped from the servants' door unimpeded. I made my way for the hedge maze, but decided to circumnavigate it for the moment, instead making directly for the mausoleum and the mysterious light. With each step, my feet disappeared into the fog, which coiled around me in unnerving tendrils. The mist seemed to test my flesh with each movement, as if feeling for a weakness, but I knew I was projecting. Fog was simply fog, no matter how disquieting it was.

As I reached the mausoleum, I slowed my steps, looking around for any signs of intrusion, but as far as I could tell, the area was silent, and I was unobserved. I crept to the entrance, my hands sliding over the cold marble and finding condensation on the surface. Before I lost my nerve, I stuck my head inside and gave it a thorough once-over, my heart thrashing in my chest. But no one was in the room.

I let out a breath and stepped within, eyes zeroing in on the candle, still lit and sitting in a window recess, where it flickered from the onset of a breeze.

I walked slowly around the small chamber. There were plaques in the wall, where the ashes of members of the family had likely been laid to rest in niches. And in the center of the room were two sarcophagi, laid side by side. I hesitated as I approached them, finding the names etched into each of them: Victor and Helena Morano. The parents of Henri and Blanche.

I swallowed hard and took a closer look to find the lid of Helena's tomb askew. My eyes widened and I rushed to its side. I could just make out the interior of the sarcophagus.

It was empty.

Perhaps I was mistaken. Was her body never recovered? She had fallen from a cliff, intentional or not. Had it been to fall into the sea? I didn't know enough of the circumstances to know for sure. Either way, I pushed the lid back into place.

I stepped over to Victor's resting place, hesitating. Would he also be missing from his tomb? His body would have most certainly been recovered. It was sacrilegious, but I had to know. I gathered my strength before I could ponder the disrespect I was about to inflict on Henri's father, and pushed on the lid. It seemed heavier than Helena's somehow, and I had to really use my strength to get it to budge. As soon as an opening was discernible, I caught a whiff of decay. I grunted, unwilling to look within the tomb, and replaced the lid. At least the siblings' father was in his rightful resting place.

My eyes found the candle again, and I frowned. Clearly, whoever had lit the flame was not in the mausoleum, so it was unlikely to be a late visit from a member of the family. That meant that it had to have been utilized as before, but by a different person. As a signal. And if whoever had stationed the candle in the window recess followed the pattern the mystery woman had used, they would be in the hedge maze.

I took a deep breath to gather my courage and left the mausoleum, making for the entrance of the maze. Medusa didn't guard the opening here, but a single marble arm reached out from the hedges as if trying to escape from being pulled back inside by the shrubs. I'd never used this entrance before, so I hadn't noticed the quirk, but it was a touch of macabre that I didn't appreciate at the moment, what with the fog sucking at my every footfall.

I stepped into the hedge maze, trying to recall how it had looked in daylight, inviting with wide aisles and cheerful greenery. It was difficult to imagine this was the same place at all. The ground churned with a heavy mist, the dark hedges appearing like impenetrable prison walls, tall and imposing, threatening. I felt like the maze would devour me if I entered, but it would plague me to no end if I left this mystery unsolved.

Determined, I pushed through the maze. I didn't meet a single dead end, this half of the maze clearly identical to the other. The designer's imagination ended, it would seem, with the statues they'd depicted throughout.

The clearing was silent as I entered it, the fog making it appear more dreamlike than before. The base of the fountain was obscured, so it looked as if the goddesses were quite literally standing on a cloud.

I circled the fountain cautiously, remaining alert for anyone who might be lying in wait nearby, but no one seemed to be around. But if they weren't here, where was the person who'd lit the candle?

I frowned, eyes roving the area more carefully, when I spotted something draped over the bench I'd previously hid behind while spying on Henri and Blanche. I sauntered over, expecting to find a discarded scarf or something frivolous from my aunt's walks. Instead, what I saw made my blood run cold.

I stopped to stare a few paces from the bench, taking in the arm flung up onto the bench, as if gripping it for dear life, trying to pull its master from the hungry fog. I didn't move for several seconds. My breathing stopped briefly as I considered who I might find at the other end of that arm. I didn't want to find out, and yet I had to.

When I next drew breath, I forced my feet to move. The fog parted ahead of me like a vessel at sea, so that when I did reach the arm, the person it was attached to was briefly unobscured.

I gagged and had to swallow several times to keep my body

from heaving. The arm wasn't even attached to the man whose eyes stared up at the sky, unseeing. The arm was casually draped over the bench, blood oozing from a bloody shoulder. The man who lay beneath it had red hair and a spray of freckles across his face. I'd never seen him before, but his likeness to the mystery woman was undeniable. A brother or cousin. What he was doing here in her stead, I had no idea, but his chest was exposed to the night air, ribs ripped aside, as if whatever had done this to him had wanted access to his heart.

I took a step back. I felt light-headed, as if I might faint, but I dug my nails into my palms to keep myself present. I circled the bench, as if I might find a clue as to why the man had been out here, and what had done this to him, when the fog revealed another secret to me from its depths. Fournier. The man's throat was gone, but he seemed otherwise unmolested. Blood trickled out from the corners of his mouth, and like the mysterious boy nearby, his eyes saw nothing.

As I gazed at the man I'd worked with closely toward the beginning of my stay at the château, I became aware of a noise emanating from the hedges around me. I blinked and took an unsteady step backward as I recognized it as a growl. The threatening growl of some beast.

Likely the very beast who had killed the men at my feet.

I willed the fog to swallow me as it had the corpses, but it passively whirled around me, unhelpful. Very carefully, as to make as little noise as possible, and to hopefully not alert a killer animal to my presence among the hedges, I crept toward the exit from the clearing.

When I stepped on a twig, it seemed to register like a blast of gunpowder in the dark. I winced and stared into the darkness.

The growling had stopped. And in a moment, in its place, I could make out the sound of crashing through the maze.

The creature had heard me. And it was coming for me.

SEVENTEEN

I abandoned all pretense of stealth and ran.

In my flight, I wasn't paying attention to where I was going. My mind reeled as I came to a stop at a dead end and was forced to turn around. I cursed myself, listening to the sound of crashing shrubs grow nearer and nearer.

Panicking and not thinking clearly, I ended up at another dead end. I wanted to scream, but that would only make my situation worse.

I stilled as the sound of destruction ceased behind me. Swallowing, I turned, but nothing was in the path. I didn't trust that the creature wasn't nearby however, lying in wait. I felt the ground around me, then lowered myself as flat as I could so that the fog swirled overhead and covered me. I pulled myself as close to the hedge as possible and pulled my legs into a ball, praying that the fog would be enough to hide me.

Branches snapped just beyond a bend in the maze, and I

focused on keeping my breathing even and low so I wouldn't give myself away. Without poking my head up, I had no way of knowing where the beast was, but hopefully it was in a similar state of uncertainty. The only problem was that if it came too near me, the fog blanketing me would disperse, leaving me without any protection. I just had to hope that wouldn't happen.

I lay there for several minutes, straining for any noise the night would offer me, but I heard nothing. I couldn't stay there forever. Had the beast given up and left? Or was it making a thorough search of the maze? If that were the case, it would eventually find me. I had no idea how long this fog would linger, after all.

Tentatively, I lifted my head, allowing my eyes to adjust to the darkness for a moment before getting to my feet. I held my breath, expecting something to come charging at me from out of the hedges, but nothing did. I was not going to let my guard down, however. I very carefully and quietly picked my way through the maze, recalling the position of its passages so I wouldn't have to make any unnecessary course corrections. I decided that it would be best to come out of the maze closest to the château, and when I skulked along the final passage, I nearly sobbed with relief. I was almost to safety—unless the creature was waiting just outside.

At the end of the corridor, I ducked my head out and, seeing nothing, took a small step out into the open. And then another. I heard something snap behind me and took off at a run, but nothing gave chase. Still, I tore through the servants' door and shut it firmly at my back, breathing heavily.

My hands shook as I climbed the stairs back to my room. But rather than shut myself away out of fear, I went to Henri's bedchamber and knocked.

After a minute, the door opened, and Henri stood before me in trousers he had likely only pulled on to answer my summons. I was distracted by the sight of his naked chest, but I shook away the feelings stirring within me, reaching forth and grabbing his arm. "Henri. I was in the hedge maze. There's something out there. It killed Fournier and another man."

Henri's eyes widened, and he pulled me into his room, closing the door behind him. He grabbed me by my shoulders and looked me in the face. "What were you doing out there? You need to stay in the château at night."

"I saw a light in the mausoleum. I had to investigate."

Henri ran a hand back through his hair. "I . . . give me a minute. I'm still waking up."

I followed him to his wardrobe, where he pulled on a loose shirt. "Fournier, you say? Are you sure he was dead and not drunk or passed out?"

"He was dead," I insisted. "His throat was . . . missing. And the other man's arm was wrenched from his body, and I think it took his heart."

Henri stared at me. "Did you see what did it?"

"No. I heard it crashing through the maze. It was growling. I don't think it was a bear, though."

Henri nodded slowly. "Could it have been a man with a dog?"

I blinked. I hadn't considered that. "I . . . yes, I suppose it could have been." I shuddered. "A man may have been behind the murders, after all. If they trained a dog or even a wild animal . . ."

Henri put a hand on my shoulder and looked me in the eyes. "I'm going to have a look. You stay here, in my room, and lock the door behind me until I return. Don't open it for anyone else."

I drew back. "Henri, you can't go out there. What if we're wrong and it's still there?"

"I'll bring a gun, just in case."

"Henri . . ." I yanked on his sleeve. "Please don't."

His jaw clenched. "I'm going, Emile. Stay here."

I let go of him and watched silently as he slipped from the room. He looked back at me once before closing the door behind him. I rushed forward to lock it.

For the next hour, I paced, unable to sit still, worrying for Henri. It seemed far too long for him to be out there in the maze by himself. What if he needed me? I should have gone with him rather than hide in his room like a coward.

Just when I had resolved to fetch Count Montoni himself, there was a sharp knock at the door. "Emile. It's me."

I sighed with relief, the tension in my chest unspooling as I unfastened the lock and threw the door open. I wrapped my arms around him. "Thank God."

Henri chuckled and patted my back. "It's okay. I'm fine."

I looked up at him. "And the bodies?"

Henri hesitated but shook his head. "Emile, there were no bodies."

I drew back, eyes wide. "No bodies?"

"I searched everywhere."

"The clearing? The arm was on the bench."

"There was nothing on the bench. I was thorough, Emile." He pursed his lips. "The fog made it difficult, but I think if those bodies were there, they no longer are."

"*If* they were there?"

Henri winced. "That's not what I meant. It's a spooky night and sometimes we see things—"

"I wasn't imagining it."

"Okay, okay," Henri said, and pulled me to him. "If you say they were there, then they were there. Somebody must have moved them. That's not something an animal would do unless it was planning to eat them. And even then, it would have to leave behind some signs."

"So, it is a man behind this." I breathed, nodding to myself. I thought of the rib cage of the man, pried open to expose his chest, where his heart had been. An animal wouldn't have done that, *couldn't* have. Only a man, a sadistic man, could have.

I looked up and found that Henri was avoiding my eyes. I frowned. He wasn't . . . hiding something from me, was he? I wondered where all the blood could have gone in so short a time. There had to have been traces of *something*. But what would he gain by lying about it? To keep me from being so upset? Or did he know something? Was this part of whatever Montoni was hiding?

"What can we do?" I asked carefully.

Henri shrugged helplessly. "Without evidence, I don't think there's anything we *can* do."

I sighed, shaking my head as I kept a watchful eye on Henri. "Poor Fournier."

"Do you have any idea who the other man was?"

"He looked like the girl. The one who tried to access your sister's room."

"A relation?"

"I believe so."

Henri frowned, considering this. That was something he hadn't known, unless he was a really good actor. But then again, maybe he was telling the truth and I was imagining his deception. I wished I could trust him completely.

After a moment, Henri shook his head. "Well, you're staying with me tonight. There's no way I'm leaving you alone."

"I was hoping you'd say that." I smiled up at him with relief.

"Yeah?"

"Yeah." I looked away. "I know it's been awkward since we . . ."

"Kissed," Henri supplied.

"Yes. Since we kissed. I just . . . I hope I didn't ruin anything or—"

"Emile. You didn't ruin anything. I just don't trust myself with you. I don't want to get hurt again. Getting close to someone is really difficult for me. And I know you still have feelings for Bram."

"Henri, I—"

"No, it's okay. I want you to figure out who you want. I don't want to force you to choose. I told you from the beginning that I was going to win you over, and that means allowing you to make the decision."

I watched him silently for a moment. He really wasn't what I'd expected. I wanted to assuage his hesitations right then, but I also knew that he was right. I did have to make a decision. And putting it off wasn't fair. If only I could see Bram in the meantime to help sort out my heart.

"Come on," Henri nodded toward the door. "We can sleep in your room."

I smiled and nodded. We walked to my room, and the moment I opened the door, I knew something was wrong. There was something in the air, something ominous, like tension.

Slowly, I walked over to my bed and lifted my light.

The sheets were ripped to shreds.

Henri went pale and held me against him as he observed the scene with horror. "I will speak to my uncle in the morning," he promised, voice unsteady. "And you are *not* sleeping alone in this house again. Understand?"

Grateful, I buried my face in his neck.

EIGHTEEN

"I think it was a warning," Henri told me the next day as we sat down to dinner and waited for the others to join us.

I nodded slowly. "You spoke to your uncle?"

"Oh, we exchanged words all right. I'm not going to tolerate you being in danger in this house." He straightened. "But I didn't tell him about the bodies. I think it's for the best if we keep quiet about that for the time being."

"You still think I was seeing things."

"I'm trying to keep you safe, Emile," Henri hissed, leaning toward me. "There's a very delicate . . . *balance* to the situation at the château. Please just trust me for now. Keeping quiet about the bodies is in your best interest."

I clenched my jaw. "Fine. For now." Although I had to wonder what sort of balance he was speaking of. Was he trying to manage Montoni? Did this circle back to what he and Blanche were talking about in the hedge maze when I'd overheard them weeks ago?

"But I told him about your bedsheets. He claims that a servant was stationed at the door, so no one could have entered the château without being seen."

Blanche chose that moment to enter and dropped into a deep curtsy before me. "Marquis."

I rolled my eyes. "Oh, stop that."

She smirked, before noting the troubled looks on our faces. "And what's this then? Did I interrupt something?"

Henri cleared his throat as his sister took a seat beside him. "We were discussing how the servant guarding the door didn't see anyone enter the château last night."

I scoffed. "Nobody saw *me* leave, did they?"

"You left the château last night?" Blanche asked, looking interested. "To see Valancourt?"

"I'll tell you about it later," Henri told her with a meaningful look.

"Will you tell her *all* of it?" I asked. "Or just the part about the bed linens?"

"Yes. Annette was in a tizzy this morning over the state of them." Blanche's face pinched, and she exchanged a quick look with Henri. There was something in that look that left me a little unsettled.

I leaned toward Henri. "Henri. The servant didn't see me outside either."

Henri hesitated. "No, he didn't. I brought that up to uncle. He's going to have someone watch the servant entrance as well, just in case. But I think it's more to keep an eye on your movements. It's probably for the best, as you're safer in the château at night. I don't want you wandering outside anymore, especially alone."

That also cut off my only escape route, unfortunately.

"So, he doesn't believe me either."

"*I* believe you. I saw your bedsheets. So did the staff. You didn't invent that."

"I suppose your uncle believes I tore them up myself?"

Henri swallowed and glanced at his sister. "I think we all know that strange things happen around here."

I scowled at his evasiveness.

"Strange things do occur around here," Count Montoni said, sweeping into the room with Aunt Cheron on his arm, looking smug, "Why, just last night, Fournier left the château. He took all his things with him and left his immediate resignation behind. There's nothing nefarious in that unless you count the ungratefulness of a servant."

I met Henri's gaze and he looked away guiltily. Fournier . . . *left.* How convenient. Just what did Henri know about this? Was he working with his uncle? Why would he when he so clearly loathed the man? Either way, a murder had just been covered up, and Henri knew something about it.

Blanche wrinkled her nose. "But uncle, Fournier wouldn't up and leave like that. He's been with our family forever. I should think we know his character fairly well. He was Henri's valet for—"

"Precisely why he left," Montoni cut her off as he took his seat. "He wasn't pleased about his demotion, and he believed to have been made a laughingstock, given that a marquis in disguise took over his former duties."

"That's not fair," Henri said.

"It sounds rather spot on to me," Aunt Cheron said with a shrug. "I don't blame the poor chap. I mean, can you imagine?"

"But what if there was foul play at work here?" I asked

defiantly, ignoring Henri as he shook his head. "Blanche's concerns shouldn't be ignored."

Montoni sighed. "Then I would say that the fog last night got to you. I can hardly blame you, especially after that prank played on your room. It excites one's imagination."

Prank? That was how he was going to play that off? Some sort of retaliation from the staff?

Aunt Cheron nodded. "I once swore that I saw a top hat moving down the street without anyone wearing it. It was dark of course, but for years, I believed what I saw. The mind plays some awful games with us when we're under duress."

"Unless there's another reason why you suspect foul play?" Montoni asked, throwing a casual eye toward Henri, before zeroing in on me.

Henri was staring at me so hard that I could feel it.

"Not at all," I said.

I stewed in my anger, but I'd done all that I could. I didn't understand Henri's insistence on keeping what I'd seen secret, but I would respect it. Even if he was obviously keeping something from me, I did believe he had my best interests in mind. I just didn't understand how. Perhaps it would be best to keep any further observations to myself. No one seemed to believe me anyway, and honesty was beginning to seem more overrated by the day. It did nothing but get me in further trouble.

Conversation moved on to other topics, but I kept thinking about Fournier and Hargrove, and how easily their murders were covered up. If Montoni had been responsible for Hargrove's murder, as Father Schedoni claimed, then it stood to reason that Montoni was lying about Fournier to cover up another murder. Could that have been Montoni in the hedge maze last night?

Could he have a dog hidden somewhere on the estate, trained and capable of tearing a man to pieces? Was that his secret? I wouldn't put it past him.

I looked up when Count Montoni clinked his glass with a fork and rose from his seat. "If I could have everyone's attention, please. I have an announcement I'd like to make."

I frowned and exchanged a look with Blanche.

"It is my great pleasure," Montoni said, "to announce my engagement to Lady Abigail Cheron."

My mouth dropped open. Had I heard that right?

Henri looked just as stunned. "So soon?" he asked once he'd regained his wits.

Count Montoni beamed. "Yes. We've decided there's no point in putting it off. We fell for each other the moment we met, and have been very happy these past few weeks. We want to extend that happiness for the rest of our lives."

I met my aunt's eyes, and she held my gaze for a moment, as if daring me to make a scene. When I didn't say anything, she smiled and looked away, as if she'd won.

Well, I wasn't going to be the one to expose Montoni's gambling problem, or his potential financial issues. It was clear that he imagined my aunt to be wealthy, but I doubted she had the money he had in mind. Her fortune was modest at best. But I figured they deserved each other, so when Henri stood to drink to the couple's health, I did as well, nodding to my aunt, who seemed genuinely surprised at my approval.

My plans for acquiring Udolpho, unfortunately, continued to look bleaker. Montoni might not have the resources to oblige my blackmailing scheme even if I did uncover something worth securing the castle. And with my aunt joining his family, Udolpho would be on her radar. I wouldn't be able to escape her notice as I'd planned.

It was likely for the best, as seeking out the answers to this family's mysteries were growing more and more dangerous. After all, protecting my life was more important than losing my freedom. In the end, what would speaking out about Fournier's body actually accomplish, aside from more scrutiny? Aunt Cheron could even use it to add to her objections to my sanity. No, Henri was probably right. I should listen to him, believe in his cunning. It might get me out of this mess, in the end.

"When is the wedding?" Blanche asked when we'd all sat down again.

"We don't wish to wait long," Aunt Cheron told her. "Two weeks should be sufficient time to arrange it. I already had my big wedding, and a smaller one seems rather appealing at the moment. Wouldn't you agree, Count?"

Count Montoni nodded, patting her hand. "Very much so. This is going to be the beginning of something beautiful."

I refrained from rolling my eyes.

I convinced Blanche to venture outdoors with me the next morning, since Henri was in town on an errand for his uncle. We walked the hedge maze, whereupon I studied the area around the bench where I'd seen the bodies of Fournier and the mystery boy. I found nothing of consequence to mark that they'd been there. We also visited the mausoleum, where Blanche said a prayer for her parents. I noted that the candle was gone from the window recess.

"I received a letter yesterday," Blanche revealed as we stepped into the library. Grimes had made tea and poured a cup for each of us. He didn't hand me my cup as he did Blanche, one of many slights I'd suffered from him since coming out as marquis. Not that I could blame him. He was likely embarrassed by my subterfuge.

"Oh?" I watched as Blanche added her customary three sugar cubes and stirred them. She smiled graciously to Grimes as we went to sit on the sofa. My eyes sought three taxidermy bats near the ceiling in the corner, which made me smile, like they were winking at me.

"Oh, yes. From Carmilla. You do remember her, I suppose?"

I groaned. "You can't be serious."

"She hinted that she would like an invitation to sup with us." Blanche grinned at me. "You, dear Emile, have an admirer."

"I already have admirers. And I actually return their affections." I also wasn't so sure that Carmilla's interest was in me, given my observations on the evening of the ball. She had been flirtatious and pleasant, but also distracted. If anything, she was likely more interested in cultivating a friendship with Blanche than with me as a suitor.

Blanche sipped her tea, then spit it out with a yelp, holding a hand to her mouth.

"Did you burn yourself?" I asked, concerned.

Blanche's eyes watered and she nodded. "Terribly sorry," she said, getting up. She still held a hand to her face.

"What can I do?" I asked, standing with her.

She shook her head and looked at Grimes. "Get rid of that batch of tea immediately. All of it."

Grimes's eyes were wide as he watched her rush from the room. I met his gaze for a moment before he set out to carry out her wishes.

I lowered myself down into my seat slowly, then gazed at my untouched teacup. With a frown, I picked it up and sniffed at the tea. It smelled strong, but nothing noteworthy stuck out to me. I took a tentative sip and winced. It did have an odd aftertaste. Slightly bitter and metallic. I set the cup aside.

"Ah, here you are," Henri strode into the room with a smile as he peeled off his riding gloves. "Was that Grimes I saw racing out of here?" His smile turned wicked. "Did you scare him off?"

I pretended to look offended. "Hardly. Your sister burned herself on her tea. I hope she's alright."

"Burned herself?" Henri glanced back as the bell rang for the front door.

"Yes. And then she told Grimes to throw the batch out."

"Oh, is the tea terrible as well?"

I shrugged. "It isn't the best."

Henri sat across from me. "How has your day been otherwise?"

"More of the usual. And your errand?"

Henri leaned forward and looked around as if we might be overheard. "There's an odd bit of news going around. The apothecary shop owner's brother has gone missing. Some think the whole family was caught up in something altogether unsavory."

"Like what?"

Henri shrugged. "Gambling, smuggling. Who knows? It's just gossip. I honestly don't know how some of these rumors get started."

So, the dead boy from the hedge maze *had* been related to the apothecary shop owner. It made me wonder what was so terrible a crime that he'd been murdered for it.

"Now see here," Grimes followed a man in a suit into the

room. "You have no right to be in here. I've told you once, and I'll tell you again: You have the wrong house."

The man smiled thinly at Grimes. "And I tell you, sir, that I do not." He stood before a side table and wrote something on a piece of paper, before setting it down. Then he wrote on another piece of paper and attached that one to the lamp sitting upon the table.

I exchanged looks with Henri. "Is everything alright, Grimes?"

Grimes looked flustered. "Just don't let him wander the house unsupervised. I'm going to fetch the count." He dashed out of the room, leaving Henri and me gaping.

We watched the man move on to a painting, where he took a moment to study it before scribbling something down and putting a paper on that as well.

"What is he doing?" Henri asked me.

I shrugged, bewildered, and stood as Henri went to inspect the papers the man had written and discarded. When I approached, Henri pulled the paper from the lamp and showed it to me. It was a tag boasting the number thirty-five.

"Say," Henri said, walking up to the man, who was now looking over a candelabra. "What is this?"

The man frowned at the tag in Henri's hand. "If you wouldn't mind leaving those be. I'm tagging all assets in the house for sale. They are to go to auction."

"Auction?" Henri's eye widened. "I think Grimes is correct, sir. You have the wrong address."

"I wish that were the case. Unfortunately, the good Count Montoni is so far in debt that he must pay it off by selling his possessions."

Henri went pale as Count Montoni stormed into the room, face red and contorted with rage.

"How dare you," Montoni bellowed. "You will leave this house at once."

"I will not," the man countered. "I have a legal right to be here. We are going to hold a public viewing to sell off your items five days hence. You may be present if you like, but I would recommend sparing yourself the indignity."

Montoni's mouth opened and closed as the man wrote another tag for the curtains. "See here: I am going to be married in a fortnight."

"Congratulations."

"What I mean," Montoni said, putting a hand on the man's shoulder, "Is that I will be married into wealth. I can pay off my debt. There's no need for this demonstration. I understand the threat."

The man paused to peer at Montoni, his jaw working for a moment. He crossed his arms and shrugged. "A fortnight will be too late. If you can't pay your debt within ten days, I can do nothing but proceed with the actions I've laid out."

Montoni nodded. "Fine. I will speak to my fiancée. I'm sure she won't have a problem with moving up the wedding. It will be as you say."

The man scrutinized Montoni for a full minute before he nodded. "Very well. Ten days. If you aren't in my office by then, no amount of prostrating will put me off any longer."

"Thank you," Montoni said, bowing as the man made his way to the door. As soon as the man left, the count ripped the tags from the furniture, a steady stream of curses issuing from his lips. When he noticed Henri and I gawking at him, he paused to point a finger in our direction. "Nothing out of you two. If your aunt finds out about this, I will tear you limb from limb, and that is not an idle threat. Do you understand me?"

"Crystal clear," Henri assured him as I nodded.

A muscle jumped in Montoni's cheek as he stormed from the room.

Henri released a deep sigh. "So, it's true then. Uncle has ruined us."

"Gambling?"

Henri glanced at me, then nodded. "I'm afraid so."

"Are you still planning on killing him?"

Henri blinked. "What did you say?"

I shifted. "I may have been in the hedge maze one night and overheard you and Blanche."

Pursing his lips, Henri turned away. "It's not what you think, Emile."

"I know." I put a hand on Henri's back. "I trust you, Henri. Whatever that was, it's your affair, not mine."

Henri scoffed. "I'm afraid you put too much faith in me sometimes. I don't deserve your esteem."

"I beg to differ."

Henri faced me, and after a quick glance at the door, pulled me into a kiss. A heated kiss that left me blushing. I clung to him afterward, unwilling to let him go. Henri's eyes stared down into mine hungrily, and I wanted nothing more than to continue attending to his lips. But we were in public, and we couldn't chance any further contact.

"We're going to pick up where we left off tonight," Henri said, his voice low.

I swallowed hard. "That sounds like a threat."

"Oh, it is. A threat and a promise."

"Please, Count, threaten me some more."

Henri laughed.

I could only reflect the desire I saw in his eyes in my own. I wanted him. All of him. But I knew that I couldn't possibly give in to my impulses until I'd spoken to Bram. He deserved that at least.

Henri seemed to read my thoughts; his mouth tightened. "Of course, I don't want to pressure you. I'll let you set the tone. You are the marquis, after all."

"Ugh," I put a hand to my head. "You and your sister are never going to lay off the teasing, are you?"

Henri's smile returned. "Absolutely not." He grabbed the sides of my face and gave me a kiss on the forehead before leaving me in the room by myself, blushing furiously.

NINETEEN

That evening at supper, it was announced that the wedding would take place the following morning. They were so in love they couldn't wait any longer to be married.

"In love with her money," I told Henri.

Henri stifled a laugh.

Any thoughts of corrupting me with kisses were postponed, as we both needed sleep for the early day ahead.

The next morning, we congregated at the nearby chapel where Father Schedoni himself officiated the wedding between Count Montoni and my aunt. The wedding was small, just the siblings, myself, and the servants, but my aunt didn't seem to mind. She was beaming from ear to ear, and I almost felt . . . *happy* for her? It was a strange feeling. She'd been a source of anxiety and fear for so long now, but she was family, and seeing her married was oddly emotional. I knew that she wouldn't be happy with Montoni. The count would be disheartened when he learned that my aunt likely did not have the money necessary to pay off his gambling debts. She wouldn't have access to my inheritance but for the amount necessary to maintain La Vallée, which she had obviously seen fit to forgo. I wasn't sure what that meant for Château le Blanc, or for Henri and Blanche. I could only hope that things would somehow work out, or that enough money would be procured from my aunt to put off creditors for a time.

That evening, we had a feast, and several neighbors arrived to partake in the celebratory dinner. As the night wore on, Montoni disappeared into his office, before Aunt Cheron, rather Aunt *Montoni*, was summoned to attend to him. Soon after, Henri, Blanche, and I were ordered to the library for a family meeting.

Grimes was in the library when we arrived, speaking with an enraged Montoni, grinding his teeth.

"What's this now?" Henri asked as he took a seat beside his sister. I sat in a chair near my aunt, who looked distracted and a little pale.

Grimes looked up at Henri, then glanced at Montoni, as if for permission to speak. Montoni waved a hand at him.

"It appears," Grimes said, clearing his throat, "that some things were found in Fournier's room when it was being cleared out, that are rather alarming."

I perked up. Perhaps there was evidence of his murder yet.

"Does it point to his current whereabouts?" Blanche asked.

"Er, no. There was some gold paint and a stash of silverware beneath his bed."

I had expected something like this. I'd given Annette the go-ahead to inform Grimes of the scheme we'd uncovered, since I didn't see the point in putting it off longer. What I hadn't expected was for Fournier to be involved. "Gold paint? What does that mean?" I asked, feigning ignorance. I glanced at Henri, only to find that he'd gone pale, as had Blanche. Was I missing something?

Montoni tsked. "What it means is that Fournier was planning to paint silverware gold and swap it with some of our very expensive gold sets."

"So, he was a thief," my aunt said, sniffing. "It makes sense that he would run off then."

I caught a shared look between Henri and Blanche before Henri smiled tightly. "I wonder why he would leave without making the switch first. He must have lost out on quite a bit of money." His tone was goading, as if trying to solicit a response from their uncle. How curious.

"That's not the point," Montoni growled. "One of our servants saw fit to try and steal out from under our very noses. And that is money that we do not have to lose, if the finances I looked over this evening are any indication."

Blanche frowned. "What are you saying, Uncle?"

"That Madame Cheron may have *exaggerated* her fortune."

"I only ever said that I was well off," my aunt protested. "I never said that I was rolling in money. And I did not expect to be married to a man in so much debt that he would need me to bail him out."

Blanche put a hand to her head. "Your infernal gambling. Why must you take such chances, Uncle?"

"Do not dare speak to me of how I conduct myself," Montoni sneered. "It's by my charity that you've been allowed to participate in this season's balls. I could have just as easily been rid of you and sent you to a ladies' seminary. Or perhaps take the veil. Father Schedoni would be pleased to preserve your virtue, I'm sure."

Blanche looked away, chagrined.

"I hold all the power here. You need to remember that. I am more powerful than the both of you. Combined. Stay in line, or I will be forced to demonstrate that strength."

Even Henri looked sickly now. His hand trembled slightly before he seemed to regain his composure. I wondered what power Montoni held over Henri's head. His power over Blanche was obvious.

"It's not my aunt's fault that you married her for her money," I said, tempting the count's wrath.

Montoni snorted. "I hardly married Madame Cheron for her money. I love the sweet creature. I am merely disappointed."

My aunt smiled, although it didn't quite reach her eyes.

"But what does this mean, Uncle?" Henri asked. "Is there enough money to satisfy creditors for now?"

"No. There is not." Montoni sighed. "I am going to lease Château le Blanc for a time. My creditors have agreed to use the rent money to pay off my debt. It will likely take a year or so."

"What do we do in the meantime?" Blanche asked, looking genuinely frightened.

"I will also be renting La Vallée for additional income," my aunt said. "And should Emile come into his inheritance, I assume he will continue the lease, and perhaps share a portion of his fortune to pay off the debt faster." She met my eyes. I blinked. She could have very well had me thrown into an institution and claimed my inheritance for herself immediately. The fact that she spoke as if the inheritance was a sure thing gave me hope. It also made me believe that she was protecting me from Montoni.

I wasn't sure why that would be the case, given our history, unless she perceived the nature of Montoni more astutely than I gave her credit for. She couldn't have been happy that he would immediately need her financial support to pay for his gambling habit. It had to make one feel used.

"But where will we go, if we cannot stay here?" Blanche wanted to know.

Count Montoni smiled grimly. "Udolpho, of course."

Henri shuddered visibly, and I felt my spirits sink. How ironic that the safe haven I had looked to these past weeks ended up being the very place I would be forced to in this trying time.

"Udolpho?" my aunt asked.

Count Montoni turned to her with a smile. "Of course, my dear. You didn't think this was my only property, did you? I have a castle in Italy, just waiting for us to inhabit it."

"A castle." My aunt's eyes sparkled.

I met Henri's gaze, and while he seemed resigned, he offered me a weak smile.

Montoni took a sip of his wine. "I was planning on spending our honeymoon at Udolpho. The countryside in Italy is stunning. Picturesque. This setback we are experiencing will extend our stay, but it need not be an unpleasant time for us."

Aunt Cheron, for I couldn't quite think of her as Aunt Montoni just yet, beamed. "Oh, it sounds like a grand adventure. Don't you think so, Emile?"

"An adventure," I echoed with false enthusiasm.

"When do we depart?" Henri asked.

"In two days. At dawn," Montoni replied.

"Two days!" Blanche straightened. "That hardly gives us time to put our affairs in order."

"Yes, best get to writing to friends and suitors at once. I'm sure you can manage that. Your lady's maid will do your packing for you." Montoni sniffed. "Of course, the staff will stay on to assist with the leasers. We will take Annette, who will also see to the comfort of Madame Montoni, as well as my own valet, Cavigni. I was thinking that perhaps we would bring Ludovico to split valet duties between Henri and Emile. Does that sound fair?"

We all nodded, although my mind was racing with thoughts of preparation and the journey ahead. With everything going on, I likely wouldn't have a chance to speak to Annette until we arrived at the castle.

"Why must we leave so soon?" Blanche asked. "Can we not wait a few more days, at least?"

"We are already cutting it close," Montoni said. "Our medicine will need to be administered in a week's time. Father Schedoni, of course, will accompany us, and will remain with us to see to our health."

I shuddered at the thought of having Schedoni on hand for the foreseeable future. And then I realized with a start that this would mean I would be leaving Bram behind. And if we left in two days, how would I get word to him? The servants would likely be too busy with arranging for the journey to be able to run into town for me.

When we were dismissed, I walked with Henri toward our bedrooms. Or *his* bedroom, rather. "You're quiet," he observed.

"It's a lot to absorb." I tried to put him at ease with a smile, but it was feeble. "I'm also worried."

"Of course you are. But it will be alright. Udolpho is . . . I won't lie, it's dismal. But we'll be together." He reached out and grabbed my hand. "I believe we can weather anything together, you and I."

I did smile at that. "I agree."

"Good. Then there's nothing to worry about." Henri sighed. "But I will miss my creations."

"Creations?"

Henri nodded. "Surely you've seen them. I take an interest in taxidermy."

My eyes widened. "Those are your doing?"

Henri chuckled. "Of course. Who did you expect created them?"

I pursed my lips, unsure. They weren't to my taste, but I'd come to enjoy the scenes over time. "They're dead animals. Isn't that rather morbid?"

"I suppose you could see it that way. I prefer to think of it as giving them a second life."

We slowed as we approached one such scene. A fox sprang from tall grass, upon an unsuspecting hedgehog. The fox's paws were outstretched, its mouth open in a snarl. I reached out and ran my hand through the red and white fur of its tail. "Yes, but you're posing dead bodies."

Henri sighed. "I know it's hard to understand, but creating these makes me feel . . . I don't know, closer to the natural world. I think sometimes we forget that behind teatime and etiquette and fancy dresses, we're all animals, a part of nature. This grounds me." He set a hand on the fox's head, almost affectionately. "I'm honoring their lives by preserving them. It makes me feel good to do something for these creatures. They're beautiful and deserve to be admired in death, not just thrown on a rubbish heap after their meat's been cut away."

I nodded slowly. I didn't want to make Henri feel like he had to defend himself. If this was a hobby he enjoyed and it gave him some satisfaction, I wanted to support it. "I like the bats in the library. I think they add a touch of whimsy."

Henri glanced up and smiled. "Thank you. I've always liked bats. Very misunderstood creatures." He sighed as he straightened. "Most of the animals I work with are misunderstood."

For a moment, I imagined that Henri looked rather sad, but I wasn't sure why. Was it because he would be leaving them behind? They had to trust the family leasing the château would respect them and not disturb them.

We began to walk along the hall once more.

I cleared my throat. I hated to bother Henri with something so personal, but I didn't see any other way around it. "I wonder if you could do a favor for me?"

Henri lifted an eyebrow.

"I would like to write to Monsieur Valancourt, to apprise him of our plans. He has a right to know."

Henri breathed in deeply and let it out with a sigh. He squeezed my hand. "I suppose it's only fair."

I blinked. "Really?"

"Well, he doesn't have much of a chance now that you won't be living in the same country soon." Henri pulled me to a stop and drew me to him so that we were face-to-face. "And anyway, haven't I earned your heart by now?"

I put my free hand on his chest. "You may be getting closer."

"Yeah?" he asked, inching his face toward mine. His eyes glanced down at my lips.

"I mean, I do like it when you hold me."

"Is that all?"

I swallowed hard as his lips brushed against mine. My body leaned into him, and I nearly gasped when he pulled away and continued up the hall without me.

"That's what I thought," he said, casually.

I glared at his back. "Tease."

"Oh, *I'm* the tease?"

Part

Three

TWENTY

"I've got that for you, my lord," a handsome man in his early twenties told me, grinning as he lifted my heavy trunk with ease and handed it up to the carriage driver.

"Thank you," I said, feeling awkward that I didn't know the boy's name. He was familiar, but I couldn't place him. I'd never been terribly good with names.

"It's Ludovico, my lord." He said, reading my dismay. "Don't fret. It's a large staff, so I'll forgive you this time." He winked and I felt my pride swell at the attention. Henri caught the look and shook his head at me.

I grinned in reply.

Montoni, my aunt, and Father Schedoni were going to ride in the first carriage in our train, while the servants would ride in the last one. That left the middle carriage to Henri, me, and Blanche, exactly how I liked it.

"It's rather exciting," Blanche said, smiling as she piled into the carriage after us and looked out the window longingly at Château le Blanc. "I love to travel. It's just too bad this will end in that terrible place."

"Is Udolpho really so bad?" I asked, skeptical.

"Whatever you imagine, it's worse," Henri joked. Or rather, I thought it was a joke.

"Best lower your expectations," Blanche examined her nails. "We won't be attending balls or parties."

I leaned back in my seat, the cushion stiff and uncomfortable. I shifted until I was satisfied. "So, it's basically no fun at all."

"Not an ounce to be had."

"Well, I plan to have fun." Henri's hand found my thigh. "Quite a bit of it, actually."

I swatted his hand away. "Scoundrel." As the carriage drove away, I gave him a quick kiss on the cheek.

Henri beamed at me.

"It's not going to be like this the entire journey, is it?" Blanche looked down her nose at us. "If it is, I think I'll take my chances with Father Schedoni and the newlyweds."

"No, you won't," Henri said dismissively.

She smiled in agreement. "No, I won't."

We all peered back out through the window as we drove away from the château. We watched it grow smaller and smaller, until a bend in the road hid it from sight.

Henri sighed. "And then it was gone."

Blanche patted his knee. "We made a lot of good memories in that house."

"And we'll make plenty more, even in a gloomy old castle like Udolpho."

"Together always," Blanche said.

"Together always, sister."

As we skirted town, I noted each building we passed, as if I would never see them again, which could very well be the case. I wondered what Bram was doing at that moment, if he was perhaps watching for the parade of carriages, whisking me away to parts unknown.

"He got it," Henri told me.

I smiled wistfully at him. "You gave it to him yourself?"

"I did. I would have stayed to observe his disappointment, but I was in a hurry."

I lifted an eyebrow. "Truly? I thought you fed off the suffering of others."

He placed a hand over his heart. "You wound me, sir."

"By speaking the truth?" Blanche asked innocently.

Henri pursed his lips. "Is this how it's going to be then? The two of you ganging up on me? Maybe I should fling myself from the carriage now and be done with it."

I shared a conspiratorial look with Blanche.

"This could be fun," she said in a fake whisper.

"I agree one hundred percent," I whispered back.

Henri just shook his head, grinning.

We stopped at an inn for the first night, and the second. On the third evening, we were too far into the countryside to secure such an establishment, so Montoni called on some friends whom he knew would put us up.

Ugo and Bertrand were brothers who owned a modest house. The servants would be forced to sleep in the barn, while the rest of us would double up in rooms for the night. The house had only one servant, who saw to all of our comforts, which I'm sure was taxing. A woman from the village came three times a week to cook, and was summoned on this occasion, providing us with tender lamb and greens, which was more than satisfactory on such short notice.

"It smells lovely," I complimented as I was served. I eyed the food with some trepidation however, as it was served much rarer than I liked, but I would eat without complaint, having burdened our hosts enough.

"Quite," Blanche agreed, lips pasted into a smile that, if I didn't know her better, appeared genuine.

"My child," Father Schedoni said, brows furrowed as he observed Blanche, "where are your gloves?"

I blinked and looked to Blanche's bare arms. Usually, she did wear gloves when out, and as I glanced around the table, I realized that Montoni, Morano, and Schedoni all wore gloves.

Montoni narrowed his eyes at his niece. "How thoughtless of you."

Blanche stood, apologizing, blushing under the scrutiny of the others. "I will fetch them right away."

"I haven't gloves on either," I said, standing with her. "I'll escort her."

Montoni gave me a passing glance, nodding.

As we left the room, Blanche sent me a grateful smile. "That was embarrassing."

I scratched my head. "You always wear gloves when out?"

"For meals," Blanche explained. "Uncle once received a sliver of silver and it got infected. He nearly lost his hand. Since then, we've been instructed to wear gloves when guests to dinner." She shrugged. "It's inconvenient, but we indulge him."

"Strange."

Blanche smiled, grabbing my sleeve. "Thank you. For coming with me. I'm afraid you're in the company of a strange family. We have our quirks."

"Like taxidermy?"

Blanche sighed. "Yes. Henri does dote on those things. I think they give him a sense of control, and an outlet for creativity. I hope they didn't frighten you. I know they can be a bit much."

"They're rather impressive, actually."

"It is an odd talent," Blanche acknowledged, "but he's skilled at it. Henri has always been fond of animals."

"You should get a pet."

Blanche raised an eyebrow. "You really think my uncle would allow an animal in the house?"

She was right. I couldn't see Montoni indulging them in that manner. He'd be more likely to kick a puppy than pet it.

When we returned to the dining hall, Bertrand was speaking in a low voice. "Yes, you'd best be careful in the woods surrounding that castle. I've heard that it's a haunt for assassins and bandits. Not a place for proper gentlemen, nor women. Stick to the main roads and do not fall for any tricks of broken-down carriages or anything of the sort. Mind your own business, and you should reach your destination just fine."

"We aren't afraid of bandits or anything of the kind," Montoni sniffed. "I am well acquainted with the area surrounding Udolpho, and the people who reside there. It's cruel to worry my new wife so."

Bertrand eyed Aunt Cheron with hesitance. "I beg your pardon, my lady."

My aunt merely nodded in response.

Bandits and thieves. What sort of place was Montoni bringing us to? It was sounding more and more like a quiet corner of the world to do away with us.

"Is there much in terms of society then?" my aunt asked Montoni, and I leaned forward, genuinely curious.

"Unfortunately, there is not," Montoni said, blowing on a cut of meat before carefully removing it from his fork with his teeth. I noticed Henri eat with the same care and almost snorted. He looked as if he thought the lamb might return to life and bite him. Blanche, I noted, didn't eat at all, but rather cut at the meat and pushed it around her plate. Perhaps it wasn't to their liking? Despite it being quite rare, it wasn't bad.

"It is surrounded by forest on three sides, and built into a mountainside," Montoni continued. "The ride is more treacherous than I like, but the view is simply stunning. As a quiet retreat, it will be like nothing you will ever experience. The perfect setting for a honeymoon."

Aunt Cheron smiled, but it did little to brighten her features. Even she was having misgivings. Udolpho Castle sounded isolated, like a prison. And I had been hoping to win the estate for my own, had been banking on it. It was strange how things turned out. As much as I was bored of the arduous journey we were currently undertaking, I suddenly wished for it to be prolonged to avoid reaching our destination that much sooner.

It was another two days before the Apennine Mountains could be seen in the distance, bringing our journey to an end. We passed through several valleys, some barren of trees, rocky and unforgiving, while others were covered in pine or fields of tall grass. There was a small village that consisted of perhaps thirty houses and a tavern, but otherwise, the only signs of civilization were farmers' cottages here and there. We ventured through a vast pine forest before trees gave way to a gorge, which we had to traverse via a covered bridge, its wooden planks rickety beneath the wheels of our carriages. It truly was an out-of-the-way area, but I had to admit that Montoni was correct about the landscape. It was majestic and beautiful and lifted my spirits, despite the situation we found ourselves in.

"And there it is," Henri said after some time had passed. I couldn't see what he was referring to, so I scooted to his side and leaned over him to gaze out through the carriage window. Night was fast falling, the sun seeming to be swallowed by the mountainous peaks ahead of us. It made for a pretty scene, pinks and oranges cooling to purples that played over the rock face. Built into the mountains looming large beyond was a sprawling castle. I gazed with melancholy awe upon the structure. Despite the beautiful colors at its back, the castle seemed to swallow the light with its moldering walls of dark gray stone. As I watched, the lights of the mountain were snuffed out all at once, sending shadows racing over the castle, as if chased by specters. I absorbed the stretches of ramparts and looming towers, the turrets that jutted up from the gloom, and thought what a lonely place it looked. As we reached the gigantic castle gates, some details began to stand out to me, such as the hunched figures along the battlements, hideous deformed stone monsters that would likely have given the gargoyles of Notre Dame a run for their money. They lurked, as if watching for travelers below and perhaps, warning them away.

Once the gates had been opened from within by unseen servants, we traveled through the courtyard, choked with weeds and grass. Inside, it seemed, would be as gloomy as without.

"Home, sweet home," Henri said, smiling thinly.

"But perhaps not for long," Blanche offered a beacon of hope. None of us replied.

The carriages skirted the end of the courtyard, coming to a stop before two large doors boasting knockers shaped like wolf heads. I felt uneasy and light-headed from the long days of travel, and I was grateful for Ludovico's help down from the carriage.

Despite night having just fallen, a chill already permeated the air, and I followed the procession of my travel companions inside the main doors, conducted by a short, round man named Bertolino, who kept bowing and scraping to Montoni as if the count was royalty.

"You'll see to the horses?" Montoni asked as Bertolino led us to a sitting room, where we sat on stiff-backed furniture that had seen better days. The dark stone walls were covered with tapestries in an attempt to hide the cold features, while a roaring fire had been prepared. I welcomed the warmth and gazed around uneasily, meeting my aunt's eyes briefly before they slid away.

"We have a very capable new stablemaster, my lord," Bertolino informed the count. "While your message was a surprise, we have no shortage of people in the village looking for employment. You'll recognize many familiar faces from years past, when Udolpho was utilized more regularly. We've only had a few days to prepare for your arrival, but I think you'll be pleased with the result. Usually, we keep the east wing completely closed up, with the furniture protected, you know. The common rooms have been aired out in anticipation, including the gallery."

"Very good. Bertolino, meet Lady Montoni, my new wife. She will be mistress of the castle, and you will see to her every comfort. The other unfamiliar face is her nephew, Marquis St. Aubert. You will make sure to give him the red room in the east wing."

Bertolino bowed deep to my aunt, and then to me, before turning a confused look on Montoni. "The red room, sir?"

"That's what he said," Father Schedoni sniffed.

Bertolino hesitated but nodded. "We can arrange for fresh bedsheets. The rest of your family will accept their usual rooms in the west wing?"

"That will do," Montoni said, waving a hand.

Henri straightened. "I could take a room in the east wing, to keep Emile company. It's no trouble."

"We aren't going to complicate the matter further," Montoni said with a finality that brooked no further arguments. "Now, I think we are all weary from our journey." Waving a dismissive hand at Bertolino, he issued his next set of orders. "Perhaps you can show Lady Montoni to her room and direct the luggage to their appropriate destinations. Then have some food sent to each of us in our bedchambers."

"Very good, my lord," Bertolino said, bowing, before escorting my aunt from the room.

I clasped my hands together tightly before me, unsure and feeling uncomfortable in this big, unfamiliar castle. Despite the fire, I still felt a draft in the room, and I wondered if the entire castle would be cold, as if it were in the very bones of the place.

"I will show you to your room," Henri offered, suddenly standing before me. He didn't look to Montoni to confirm that the action was acceptable but instead helped me to my feet and led me from the room, holding a lantern to see by.

The halls were dark and narrow, and I tried to pay close attention to where we were going so I wouldn't get lost in the night. I kept telling myself that the castle would look more like a home by the light of day, but I wasn't sure. It just didn't feel hospitable.

"I'll come to your room when I can," Henri said, glancing back at me, the lantern light chasing the shadows from the planes of his face. "I don't know why uncle gave you a room so far from everyone else, but it *is* a big room. You'll be quite comfortable there, I'm sure."

"I'm sure," I repeated.

Henri stopped and turned to look at me. He put a hand on my shoulder and smiled encouragingly. "I know that it looks dismal right now, but it won't be that bad. We'll be together. There's plenty to explore and keep us occupied. I'll show you the library in the morning. It's immense."

"A library?" I asked, perking up. Now that I was no longer a servant in disguise, and had no social engagements, I would actually have time for such diversions.

Henri grinned. "That's my boy." He leaned forward until our foreheads touched and he searched my eyes. "You're not alone here. I don't want you to feel like you're locked away. Any time you feel like that, I want you to seek me out, okay?"

I let out a deep sigh, then nodded. "Thank you."

Henri pulled away and we continued to my room. Just when I thought that the castle couldn't possibly extend any farther, we climbed a staircase and stopped before a door with a brass knob.

I held my breath as Henri slipped inside and began to light candles. It was a large room with a narrow window at the far end. The fourposter bed was draped with red sheets and curtains, while a matching rug encompassed nearly the entirety of the stone floor, reminding me of a pool of blood. A table was positioned near a large fireplace, with an ancient-looking chess set atop it, pieces scattered about the board as if in the midst of a heated game, even now.

"I'll send Ludovico to start a fire," Henri offered. "It'll seem rather cheery after that."

"Alright."

"Unless you want to start one yourself? I have it on good authority that you make quite the roaring fire."

I snorted. "I have been known to make a fire here and there."

"You know the tricks of the trade. So manly."

"That's me. Manly, through and through." I knew that Henri was trying to break the tension, that he wanted me to feel comfortable, but I was far from it. In a moment, despite myself, I began to shake. I wasn't sure if it was from the cold of the room or from fright and stress, but Henri was upon me in an instant, running warm hands over my shoulders. He leaned down and kissed me softly on the lips, his eyes full of tenderness.

"I'm okay," I assured him. "I'll get used to it. I just . . . I'm tired and hungry."

Henri watched me for a minute. "I think we're all tired and hungry. When Ludovico comes for your fire, I'll make sure he brings along your supper." He hesitated. "Perhaps it would be best if I left you to your own devices tonight, since my uncle might be more observant of his surroundings than usual. Would that be alright?"

"Yes, of course. Like I said, I'm tired anyway. I'll probably fall right to sleep after dinner."

"Okay." Henri reached out and squeezed my hand briefly before heading to the door. He paused on the threshold. "Good night, Emile. I'll see you in the morning."

I nodded, and he left me alone.

Releasing a sigh, I walked the room slowly, in a circle. It was clean and well cared for, at least. Once a fire was started, it really would be cozy.

I stopped to stare once I noticed a second door to the room. I didn't know where it led, but I didn't like the idea of someone having access to the room from another part of the castle. I approached the door and fingered the bolt, which looked weak and rusted through. I doubted it would be much use if I fastened it, but I did so anyway.

It was less than half an hour before Ludovico arrived with a cold meal and a goblet of wine. I was more thankful for the wine than anything, reveling in its warmth as it spread through my chest. It served to relax me, and once the fire had been built and was roaring behind the grate, I begged Ludovico to sit with me for a time.

"Annette has told me a lot about you, my lord," Ludovico ventured as he replaced the chess pieces on the table to their starting positions.

I squinted at him. "With Annette, that could be a good thing or a bad thing."

Ludovico snorted. "Very true. And she would probably scold me for saying so, but I think she rather thinks very highly of you, my lord."

"Please call me Emile," I said, happy to hear that Annette held me in such regard. "I understand that we've been communicating through Annette for a while. It's about time we met."

"Quite right. But I don't think we were much help, I'm afraid. If Montoni was hiding anything of consequence, we didn't unearth it." He cocked his head as he finished setting up the chess pieces. "If you don't mind my advice, I would be careful looking into the count while you're at Udolpho. There seem to be eyes and ears everywhere. And we are rather isolated here."

I nodded slowly. "I'll keep that in mind."

Ludovico smiled. "Annette did tell me to keep an eye out for you, though, so don't think you have no allies here."

"I'm glad that I can count on you, Ludovico."

"Do you play?" he asked, gesturing to the chess set.

"I do, but not very well. My father would always trounce me."

"Well, if you would ever like a game, I promise to go easy on you. I've played all the servants at the château who would, and even Dr. Valancourt once. I could help you improve if you'd like."

"I would like that very much. I believe I saw a chess set in Bram's . . . er, Dr. Valancourt's office."

Ludovico sent me a knowing look. "Ah, yes. Annette has told me about Valancourt. Lady Morano and her brother have discussed him at length, and Annette can't hold her tongue around me. Fair warning."

I straightened. "I'll have to be careful about what I say around the both of you then. I wish Lady Morano was as discreet. Apparently she holds Annette in high esteem if she talks so loosely about my love life around her."

"Annette may speak plainly about these things to me, but I assure you that it goes no further. Lady Morano understands that she's trustworthy, and Annette knows that I am as well."

"Then I trust the judgment of my betters in this matter."

Ludovico smirked. "How do you feel about being so far away from Valancourt now?"

With a sigh, I plopped onto my bed, smoothing my hands over the sheets distractedly. "Honestly, I'm not sure where this leaves us. I miss him already, quite terribly. He's so warm and genuine, and when he gets excited about something, he's so animated. You should have seen him on the way to the opera . . ." I shook my head. "But that could very well be a lost cause. I wish he was here, but he isn't."

"But Count Morano is here."

"Count Morano *is* here," I agreed, looking up to meet Ludovico's eyes. "And I like him very much as well, for different reasons. I think my time here would be better spent acquainting myself with him than pining for a man I have no hope of seeing for quite some time."

"It's okay to miss Valancourt though," Ludovico offered. "He'll still be there when you leave this place."

I smiled thinly, an ache forming in my chest. "I hope you're right."

Ludovico took his leave after a while, and I was thankful that his presence had lifted my spirits, despite reminding me of my separation from Bram. I hoped Bram would wait for me, selfish as that was, but I also had to be realistic. He had seemed skeptical of a future between us the last time I'd spoken with him, after he'd discovered that I was a marquis. Maybe this was yet another sign that we weren't meant to be together, even if the thought made me want to lay down and cry.

I locked the door after Ludovico. This one, at least, had a sturdy lock. Then I stared into the fire as I finished my meal, wishing I had more wine to get me through my first night. As I slipped beneath the cool sheets of the bed, I heard the wind howl through the castle, and I recalled Annette's warnings of it being a haunted place.

"A place is just a place," I told myself as I closed my eyes, exhausted. "And a place cannot hurt you."

TWENTY-ONE

I wasn't sure what woke me. A noise, perhaps, or a vague sense that I was in an unfamiliar place. Either way, I found myself bolt upright in bed, staring into the corners of the dark room, where the dying embers of the fire could no longer reach. It took me a moment to remember where I was, and then the knowledge did little to appease my mind.

I heard a howl outside and I pulled my sheets up to my eyes, wondering if the noise was the wind, as before, or actual wolves prowling the forest. The sound seemed altogether too real to be anything but the latter.

Glancing at the fire, I decided that I could throw another log or two on to chase some of the shadows from the room. Perhaps that small comfort would be enough to calm my racing thoughts and deter my imagination from running amok.

I crept across the room and set to work on the fire, making sure the new logs I'd added caught fire and would renew its strength. After fussing with a fire poker for some time, I stepped back and reveled in the warmth of the flames. My eyes drifted to the second door I'd noticed, and I frowned. I stared at it for a moment before approaching and touching the bolt. I could have sworn that I'd bolted it, yet it was now unlocked.

Feeling uneasy, I ventured to the main door to find it locked. I must not have bolted the second door. That was the only explanation. There were only the two doors, and if I'd locked both of them, no one could have gained access to my room in the night.

I heard something then, through the second door. A moaning. But no, it hadn't come from the door, but from the walls themselves. I stepped back, my hair standing on end.

The wind. It had to have been the wind. There was some sort of gap in the wall, and when the wind blew through it, it sounded like moans. It happened in old houses all the time.

I swallowed hard, panic clawing at my chest, despite trying to reason my fears away. I'd been so tired that I could have easily thought about throwing the bolt without actually doing it. No one could have been in my room while I'd slept. And it had been the wind blowing through the castle that had awakened me.

True fear crept up my spine as I realized how far from the rest of the household I was in this unfamiliar castle. I felt myself sweating as paranoia set in. I knew that I couldn't stay in that room for another moment.

I threw on a cloak and lit a candle before slinking out of the room, making sure to close the door firmly behind me. Once I was in the hallway, I stared around myself with unease. Everything was so still and dark. It was an eerie feeling, and I didn't like it one bit. How could Montoni send me so far from the other rooms? It was cruel. I wasn't sure if I could take it.

Steeling my nerves as best I could, I descended the staircase and followed the halls the way I remembered, back to the main sitting room. Thankfully, I hadn't gotten turned around, but rather found myself in the exact place I'd meant to go.

"My lord?"

I started as a shadow fell across me, and I wheeled to find Annette staring me down, eyebrow raised.

"You scared me, Annette. Make some noise in the future."

Annette snorted. "Couldn't sleep either, could you, sir?"

"I slept a little."

"More than me." Annette shook her head. "To be back in this place . . . ugh. How I hate it here. It's so depressing." She squinted at me. "You haven't seen any ghosts, have you? You look like you've seen a ghost."

"I . . . no. I haven't seen any ghosts." I'd maybe heard one, but I wasn't going to invite Annette to feed my already-vivid imagination.

Annette shrugged. "Well, give it some time. It's only the first night, after all. And you're in the red room."

I blinked. "What about the red room?"

"Nothing," Annette said innocently.

I narrowed my eyes.

"I spoke to Ludovico," she said, changing the subject. "What's the plan now that we're at Udolpho Castle? I don't see how finding anything on Montoni would give us any leverage out here."

I glanced around the room, recalling Ludovico's warning about eyes and ears. "You're right. I don't think there's anything to be gained here."

She squinted at me. "Just what did you hope to find on him? And no more holding back like you did with your title. That's not the sort of thing partners keep from one another. It doesn't exactly instill confidence."

I winced. "You're right, Annette. I am sorry about that. It was of the utmost importance for me to keep that detail secret. From everyone."

"Yes, I've had the *pleasure* of seeing to your aunt. I would have run for the hills myself if I'd been in your shoes. She and Montoni deserve each other if you ask me."

"I'm not sure anyone deserves to suffer under Montoni, even my aunt." I sighed. "I truly am sorry for the subterfuge, Annette. Can you forgive me?"

Annette watched me for a moment before giving a sharp nod. "Very well. But I am sticking my neck out for you, so I expect some transparency. Of course, the silverware plot led nowhere." She shook her head. "I still can hardly believe that Fournier was caught up in that business."

I hesitated, wondering if I should inform her that Fournier was dead, and that I believed Montoni was covering up his murder, and decided to share some of my thoughts on the matter. I did just agree to share information with her, after all. But perhaps I could leave out the more worrisome details. "I don't believe Fournier merely left the château. I believe he was removed by Montoni."

"But whatever for?"

I shrugged. He had clearly been meeting the red-haired boy in the hedge maze. I wasn't sure the significance of that just yet. "I'm not sure. But finding the silverware in Fournier's room was certainly convenient. I wouldn't be surprised if it had been planted to explain away his disappearance."

Annette pursed her lips, absorbing this. "And what do you hope to accomplish now that we're at Udolpho, my lord?"

"I believe my only hope now is to wait out the next five months until I can claim my inheritance. I appreciate your help, Annette, but I'm not sure there's anything else to be done."

Annette cocked her head. "My lady said you would need to be married to collect your inheritance."

"I . . . yes, that was my aunt's wish, but there are no balls out here. There are no eligible ladies to court. I hardly think I have to worry about that now."

"Maybe. But Montoni's a shrewd one. I wouldn't rule out some new scheme, especially if he's desperate for money." She stepped closer to me, lowering her voice. "Maybe I'll keep an eye out, just in case. I always liked Fournier, and if he had anything to do with his disappearance, I would like to get to the bottom of it myself."

"Just don't take any unnecessary risks. I would hate for anything to happen to you."

"Aw, lord, you're making me blush." She grinned. "But enough prattling on. Did you come this way looking for the kitchen?"

"No, I was not. I was going to see Count Morano. I must speak to him about something."

Annette smirked. "If you say so, my lord."

I glared at her. Now that I knew that she talked with Blanche openly about my affairs, I didn't feel quite so bad about all that I'd withheld from her over the past few weeks. I suppose it shouldn't have been a surprise that they were so close, given how they'd previously had a laugh together over my fire-making skills.

"I do."

With a roll of her eyes, Annette turned and started for a doorway on the other side of the room. "Follow me."

The journey to the rooms in the west wing was substantially

shorter than the one to mine. Annette pointed out the rooms for each of the guests, in case I should need them, then bid me good night, leaving me to my own devices.

I lingered outside of Henri's door until I was sure Annette had gone, then knocked tentatively. Now that I was there, I felt silly for disturbing him. He was going to think that I couldn't go a single moment without him, and he had a big enough ego already. But when he didn't answer, I hardly cared. I knocked louder and then pushed on the door. It gave way, and I ducked within to find a dwindling fire.

I glanced toward the bed, feeling apprehensive. "Henri? Are you asleep?"

I crept across the room as silently as I could. Maybe I could slip into bed with him. Perhaps lying with him for a time would put my mind at ease. But when I reached his bed, I found it empty.

I frowned and looked around the room. Those were Henri's trunks. Those were his clothes strewn about the floor. But where was Henri? And at this time of night?

I eyed the discarded clothing warily, imagining him running about the castle without them. Blood rushed to my face as I tried to banish the images I'd conjured, knowing full well he'd have changed into something appropriate for wandering these drafty halls.

I heard a sound from the hall and stepped out, wondering if it was Henri returning from some brief errand, but it was only Bertolino, standing in the doorway of Montoni's room.

"What do you mean 'missing'?" Montoni's voice bellowed loud enough for me to hear.

I stepped closer to the wall, unwilling to be observed. I was too far away to hear most of what was said, but I caught snatches of conversation. "Who was on watch?" and "a thorough search in the morning" were other bits I was able to make out. Clearly, something had been stolen. Something valuable. Perhaps one of the servants had used the chaos of our arrival to mask the crime. Either way, Montoni did not sound pleased. When I heard a glass crash into the wall, I ducked into Henri's room, lingering for a few minutes before stepping back into the corridor.

A howl from outside sent a shiver down my back. In rapid succession, other howls joined in with the first, chasing me all the way back to my room.

"Last night?" Henri grinned at me the next morning as he loomed over my bed, holding a breakfast tray. "Were you planning on having your way with me finally? And I missed it?"

I sighed. "It's not funny. I was scared out of my mind."

Henri sat on the edge of my bed and set down the tray. I eyed the eggs and bacon with longing, but I refused to partake of anything until I got to the bottom of why Henri wasn't in his room last night.

"I didn't mean to diminish how you felt," Henri said, placing a hand on my arm. "It's just usually me coming to you. It's a nice change."

"And you were . . . ?" I didn't know why I found it so surprising. They were clearly close.

Henri shrugged. "Getting a glass of milk, emptying my chamber pot . . . a number of things." He tilted his head. "What did you think I was up to? Sneaking off for a secret rendezvous with another boy? There's no one around for literally hundreds of miles who would interest me."

"No? Not even Ludovico?"

Henri snorted. "Don't get me wrong: He's nice to look at. But he's completely mad for Annette."

"Annette?" My eyes widened. "Really?"

"Really."

"Does she . . . know?"

Henri rolled his eyes. "Yes, she knows. Unless she's hopelessly daft." He considered. "Which she might be."

"She is not," I slapped his arm. "Annette is a sharp girl."

"I know." Henri grinned at me. "But my point is, out here, I only have eyes for you, because you're all that's available."

"That's one way to boost my confidence. And if I was the last man on a desert island, you'd choose me too, I suppose?"

"See? You're sharp too." He watched me eat, choosing a piece of toast for himself. "What was it you wanted to ask me?"

I raised an eyebrow. "Ask you?"

"Last night, when you came to rouse me in my bedchamber."

I swallowed a mouthful of bacon. In truth, I was rather embarrassed about the previous night. Clearly, no one had been in my room, and I certainly hadn't heard a ghost. It had been my imagination running away with me. I didn't need Henri teasing me about how I was afraid of the dark or some such nonsense.

"You know, I don't even remember," I told him.

Henri put a hand on my knee. "If you want to sneak into my bedroom at night, you don't have to make up excuses."

My face burned. "I'll keep that in mind."

"Please do."

For the rest of the day, Henri offered to show me around the castle to better acquaint me with my surroundings. Blanche, unwilling to be left out, invited herself along for the tour.

The first thing we did was climb the stairs to the ramparts. It was pleasantly warm, and looking out past the castle, I gazed on the forest of pines and rugged landscape. It was a breathtaking view. I had dabbled in painting before my father had died and thought that perhaps I would pick up the brush again. I would have no end of inspiration here. Looking behind me, I could see mountains loomed over the castle. I had to crane my neck to take in their full majesty.

"See?" Henri said, sliding his arms around my waist. "Not so bad."

I smiled, leaning back into him. "Maybe." The truth was, in the daylight, the castle retained its air of dread and gloominess. However, superstitions and fears that plagued people at night were chased back to the shadows. I wasn't afraid of the castle, and that was important for my happiness and comfort.

I eyed one of the gargoyles with interest. It was round and vaguely owlish, with a devil's tail and a snout, but it was actually kind of cute. Less scary and more curious.

"See that turret?" Henri asked.

I glanced up and followed where he was pointing, to the east wing, near where my bedroom lay. A thin, spindly turret rose from the surrounding castle like a volcanic plume. "Yes, I see it."

"We've never been in there. The only place we haven't been able to explore."

"Oh?"

"It's not for lack of trying," Blanche helped. "It's locked. And even when we've forced the lock and gotten into plenty of trouble for doing so, it's reinforced somehow."

"Won't budge at all," Henri agreed. "I'd like to find a way in, though. Maybe during our stay this time."

I gazed up at the turret again, shielding my eyes from the sun. "What do you think is in there?"

"Probably nothing at all. But I intend to investigate that nothing if it's the last thing I do."

I grinned at him. "So adventurous."

"That's me," Henri said, puffing out his chest. "Adventurous, daring, charming . . ."

I rolled my eyes, earning a chuckle from him.

"How was the red room?" Blanche asked casually, leaning out over the stone to assess the sizable drop below.

"Why is it called that?" I asked, frowning and pulling away from Henri. "And why was Bertolino so startled that I was to stay there?" I turned to watch him fidget.

"It's just . . ." Henri scratched the back of his neck.

"It was our parents' room," Blanche blurted. She looked away. "They were very happy in that room. It's isolated from the other rooms, but they preferred it that way."

I nodded slowly. "Did anything . . . strange happen in that room?"

"What?" Henri frowned. "No. Why?"

Blanche tilted her head. "It's where father . . ." She looked up and caught Henri's eyes, then glanced away.

Even though she'd let her voice trail off, my mind filled in the blank for her. It was where their father had killed himself. I wasn't sure how I felt about sleeping in a room where a man had died, but I didn't believe in ghosts. It was only a room.

"You promised to show me the library," I reminded Henri, changing the subject.

Henri smiled gratefully. "You're going to love it." He pulled me to him and pushed a strand of hair out of my face. "Just don't get so wrapped up in books that you don't have time for me."

"Never," I promised, gazing up into his eyes. It was strange how easy things had become between us. My misgivings about him seemed insignificant to the peril of my current environment, even if I did feel like he was holding back. If he was wise to what his uncle had been doing back at the château, I couldn't fathom his reasons for protecting those secrets. I wondered, not for the first time, if there was a chance of a future with him. I wasn't sure how that could come about. I would need to secure my inheritance before even pondering next steps, but I thought perhaps that would be worth pursuing. I wasn't trying to steal Henri's inheritance anymore, and likely never would have considered it if I'd seen Udolpho beforehand, so I didn't feel like my life with him would be built on lies. And yet, there was still a mystery shrouding him that I felt needed to be unraveled.

The library was impressive. It was two stories with a winding staircase leading up to the second floor. I'd never seen so many books in one place before, everything from histories of obscure African tribes to first editions of rare novels. I pored over the spines for nearly an hour, despite my fear that Henri and Blanche were growing bored. I set a small stack of books I'd selected onto a desk on the first floor, before a globe that was half as tall as me.

"I'll come back for these," I said, patting the books lovingly. I still had a quarter of the book on lunar goddesses to get through, not that it was a long book—it was just tedious, so I could only bare small chunks at a time. But I figured if we were going to be here for several months, it wouldn't hurt to stock up on reading material now.

Blanche blinked lazily at me. "No, please, why not read them now? I want to see exactly how boring a tour Henri can possibly give."

"Be nice," Henri said. "And anyway, I don't recall ever actually asking you along."

"Right. I should probably go have fun with Father Schedoni. He's sure to be the life of the party."

The library doors banged open at that moment and three servants entered, Bertolino among them.

"Good day, my lords. My lady," Bertolino greeted us. He gestured for the others with him to climb the staircase to the second floor.

"What's this, then?" Henri asked.

"Inspection. We're making sure the castle is in tip-top shape for our guests. Can't have anything overlooked."

I narrowed my eyes. This was likely part of the search for the lost item I'd overheard him talking to Montoni about. As I watched Bertolino walk the room, I wondered what could have been lost. He wasn't being very thorough. He was more concerned with the drapes, large bookcases, and trunks than with the desk or the shelves themselves. It couldn't have been a small item they'd misplaced then.

In a few minutes, the servants left.

"That was strange," Blanche said, sending her brother a worried look. "I wonder if we should be concerned."

"Surely not," Henri said. He smiled and put a hand on the small of my back. "What do you say we see the northeast turret? It was one of my favorite places growing up. It has a telescope, you know."

"Oh?" I allowed him to lead me from the room, knowing that I would be spending a lot of time there in the near future.

As dusk descended over the castle once more, I found myself seated in a drab, windowless room for supper. Overhead, a chandelier of somber glass observed us, candles lit along its arms and sending shadows dancing across the table. Additional candles illuminated the room from candelabras lined around the perimeter. Despite the hundreds of flames, I could still feel the gloom of night choke the castle around us.

"What do you think of the castle so far, Madame Montoni?" Blanche asked my aunt politely as salads were produced to begin our meal.

My aunt chewed slowly, as if forming her thoughts before swallowing. "It is much bigger than I thought it would be. It must have been difficult to build way out here."

I tried to hide my smile. Nothing in her words could be considered an insult. Very tactful.

"Stone was cut from the mountain itself," Montoni said. "It would not have been a struggle to assemble, given the material available right here." He took a sip of his wine. "And this castle has stood for centuries. It is a fortress, able to withstand the most perilous siege."

I refrained from rolling my eyes. The castle had clearly been around for centuries. One look at it could tell that much.

"Do you think you'll like it here, Emile?" my aunt asked, shifting the conversation to me.

I swallowed a piece of lettuce and pasted on a smile. "I love the library. Just try to make me leave it."

My aunt noted my ambiguous response as well and lifted her glass to me, as if I'd scored a point.

"Yes, let's all toast to this great castle," Montoni said, raising his goblet. "To the majesty of our ancestral home. To Udolpho Castle."

We all complied. "To Udolpho Castle," I said, my voice blending with those in attendance. I looked around the table and frowned, suddenly noticing the monk's absence. "Where is Father Schedoni? Is he not joining us?"

"No, he's not. He's seeing that our rooms are ready for tomorrow night's injections. Emile, I trust as our guest, you'll be willing to help."

I offered a stiff nod in reply. Blanche winced. "Tomorrow night? Already?"

"Uncle," Henri said, looking down at his plate. "Can we not forgo the injections tomorrow night? We're at Udolpho, after all. It's so isolated out here."

"What does that have to do with it?" Montoni snapped, glancing at my aunt. "It's not a matter of who's around. The injections are for our own good. And besides, have you forgotten the people in the village below? We aren't completely alone."

Henri nodded, then met my eyes briefly. I hated that I would see him in pain again so soon, and I was also proud that he'd brought it up to his uncle. But the outcome wasn't unexpected.

Montoni cleared his throat as he glanced up the table in my direction. "Emile, your aunt and I have been talking. About your future."

I tensed as his eyes found mine, piercing and dark. I was silent as I waited for him to continue, noticing my aunt shift uncomfortably from the corner of my eye.

"Since there is no social scene in this remote area, and we would like you wed by the time you come of age, an elegant solution has been determined for you."

"Determined for me?" I echoed, swallowing hard.

"Quite. You are in need of a wife; my niece is in want of a husband. A union between the two of you would intertwine our lives even further. It would be very advantageous."

Cutlery clattered across the table, and I looked up to find Blanche pale, her fork having fallen from her hand.

"That's not funny, Uncle," Henri said, glaring at Montoni.

"It's not a joke," Montoni said, smiling. "All of our finances will be combined, and we will have four estates to run in total, giving each of us houses to oversee, with Udolpho remaining a retreat. Lady Morano and the marquis are already acquainted with one another, and are fond of each other. Unless I misconstrue? I don't see why this shouldn't be the happiest of occasions."

My jaw twitched as Blanche turned her head and blinked away tears.

"No," I said, sitting back.

"No?" Montoni seemed amused. "You think you have a choice in the matter?"

"I do. I won't sign any documents to legalize a marriage. I won't marry her. I will only marry for love."

"For *love*," my aunt scoffed. "You know full well that that can never be."

I felt myself turn red as Montoni regarded me coolly. "Your aunt is correct. A man with your title must be strategic. Society demands as much. Your heart cannot factor into it." He swirled the wine in his goblet. "And the sooner you sign those papers and marry my niece, the sooner you can return to France. You can even have your choice of estates."

Aunt Cheron straightened, meeting my gaze. "I've always told you that I don't care how you conduct your life, so long as you don't start a scandal. You and Lady Morano may not love one another, but it's the perfect foundation for happiness."

"And what of me?" Blanche asked. "Does anybody care what I think? I want a real marriage!"

"And if there's no love between the two of you, I'm sure you can both see anyone who strikes your fancy," Montoni said dismissively. "Just keep it quiet and provide the family with an heir."

Blanche slammed her fist onto the table and rushed from the room.

Montoni waved a hand in her direction. "She will get over it. You, Emile, have a decision to make. I expect you won't disappoint us with an unfavorable answer."

"I'm afraid that my feelings are in alignment with your niece's," I told him, standing and tossing my napkin onto my plate. "Good night."

I stalked from the room and leaned against the wall once I was out of earshot. I took several deep breaths. So, it had finally happened. The ultimatum was before me, and Blanche was caught in the crossfire. Why did my aunt have to insist on marriage? The only reason this was even happening right now was because of Montoni's gambling problems. He should be the one forced to face consequences, not the rest of us.

How I hated Montoni. And my aunt. They *would* wait until we were isolated to make this demand of me. I was at their mercy, in enemy territory, and stuck inside a prison in the form of a castle.

And I didn't see a way out.

TWENTY-TWO

"It's so unfair," Blanche said, dabbing at her eyes the next afternoon.

"I know," I said, leaning back into her pillows as we stared at the foot of her bed, wallowing in our sorrow together.

"I had such dreams," Blanche confessed. "A man would allow me to be *me*. We would go on adventures together and we'd be unstoppable. He would meet my strength with his own fire."

I nodded numbly. "Your dreams should be realized, Blanche. I won't sign those papers."

She seemed not to have heard me. "Now, they want to relegate me to a . . . a prop to help secure the family fortune, thrust on the first man to come along." She glanced at me. "No offense."

"None taken."

"But once my uncle's mind is made up, he gets what he wants. You must sense that we're prisoners here. We're either leaving here with wedding bands, or we're not leaving at all."

I shook my head. "I'm prepared for what may happen to me.

But you need not share a miserable fate for my sake."

"What do you mean?"

"If I refuse, I'll be sent to an asylum. But maybe that's inevitable. At least that way, your life wouldn't be ruined as well."

"Emile." Blanche sat up and covered my hand with her own. "You're not going to an asylum. Don't be ridiculous. I would be willing to give up my happiness to prevent that."

"That's kind of you, but I'm afraid the two options before me both lead to misery. My fate won't be kind. Your life still has possibilities, provided that I don't agree to marry you."

Blanche pursed her lips. "I'm sorry, Emile. I hate that I'm the cause of your worries." She shook her head. "But I am fond of you. I want you to know that. I don't blame you for a thing."

"I know." I sighed. "I like you too, but I'm of the same mind. I don't want to have to lie all my life. I don't want to be coerced into a loveless marriage."

Blanche squeezed my hand.

A soft knock at the door interrupted our shared disdain for Montoni, and Henri peeked his head in.

"Ah," Henri said, surprised to see me. "I wondered where you'd gotten off to."

I smiled thinly. "Why, if it isn't my future brother-in-law."

Blanche scowled.

Henri sent us a sympathetic look, then held up a bundle in his arms. "I brought you those books you left in the library yesterday," he told me.

I accepted the stack. "That was thoughtful. Thank you."

Henri looked us over, frowning. "Come now, what's this?"

"Oh, just indulging our mutual misery," I said.

Henri chewed on his lower lip as he regarded us. "You know,

I've been thinking our dilemma over, and perhaps it's not as bad as we imagine."

"Oh?" Blanche snorted. "I'd love to hear this."

Henri strode to her side. "The problem we face is that you'll be tied together in matrimony. That's it. Your lives will always be connected. But is that really so terrible?"

I glanced at Blanche. "It's not. But it's much more than that."

"In your minds maybe," Henri said. He placed a hand on Blanche's arm. "But even if you're wed, you can still conquer any man you desire. You can fall in love and be swept off your feet and do everything you've ever wished to. You won't even have to stay at the same estate as Emile. You can travel the world, and foreign princes would fall madly in love with you."

Blanche laughed harshly. "You're right. Why didn't I think of that before? All I have to do is forfeit my integrity and cheat on my husband at every turn."

"Society doesn't give people much of a choice," Henri said. "How many couples are in loveless marriages? How many married men pay for whores and have mistresses?"

"Oh, yes. Whores and mistresses. You must have such a high opinion of me, Henri."

Henri groaned. "You know what I'm saying. Life doesn't end with marriage. Love doesn't have to be out of your grasp just because you've married. It's not a death sentence, and you don't have to be miserable." He gestured to me. "You'd be marrying a good friend and have that security. Meanwhile, you won't miss out on life. Countless others have found ways to navigate happiness while married. Why not you?"

Blanche seemed to consider what he was saying, but she wasn't convinced. "Who would I be left with in this scenario of yours? The men who would be interested in the sort of affair I could provide aren't exactly princes." She turned her nose up at him. "And besides, I would still have to keep Emile's secret while navigating those waters. And that's not even considering *you*."

Henri blinked in astonishment. "Me?"

"Oh, yes. You'll have to marry one day as well, and just what will you tell the future Countess Morano about Emile?"

Henri shrugged the thought away. "Haven't you been listening to me? Many people are in loveless marriages. I would simply have to find a wife who cared for status and comfort above all else. That shouldn't be hard."

Blanche rolled her eyes.

"And what of me?" I asked.

Henri grinned. "Isn't it obvious? We could be together, forever. You and I." He grabbed my hand, and I yanked it away.

"Are you serious?"

"Well, I mean, it's going to happen. I just want to—"

"Force me into a loveless marriage? With your sister?"

Henri took a deep breath and let it out slowly. "We can do all the things you want to do too. Why are you both so hung up on the authenticity of this marriage?

"You want us to just throw what's proper to the wind?" I scowled. "I don't like it, Henri. It feels wrong. How could I ever give myself over to something that's so fake and manipulative . . . it would seem more like I was giving up than living. I want to have an authentic life."

"Oh, okay. Marry the love of your life then."

I frowned. "What?"

"Just marry the love of your life. When you make a decision on who you love."

I didn't care for the exasperation I saw in Henri's face. I felt like he was talking down to me. "Stop talking foolishness. You know that I can't marry who I love, whoever that might be. Men can't marry one another."

"Exactly. Your authentic life can never be, Emile. I'm sorry, but it can't." He turned to Blanche. "And how many couples do you know who are actually happily married?"

"My parents were," I said.

"So were ours," Blanche said, smiling sadly. "And that's the sort of life I want, brother. The happiness they shared."

"Yes, well, our mother wasn't as happy as she let on, was she? Or she wouldn't have thrown herself from a cliff."

Blanche paled.

"And you," Henri pointed a finger at me. "What do you expect is going to happen? No matter what, you aren't going to get the life you want. This is a solution that will work."

I scowled. "You cannot believe we would truly be happy."

"Of course we can be happy! We'll have each other." He grabbed my hand. "Emile, I want to be with you. I hate to be blunt, but you have to know that your dreams can never become a reality. This is the best we can hope for."

"So, I should just grow up and ruin your sister's life?"

Henri's cheek twitched. "Blanche will be happy as well. I will see to it that she is happy."

Blanche stared up at the ceiling. "Maybe I could be happy. It's not what I wanted, but . . ." She sighed and turned to me. "We have some time to come up with alternate solutions, Emile. But we won't have long. Let's think on it. And in the meantime, maybe we . . . consider this. Try to reconcile with it."

I pushed myself out of her bed and headed for the door.

"Emile!" Henri called after me.

But I didn't stop. I didn't stop until I reached my room and threw myself down onto my bed. Henri was manipulating the situation. He'd seen that Montoni's proposition was advantageous to him and was now trying to convince us that it was for the best. He didn't care if his sister would truly be happy. He didn't care about me either. He was just being selfish.

What I didn't want to face was the truth. Henri was right. I couldn't marry who I loved. My life would never be the idealized version I'd conjured in my head. Society just wouldn't permit it. Montoni's plan could work to our advantage. It was true. I could perhaps even like the sort of life that Henri envisioned for us, even if it wasn't a traditional happiness. We could be happy together in a scenario where we were all a part of each other's lives, yet fulfilling certain societal obligations. We could live our real lives out of the public eye.

The only flaw in Henri's plan was that I did not trust Montoni. How could I believe that once I signed that marriage certificate, Montoni wouldn't immediately kill me? He'd done it before, likely on multiple occasions. If he was worried about my aunt or other witnesses, he could just as easily resort to committing me to an asylum. My estate and inheritance would be in Blanche's hands either way, and Montoni would seize control of them.

I couldn't allow him to have that power over me.

I pulled a pillow over my face and screamed into it. This family . . . this whole situation . . . I needed to get away from here. I needed to escape, disappear into obscurity until I could claim my inheritance, as was my original plan. It was the only way I would get out of this sane, and able to live a life as *I* wanted to live it.

I just didn't know how I was going to make that happen.

"You're late."

I shrugged off my coat as I watched Father Schedoni toss an empty syringe into a waste basket. He glared at me. "You need to take this seriously, boy. There will be mighty consequences if you fail to perform your duties."

I looked past Schedoni to where Henri lay on his bed, propped up against his pillows, shirtless and already sweating.

"You are addressing a marquis," I told Schedoni. "You'd best remember that, Father."

"A marquis." The monk sneered. "Yes, my lord."

"Is my aunt attending to Montoni tonight?" I asked him.

Schedoni regarded me with narrowed eyes. "Your aunt has partaken in too much wine and will be resting while I take care of the count. Not that it's any of your concern."

I frowned, unsettled. My aunt had certainly not seemed inebriated at dinner. She had probably been given some sort of sleeping draft. That would certainly be one way to ensure she didn't see or hear anything she shouldn't. As soon as Schedoni had left the room, I stared at the syringes he'd left behind, as well as the water basin on the side table, bracing myself for another long night.

"I know you're upset with me," Henri said, his voice weak. "I'm sorry, Emile. I want you to be happy. And I think I can make you happy. The circumstances to make that happen were never going to be perfect."

I snorted. "Well, we agree on something then."

"Please, Emile. Please just think about it. I can't see an alternative where we both live the rest of our days together, can you?"

I closed my eyes, not wanting to think about how society had turned its back on us, because of who we loved. That was why I was in this situation, at the mercy of a conniving man who wanted me to marry his niece for my fortune. I wanted nothing more than to spurn that society for what it had done.

"Do you remember when I told you that we should just keep going?" Henri asked. "When we rode that horse out for that picnic?"

I continued to stare at the wall, refusing to look at Henri. "The horse's name was Stormy."

"Stormy, that's right." Henri smiled weakly. "I said that we could start over somewhere. It would be just the two of us, loving each other, even though we had no money."

I felt my throat growing thick at his words. That was the first time I'd considered that Henri could be my future.

"I just want us to be happy, Emile. I want us to be together."

I sighed and put a hand to my head. "I know you do, Henri. But I can't trust your uncle's word." I turned to him. "We would be at his mercy. I would never be able to let my guard down. He could make me disappear like he did with Fournier, or even throw me into an asylum, and we would be powerless to stop him. What happens when he goes through my money and I'm no longer any use to him? You think he will let us be?"

Henri's tight smile turned into a grimace, his head snapping back as a sharp gasp escaped him.

I was at his side in a moment. I ran a cool cloth over his forehead. "Are you alright?"

Henri nodded. "The window. Close the window."

I made my way to the window and looked out into the darkness around the castle. It was so complete that I could make out nothing, save for the stars overhead. And the moon. The moon was full and bright, glowing as if with some mystical energy, pulsing as it watched over the quiet world.

I closed the drapes and turned to find Henri half out of bed.

"Henri!" I ran to him as he vomited on the floor.

I pushed him back into bed and wiped his mouth. He looked terrible. His hair was stuck to his forehead with sweat, and he seemed unable to focus on me. I kissed his forehead. "You're alright," I told him. "I'm right here, okay?"

Henri didn't respond but lolled his head back and forth.

I hesitated, wondering if I should fetch Father Schedoni. I glanced down at the vomit on the floor, realizing that I would have to clean that as well. I blinked, staring at the blood mixed in with mucus that gleamed silver.

"Emile," Henri gasped. "I . . . I need another injection."

"So soon?" I asked, glancing at him, worried. I felt his forehead. He was burning up. "I . . . I'm going to get Schedoni."

"No." Henri's hand found mine. "No, please. Stay with me."

I swallowed hard, unsure, but I nodded. I sat at the edge of his bed and watched his eyes. They were completely black and seemed to glow at the edges, a yellow creeping in, as I'd noticed once previously. Maybe he did need another injection.

A garbled noise issued from Henri's lips, which I realized was him trying to speak.

I shook my head, deciding that I needed to give him more medicine. I prepared a syringe and plunged it into his arm. After a minute, Henri seemed to relax, although his breathing remained labored. He closed his eyes, but I'd glimpsed their return to a normal color beforehand.

In the clear for the moment, I set to work on cleaning the rug, hoping that had been the worst of it.

After worrying over the rug for some time, I realized that I would need some sort of cleaning solution to save it. As Henri seemed to be doing alright for now, I made my way down the hallway, toward the staircase that would lead to the kitchen and workrooms. I must have taken a wrong turn, for I suddenly found myself in a gallery, the light of my lantern faintly cutting through the darkness.

I walked slowly into the room, holding my lantern up to view portrait after portrait, surely ancestors of the family. I paused as I came to Countess Helena Morano, Henri and Blanche's mother. She looked the picture of beauty and was clearly happy with an easy, wide smile—a smile that reminded me quite a bit of Henri.

I stepped back and stared at the painting. I couldn't help but wonder if there was something more to her story. I was in a precarious situation myself, and even people I cared for were ushering me into a life that I had no desire to step into. Despite that, I wouldn't take my life to escape that fate.

I would never know the answer. What had been going through her head when she'd leaped from the cliff was something only she knew and had died with her.

I heard a shuffling up ahead of me and blinked. I held the lantern up, but of course, the light didn't penetrate far into the gloom. I thought I was alone, but perhaps I was being observed by someone, a servant perhaps, although I didn't know why they wouldn't have a light to guide them.

"Hello?" I called out tentatively. "Is anyone there?"

No further sound came to me, but I knew that I'd heard something. I took several more steps into the room, illuminating more grim faces and haunted eyes. In the window at the far end of the gallery, I saw a pool of moonlight gather on the floor as a cloud moved aside.

I paused, about to turn back to try to locate the servants' area once more, when my eyes landed on a tapestry on the wall. It billowed, as if lifted by a breeze, revealing a recess in the wall. I took a step toward it, wondering if perhaps there were passages within the castle's walls that no one knew about. Perhaps I could even use such a passage to escape the castle and flee. But as I drew closer, I checked my expectations. This was more likely a damaged area of wall that had been covered. It was likely nothing of consequence.

I reached out for the tapestry and pulled it aside.

My eyes widened and my mouth dropped open in horror. A corpse. I was staring at a corpse.

I swallowed a scream. My hand clenched my lantern as I numbly took in the skeletal form before me. It was a woman's body in a threadbare lavender dress, with blonde hair clinging to her scalp in clumps. The skin stretched tight across her bony arms and face, where sunken eyes remained closed, and lips receded from ghoulish teeth. She was an unnatural yellow color as she sat in the recess, legs pulled up to her chest, head resting against her knees, as if only asleep. She had a locket around her neck, similar to the one I'd found in Henri's coat pocket once upon a time.

I reached out for the locket, curious, my mind not quite coming to terms with the fact that I was looking upon a dead body. An inch away, I hesitated, remembering myself. I couldn't very well touch a corpse, no matter how much I wanted to have a look at that locket.

The corpse's eyes suddenly snapped open and stared back at me. Her mouth fell open in a moan.

I fell to the floor, unconscious.

TWENTY-THREE

When I came to, I found myself in darkness, my lamp having gone out. I lay on the floor, dazed for a minute, until I remembered where I was and what I had seen.

I sat up quickly, staring at the tapestry hanging upon the wall, and gulping in deep breaths of cool air. Had I actually seen that? Or had it been my imagination, ignited by the Gothic atmosphere of this place?

I reached out and, despite my better judgment, flung the tapestry aside.

The recess was empty.

Letting out a breath, I slumped back against the floor. I stared at the ceiling, wondering if perhaps I had imagined the corpse. A corpse couldn't move, after all, and that had definitely been a corpse. No person could have lived looking the way she had.

Once I'd calmed myself, I retraced my steps back to Henri's room. I gave up on looking for anything to clean the rug. The servants would have to see to it in the morning.

Luckily, Henri was in a fitful sleep when I slipped back inside and as nearly two hours had passed since I'd last given him an injection, I administered another.

Henri awakened as I pulled the syringe from his arm and I smiled down at him, smoothing his hair back. "Hi," I said.

"Hi," he returned, watching as I tossed the syringe into the trash bin. "How long have I been asleep?"

"A few hours. Close your eyes. You can use the rest."

Henri shook his head. "I feel like I'm burning from the inside out. I hate this, Emile. I don't want to have to do this every month. I'd rather be in chains."

I retrieved a damp cloth and dabbed at his forehead. "I'm here with you, Henri. Just rest."

"I'm a monster, Emile," Henri said, leaning back into his pillow. "You should hear it from my lips if you're to be stuck with me. I'm a monster and I get insanely jealous and I get angry and I'm mean. I don't deserve someone like you in my life. Not one bit."

"Henri, you're feverish. Stop talking."

"I almost didn't give Valancourt your letter. I was so worried that you'd still choose him over me. I considered just tearing it up and leaving him in suspense. But I had to give it to him. You'd made me promise."

I swallowed hard. "I appreciate that you did, Henri. That was probably very hard for you."

"I'm a terrible person," Henri cried, turning away. "If I weren't such a coward, I would follow my parents' examples."

I was speechless at this outburst and grabbed his hand, squeezing it hard. "You must never think such things, Henri. Promise me you won't consider them. I know you'll keep your promise."

Henri's lower lip quivered. "I promise, Emile."

"Good." I kept holding his hand, and soon enough, he fell back to sleep, and I slumped back with a sigh.

It was no wonder that I'd imagined living skeletons, I thought tiredly as I rubbed my forehead. I was under so much stress. It was a miracle that I hadn't caved under the pressure long ago.

When the sun finally sent beams of light through the dark hallways of Udolpho, I crawled into bed next to the still-slumbering count and held him. He smelled of sweat, but I didn't mind as I curled into him. I rested my hand over his heart, and felt a steady pulse beneath my fingertips.

I was still upset with Henri for trying to talk me into this arranged marriage with his sister, but I couldn't hate him. I understood where he was coming from, but that didn't mean that I would give in to his wishes. If anything, him backing Montoni's plan was a sign that I needed to let him go. I needed to leave this place, even if I had to do it on my own.

I began my preparations to flee Udolpho that afternoon. I secreted a store of food for a pack I'd made, and I hid it beneath my bed. I wrote a letter for Henri, knowing that I couldn't leave without saying something to him. But I still needed to find a way out of the castle that wouldn't be guarded. I knew that I likely wouldn't be able to escape that night, but if I did find a weak point in the castle's defenses, I wanted to be ready to take advantage of it at a moment's notice.

I wandered the castle with a notebook, making notes of the halls and rooms, staircases and exits. If I was to find a way out, I would need to have some basic knowledge of the layout. The problem was that it was so sprawling. But, I realized, that was how I could likely find a place to flee. With so much ground to cover, the servants would be spread thin. I merely needed to exploit that in an area where escape was possible.

It took me a little over a week to create a coherent map of the place, between my obligations to appear for meals, where I feigned warming up to the idea of an arranged marriage and avoided Henri. I knew that I couldn't give Henri the chance to change my mind. I understood why he wasn't opposed to Montoni's plans, but I couldn't compromise, given Montoni's untrustworthiness.

I hadn't forgotten my earlier musings that perhaps there were passages in Udolpho that the inhabitants were unaware of. An ancient castle such as this would likely have some concealed way to leave, should it come under attack. I searched in the cellar first, but only found casks of wine, a dusty harpoon canon, and mildewed furniture in storage. I explored the east wing, which Bertolino had mentioned had been closed up while Montoni had been away, thinking that perhaps some area had weakened that I could exploit.

As the sun began to lower in the sky on my eighth day of exploring, I suddenly found myself in a courtyard that I hadn't known existed before. I gained access from a door near my bedchamber, surprised to find myself outdoors once I stepped through it. The courtyard was small, and grass grew through cracks between stones, evidence to its neglect. Part of the castle had caved in nearby, and I picked over this area, but it didn't amount to much in terms of escape possibilities.

One thing that I found peculiar, however, was a statue in the center of the courtyard. It was once again of the three goddesses from the hedge maze at Château le Blanc. Selene, Hecate, and Artemis. The lunar goddesses. I examined the statues closely, noting that they were mostly in the same positions as the others I'd seen, except that rather than Artemis holding up an arrow for consideration, she had one notched in a bow and aimed up at the sky.

"Why are you here?" I asked the statues.

But, of course, the stone figures did not answer.

That evening, I resolved to finish the book on lunar goddesses I'd taken from the apothecary shop. Their appearance here was too coincidental. They had to have some special meaning to the family, and I was too curious to ignore it, even if it temporarily sidetracked me from my immediate quest.

Most of the book had related lore and tales of the goddesses, and by the time I reached the final chapters of the book, I decided that it wouldn't contain any information worth the time. But then I paused on a section that spoke of "The Children of Hecate." They were witches, sworn to the lunar goddesses, perhaps even descended from their bloodlines. Their mission was to seek out and expose the enemies of the goddesses, to "never let them have a moment's rest," should they find comfort in the world, since "death was too merciful for their crimes." In return, additional secrets of the occult were bestowed upon the witches.

Apparently, the mortal world wasn't worth the attention of the goddesses, so they had their subordinates do their dirty work for them. They would have made good aristocrats.

I was just finishing the book when a soft rap from my bedroom door forced me to set it aside. I hesitated as I sat up in bed, wondering if it was perhaps Ludovico or another servant, come to check on me.

I opened the door to find Henri staring in at me with a crooked grin. "You've been avoiding me," he accused, pushing his way inside.

I sighed as he walked around the room, as if he were searching out any changes I had made. He stopped at the chess table. "Do you play?"

I hesitated. "Barely. Ludovico promised to play with me, but your uncle has kept him rather busy. I think you'd call what I do blundering."

Henri laughed. "Good. I hate losing."

"So I've seen."

The smile dropped from Henri's face. "Come. Let's not talk about that now. It clearly upsets you and . . . can we just be with each other right now?"

I wanted more than anything to forget my troubles, but Henri was part of them. I'd been turning the possibilities of life with Henri over in my mind this past week, and I realized how well Montoni's plan could work, if not for Montoni's involvement. But there was no remedy for that, so the entire plan had to be thrown out, and perhaps, my happiness with it.

Noting my distraction, Henri took a step toward me. "I have a surprise for you."

I narrowed my eyes suspiciously. "What?"

"You'll have to follow me to find out."

I scowled, and watched him walk to the door, grinning back at me from the threshold before he slipped into the hall, leaving the door ajar behind him.

I'd never been good at leaving something undone. I was too curious. So, I followed him. As soon as I was in the hallway, Henri was at my side, his arm slipping around my waist. "I know that this dreary castle can be tiresome. I just want to remind you that that's not all you will find here."

I was silent as he led me through the dark hallways with a lantern in hand, and up to the ramparts, where a breeze cut through my clothes. "Is it much farther?" I asked, exasperated.

"Not much." Henri led us to a turret and up a winding staircase. It was one he'd shown me previously, with a telescope and star charts on the walls. It was a lovely room, but I didn't have the patience for it at the moment.

"Henri, I'm not . . ." I paused as he pulled aside a curtain to reveal another staircase. But weren't we already at the top of the turret? I frowned.

Henri nodded toward the staircase and held out his hand. "Come on."

With reluctance, I gave in, and he led me up the staircase.

We came out on top of the turret, jagged stone partially obscuring the view around us. I wondered what Henri could have possibly had in store for me when I noticed blankets sitting out on the floor.

I blinked. "What is this?"

"A reprieve from your miserable apartment below," Henri said, walking over to the blankets and pulling one over his shoulders.

I rubbed at my arms as I followed his example, cocooning myself from the chill of night.

"When I couldn't stand this suffocating castle as a boy, I would sneak out here," Henri confessed. "It wasn't just the telescope below that made me love this turret. It was this view, the freedom I found when I was no longer smothered by dark stone and shadows." He took a deep breath and let it out, eyes fixed overhead. "I would just lie here and watch the sky for hours until I fell asleep."

I looked up and gasped. I hadn't noticed the brilliance of the sky earlier, purples and blues lit by millions of shiny pinpricks. I felt like I could hardly comprehend what I was staring at.

I turned to face Henri. He was closer than I'd thought. "Not everything is terrible in the world, Emile." He pushed a strand of my hair back from my face.

I swallowed hard. "Henri, I . . ."

But my words were cut off as Henri's lips covered mine in a slow, tender kiss that burned me from the inside out. I was panting by the time it ended, but Henri didn't push it any further than that. He pulled me into the crook of his arm, and we watched the night sky together, warm beneath our blankets.

The next day, I combed through the library, hoping to discover some portal that would manifest upon pushing on a bookshelf or disturbing a particular novel, but nothing appeared. I was about to give up my search when I recalled the recess in the wall of the gallery. I shuddered when I remembered the skeleton that had seemed to come alive, but I knew that was just fancy. No visions would plague me in the middle of the day, with sunlight streaming in through the windows. The recess, however, had been real.

I retraced my steps to the gallery, mulling over the previous night with Henri. I'd wanted to tell him everything that I was feeling, had considered begging him to flee with me, but I hadn't the courage. I couldn't trust that Henri wouldn't impede my escape. As much as I enjoyed his company, and how he treated me with such tenderness, I couldn't give myself over completely to someone who was clearly still harboring secrets from me. I was still unsure of the extent of Henri's knowledge of Montoni's activities, including the murders he'd committed. That didn't sit well with me. Until he confessed everything he was holding back, I wouldn't be able to let him in the way he wanted me to.

I sighed, trying to slough off the feelings of warmth thinking about Henri had allowed to creep in. I couldn't let my resolve waver. If last night had illustrated anything, it was how dangerous Henri was. He could make me forget myself. I couldn't afford that. Not now, not ever. I would find a way out of this infernal place if it was the last thing I did, even if it meant hurting Henri and leaving him behind. Hadn't that been Bram's advice? Take what you need to and look out for yourself above all others?

The thought of Bram sent a pang through my chest. I missed him as well. His kind heart, his astute advice. He seemed to have the ability to cut through the noise in my head, to get to the truth with little effort. If he were here, he would uncover a way out of this mess with ease. If I did manage to escape, would I be able to find my way to him without Montoni's forces tracking me down? If I was to lose Henri, I didn't want to lose Bram as well. My heart ached terribly at the thought of losing either of them, even if that was the inevitable outcome of a heart torn between two men.

Still attempting to put my thoughts of romance aside, I stalked into the gallery. It continued to be dark and foreboding during the day, but the small amount of light from the opposite end of the room was enough to fuel my resolve. I went directly to the recess before I could think about what I was about to do, or what I might find, and flung aside the tapestry.

The recess was empty. Of course it was. As I examined the

small space, I saw nothing to indicate that a body had occupied the space recently, not even a strand of hair. Getting to work, I felt about the interior of the space, pushing and prodding. After a minute, I wondered exactly what I was looking for. A hidden spring? A button? The penny dreadfuls I'd consumed throughout the years had been vague on this point. Eventually, I pushed on the back of the recess and gasped as I found that it moved under my weight. I stopped and glanced up the gallery to make sure I was alone, and then squirmed into the recess, pushing into the back wall all the while, a grinding noise issuing forth that set my teeth on edge. Before I knew it, the wall had moved a good six feet, revealing a gaping passage to the right. I hesitated only a moment before crawling inside.

There was enough room to stand, and I drew up to my full height as the sound of stone scraping behind me recalled my attention to the recess. The backing of the recess was returning to its initial position. I swallowed hard as the last vestige of light disappeared, leaving me in complete darkness. It had been foolish of me to venture forth without a lantern, and apparently I was to pay for it. I felt along the wall that had closed before me, and found a stone that shifted beneath my touch. Pressing on this, the recess began to withdraw into the wall again. Satisfied that I wasn't completely trapped, I turned to examine the passage ahead of me before the light disappeared once more. That was when I noticed a torch perched in a sconce on the wall. I grinned as I hefted it from its cradle and felt in my pockets for a light. Luckily, I'd had the foresight to keep a flint handy.

The torch roared to life before the light faded again behind me, and yet I hesitated to push forth into the unknown. I had to do so however, if I was to find a way out of the castle and escape my captors. Muttering a nonsensical prayer under my breath, I proceeded along the secret corridor.

I stumbled across many turns and bends, and the path sometimes led me up or down flights of stairs, but it never branched off, so I wasn't worried about losing my way. I paused often as I came across points of light in the walls. The first time I noticed a stream of light penetrating the dark space ahead, I stopped to examine its source. Lining my eyes up with the holes, I found myself peering out into a study. I wasn't sure whose study it was, or where in the castle it lay, but I was intrigued and made a note of the room's contents should I see it from the other side.

After this discovery, I gazed out upon a sitting room, the dining room, and then a bedroom. I knew where the dining room was located and was distressed to imagine someone spying on the family as they sat to eat, but I was even more disturbed by the sight of the bedroom. From the trunks, I was able to determine that this was Blanche's room. I was in the west wing then. And as I moved up the corridor, I found views into Montoni's chamber, Schedoni's, and even Henri's. I bristled as I stared into Henri's room. He was flopped across his bed, reading. It didn't sit right with me that someone could look in on him whenever they wanted. But then again, someone could do the same to me, I supposed.

I shuddered as I continued my trek through the passage. I ran across doors, all locked, and more spy holes, until I finally came to a sight I was familiar with. Back in the east wing, I looked in on my own room. From the point of view afforded to me, I determined that I was staring out from the direction of the fireplace. I saw a door nearby, but it wasn't situated correctly to be the second door in my bedchamber. I still hadn't a clue where that led.

It wasn't much farther up the tunnel when I came upon a dead end. I felt around the wall like I had at the beginning of this journey, and found a loose stone once more. Pushing on it, a scraping sound resounded, until a recess was revealed to me. I wasted no time in scrambling into the space, anxious to be out of the dark tunnel. I blew out the torch and tossed it back into the corridor before it was closed off to me, then scooted out of the recess to find myself in a circular room. There was a door ahead of me, and winding stairs going up into darkness. I tried the door and found it unlocked. When I pushed through, I found myself standing outside, near the courtyard I'd discovered earlier with the goddess statues. I gazed back at the room I had just left and lifted my head to follow a sizable turret jutting into the sky.

So, now I knew of two ways by which to enter the secret tunnels. That was a good start.

Before I was missed, I made an appearance to take tea in the drawing room with my aunt. Blanche played at the piano, the atmosphere of Udolpho clearly coloring her music choices, melancholy and dark. She didn't leave her seat the entire time I was in the room, and I decided that it must be that she didn't wish to speak to me. Which was fine.

I wanted to take another tour of the secret passage before night fell, but first I stopped in my room to examine the fireplace. It took careful scrutiny, but eventually I found two small holes to the side of the chimney chute. I plugged them up with tissue. If someone wanted to spy on me, they would have a hard time locating the holes, and would leave evidence behind.

Next, I unbolted the second door in my room and stepped into a winding staircase. I frowned, and followed the staircase upward at once, to a door that I discovered led out onto the ramparts.

Satisfied, I followed the stairs past my door to the bottom stair, where another door lay. This one led out into the hallway beneath my room. I began to ascend the stairs to my room, when I noticed a recess in the wall similar to the one in the turret I had exited the passage from. Hesitating, I reached into the recess and pushed against the stone backing. It shifted easily.

Excited by this new discovery, I returned to my room to retrieve a lantern, then entered the recess, pushing the backing in far enough to allow for me to squeeze into the perpendicular passage. Like the other, I was able to stand just inside the opening and gaze down a narrow corridor. This one, however, did not go far. I very quickly found myself before a door.

It was locked.

Frustrated, I shook the doorknob, to no avail and let out a sigh as I leaned against it. I stood there for a minute before I realized that I heard something within. Was it voices?

I pressed my ear against the door and could make out some low noises, like moans. Was a person locked in the room? I stood back and stared at the wall. Should I call out? If it was Montoni or some schemer, I would be giving away my advantage, but if someone was in trouble, I couldn't just leave them, could I?

I took a chance. "Hello?" I called out. "Is someone there?"

No reply came. I rested my ear against the solid frame of the door once more and continued to hear noises within, muffled and troubling.

Putting my eye to the keyhole, I tried to see inside the room, but only a yellow haze greeted me. The chamber beyond was lit. That implied that it was occupied or, at least, active. I frowned as I stood, wondering how I could enter the room, before giving up, deciding that I would have to think on it.

Since I had plenty of time before dinner yet, I traversed the first tunnel I'd discovered once more, stopping to listen at every door I came across, should I find that more were occupied and perhaps holding prisoners. Udolpho was a castle, after all. Didn't all castles have dungeons?

I discovered nothing new this time around. I did take the time to look on each room with peepholes, even as I realized by doing so, I was invading the privacy of others in the way I abhorred the idea of someone doing so to myself. But I couldn't help myself. And anyway, I didn't have malicious intentions.

Blanche was getting her hair brushed by Annette, who prattled on with a constant stream of conversation, but Lady Morano didn't seem to be listening. She was staring at her reflection in the mirror, as if lost in thought. Her eyes looked sad, tired, and I wondered what she was thinking about. The life she would be giving up if she were to cave to her uncle's demands? She was as much a victim in this as I was, and I empathized with her. But I had to put myself first. Even if she saw the advantage in our attachment, I couldn't allow my future well-being to fall into the hands of Montoni. Even for her happiness.

Blanche picked up an envelope sitting on her bureau and tapped its edge against the surface momentarily before Annette raised an eyebrow at her. "Another letter from Carmilla, my lady?"

"That's none of your concern," Blanche said, setting the envelope back down.

"Keeping secrets from me now, are you?" Annette teased. "You know you can hardly scandalize me. I've seen it all."

"That, I believe," Blanche smiled into the mirror thinly, her eyes lingering on the letter.

Henri wasn't in his room. Neither was Father Schedoni. My aunt and Montoni, however, were, and their topic of conversation was of interest, as it pertained to me.

"I don't see the advantage of allowing this to drag on," the count was saying. "If your nephew doesn't consent to marry my niece, there is nothing left to say on the matter. We will need to sidestep the boy entirely."

Aunt Cheron's jaw twitched. "Oh? And these documents you want me to fill out are for our future happiness, are they? I was always prepared to send Emile into the care of an institution if he couldn't grow beyond his perversions, or at least sire an heir, but that was always intended as a temporary measure. What you're proposing is cruel."

Montoni sniffed. "It's just a formality. Should you accept the inheritance, we must be prepared for any eventuality. If you should die, the money would need to go somewhere. I would think you'd *want* your husband to inherit it."

"And trust that you won't use these documents to rid yourself of us both? You must think me an imbecile."

"No. I think you as hardheaded and suspicious as your nephew."

My aunt scowled. "And anyway, this doesn't address the fact that there is no heir to my bloodline. After a temporary stay at an institution, I'm sure my nephew would be too fearful of returning. He would fall in line and do his duty."

I closed my eyes. So Montoni wanted me locked up for the rest of my life. That was what I had to look forward to if I didn't give in to his demands and marry Blanche. A bleak future, indeed.

"I won't take that chance," the count returned. "And our families are united under our marriage, Madame Montoni. Don't forget that. My niece and nephew are your family now too. You must think of them as much as Emile."

"Emile is my blood. He will always come first. I cannot forget that my brother put him under my care. I will do what's right for him and the bloodline. And signing those papers is not to his, nor my, advantage."

I didn't see the blow coming until my aunt sunk onto the bed, a hand at her cheek. I watched in horror as Montoni slowly lowered his open palm. He glared down at her menacingly. "I have ways of making people change their minds," he said through clenched teeth. And then he stomped from the room, slamming the door shut behind him.

My aunt flung herself onto the bed, sobbing into the pillows as I watched helplessly.

If I hadn't known the extent of Montoni's cruelty before, I did now. He was a monster. He did not have my best interest in mind, nor my aunt's. All he cared about was taking my inheritance for himself, as I'd suspected.

A hand suddenly clamped over my mouth, and before I'd regained my wits enough to struggle, strong arms pinned my own arms against me, pulling me from the spy holes and into the darkness.

TWENTY-FOUR

I realized too late that Montoni must know of these passages, and I struggled against him as I was dragged deeper into the passageway. With dawning horror, I knew with certainty that if I died here, my body would never be found.

But I was helpless in the iron grip of my enemy.

"*Shhhhh,*" a voice whispered in my ear. "It's only me."

I blinked as my ear was tickled by the breath of my captor. While his voice was low and gravelly, I would know it anywhere, and relaxed in his grip.

He let me go and I turned to find Henri grinning at me, a finger held to his lips for silence. He gestured to the spy holes, and I realized that he'd covered my mouth to prevent me from crying out and giving myself away. I'd been so immersed in the scene unfolding between Montoni and my aunt that I hadn't heard him approach.

I slapped his chest. "You scared me," I mouthed.

Henri's grin only widened, and he pulled me to him, bringing his mouth close to my ear once more. "I'm sorry. Forgive me."

I shivered and pulled away from him. "What are you doing here?"

"I could ask the same of you."

I pursed my lips and watched him approach the peep holes I'd been gazing through, observing my aunt crying on her bed.

"What happened?" he asked as he stepped back.

"Your uncle is going to put me in an institution for the rest of my life and kill my aunt so he can have my inheritance."

Henri's eyes narrowed. "I hope you're kidding."

"I'm not." I hesitated. "I mean, that's what it sounds like, given the documents he wants my aunt to sign."

"That's not going to happen," Henri growled, grabbing my arm. "Emile, I am going to protect you. Even from my uncle, if need be."

"Even if I don't marry your sister?"

Henri sighed and ran a hand back through his hair. "I just want you to consider it, and what it could do for our future."

I scowled. "You're not going to convince me to go through with it."

"And I'm convinced you'll change your mind. Blanche has."

"Has she?" My mouth twisted with disappointment. "That's unfortunate."

"No, it's not."

I shook my head. "How do you know about these passages?"

Henri rolled his eyes at my change of subject. "I spent time here growing up. Of course I know of them."

I frowned. "Wait. Were you *watching* me?"

"Of course not. I'm a gentleman." He raised an eyebrow, and

I heard the implication in his words. *I* had been caught watching people. It wasn't an admirable act, and I flushed in response. I was hard on Henri's manipulative behavior, but at the end of the day, he was respecting the privacy of others and I was not. I had come to admire Henri's cunning, but perhaps I had taken that admiration and pushed it too far myself. I didn't want to think of myself as a bad person, but would a good person be sneaking around, watching people like I had? And here Henri was, catching me in the act and forgiving my behavior without even having to be asked. He understood me.

Henri waved a hand. "Anyway, I know how resourceful you are and that you'd find this tunnel, at the very least."

"*This* tunnel?" I stepped forward. "So, there are more?"

"Of course. This castle is ancient, and it was politically advantageous. Kings and queens stayed here. Generals, captains. My ancestors built these to learn their secrets."

I hesitated. "Your uncle knows of them too, I suppose?"

"Not this particular passage, so far as I know. I only ever see him using . . ." He let his voice trail off.

I crossed my arms. More secrets. Of course. "Okay. Just tell me this much: Is there a secret way out of the castle?"

Henri's face darkened and I noticed a muscle twitch in his cheek. "No. Not that I know of."

"You promise?"

"I promise."

I nodded, satisfied, then turned and began to walk back up the tunnel. "Thank you for your concern, Henri. I'll see you at supper."

Henri grabbed my arm to stop me. "Don't run. Please. We'll find another way."

I shrugged him off. "You've already made it clear what that

way is, and I'm not interested."

I stalked away, and this time, Henri didn't try to stop me.

As Ludovico coaxed the flames in my fireplace that evening, I hovered over him, gazing at the spot where I'd plugged up the peepholes. They were still covered, so at least no one had been watching me as I'd changed before dinner.

"How long have you worked for the family?" I asked the servant.

Ludovico glanced up. "Six years, my lord."

Six years? He must have started serving the family fairly young.

"Have you been to Udolpho before?"

Ludovico nodded. "Yes. I come at least once a year."

"And have you heard anything about secret passages?" I asked casually, examining my nails. "Or any hidden rooms?"

Ludovico's eyes flickered to the second door in my room before he looked away. "No, sir. Why do you ask?"

I narrowed my eyes. "You are a terrible liar, Ludovico. What do you know?"

"Nothing. I swear it."

"On Annette's life?"

Ludovico's eyes flashed. "That's not fair. I've only heard rumors of them. I've never seen anything myself."

I smiled triumphantly, knocking on the second door. "What do you know of this?"

"It leads to a staircase."

"And a secret tunnel."

Ludovico frowned. "I don't know about that. Annette opened the door at the top of the stairs. It leads out onto the ramparts."

I straightened, examining Ludovico in a new light. "Annette can pick locks?"

"Pick locks, sir? My Annette? Hardly. She has a master key."

"A master key?"

Ludovico nodded, before looking at me through suspicious eyes. "Why?"

"Because. You're going to fetch her immediately. But say nothing to her or the family about it."

Ludovico pursed his lips. "My lord, I . . . I need this job. As does Annette."

"You won't lose your jobs. If we're discovered, I'll say I coerced you and take all the blame."

"Does this have something to do with secret passages?"

"It does," I said, watching a glimmer of excitement light his eyes.

Ludovico feigned indifference. "Oh, very well."

I smiled after he left, throwing on a cloak and grabbing a lantern. It seemed I waited an interminable amount of time before he returned with the lady's maid, who was clearly annoyed by my summons.

"What's this now?" she demanded, looking me over. "I suppose you want me to sit primly while you play with my hair and try out makeup on my flawless skin."

"Flawless skin?" I asked innocently as she glared back at me. I just couldn't help myself when it came to Annette, it seemed.

"He wants to borrow the master key," Ludovico told her, delighted. "He's found a secret passage."

Annette drew up. "What? You can't be serious." She squinted at me. "Are you serious?"

"I am," I said. "I found a door, and I think someone needs

help on the other side."

"Then why didn't you send for Count Morano?"

"Because I don't trust him. Not completely."

"And Lady Morano?"

I shrugged, looking away. "She has her own concerns at the moment."

"That she does," Annette agreed, watching me. "I've been trusted with this key, my lord. I don't like abusing that trust."

"Does it open every room in the castle?" I asked, wondering if I could try every door I'd come across in the secret passage.

"No, it opens most rooms. I need it for the workrooms and the like. Several servants have them. It's the skeleton keys that open every door, and only Count Montoni and Bertolino have those."

I nodded. "It would mean a lot for you to help me, and perhaps another poor wretch trapped in this castle."

She lifted her shoulders in a shrug. "Oh, very well. I knew these walls held secrets. I don't mind knowing at least one of them in exchange for the use of my key. Perhaps we'll find something incriminating on Montoni yet."

"Thank you." I grinned at her and led them through the second door and down the staircase. I crawled into the recess and pushed the back in while Annette and Ludovico watched in amazement.

"There really is a secret passage," Annette stated the obvious as she crawled in after me and into the corridor beyond. As soon as Ludovico followed us inside, the recess closed behind us, and we relied on the lantern light to bring us to the door I'd discovered previously. I placed my ear against it and listened for the moans I'd heard before. They were softer than before, but they were still there. A quick peek through the keyhole confirmed the light beyond yet burned as well.

Annette pulled a key from her skirts and turned it in the lock dramatically. "One unlocked door at your service, my lord."

"Thank you, Annette." I stepped forward and turned the doorknob, earning a squeal from the hinges. I winced at the noise but pushed it open the rest of the way to reveal a small laboratory. I frowned as I stepped into the room, glancing around at the torches burning in sconces on the walls, and another small fire on a large table in the center of the room beneath a glass beaker. There were tubes and glass orbs filled with liquids of various colors, some of it bubbling, while others sat in placid contentment.

"What is all this?" Annette breathed, squeezing past me. She grabbed one of several books on the desk and I peered over her shoulder as she opened it, finding it to be a notebook full of chemical formulas. Each entry had been signed by a Henry, but not in the manner which Count Morano spelled his name, nor was it his handwriting.

"It's like a mad scientist lives here," Ludovico observed.

I nodded distractedly as I circled the room, wondering where the moans I'd heard had issued from. There were two doorways in the room, so it could have come from either of them, but I had a sneaking suspicion that the moans I'd heard had been the burbling of these various liquids.

Annette suddenly gasped and I hurried to her side. She had opened a leather case and inside were eight syringes, identical to the ones I used on Henri when he was sick. A black liquid filled the syringes, appearing green in certain moments as the firelight flickered. Annette lifted her eyes to meet mine and held them momentarily. "Is this where it comes from? The medicine?"

"It looks like it," I said, swallowing hard. "But I still don't know what it is."

It occurred to me that there could be something here incriminating to hold over Montoni. Escape was proving difficult, but should Montoni threaten to kill me or have me committed, I could perhaps find something to dissuade him, something that would ensure I could take him down with me if he didn't relent.

I began to rifle through drawers and Annette, seeming to understand, began to go through them as well. Ludovico continued paging through the notebook, scanning pages with a furrowed brow. Unfortunately, I found nothing useful in the drawers but more equipment.

I turned my attention to one of the doors and tried the handle. It was unlocked, so I stuck my head inside, but not before we discerned voices approaching from the other door.

". . . need to make sure there is enough for another year," I heard someone say. "We can't be traipsing back and forth from Château le Blanc to Udolpho constantly."

My blood ran cold. I knew that voice. It was Montoni.

I gestured wildly to Annette and Ludovico, and they hurried to the door where I stood as we heard a key scraping against a keyhole. I had just closed the door softly behind us when we heard the other door open. With a wince, I extinguished my lantern, plunging us into darkness, save for the golden light leaking from beneath the door.

Annette attempted to control her ragged breathing beside me as Ludovico gripped my arm so tightly that it made my hand go numb.

"Of course we will need more donors to make enough antidote," another voice said as two footsteps were heard sweeping through the room.

I bristled as I recognized Father Schedoni's voice. This was the medicine he provided, so it made sense that he would be involved.

"And there's still no advancement on a cure?" Montoni asked.

"I'm afraid not. I have some of the brightest minds working on it, Henry chief among them, but also Griffin, Lidenbrock, Moreau, Clerval . . . we haven't made much headway. I'm not sure at this point there is a cure to be had, at least not with the current tools available."

"Yes, well, I have a very long time to let technology catch up, don't I?"

"I should hope so, my lord."

I tilted my head curiously. Wasn't Schedoni wary of modern medical advancements? Didn't he hearken back to a day of traditional medicine? If so, why was he conferring with scientists?

The footsteps neared the door I was crouched behind, and even though Montoni and Schedoni couldn't possibly see me, I crouched low as I ventured farther into the room, Annette and Ludovico carefully following. I felt a pillar nearby, relief washing through me as we ducked behind its cover. I leaned against the pillar, staring into the utter blackness of the room, knowing not what was in front of me.

Suddenly, the door to the chamber began to swing open and Annette squeezed her eyes shut, burying herself into Ludovico's chest as light entered the room. A lantern was brought inside, chasing away the shadows, but thankfully, whoever wielded it remained on the other side of the pillar and did not see us. Yet.

"This one will expire soon," Schedoni said offhandedly as he and Montoni paused just inside the room. "Securing three new subjects would be ideal."

"Mm. True. Send Orsino with some men. And tell them to get far enough from Udolpho to avoid suspicion."

"Of course, my lord. It will be done."

I listened with rapt attention and glanced over at Ludovico to find Annette still pressed into him. Ludovico himself was white as a ghost and stared straight ahead with wide eyes, his mouth opening and closing as if he were a fish gasping for air.

Frowning, I followed his gaze and my stomach tightened. Before us stood iron bars, sectioning off the rest of the room. Within that chamber were eight smaller rooms, also barred like jail cells, with benches, filthy mattresses, and manacles hanging from the walls. A dungeon. So, the castle had one, after all.

My eyes drifted to the only cell with an occupant. A man leaned against the back wall with his arms fastened over his head by the manacles there. He was naked, but I couldn't see his actual skin, for he was covered head to toe, in small black and green growths.

My heart seized and gooseflesh ran across my entire person as I stared at this man, who I could only tell was a man from the tuft of black hair atop his head. A moan escaped the poor prisoner, further sending my body into a state of disbelief.

I swallowed hard.

Annette began to lift her head, but I reached my hand out to stay her. If she saw the monstrous sight before us, I wouldn't put it past her to scream and give us away. I wasn't far from it myself.

Another moan issued from the prisoner, and he shifted, his manacles clanking overhead. As he settled back again, I noticed that the boils were moving, wriggling. I briefly recalled the spiders pouring out from the suit of armor at Château le Blanc and shivered, before realizing that what was covering this man was even worse. They wiggled and coiled like maggots, only with slippery dark flesh.

Leeches.

I couldn't help it. I lifted a hand to my mouth to stop myself from screaming. Ludovico's hand dug into my leg, keeping me grounded, but I couldn't look away from the man, whose whole body suddenly seemed alive with the leeches, the light from Montoni's lantern making them gleam like glittering beads on a dress, but alive as they burrowed deeper into the man's flesh.

My breathing was becoming more labored, and I feared I would give us away, after all, when the lantern finally retreated, and the door closed behind Montoni and Schedoni. We were left in complete blackness again, but I was grateful for the darkness now, for it meant that I didn't have to look upon the poor wretch being drained of his blood, alive, at the mouths of hundreds of squirming parasites.

I felt faint and leaned into Ludovico until the voices of Montoni and Schedoni disappeared, the sound of another door closing signaling their departure.

"Are they gone?" Annette asked after another few minutes.

"They're gone," Ludovico confirmed, getting to his feet. "You're both alright?"

I nodded before I realized that he wouldn't see the motion in the dark. "As okay as I'm going to be." My voice shook, as did my hands as I attempted to relight my lantern. It took three tries before I managed, sending a dull light throughout the chamber.

"No, don't look," Ludovico told Annette, turning her away as another moan was loosed from the prisoner.

"How is he still alive?" I asked, swallowing.

"That's why the victims need more prisoners. Spread over

three people, the victims might live for a while, especially if they give them breaks between feedings."

My stomach lurched and I stumbled across the room, where I vomited in a discreet corner.

"Dear God," Annette cried, confirming that she had seen the prisoner for herself. "Can't we . . . do something for him?"

"How would we get him out of the castle undetected?" Ludovico asked.

"I can't even get myself out," I agreed, wiping my mouth as I looked back at Annette. "We're all prisoners here. Some of us more so than others."

Annette was pale as she drew in a deep breath. "My lord, you . . . you have to escape. I've heard things, about what the count wants your aunt to do."

"I know." I looked away. "And I'm trying. I just can't find a way out."

"Montoni is a villain," Ludovico said, shaking his head. "I just thought he was an unfeeling man. But he . . . he's planning to kidnap people. He's killing them. And for what?"

I glanced up and met Annette's eyes.

The antidote.

I shook my head slowly. What was going on around here? What were those leeches for? To extract blood from their victims? To use that blood for the antidote? Or was the blood for something else entirely? And why not extract the blood in a more direct way? Why use leeches at all?

"We'll help you get out," Annette said.

I looked up. "What?"

"We'll help you, sir," Annette repeated, grabbing Ludovico's arm and lifting her chin.

"But . . . how?"

"Oh, I have an idea. Give me a week to set things in motion."

My heart sped up. Was she serious? Could she help me? A surge of hope coursed through my veins as I smiled at her gratefully. "Thank you, Annette."

"Don't thank us yet." Annette's lips drew into a tight smile. "Once you're outside these castle walls, you're on your own. And we're a long way from proper civilization. The rest is going to be up to you."

"I can manage," I assured her. "After all, I managed to run away once before."

"Yes, well, do a better job of staying hidden this time."

I nodded. "Yes, ma'am."

TWENTY-FIVE

ater that week, I complained of a headache after dinner and
turned in early. I left the note for Henri on my bed, where
he couldn't miss it, before I ventured to the main hall. As promised, Bertolino was nowhere in sight, likely being distracted by
Annette.

I hoisted my pack on my back. I'd kept it as light as possible,
but it was still filled with enough food for a week. It also contained one of the notebooks from the laboratory. I hadn't found
anything damning in its contents as of yet, but given what I'd
seen in the dungeon, I had to believe something within its pages
was enough to warrant an investigation. It was just the leverage
I needed to be free of Montoni's malevolent schemes if I could
escape with it.

With a cloak across my warmest clothing, I slipped out the
door and into the courtyard beyond. I kept to the shadows as best
I could as I made my way to the front gates of the castle. Once

there, I waited for Ludovico. It took ten minutes before I finally spotted the man. I rushed over to him, and he looked around, as if watching for signs of being discovered.

"Well?" I asked him.

Ludovico nodded to me. "The guards are all asleep from the tranquilizer Annette gave me. I put it in their tea. Everyone's out, but I doubt they will stay that way for long."

I clapped him on the shoulder, thankful. "And the gates?"

"I opened them just enough for you to slip outside. As soon as you're gone, I'll close them behind you."

"Thank you, Ludovico," I said, sighing with relief and giving him a brief hug. "I'll find a way to repay you one day."

Ludovico smiled shyly. "No need, my lord. Just stay safe and get as far from the castle by morning as you're able."

"I will. Tell Annette thank you for me. And . . ." I hesitated. "Tell Henri that I'm sorry. Blanche too."

Ludovico nodded once, and I turned to slip out through the castle gates. I gave one last look around the courtyard before I ventured outside. The doors closed behind me, and I ran from Udolpho, stumbling over rock and debris, until I reached a cusp of nearby pines. There, under the shadow of the trees, I looked back one last time upon Udolpho Castle, its terrible, imposing stature, and turned into the darkness of night to disappear.

I seemed to walk for hours before my feet began to ache, but I tried not to dwell on it. I kept a steady pace, using the light of the moon to guide me. I stayed on the main path for now, although if I detected any sign of pursuit, I would need to cut into the woods. But no matter what, I would have to cross the gorge ahead, and the only way I knew to do that was through the covered bridge we'd used on the journey in. That would be the one point where

I could be ambushed easily, as I had to utilize the structure. Once I was past that, I could go in whichever direction I wished, and likely evade detection.

My breaths came out in puffs of white clouds as the temperature began to drop with the night's progression, but I remained alert and eager for the trek ahead. Freedom was upon me, and I only needed to press on to realize it.

I could do this. I could escape. No asylum. No threats. No Montoni holding my life in his hands. I was going to leave all that behind, just as soon as I managed to leave this part of the country behind.

A wolf howled, long and mournful, into the night, earning the response of several of its kin. I shuddered at the sound as I became aware, all at once, of the sounds of the woods. When I'd imagined fleeing the castle, I hadn't considered that I would not only be on my own among the elements, but I would have to contend with a wilderness that consisted of hungry creatures. I closed my eyes as I recalled the hand I'd found a week into my stay at Château le Blanc. A bear attack, if the gendarmerie could be believed. Even if I suspected Hargrove as its owner, I couldn't dispute the danger of traveling the country alone at night, defenseless.

I felt as if I were being watched suddenly, and I paused to gaze back into the woods from whence I came. I saw flashes of things in the night, but nothing clearly enough to give shape, if I saw them at all. Nevertheless, the impending dread I felt pushed me to quicken my pace. My imagination was surely driving me to see things that weren't there, but my instincts screamed at me to run, run, run.

The wind whipped at my hair, and I stumbled as I hastened

along, suddenly emerging from the woods to find that I had reached the covered bridge.

I nearly sobbed in relief as I ran for the sanctuary of the structure on trembling legs.

Something growled behind me in the woods, and I looked back over my shoulder to see yellow eyes staring back at me from the shadows of the trees, eyes that bored into me with rage and promise.

I nearly collided with the wall of the bridge, and twisted inside so that I was under the roof, a feeling of safety rushing over me. I let out a deep breath as my heart returned to its normal pace, but as I gazed back out the way I'd come, I couldn't help but feel that I was not out of the clear. The covered bridge wasn't a shelter at all, really. Animals likely used it to cross the gorge themselves. Any illusion of protection I felt was merely that—illusion. I had to press on, until I reached the village at the very least, if I wanted to find any sort of true safety.

Having caught my breath, I turned and walked across the bridge, the wooden planks creaking beneath me. Now that the sky was blotted out overhead, an inky blackness gathered around me. Up ahead, I saw the moonlight resume beyond the bridge, but something about the darkness suddenly made me uneasy.

A scraping sound resounded behind me, and I stopped, turning back the way I'd come, expecting an animal, a bear perhaps, to be standing in the doorway, but nothing was there.

"Get ahold of yourself," I muttered, adjusting the bundle on my back. I shook my head and proceeded.

I stopped as a series of thumps drew my attention overhead. It sounded like something was on the roof.

Swallowing hard, I tilted my head to listen, but the sound stopped. A trickle of sweat collected on my forehead and dribbled down my nose, where I swiped it away with an irritated gesture. I had the impression that I was being stalked. Something was playing with me. But that had to be a ridiculous irrationality.

I continued up the tunnel again and was met with the accompanying sound of thumps overhead. I picked up my pace, as did the noises, keeping up with me until I was running outright. But then they stopped.

I paused, just fifty feet from the other side of the bridge. I cocked my head. "Hello?" I felt stupid for calling out. If it was an animal out there, did I expect it to respond?

But I did get a response, of a sort. Thick claws tore into the side of the bridge, splintering wood under the force of the blow.

I squealed and sprinted to the other side of the bridge, as if safety magically awaited me there. A mere few feet away, a dark figure leaped into my path, crouched low and menacing. I stopped short and stared, eyes going wide, my breath dying on my lips.

Covered in black fur and staring at me with glowing yellow eyes was a demon. Its ears were long and pointed, its muzzle resembling that of a wolf. As it drew itself up to its full height, I realized that it stood well over seven feet and was heavily muscled beneath that pelt of fur. Its hands curled into fists, razor-sharp claws digging into its palms as it stared me down. While I watched with horror, the beast opened its jaws, revealing rows of sharp, jagged teeth meant for nothing but tearing flesh from bone.

I stumbled back until my back collided with the side of the bridge, my arms stretching out as if to assure myself that what I was looking at was as real and solid as the wall. Then, the creature raised its head to the sky and loosed an unearthly howl that sent my whole body into a shocked tremble.

I was going to die. I was staring at a monster, and I was going to die.

As its head returned to assessing me, I swear its muzzle twisted into a smile.

I didn't dare move as it regarded me, but the moment it took a step in my direction, I flung myself back the way I'd come, across the bridge, faster than I'd ever run in my life. My pack fell from my back, but I hardly noticed as I pumped my arms, trying to escape the monster, even if I had no earthly hope of doing so.

I didn't hear pursuit at first, as if the creature was startled that I'd dared to run. But halfway across the bridge, I could hear its claws digging into the wood as it gave chase. It snarled at my back, and as I shot out from the cover of the bridge, I felt the heat of its breath on the nape of my neck.

The creature's strength was astounding as it swatted me with a hand. I careened across the ground, the wind knocked out of me, rolling to a stop on the path with a groan. I twisted to get back to my feet, but the monster was already there, growling as saliva dripped from its gaping maw.

I knew I was about to die as the creature prepared to leap, then launched itself directly at me. I squeezed my eyes shut, waiting for the blow that would end my existence, but instead, heard a startled grunt and thud as the body landed off course.

Opening my eyes, I saw that another monster was grappling with the black demon that had been stalking me, this one a chocolate brown. The monsters snarled as they clawed at one another, jaws snapping, searching for tender flesh to sink their teeth into.

I was paralyzed with fear as I watched them engage in battle, but then I realized that this was the moment I'd needed to escape. My legs took some convincing to carry my weight again, but once they did, I ran back to the bridge, hoping to cross it and disappear into the woods beyond before the monsters had finished their struggle. With any luck, the winner would be content with the carcass of its enemy for sustenance and allow me to disappear into the night.

It was all I could hope for, because if they decided to pursue me, I had no chance whatsoever.

Before I even reached the bridge, I heard a high-pitched whine. I didn't look back, refusing to face my death again so soon, but like a graceful feline, one of the demons dropped into my path, cutting me off from escape.

It was the black monster.

I staggered back, then fell to the ground, glancing over my shoulder to find the brown demon lying on its side, although it was no longer in the shape of a demon, but rather that of a large wolf. A wound in its neck seeped dark blood as it stared back at me, mouth agape, gasping for air.

I swallowed hard and faced the black demon once more, only to watch as fur retreated into its skin. Its ears sunk into its skull, along with its muzzle, teeth shrinking to fit a very human-looking mouth. Its stature reduced in size as legs snapped and cracked in time to bones readjusting to new shapes. I crawled back as its claws retracted into human fingers, ordinary with trimmed nails. The yellow disappeared from the eyes of this face that I knew, a cold stare falling back into place, as if it had never left.

"It's time to return to Udolpho, Emile," Count Montoni said, glaring down his nose at me. "Now, get up."

Part
Four

TWENTY-SIX

I knelt in the road, my hand running over the neck of the wounded wolf. *Werewolf*, I realized, glancing back at Montoni, who watched me with his teeth clenched. He was naked and stood in the middle of the road as if nothing whatsoever was the matter. As if he weren't a monster.

Turning my attention back to the brown wolf, I gently probed the wound at its neck. It seemed to have stopped bleeding, but it was a nasty wound, flesh torn open viciously by Montoni's merciless teeth.

The wolf whined deep in its throat as I ran a hand over its muzzle, earning a lick. My eyes narrowed. "Who are you?" I asked it. I got to my feet and stared at the wolf, its yellow eyes staring back into mine.

I glanced back at Montoni. "Who is that?" Even though, in my heart, I already knew.

Montoni sneered. "Who do you think it is? My nephew, of

course. Choosing poorly, as per usual."

"You would kill your own nephew?"

"He'll live," Montoni said dismissively. He glared at Henri. "Shift. Now."

The popping and cracking noises that came to my ears made me tense, but I remained still, closing my eyes and unwilling to turn and watch Henri while his body realigned itself into a human being. When the noises ceased, I turned to find Henri lying naked on the ground, eyes shut.

"Henri!" I rushed to his side and grabbed him by the shoulders, shaking him roughly.

"He's only fainted," Montoni sighed, as if I was testing his patience. "It takes more than that to kill one of us."

I watched Henri's eyelids flutter briefly before I noted the rise and fall of his chest. Montoni was correct. Henri was alive. He looked terrible though, his skin pale and clammy, the wound at his neck caked with blood and impossibly shredded. I swallowed back the bile that rose in my throat before I realized just how naked Henri was.

I turned my head away, but I needn't have been so embarrassed. Henri's legs were turned to conceal himself. Montoni was just as naked, but he didn't seem to care in the least. Nor did I. I was too concerned with what poor shape Henri seemed to be in. I'd never imagined seeing my headstrong suitor in such a vulnerable state. It wrenched my heart.

"Put him on my back," Montoni commanded. "I'll carry him."

I looked up to ask what he meant, only to find his body shifting once more. I couldn't watch. While Montoni changed, I slid the cloak from over my coat and wrapped it around Henri as best as I could manage. When Montoni lowered himself beside

Henri's prone form, I dragged his dead weight, lifting his surprisingly heavy body onto the black wolf that was his uncle.

Montoni got to his feet with a warning growl, meeting my gaze with an animal one. Then he sauntered into the woods and I followed, shivering in the chill air.

As we approached Udolpho, I lifted my eyes to that dreaded stone edifice I had fled, and I shuddered. This time, when I passed through its gates, any illusion that I wasn't a prisoner would be shed. I would be, watched carefully with no chance for escape. Before, at least I'd had hope. Now, I had none. I was truly at Count Montoni's mercy. The monster. An actual monster.

I had been expecting to uncover something damning about Montoni, but I'd been expecting something more pedestrian. This was beyond my ability to comprehend. And then there was Henri.

I swallowed hard as I glanced at him, eyes still closed to the night air, face shadowed. My Henri was . . . it was impossible to wrap my head around it. He was a monster, as well. An abomination. All those times he'd tried to warn me what a monster he was, this was what he'd meant. This was what he'd been hiding from me. The monster inside of him was the wolf, and I'd seen it firsthand tonight. And yet he'd tried to protect me. Even in the form of a demon, he'd come between me and Montoni, had fought for me. As much good as that had done.

"You will go inside now."

I turned back to find Montoni had returned to his human form and held an unconscious Henri in his arms. I felt pity for my aunt, who'd married this villain, not knowing what he truly was. This abhorrent creature was a part of my family, and he seemed just as indifferent to his own blood as to his new wife.

When I hesitated, Montoni glared at me. "Don't make me

come after you again. Next time, I won't be so merciful."

I nodded numbly, finding myself unable to speak in his presence. I quaked with fear as he walked casually along the wall of the castle, likely to enter from a more discreet entrance, some hidden passageway undetected by Henri or myself.

Gathering my resolve, I approached the gate and hailed a man on the ramparts, who signaled that the gate should be opened.

Immediately inside, I was met by Bertolino, who scowled at me. "You have caused quite a commotion," he scolded. He gestured to the men around him. "And the rest of them, all useless, falling asleep when they're meant to be vigilant. I don't know what has come over this place of late."

I didn't reply, but I allowed him to escort me within, where I perched on a sofa in the sitting room as the fire warmed my cold and weary bones. But it did little to thaw my fear.

Werewolves. *The family are werewolves. Henri is a werewolf.*

I hardly knew what to think. Werewolves were creatures of legend. They were not real. But, unless my senses deceived me, I had been in the wrong. The creatures existed. It made me wonder what other horrid things spun as fairytales were also true.

I cradled my head in my hands, unable to rid myself of the sight of Montoni's horrible muzzle full of flashing teeth, and those wicked claws. How could I sleep knowing that those monsters resided under the same roof as myself? And to think that my aunt shared his bed. The idea that such a dangerous man lay beside her as she dreamed made me shudder.

"Hello, Emile."

I glanced up and flinched at the sight of Blanche in the doorway. She noted my reaction and looked away.

"I suppose you're one of them too?" I asked.

Blanche sighed and sauntered into the room, taking a seat in the chair across from me. She watched me for a moment before drawing a deep breath. "Emile, you understand that we couldn't tell you. No matter how much we wanted to, Henri most of all."

I returned her gaze unflinchingly as I absorbed her human appearance. She looked like a human girl, beautiful, harmless. But beneath that flawless skin, a monster lay in wait. A monster capable of ripping a man to shreds.

When I didn't respond, Blanche leaned back in her chair. "It was years ago, centuries, when our ancestor came upon a young woman alone in the forest, strolling beneath the light of the full moon. Her skin glowed like that heavenly body, and she was perhaps the most beautiful woman he had ever laid eyes on. As no one else was around, he thought he could take advantage of their isolation, and forced himself upon the woman, not knowing who she was, nor caring."

"What does this have to do with anything?" I asked, frowning.

Blanche smiled wistfully and continued. "The woman was Selene, goddess of the moon, come to walk among humans for the night. When she was attacked by my ancestor, her sister goddess, Artemis, went for help, and found it in Hecate. Returning to their sister, Artemis shot an arrow through the man's arm, charmed with a poison, while Hecate conjured a terrible magic to curse the fool for daring to attack their sister. And so, the man was cursed, as were all his descendants. They would know fear and tremendous pain when the moon burned full in the sky. Their bodies would contort and reshape themselves into the forms of wolves, and they would destroy the human world around them in a haze of anger and unabated hunger."

I sat forward. "Are you telling me that the lunar goddesses

actually cursed your ancestor? To turn into a werewolf on the night of the full moon?"

"Yes. Near this very castle."

I met Blanche's passive gaze with horror, but also with unchecked curiosity. Her story was farfetched, but I'd also seen the result of the alleged curse with my own eyes. "There is no full moon tonight," I pointed out. "Yet Montoni became a . . ." I let my voice trail off.

Blanche nodded. "Yes. During the full moon, the change is forced upon us. Otherwise, we are able to change at will while keeping our wits about us. We can move between man and wolf, and in between. But during the full moon, we are little more than animals. We have no recollection of the havoc and mayhem we cause."

"Yet you haven't . . . wait. The medicine. It stops the transformation."

"Yes. It's very painful, but it keeps us from being forced to change into mindless beasts."

I ran a hand back through my hair. It was strange to talk about such fanciful things as if they were real. Because they *were* real. "What is the medicine?"

Blanche shrugged. "Father Schedoni secures it for us. I have no clue what it is, but it burns like silver under my skin. My whole body feels as if it's melting with it."

"The silverware!" I sat up, recalling the myths I'd heard of werewolves and their aversion to the metal "That's why it's gold at the château and here. Not to show off, but to allow you to eat unimpeded."

"Yes. And it's why we must wear gloves when we eat out. It's really the only time it comes up."

I frowned. "But why silver?"

Blanche waved a hand dismissively. "Who knows? Some have speculated that it's because it can reflect the full force of the moon. Perhaps there's some other connection we're unaware of. All I know is that I can't stand it." She paused. "And it can kill us."

I swallowed. "Can it?"

"Yes. Through the heart, through the head. I've seen the result myself."

I stood and began pacing. "Wait a second. Fournier was accused of trying to steal the goldware, but that's not true, is it? What was that?"

Blanche sighed, leaning back in her seat. "He was going to replace the goldware with silverware to expose us."

"But why?"

"For the same reason I came to find that Hargrove spoiled several batches of tea with trace amounts of silver. If we were exposed, if the household staff witnessed something supernatural, it would call attention to us. We might even shift from the surprise and pain. And then, we would be forced into hiding. We would have to leave the comforts we'd secured for ourselves over the years."

I pursed my lips. "I don't understand. Were the servants catching on? Were . . ." I blinked. The mysterious woman in the hedge maze. Her brother. They had been meeting with Hargrove and Fournier. The woman herself had tried to gain access to Blanche's room. "The apothecary shop owner . . ."

Blanche nodded sadly. "I don't know who she was, or her brother. Red hair is often the mark of a witch. They were likely guardians of the lunar deities, and thought that we were getting too complacent in our lives when we were meant to suffer for our ancestor's sin. They must have recruited Fournier and Hargrove to their cause." I recalled the book I'd perused. The Children of Hecate, sworn to expose the enemies of the goddesses, for "death was too merciful for them." The injections had allowed them to grow complacent, surrounding themselves with wealth and community, when they were meant to suffer as outcasts for eternity. If the witches were to learn more of the arcane arts from the goddesses, it was their duty to ensure the Montoni family was exposed and driven from their comfortable lives.

Blanche shrugged. "I don't know how Montoni knew, but he killed them all: Hargrove, Fournier, the strangers. He's a very angry man, angry at the curse, angry at the world."

"But you're not angry?"

"Me?" Blanche chuckled, although it held notes of bitterness. "Of course I'm angry. But I'm not homicidal. I wouldn't harm anyone. At least not unless it was the full moon. I just . . . I just want to find a cure. I want to be rid of this curse. I pray to the goddesses all the time, begging their forgiveness, asking them to lift the curse."

"But they never do," I said.

"No, they do not."

"And Henri?"

Blanche grunted. "Henri is somewhere in between our uncle and me. He wouldn't kill anyone either, but he likes the wolf. He enjoys running around the woods at night, alongside other animals, feeling an affinity to nature. I don't know if he would take the cure even if there was one. But he's a good soul, Emile. He does not share our uncle's bloodlust."

I nodded slowly, thinking about the taxidermy animals at Château le Blanc and how it felt like the wilderness had been brought indoors. "Yet you live with the blood of your uncle's crimes. You overlook his murderous rampages. He has killed, Blanche. He's killed people you know."

She looked away. "I know that. It's not . . . it's not easy to live with that, Emile. Henri and I have spoken about killing our uncle, but he's too powerful. He has the strength of three of our kind, if not more, as the alpha has always held that power. So, yes, he murders, and we must live with that guilt. What other choice do we have? He has many allies, while Henri and I are alone in our struggle. If you knew how many times Henri has been beaten at Montoni's hands when he's tried to interfere . . ." She shook her head. "We are powerless to stop him, Emile."

I closed my eyes, trying not to conjure images of Henri's throat, ripped open at the bridge. Henri had indeed been keeping secrets from me, but I understood why he couldn't divulge them. I wasn't sure I would have believed them even if he had.

"What of the legends of a werewolf's bite? Can you make more werewolves that way?"

"The curse is passed through our bloodline. Sometimes when we mate, like my parents, we create a new wolf. But it's not something we take lightly. It is a curse, after all. And only the alpha is strong enough to pass the curse on to another through a bite. Currently, that's our uncle. The rest of us aren't strong enough." She shifted. "The bite has to have several minutes to flow through a person's bloodstream to infect them, which is why none of the men Montoni killed at the château transformed. He finished killing them well before the curse could take hold. He is always careful that way." She let out a breath. "My parents thought that the curse was stronger the nearer they were to this castle, the point of origin of the curse. But I'm not sure if there's any truth to that. Nevertheless, traditionally, our family weds at Udolpho if a new wolf is to come of the union."

My aunt was ignorant of the curse then, as I'd surmised. She'd just been a convenience to Montoni. Like me.

I sat forward. "Do you know why there's a man covered in leeches in the dungeon?"

"Leeches?" Blanche wrinkled her nose and sank back in her chair. "What are you talking about?"

I watched her for a moment, seeking a tell in her reaction, but she seemed genuinely ignorant of the prisoner. "I had a notebook," I said slowly. "I lost it when Montoni chased me at the bridge, but there are more of them. I think they could provide insight into the antidote you take. Annette can show you where they are."

"Thank you," Blanche said, eyes wide with surprise. "That could be very helpful."

I nodded, watching her for a moment as I absorbed everything she'd relayed to me thus far. Of course my plan to expose Montoni was out of the question. Even if I could escape the castle with another notebook, I couldn't very well hand over such evidence to the authorities, since it would also implicate Henri and Blanche. If they even took it seriously. "Would you have told me what you are before you forced me into marriage?"

Blanche looked away as if I'd struck her. "I . . . I don't know. Would there have been any need? We likely won't produce an heir. Not together, anyway. And I never plan on changing into a wolf. Ever. I take the antidote every full moon. I want nothing to do with the beast inside me."

"Would Henri have told me?"

She hesitated. "I'm not sure, Emile. I think . . . I think he wants to share all of who he is with you. I think he's just too scared."

I closed my eyes. "And where is he now?"

"I . . . I think he's been put in the dungeon in the west wing. It's under our apartments, down a hidden passage. We've had to be chained up there before, on nights with the full moon before the antidote became readily available to us."

"Will you take me to him?"

Blanche looked around, as if we might be overheard. "Tomorrow."

I nodded and watched as she got to her feet. She headed for the door.

"Blanche," I called after her.

She paused to glance back at me. "Yes?"

"Thank you."

She held my eye for a moment before leaving the room.

I leaned back into the sofa and sighed. It was a lot to take in. A whole world of supernatural machinations suddenly come to life. I needed the night to absorb it all before I saw Henri in the morning. I wasn't sure what to think, but I was worried for him. The way he kissed me, the way he held me . . . hadn't seemed like the work of a monster. But I'd also seen him struggling against his uncle, claws raking with deadly accuracy.

I shuddered, wondering just what sort of world I found myself in now.

TWENTY-SEVEN

Montoni watched me as I lifted a cup to my mouth at teatime the next afternoon. He seemed to expect something from me. Maybe he thought I would run from the room screaming as soon as I laid eyes on him. I'd certainly felt the urge to flee. My body knew now that he was an alpha predator, and being so close to him made my hair stand on end. But I wouldn't give him the satisfaction of seeing me cower. I met his eyes with a level gaze.

"Bertolino, you may leave us," Montoni said.

Blanche shifted in her chair uneasily as the servant scurried from the room, closing the door behind him.

My aunt added a cube of sugar to her teacup, oblivious to the tension in the air. "A little strong, isn't it?" she muttered, giving it another taste, and deciding it was good enough, taking a healthy sip.

"Do you have something to say, Emile?" Montoni asked.

My eyes darted to my aunt, who frowned, before finding the

count again. "No, I don't think I do."

"You don't find me disgusting? Abhorrent?" He leaned forward. "Monstrous?"

"What are you going on about?" Aunt Cheron wondered, watching the proceedings with confusion. She turned to me. "Emile?"

"How is your cheek, Aunt?" I asked.

Her hand flew to her face, where she had done a worthy job of covering up the bruise, but it still swelled. "Clumsy of me. I should have had a light."

"Indeed."

I found Montoni's eyes again and wondered what he was playing at. He couldn't intend to reveal what he was to my aunt. I was sure she didn't know. There was no way she could have carried on as she had with the knowledge.

Montoni picked up his teacup and swirled the contents. "It seems that I cannot let you leave, Emile. You've put me in a difficult position, but I do think something can be worked out. However, I must now insist on a marriage to Lady Morano if you ever wish to leave these walls again."

Aunt Cheron was staring at me in wonder. I couldn't tell what she was thinking, but clearly she realized that I had come into knowledge of a secret that Montoni could not let out. I had some power over him now. Little did she know, he could end me in an instant if he chose to.

"He won't say anything, Uncle," Blanche spoke up. "Even if we weren't to marry, he has too much affection for us to hurt us."

"That may be so, but I want assurances." Montoni set down his teacup and tapped its side. "It has also occurred to me that if you are no longer going to be taken out of the picture, the inheritance will go to you, after all."

I blinked, unsure. I sent Blanche a questioning look, but she seemed as clueless as I.

Montoni smiled at my confusion. "I don't like complications, Emile. I am a simple man. If I want something, I take it. I remove any obstacles, any extra pieces on the board, so to speak. And as I come to these conclusions, I realize that I really have no further use of your aunt."

My eyes widened and I sat up. "No. I beg you. Don't . . . don't hurt her."

Aunt Cheron stiffened and stared at Montoni. "What are you saying? That you would murder me in cold blood?"

Montoni's smile widened. "Oh, the blood will be warm."

Cheron paled and watched him uncertainly, as if trying to read into his words.

"No," I said, standing. "I will keep your secret. I will . . ."

Montoni raised an eyebrow. "You will what?"

I hesitated, looking at Blanche. Could I marry her? Even for the life of my aunt? A woman who had been cold to me my entire life, who had threatened to confine me to a mental facility? It would mean tying myself to Montoni for life. Who knew what he would do even if I did comply?

With a sigh, Montoni waved a hand at my aunt. "But alas, Father Schedoni has need of some subjects for an . . . experiment. Madame Montoni would fill that position very adequately."

I swallowed hard. The leeches. He didn't know what I'd seen in the dungeon, that I was onto him in that regard. I wouldn't rise to the bait and let him know that I'd seen more than he already knew. That would give him even less incentive to keep me alive. But I knew that he meant to drain my aunt of her blood

for whatever he was doing. It had something to do with the antidote, but I couldn't quite make it out. What was he doing to them?

Aunt Cheron laughed, but it was a weak laugh. "What are you
all going on about? Is this some sort of prank?"

Montoni slammed his fist onto the table and we all jumped.
"Shut. Up," he ordered my aunt. "I've had enough of your prattling." He swiveled his head in my direction. "In a fortnight, we
will hold a ceremony for your marriage. If you do not go through
with it, the rest of your stay here will look very different. And it
will be indefinite."

I met my aunt's eyes momentarily, holding them, before turning to Montoni. I took a deep, shuddering breath. "I'll marry her."

Montoni paused. "What was that, Marquis?"

I sat up straighter. "You win. I'll marry Blanche." I glanced at
Lady Morano's startled expression before returning Montoni's gaze.

"Oh, Emile," my aunt said softly, a hand to her chest. She
looked torn. This was what she'd wanted for me, for our family.
But this certainly wasn't how she'd pictured it, despite her own
coercions.

A sly smile spread over Montoni's lips before he gave me
a nod. "A wise choice. Still, I think your aunt would benefit
from . . . fresh accommodations until then. Wouldn't you agree?"

He meant the dungeons, of course. I glared at him. "Even if
you were only a man, you'd still be a monster."

Montoni barked out a laugh. "You seem to be under the false
impression that you have any power here." He held up a hand
and we all watched silently as his fingers elongated into claws,
hair sprouting from his skin, nails sharpening to points. "Or have
you forgotten already?"

My aunt slumped forward in her seat, her head hitting the

table with a dull thud and rattling the saucer beside her.

"I saw that coming." Montoni smiled grimly, reverting his hand to its human form. "I honestly thought it would be much sooner. Maybe a little backbone runs in your entire family."

"Better than a curse," I said.

Montoni tossed his napkin onto his plate and stood with a humorless grin. "What you call a curse, I call a gift." He strode from the room. "Unfortunately, it seems that I'm the only one in this family worthy of it."

Blanche reached across the table and grabbed my hand. "Emile . . ."

"It's okay," I said, sending her a tight smile. "He needs to at least think I'm willing to go through with this. If anything, it'll buy us some time."

Blanche worried at her lower lip while I wondered just what I would be able to do with that time. My choices were limited. I was trapped here.

"Maybe Henri will have an idea," Blanche suggested.

"Maybe," I said, not believing it for a second.

Blanche didn't send for me that evening. I paced my room until well after midnight, before I gave up, realizing that she wasn't going to bring me to see her brother tonight. I was anxious as I slipped into bed. I couldn't get the image of Henri wrapped in chains out of my mind, nor my aunt having leeches applied to her skin. If anything, perhaps the impending nuptials had spared my aunt that particular fate.

What a villain Montoni turned out to be. And it seemed that I was to be tied to him forever. Could I actually go through with this marriage to Blanche? In the end, I might not have a choice.

I lay on my bed, cold despite the fire Ludovico had stoked for me. The whole castle was drafty. I could hardly imagine it was livable in the winter months. But if I was to spend the rest of my life behind these walls, I would find out soon enough.

I was just drifting off to sleep when I discerned a tapping noise in the room. Was it rain on the roof perhaps? I tried to ignore the noise, cocooning myself deeper into my bedsheets, when I heard a creak.

I froze. The creak had been close. In the room, in fact.

I didn't dare move, let alone breathe, but I kept my eyes wide open as I watched something appear out of the corner of my vision. A figure dressed all in white glided across the room.

I squeezed my eyes shut. Given our conversation at dinner, I gathered that Montoni needed me alive, for now, if he wanted to see any of my money. He wouldn't dispatch an assassin to murder me in my own bed in the middle of the night.

But who else would be in my room at such a late hour? A servant sent to check on me? Perhaps to ensure that I wasn't trying to escape once more?

I heard another creaking, almost like a groan. The blood curdled in my veins.

Could it be a . . . ghost? Annette had warned me that the castle was haunted, but after all I'd seen . . . the peculiar behavior of the family had been explained, the moans I'd chalked up to the wind, or perhaps echoes from the dungeons. I couldn't deal with ghosts on top of werewolves, but why not? What was one more unearthly being? And maybe it would help me. If it was the ghost of the late Count Morano, who'd died in this very room,

perhaps he would be willing to assist me in my current predicament, for the sake of his children.

Opening my eyes, I slowly sat up, gaze sweeping the room.

I saw nothing.

The fire was still roaring, chasing back most of the shadows.
I hadn't imagined the figure, had I?

Tentatively, I rolled out of bed to check the doors. Both were
locked. With a frown, I returned to my bed. It had to have been
my wild imaginings. I'd had a shock, and the supernatural was on
my mind. Or maybe I had simply drifted into a half sleep without realizing it. I was safe, I assured myself, locked in my room.

But sleep did not come easily.

I was beginning to wonder if I would have the chance to see
Henri at all before the dreaded moment where I would bind
myself to this family. Montoni seemed to be keeping his niece
close, and whenever I did manage to exchange some words with
her at meals, it was always to hear that she couldn't manage it
just yet. I wasn't even sure *she'd* been able to see Henri. It made
me frantic. I reread the book on lunar goddesses from cover to
cover multiple times, trying to discern any hint of a werewolf
curse in its pages, but I found nothing. And for a family of werewolves, their library seemed short in supply of any books on
the supernatural. I spent most of my days searching for secret
passages I may have missed. I attempted to locate the passage
to the dungeon in the west wing myself, but I'd been unable to
find it, and it was far too busy in that wing to chance lingering.
The servants' master keys had been taken away, clearly as a pre-
caution should they choose to aid me. Without Annette's key, I

no longer had access to the laboratory where my aunt would be held captive, so I utilized the one passage that I could, spying on Montoni and Schedoni through peepholes. Unfortunately, they were rarely in their rooms, and when they were, nothing of consequence occurred. I felt useless, knowing that Henri and my aunt were being held in cells somewhere, but there was nothing I could do.

The servants seemed to be under the impression that they had left the castle for a time, given what Ludovico had told me during his evening visits. They seemed to be divided into two camps: either under Montoni's thumb like Bertolino, or ignorant of his crimes. Only Annette and Ludovico knew the truth.

I was pacing my room, as I found myself doing often these long days, when Ludovico arrived later than usual one evening, breathless, to escort me to Blanche's bedchamber. "Lady Morano apologizes for the delay," he said as he led me to the west wing. "She was indisposed for a majority of the week."

"I know," I sighed. "Thank goodness she's found an opportune time. What of Montoni?"

Ludovico hesitated. "The lady was with her uncle in his study for a long while earlier tonight. I heard shouting but couldn't make anything out."

I bristled. "He really is an overbearing monster."

Ludovico didn't reply but continued to guide me in silence. We waited on the landing below Blanche's room until Annette came out to look over the balcony railing to ensure we were there. Lady Morano came out a minute later wrapped in a black cloak.

"Ludovico, help Annette," Blanche ordered the servant. "She has a job for you."

Ludovico bowed, then disappeared up the stairwell.

Blanche turned to me and looked me over. "Well? Are you prepared to see him?"

"Should I have need to prepare myself?"

She smiled thinly. "I don't think my uncle would hurt him any more than he already has."

I nodded stiffly, not quite sure of that assessment, as she led me through a doorway with a short hall. There was a door at one end, but she ignored this, instead gesturing for me to help her remove a painting in a large gilt frame, covered with a black veil. Once removed, there was a large enough recess to stand in.

"It's through here," she said.

I nodded and, curious, lifted aside the veil from the painting. A gentle tug removed the entire cloth, leaving me to gaze upon one of the ugliest pictures I had ever beheld. It was the portrait of a man in a suit. Based on the fashion, I would have assumed him to be in his early twenties, but he looked much older, and wretched. His hair clung to his scalp in chunks, his teeth were rotted and mostly missing. His face seemed paralyzed in a grotesque grin that was ghoulish, matching the rotting flesh of his face.

"Don't," Blanche said, throwing the veil back over the picture. "It'll give you nightmares if you gaze on it for long."

"My whole life is a nightmare," I muttered, following her into the recess. We pushed on the backing in unison, and the ensuing grinding sound made me wince. Was Montoni in his room? Would he hear us?

"It's okay," Blanche assured me. "I had to wait so long because I needed to make sure he would be out for a time."

"Ludovico said you were fighting."

Blanche shrugged as an opening appeared in the wall to

our right, and we stepped through. A torch was lit just inside. "Obviously, the ultimatum he gave you was awful."

"I've been trying not to think about it."

"He's also been lying to us. Annette showed me the laboratory before her master key was taken. I was able to look through some of the notebooks you mentioned. The antidote appears to be silver."

I raised an eyebrow. "But I thought silver could kill you?"

"Apparently the silver in the antidote we're given has been diluted and filtered through blood . . . other people's blood, and then harvested via leeches. It's so painful because they are literally filling our veins with poison." She shuddered. "I don't think I can take the antidote knowing where it comes from. My life isn't more valuable than anyone else's. People shouldn't have to die so I can carry on, as is clearly happening. I would rather . . . I would rather be in chains."

I tried to banish images of the man I'd seen covered in wriggling leeches as the recess filled in behind us. "You're a brave woman, my lady."

Blanche rolled her eyes. "Yes, well, let's hope we won't have to test *how* brave." She gestured up the passageway. "Come. My brother should be up ahead."

"You're sure he's down here?" I asked, following her. I grazed the wall as I walked, and grimaced as the stone was slimy and wet to the touch. In fact, the whole passage smelled of fungus and rot. And Henri was being kept imprisoned in a place like this?

At the end of the passage, a doorway to the left opened up into a larger room, much like the dungeon I'd discovered beyond the laboratory. Torches illuminated the walls from sconces, sending flickering light over the dreary, grimy room, and gleaming on bars that looked brand new. Beyond the bars, Henri paced back and forth like an animal in a cage.

"Henri?" I whispered.

Count Morano looked up, then beamed. "Thank God you're alright." He rushed to the bars. "I was so worried."

"You're the one in the dungeon," I told him, looking him over. His white shirt and tan pants were stained with dirt, and his hair was mussed, but he otherwise seemed in fine condition. A bandage covered the space between his shoulder and neck, yet blood still seeped through the cloth. "That monster," I hissed, reaching out to touch the bandage.

Henri swallowed hard and put a hand over mine. "It looks worse than it is. It'll heal on the next full moon. The full moon always restores us." He lifted the edge of the bandage to allow me a glimpse of several jagged cuts in the process of healing. The deepest wound still appeared raw, but they didn't look swollen or infected. If I didn't know any better, I would say these wounds were a month old, not a mere week.

"Uncle lost an arm once," Blanche added. "To a witch."

"He grew it back?" I asked, bewildered.

Blanche shook her head slowly. "No. He claims it was the same arm. He'd buried it across town, where no one could find it and discover his secret. Burned it until it was unrecognizable. But he swore it found its way back to him, as if pulled by an invisible string. As soon as it reattached itself, it just healed as if it had never happened." She shrugged. "But that's nothing. We can die and be revived on the next full moon. So long as it's not silver that kills us. We also age slower. Especially in old age, our bodies fight off mortality's effects, giving us extraordinary lifespans."

"That is . . . remarkable. And terrifying."

"Too terrifying?" Henri asked softly.

I looked up to meet his eyes. They were the same brilliant green that I remembered, but there was something in them that I wasn't accustomed to finding in their depths. I thought it might be fear. It was strange to think that this man was a wolf the other night, that I'd seen him tearing into his uncle ferociously, to come to my aid. It was hard to reconcile that beast with the handsome, very human man who stood before me, unsure and looking so fragile.

My Henri.

Henri laced our fingers together and swallowed hard. "Emile, I . . . I'm so sorry. I wish I'd had the courage . . . I wish I'd been able to tell you what I am. A monster."

My heart squeezed in my chest, and I reached in the cage with my free hand to cup his cheek, covered in stubble. "No, Henri. You're no monster."

Henri's lips quivered and he looked away, blinking back tears. "I don't deserve your generosity. I know that you've never loved me, and I've been terribly unfair to you. I kept you from Bram, I turned you over to your aunt because of my bruised ego, I tried to force you into a relationship when you were in no position to say no . . ." He put a hand to his head. "I am scum for what I've done. I'm so sorry for the pain I've inflicted. I never should have tried to force you into a life I would benefit from. I know it would have made you miserable, and it was wrong of me to push you." He took a shuddering breath. "I'm sorry for the lies and subterfuge. I was lonely and you were the best thing that's ever happened to me. I didn't want to lose you. It was selfish. I only wish I'd assisted you in escaping Udolpho sooner."

I squeezed his hand. "Henri . . . I can't say that I wouldn't have behaved in the same manner. The curse is a lot to bear, and it makes truth hard to come by." I paused. "And I won't forget that you came for me. You fought with your uncle for my sake." My eyes found his bandage. "You're hurt because of me."

Henri shook his head sadly. "When I read the note you left for me on your bed, and heard my uncle howl outside the castle gates, I knew he was going after you. I couldn't sit by, not knowing what he would do once he caught up to you. Intervening was the least I could do. And if I was stronger, perhaps . . . perhaps you would be far from this place by now."

"You can't blame yourself."

Henri let out a shaky breath and pulled away from the bars, dropping my hand in the process. He appraised me and nodded to himself. "The thing is, Emile, if you don't go through with this marriage to my sister, I don't know what my uncle will do. I don't think he'll give you another chance. You have to leave."

I drew back. "I've already tried."

Henri shook his head. "I've written to a friend who can help you on your journey away from here. He's waiting in the village for you, sitting in the pub every evening. You only need to make it there. We have a plan to get you out of the castle." He nodded to Blanche behind me. "With a carriage, you needn't worry about stumbling through the woods, being stalked by my uncle."

"A carriage?" I asked, frowning. "How would you manage that?"

"Details can wait. But you have to flee and get to safety. Leave and never look back."

I felt my stomach drop. "What are you saying?"

Henri's throat worked for a moment. "I'm saying that I never wanted you to leave me, Emile, but I've come to understand that I have to let you go. You need to escape and forget all about me and this accursed family."

"But how could I ever forget you?" I asked, reaching through the bars for him. "Henri, I . . . I'll come back for you."

"And you'll be in no better place than before." Henri shook his head. "No. You must disappear, at least for a time. You will never be safe so long as my uncle watches for you."

"I can't do that, Henri." I felt my throat closing. Tears welled in my eyes. "I can't just leave you like this."

"You can, and you will," Henri said. He clasped my hand and held it, looking me in the eyes with tenderness. "I love you, Emile. And I wish you well. Have a good life, the life you deserve."

"Henri . . ."

Henri dropped my hand and turned away. "Get him out of here, sister. Make sure he gets to safety."

"Henri," I repeated. "Please, Henri . . ."

Blanche dragged me away with more strength than I imagined her capable of. She led me back the way we'd come, and dazed, I allowed her.

A few minutes later, I was sitting in a chair at her vanity, staring at my reflection in her mirror. Could I do it? Could I leave my aunt to the mercy of Montoni? Could I leave my friends behind? Could I leave Henri behind and simply move on with my life? "Blanche, this isn't right."

Blanche stood over me from behind. She reached forward and hugged me. "Honey, it's the only way this ends well for any of us. Me, my brother . . . we can't escape the curse. But *you* can. And knowing that you're out there somewhere, thriving, would make it bearable. For both of us."

I swallowed hard. "My aunt . . . I can't let her die here."

"Don't you worry about your aunt. My uncle will be so distracted by your escape that it'll give me a window to spirit her from Udolpho. I promise to make sure she gets away from here. But I am sending Annette with you. It's become too dangerous here, and I need to ensure her safety as well. I would never forgive myself if anything happened to her."

I nodded slowly. The tears came then, and I buried my face in my hands. "I can't just leave him, Blanche. I can't."

"We need you to live," Blanche soothed me, stroking my arm. "That's the best we can do right now. Maybe someday, years from now . . ." She let her voice trail off, neither of us believing the lie.

"I'll miss you too," I said, drying my eyes with my sleeve. "You've been a good friend."

Blanche smiled thinly. "Thank you for saying that, but I haven't been proud of some of my choices. I should never have been willing to trade your happiness for my own compromised freedom."

I patted her hand and we gazed at each other in the mirror for a moment.

"Now," Blanche said, clearing her throat, "we need to get you ready."

"Ready?"

She nodded. "For your escape."

I watched her warily as she pulled a dress from her wardrobe.

"And what did you have in mind?" I asked.

Blanche grabbed scissors from her vanity and winced as she held it to a lock of her hair, as if poised to lose a limb. "You are going to leave this castle as me."

The scissors made a loud snipping sound, and I watched a long lock of blonde hair fall to the ground.

TWENTY-EIGHT

I stared at my reflection. I did good work. It wasn't perfect by any stretch of the imagination, but with a cloak, and a hood pulled low over my face, I could perhaps pass as Blanche. I puckered my red lips and resisted the urge to touch my powdered face. Blanche tucked another lock of her hair inside my hood, and I winced as I eyed her severed hair. It wasn't cut evenly. It was crude and . . . terribly short. It actually kind of suited her, but it needed to be cleaned up, desperately.

"There's no way your uncle won't know you helped me," I pointed out.

"And it's too late now," Blanche retorted, grinning at me. She patted the edges of her hair, scowling. "I won't do as good a job as you, but I'll fix it as best as I can." She straightened. "Now, remember: You need to go into town to be measured for adjustments on a dress for the upcoming nuptials, since that scoundrel of a marquis has agreed to marry you."

"A scoundrel, am I?"

She ignored me. "Annette will do all of the speaking for you, since a lady shouldn't have to speak about fittings and the like to a servant, and if the point is pushed, you have a cold and lost your voice. Annette will accompany you, but they will send a driver with you. You will need to keep up appearances until you get to the village, at the very least. Hopefully, when you don't return to the carriage, and the driver returns to inform my uncle, it will be far too late to track you down."

"Hopefully," I agreed. "I foresee plenty of places for this plan of yours to go wrong."

"Then we will simply have to hope that all goes right." Blanche turned me around to face her and smiled as she looked me over, a touch of sadness coloring her eyes. "It has truly been a pleasure to meet you, Emile St. Aubert. Take care of yourself."

I pressed my lips together to check the sob I felt gathering in my throat. I nodded and we hugged our goodbyes.

Fifteen minutes later, I was waiting in the courtyard for the carriage with Annette, all having gone according to plan thus far. It was dark and drizzling, which worked in our favor, for I kept my hood low without suspicion. I realized that if we were caught, it wouldn't be just Blanche and I who would find ourselves in trouble, but Annette as well, whose place here was precarious. She could end up with my aunt as a specimen if this went awry, which was clearly why Blanche had insisted on her traveling with me. I was glad she'd had the foresight. Having Annette at my side during this trying time was certainly a comfort. And if things continued to go right, Ludovico would join us with my aunt at some point in the near future.

"Can you believe that Ludovico locked me in a closet when

he learned of the plan?" Annette snorted as we watched for the carriage. "He honestly thought that would keep me from fulfilling my duties."

"He was worried about you. This is dangerous," I pointed out.

Annette waved a hand dismissively. "Yes, well, once he realized this would also see me to safety, he changed his mind. He's lucky he's so adorable. No man gets to tell me what I can and can't do."

I stiffened as a carriage turned the corner, a horse clopping leisurely. As it pulled up, Annette opened the door for me before the driver had a chance, and I climbed inside.

"My lady," the driver bowed to me as he helped Annette within. "The roads are wet, so it may take longer than usual." He watched me for a moment until Annette cleared her throat.

"Her ladyship cannot speak," Annette told him. "Voice is gone from a cold. Not that she would wish to speak on such matters with a driver."

"What matters?"

Annette leaned close to the man, conspiratorially. "Wedding things. What this trip is for. Haven't you heard? She's going to marry the marquis."

"The marquis? That lout?"

I held my tongue, although I very much wanted to know how my reputation had been sullied in such a fashion. It was probably Bertolino's doing. He'd never liked me.

Annette snorted, sending me a pointed look. "He'd be lucky to have her, wouldn't he? Any man would."

The driver smiled encouragingly at me. "I'm sure he will make you very happy, my lady. We'll get you to town, in no time."

I dipped my head as elegantly as I could, the man quickly

closing the door on us and climbing atop the carriage. With a click of his tongue, we were off.

I watched with apprehension as we approached the castle gates, imagining that they wouldn't open. So many things could go wrong. The porter might come out to question the journey, Blanche might be discovered inside while she was supposed to be in this carriage, Montoni might come to see me off . . . but none of those worst-case scenarios came to pass. The gates opened and we passed through without molestation, and then we were on the winding road through the forest, and on to the village beyond.

I had another moment's fear when we approached the covered bridge some minutes later, the site of that horrible confrontation with Montoni in his monstrous form, but once more, we traversed the gorge with no problem, and were on our way to safety.

I watched the dark forest that swept by the carriage as we continued on our way. The lantern that rocked beside the driver gave the shadows life around us, and I was certain on more than one occasion that I saw a large black wolf flanking the carriage, but it was most likely my mind imagining the worst. After all, given what I'd seen previously, Montoni would have no qualms attacking the carriage outright and killing everyone in my company.

Soon, the soft glow of the village could be seen ahead like a mirage in a desert of shadowy forest. The lights seemed warm and safe, and the nearer we drew to them, the more the knot in my stomach uncoiled, until the carriage was gliding along the streets between houses.

"We made it," Annette stated the obvious, peering out the window. "My mistress is a clever one, is she not?"

"That she is," I agreed, smiling.

The carriage stopped outside of a two-story house with a sign promoting it as a shop that combined several specialties, including dresses. The driver was much quicker to attend to the door this time, and helped Annette out first with a polite nod, before reaching a hand in to me. I hesitated, then reached out for his hand, allowing him to guide me down the steps and onto the pavement beyond. I snatched my hand back as soon as was polite, thinking how thick and graceless my hands looked compared to the slim hands of Lady Morano, even under the protection of gloves. I hardly believed that my disguise would work on the driver, but he dipped into a reverent bow as I stepped past him, taking care to keep my face shadowed beneath my hood.

"We have some additional items to shop for while we are here," Annette told the driver. "It may be some time before we return."

"I'll be here," the driver replied, tipping his hat to her. "Take all the time you need."

We walked around the side of the building and kept going past the door. We rounded the house and moved quickly on through the neighborhood, making a beeline for the tavern. I paused in a dark alley on the way to rid myself of Blanche's dress and gloves, revealing a thin shirt and trousers beneath. Once I'd discarded Blanche's lovely hair, I replaced the cloak and scrubbed at my face with the help of a puddle and a kerchief. It wasn't perfect, with lips a little too red and uneven skin, but I looked far more like myself than before.

"Do we know who we're meeting?" I asked as we stepped into the pub. The lighting was dim among the tables, brightening at the counter where a man was busy scrubbing at a stein.

"I haven't a clue," Annette whispered back to me. "Only my lady said you would know them."

"Well," a familiar voice said at my back, "you left town so

quickly that I wouldn't be at all surprised if you'd forgotten me."

I whirled around to find Bram standing there, beaming at me. I didn't think about what a scene I would cause, I merely reacted, throwing myself into his arms and squeezing him. "Bram! Is it really you?"

"Of course it's me," Bram chuckled, hugging me back. After a moment, he extracted himself from me and nodded to those who'd stopped to stare at the display, before smiling down at me, his dimples showing deeper than ever before. "You're glad to see me, I take it."

"Glad to see you?" I echoed. "I've never been happier to see someone in my life. But how did you come to be here?"

Bram grabbed my arm and gestured for the door. "We can talk about that on the way. For now, we should continue moving. I have two horses at the edge of town, waiting."

"Horses?" Annette shrunk back at the word. "I've never been one for horses."

"You'll ride with me," I told her, sending her a reassuring grin. "I'm a very good rider. You'll be safe."

Annette winced but bobbed her head in assent.

I walked alongside Bram, itching to grab his arm, but knowing that it would only attract attention. "How are you here?" I asked again.

Bram glanced at me, then shrugged. "Henri said you would have need of me."

"Henri?" I frowned. "Henri sent for you? And you came?"

"If there's one thing I can trust about Henri, it's that he would only write to me, of all people, if the situation had become dire and you really needed me. I followed his instructions to wait at the pub each night for your arrival."

"How long have you waited?"

"This was only my second night. I was expecting to wait longer."

I swallowed hard, my mind racing at these revelations. Bram had come for me when summoned. He'd left his responsibilities behind, dropped everything, to see to my safety. I really didn't deserve that sort of devotion from him. What would he think when I told him about how close I'd become with Henri? He would despise me, thinking all this trouble was for nothing.

And Henri had called on a rival suitor for help. It was almost unfathomable to me that Henri would deign to do such a thing. He'd set aside his pride for me. When faced with my peril, he'd chosen to keep me safe, putting me above everything. How could I ever repay that?

We reached the horses before long, and I rode with Annette clinging to me some forty minutes to a farmer's barn. Bram had rented it for the week and had been staying there during the day. Now, we would rest until morning before continuing on our way, safe in the knowledge that we were far from Udolpho, and out of the way enough where it would be difficult to discover us.

"What has been happening at Udolpho Castle?" Bram asked as he seated himself upon a barrel of hay. Annette had settled into a corner of the room far from us, to give us privacy.

"A lot," I said vaguely, running a hand back through my hair. "I hardly know where to begin."

"Was my involvement truly necessary?"

"Yes, I'd say that it was." I sighed. I wasn't sure what to tell Bram. I couldn't reveal that the family were werewolves. It would not only require a dramatic suspension of disbelief but also put Henri and Blanche at risk. Their uncle aside, their secret was a dangerous one, one that could get them killed. "I don't want to go into details, but suffice it to say that Count Montoni was holding me there against my will. Even now, Count Morano and my aunt are his prisoners."

"Prisoners?" Bram straightened. "Surely you jest."

"I do not. There is a plan in place to extricate my aunt from the dungeon, and I don't think any harm will come to Henri, but . . . it has been a trial."

Bram looked pale, and the muscles in his cheek twitched. "That monster. The gendarmerie will see to him if it's the last thing I do."

I blinked. How right he was. Montoni *was* a monster, but getting the authorities involved would only end in tragedy, and not in our favor.

"For now, I simply want to reach safety," I told him. "I haven't had time to plan my next steps. But Montoni is a very dangerous man, Bram. He shouldn't be trifled with. Promise me, for now, that you'll not raise a hand against him."

Bram hesitated but nodded. "Very well. You're more acquainted with the details. But I will hear a full account from you, and soon." He reached out and touched my arm. "We can figure out how to proceed together."

I melted under the tenderness I found in his eyes, and guilt immediately made me shudder under his gaze.

"I've missed you," Bram said, beginning to stroke my arm. "I wasn't sure I would ever see you again. You left me with a broken heart. I thought I would hear from you once you reached Udolpho. When I didn't, I wasn't sure what to think." He shook his head. "I was going crazy for a time, Emile. Not a day has gone by when I haven't thought of you."

I blushed and looked away. Bram dropped his hand and cocked his head. "You don't feel the same."

It was a statement more than a question, and I knew he felt the distance between us. "So much has happened to me," I said softly. "And it wouldn't be fair if I didn't tell you that my affection for Henri has grown into something more."

Bram closed his eyes and nodded. "I was afraid of that. And is there any hope for us to rekindle what we felt?"

It suddenly hit me that Henri handing me off to Bram was perhaps his way of pushing us back together. If Henri truly never expected to see me again, and wished only for my happiness as he'd proclaimed, this was likely where his mind had settled. My heart lurched in my chest as I thought of Henri making that sacrifice, his very happiness, to see me safe. And here I was with his rival. I knew then that I couldn't leave Henri to the mercy of his uncle. I had to do something. I just wasn't sure what.

And Bram deserved better. Even now, I felt safer with him than I'd felt in weeks, and I knew that his words and touch could both soothe my soul in ways Henri couldn't. As much as I longed for Bram, it wasn't fair to lead him on if I continued to think about Henri. If only I didn't have to decide between the two.

"I'm not sure," I said, honestly. "As you've pointed out, I have changed. Your advice was part of that change, so it might be to your liking. But I can't promise it will be as before. I'm sorry you came all the way out here to—"

"Do not apologize," Bram cut me off. "You can't promise yourself to me if your heart is in conflict. I won't press the issue." He hesitated. "But I will admit that I was wrong about Henri, in some respects."

"How so?"

"In his letter to me, he apologized for his slander of my father's practice. He said that he'd been trying to save face in the moment, when pressed on why his family utilized Father Schedoni instead of my father, and in doing so, came up with a response that he thought would appease the inquirer. He said that making Schedoni seem like the only option for his family was important for his family's safety, whatever that means. But he never thought that his foul words would spread through town like they did. He claims to have tried to stop them, but I'll never know if that's true." He shrugged. "I might not understand his motives, even now, but I do regret our friendship ended the way it did. It was only his treatment of you that renewed my loathing for him."

"He has quite redeemed himself," I assured Bram. "He has saved me from misery. And in my place, I'm afraid he's going to suffer greatly."

"I'm not sure how you can so easily forgive someone who tried to force you into an inappropriate relationship when you were powerless to refuse."

"It wasn't easy. But he's earned my forgiveness. And my gratitude. Perhaps even my heart." I shrugged helplessly. "I don't know how to explain it. He's done some terrible things. He's acknowledged that. I never expected to be able to look past them, and yet . . . I've seen him grow. He's genuinely remorseful for his actions. I'm willing to give him another chance, and I'm glad what you've relayed to me has confirmed that he's willing to try to be a better person."

Bram nodded slowly, then patted my hand. "I may not completely understand, given how I saw him treat you, but I trust your judgment, and ultimately, it's your decision whether to forgive him or not." He paused. "However things turn out between you and me, know that I will always come to your aid, Emile. You will always have my esteem, and my affection. I will never again let what happened between me and Henri happen between me and someone else I care about."

I smiled, my eyes misting over. I reached up and hugged him, and he hugged me back. I tried to put as much feeling into the embrace as I could, to let him know how much he meant to me, how much I was sorry that I couldn't give him a full account of my heart. "I'll always be there for you too, Bram."

He smiled into my hair. "I'm happy to hear you say that."

A resounding crack from across the barn sent us to our feet in an instant. I watched, eyes wide, as the door to the barn shuddered under the weight of something massive, several boards cracking in its wake.

"Oh God," I said, clinging to Bram.

"What is it?" he asked, pushing me behind him.

"It's Montoni. He's found me."

TWENTY-NINE

A menacing growl reverberated through the night air as the door shuddered once more under the weight of Montoni, more wood splintering as it buckled in at an alarming rate.

"What do we do, my lord?" Annette asked, frozen in place, staring at the door.

"Up in the hay loft," I ordered her, pointing to a nearby ladder. "He's not here for you."

Annette obeyed immediately, scrambling up without another word.

"How is *that* Montoni?" Bram asked, hands on my shoulders. "Surely it's some demon."

"He *is* a demon," I told him, beginning to shake. Montoni was man *and* beast. A terrible combination, I realized, closing my eyes. He could have inquired in town after strangers staying nearby, then simply tracked the horses. I'd led him right to Bram.

There was a shout outside the door, followed by the blast of a gun.

I rushed forward, Bram at my side, and peered out through the gaps that had been created in the door as it had begun to cave, but the darkness was too thick to see anything of consequence. There was the sound of a struggle, and then no sounds at all.

I swallowed hard and looked at Bram. "He wants me. If I go out there, he'll—"

"Absolutely not," he cut me off.

"But, Bram, you don't understand what he's capable of."

"If this door is any indication, I have some idea, and I'm not sending you out to anything capable of causing that sort of damage."

I pursed my lips, wondering how I could make him see how futile this was. Montoni would get in if that was what he wanted. It was only a matter of time. Nevertheless, we pushed against the door to brace it against another barrage.

After a minute, all yet remained still. I began to wonder if perhaps the farmer had wounded Montoni. But then why hadn't the farmer come to check on us?

He might be feasting on the farmer, I suddenly realized, my stomach churning. Yet another victim of this monster's nefarious appetite.

Looking up at the door, I gasped as I saw a yellow eye staring in at me. I stumbled back, falling to the ground as Montoni renewed his assault on the door. The door was barely holding together at this point. Bram suddenly cried out, falling back and holding a hand to his arm, his face contorted with pain. I rushed to his side and ripped a strip of fabric from the bottom of my shirt as I noted blood seeping from between his fingers.

"Bram," I cried, wrapping the cloth around his arm.

"It's okay," he gasped. "He just scratched me."

I watched the white cloth blossom with red. "It's deep."

"I'll live." He grunted, pushing himself to his feet.

The door buckled completely under the next blow, shards of wood and debris whipping past me, making me yelp. One large timber of wood slammed into Bram's forehead, and he sank to the ground, unconscious.

"No!" I screamed.

Montoni leaped into the barn and crouched before me, baring teeth dripping with blood. He circled me, growling threateningly while I quaked in fear.

"I give up," I told him, voice tremulous. "I'll come with you right now, and I won't try to leave again."

Montoni tilted his head, watching me, then drew himself up to his full height. He held a claw out to me, a talon two inches long reaching out to my face.

And then I fainted.

When next I came to, I found myself on a cold stone floor, my head propped on a pillow. I opened my eyes to find that pillow was actually someone's lap. Henri's lap.

"See? He's coming around now. No permanent damage."

I blinked and lifted my head to find Montoni leaning against the opposite wall, watching me with a knowing smile.

"What?" I asked groggily, struggling to sit up.

Henri helped me, smiling reassuringly. "You're okay."

"For now," Montoni added, earning a glare from him.

"Where are we?" I demanded, gazing around the unfamiliar circular room.

"In the locked turret," Henri told me. "It seems that we're going to be *confined* here for the foreseeable future."

"Confined," Montoni chuckled. "I like that." He examined his nails, as if this was an everyday occurrence, locking people in dungeons. And it seemed to appear that was the case. "But hardly for the foreseeable future. I'm not a cruel man. I think a week will do. I'm sure by then, you will have learned your lesson."

I squinted up at him. "That's mighty generous for a madman."

"I am nothing if not generous," Montoni grinned with a mocking bow. He raised an eyebrow at Henri. "But of course, my nephew will understand the significance of a week."

My eyebrows drew together in confusion as I glanced at Henri uncertainly. He'd gone pale at his uncle's words, and my stomach pinged with unease. "Henri? What does he mean?"

Henri met my eyes and then bit his lips. "In a week, it will be a full moon."

"Right you are," Montoni clapped. "And since you've both been very naughty, I'm afraid I'll have to withhold the antidote for the night."

I stiffened as what he was saying began to register. My mouth went dry. Henri would turn into a werewolf in a week's time, on the night of the full moon. Without the antidote, there would be no suppressing it. When he turned, he wouldn't be in control. And I would be locked in here with him. . . .

Montoni procured a slip of paper from his pocket. "Of course, should I find a signature on these papers . . . I might be willing to change my mind."

I closed my eyes. La Vallée. My inheritance. My livelihood. Of course he would hold those over my head. "After all this, you still want me to marry your niece?"

"Marry my niece!" Montoni laughed without humor. "I think we're past that, don't you? No, monsieur. This will leave your inheritance to me. You will not see a penny."

I swallowed hard and opened my eyes, glaring at him. "Fine. I'll sign."

Montoni lifted an eyebrow. He stepped forward and handed me the document.

I signed it and threw the pen back at him.

"See? That wasn't so hard," Montoni said, retrieving the pen and pocketing the document. He turned to walk down the staircase. "Enjoy your meal, nephew."

"Uncle?" Henri called, voice rising.

Montoni paused on the stairs and glanced back at us. "I never said I'd let you go if this was signed. But I appreciate your cooperation, marquis." He laughed at my stunned face. "Enjoy your final week." He continued down a step before turning to us once more. "Oh, and if you find yourself wishing for a friendly face, you need only look out your window."

He disappeared from sight, and we listened as he locked the turret door, trapping us inside together.

I turned to meet Henri's eyes. They swam with tears, but he tried for a smile, even during this unspeakable time. The boy who now held my heart, after such a painstaking journey to unravel all of his secrets, who in a week would destroy me through no fault of his own.

"I'm sorry, Emile," he choked out, running a hand across my cheek. "I'm so, so sorry. I thought I'd be able to get you to safety, yet I've only made things worse. Again. Maybe that's my real curse. Never being good enough to save the day."

"Stop that," I ordered him, slapping his hand away. "We've been in bad situations before."

"But this is so much worse, Emile. I can't . . . I won't be reasoned with when I change. I'll . . ." He swallowed hard, his eyes watery. "Emile, I . . ."

I shook my head, unable to speak. We would find a way out of this situation. We *had* to.

I got to my feet and stumbled over to the sole window in the room and gripped the bars fastened there. The blue sky and the mountains seemed to mock me from my prison before my eyes fell on something just outside the window. A pike peeked up from a neighboring rampart with something run through it.

A cry caught in my throat, and Henri was beside me in an instant, holding me as we gazed out over the ghastly sight together.

A head was perched atop the pike, its barbed end sticking out cruelly from its skull at an angle. Its eyes were rolled up in its head, its mouth hanging open, revealing a bloated, purple tongue. But even in this state, I recognized the face of the man staged before us like some ungodly totem.

It was Bram.

THIRTY

The only respite from the cold, claustrophobic prison we occupied was that single window to the east, but I couldn't peer through it, no matter how much I needed a glimpse of blue sky, a sliver of hope, for the mocking head of my former suitor awaited me there.

When I closed my eyes, I still saw it, the gleaming bone dangling from his neck, the skin torn from where it had been rent from the rest of his body, much like that hand I'd found on my first week at Château le Blanc. It must have been a horrible, painful death, and I hadn't been conscious to even offer him some comfort with my presence. He'd died alone in a vain attempt to aid me, a man who didn't even return his affections as before.

Guilt and pain ate away at me so that I almost didn't mind the fact that in just a few more days, I would be murdered by my other suitor. At least then I wouldn't keep imagining my friend's final agonizing moments.

I could only hope that, at the very least, Annette had escaped.

Henri tried forcing his way out from the turret, changing into a half-wolf, half-human monstrosity with chocolate-brown fur, and using his sizable strength, but it wasn't enough. The door could have been a part of the stone wall itself for all it moved.

I sighed as he climbed the stairs up to me once more, looking defeated. Even covered in fur, I could tell how he was feeling.

"How can you stand to look at me?" he asked after he transformed back into his human self from the half-wolf. "I'm monstrous. And now you see how truly monstrous I am. I never exaggerated that point."

I put a hand to his shoulder, smiling lightly as I looked up at him, my brave, tortured boy. "It's only when you've treated me poorly that you've been a monster, Henri."

Henri looked away. "I . . . I know. And I will regret those moments of weakness for the rest of my life. Long after . . ." He closed his eyes and shuddered. "I will be better."

"I know you will."

"But Emile, I cannot vanquish the beast. The actual beast that lives in my bones and my muscle. It will not be denied on the full moon."

"I don't suppose the lunar goddesses will have any say?"

"The lunar goddesses laugh at our pain and misfortune." Henri scowled. "They are like all gods, fickle and careless. They did this to my family, then left, probably never thinking of us again."

"Bram said something similar about our social class," I mused.

"I . . . yes, Bram . . . I'm sorry you had to see that. He didn't deserve that death. He was a good man."

"He was," I agreed, heart stuttering painfully at his memory. I still couldn't quite wrap my head around the fact that he was gone. It didn't seem real. I was afraid that if I admitted the reality, that I wouldn't be able to stop screaming. "And he forgave you in the end, you know."

"Yes, he always was better than me." Henri smiled wistfully. "I guess you two have that in common."

I didn't correct him with "had."

"You liked him then?" I asked. "You considered him a friend?"

"Of course I did. If not . . . if not more." Henri rubbed the back of his neck. "He was the first boy I ever had romantic feelings for. He was always so nice and generous, smart . . ." He sighed. "I hated that my secrets destroyed that friendship and any potential it may have had. But if it had remained intact, then perhaps I never would have been entangled with you." He grinned at me. "And I very much enjoy our entanglement."

I snorted, before remembering that any form of "us" we had left would be only a few paltry days long. Very soon, I would be yet another boy whom Henri had lost to his curse and his family's secrets. It was tragic.

"There's some sort of tumbler," Henri said, staring down the staircase. "There must be a secret switch on the outside, something that keeps the door bolted in place. If only we could find it."

"It doesn't matter," I said. "Even if we find it, we're in here. The keyhole and whatever locking mechanism Montoni uses, is out there. None of his servants are going to help us."

"Ludovico could help."

"Maybe." I turned back to a sheet of paper, where I was scribbling notes out for Ludovico with charcoal. We'd found several worn books and art supplies in the cubbies of this room, as if it had been lived in, or used for storage. I'd begun throwing balled-up paper out the window, in hopes that he would find one of our messages recording our location and our need for the antidote. I threw them far and wide, folding some of them in such ways that the wind carried them even further. If but one of them would find friendly hands . . . But if Montoni or his goons discovered them, they would round up any evidence and any hope would be vanquished.

"Well, I'm not giving up," Henri insisted. "There has to be a way."

I lay back on the sparse amount of hay I'd managed to collect for a pillow these past few nights, giving my hand a break from writing. I gazed at the ceiling, trying hard not to notice the expanse of blue sky beckoning from the nearby window.

Henri sighed as he observed me. "Emile, you can't keep torturing yourself over Bram. You didn't kill him."

"I know, but I should have been the man he wanted me to be. I wasn't able to express how I felt about him. I liked both of you so much, and the way I spoke to him, it was like my heart betrayed me in the moment. I didn't realize until he was gone how much him not being in my life would hurt." I swallowed past a lump in my throat. "I'll never forgive myself for that."

I closed my eyes and felt Henri's hand on my arm. "Emile, you can't force your heart to reveal itself to you if it's not ready. That's not how love works."

"I know, but I feel like such a failure. Everyone I care about is either dead or in trouble. Blanche has likely traded her rooms for the dungeon you've been occupying. I feel like everyone I come into contact with suffers."

Henri was about to reply when my eyes found etchings on the ceiling. I held up my hand to silence him as I craned my neck and got to my feet. I reached up on tiptoes to graze my fingers over one of the marks. "Aren't these . . . tally marks?"

Henri's brow furrowed. "Looks like."

Frowning, I scanned the ceiling, where the four lines with another line crossing through them, ran the length of the room, and even spilled over the walls in some areas. They'd been drawn with the same charcoal I used now. I glanced at the sheets of paper and books. "We're not the first to be locked up here."

"Probably not, knowing Montoni. The dungeons probably overflowed at times. Maybe someone was in here all those times Blanche and I tried to break in, hoping we would free them."

I followed the tallies to one corner where they continued to run down the wall and gasped when I noticed the edge of a piece of paper sticking out from behind a loose stone. I pried the stone loose and grinned as I unfolded the paper, eyes roving across the page eagerly. My jaw grew slack with each additional line until I let my arm fall to my side. "Henri."

Henri was beside me in a moment. He frowned down at the paper in my hand and snatched it from me, eyes running over the words there.

Henri's eyes widened, the color draining from his face, his throat working. "This can't be."

I pursed my lips. "Your mother . . ."

Henri glanced up and met my eyes. "My mother was a prisoner here." He sank to his knees, as if standing was too much for him, and read "I only wish that my loves, Henri and Blanche, knew how much I regret even considering leaving them behind. Seeing them grow up from afar has been my greatest joy in my prison."

He pushed his face into his knees, his body shaking with silent sobs.

I sat beside him and rubbed his back, looking around the

small room. Based on the tally marks, she had spent years in this cell. I wondered how she eventually met her end. Had Montoni had enough of her? Found her captivity too risky? Someone other than Montoni had to have known she was here, for he was frequently out of the country. It wasn't only the count who was culpable for this.

Henri looked up after a time and wiped away his tears. "My uncle always said that they found her so shattered and broken at the bottom of the cliff that he drove a silver spike through her heart to end her pain and honor her wishes."

"I'm so sorry, Henri."

"But she could still be alive. Don't you see? Maybe she escaped or . . . or was moved to another part of the castle. Maybe the tower became too risky."

"Maybe," I agreed, not holding out much hope. But this hope wasn't mine to extinguish. Henri could use some of that right now. We both could.

I watched the moon through the window the next few nights, taunting me as it continued to fill out. As we spent our last day in the cell, awaiting dark and that fateful hour when Henri would shift into a mindless monster, we sat in silence. Henri held me against his solid chest as I listened to his heart pound beneath my ear. I felt oddly at peace, like a quiet was coming over my soul, and I tried to trick myself into believing that it even felt right to face my end here and now, at Henri's hands. But it would never feel right to be a pawn to a cruel man such as Montoni. I wondered if he would come out to watch, perhaps linger on the ramparts as he listened to the sounds of his nephew transforming and then murdering me. Of course, that couldn't actually happen. Montoni would require the antidote during the night and would be indisposed, but that didn't stop me from imagining the worst of him.

Henri reread his mother's note, as if memorizing her words, the slant of her hand. I couldn't blame him for soaking it in, finding joy in the words left behind by one he'd loved so dearly. His distraction had made me feel oddly lonely these past few days. I had no parents. No one would miss me when I was gone aside from Henri and Blanche, and perhaps my aunt. That was why disposing of me would come so easily to Montoni, and why he could step into my inheritance without a fight.

The shadows in the tower grew longer and eventually darkened to pools that covered the walls. I shrunk deeper into Henri, watching the sky fade into darker shades of blue with each passing minute, trembling with the knowledge of what was to come.

I didn't dare look at Henri when he began to pant and slunk off into a corner with a grunt. It was strange that I wanted him to continue to hold me, even as he became the thing that would be my destruction. He was sweating already, the change pressuring him to give in, as I glimpsed the moon in all of its glory outside our window, glowing radiantly, as if offering me solace in my last few minutes of life.

A clank from below gave me pause and I tilted my head, listening. It was a sort of crushing noise, like stone rubbing against stone. And then someone was standing at the top of the staircase, bathed in shadow. I stared at the figure, wondering if I was seeing things, or perhaps, being visited by Death, waiting patiently for Henri's teeth to sink into my throat so they might ferry my soul to the underworld.

"My lord?" A hand reached out and I blinked at it in disbelief as I recognized Ludovico standing before me, looking shaken as he stared off into the corner, where Henri was panting loudly.

I leaped up and grabbed the item he held out to me, a leather case. I flipped it open with shaking hands to find eight syringes carefully tucked within, filled with blackish-green liquid.

"Ludovico, I could kiss you," I said, pulling out a syringe and tapping the glass tube. "We're saved. We're going to get out of this." I released the tiniest drop of antidote before I turned to Henri and froze.

Henri's body cracked as the fingers in his bones elongated, his nails curling into deadly claws. His mouth pushed out from his face, teeth stretching into monstrous jaws while brown fur sprouted from every inch of his skin. He cried out, a sound that devolved into a gurgle in his throat, before resonating as a deep rumble.

I wasted no time. I lunged at Henri and sank the syringe into his arm, pushing the plunger in one fluid stroke. I stepped back and watched him for signs of the wolf retreating, but his eyes began to glow a golden yellow and his ears curved upward.

I cursed, grabbing another syringe and turning to him as he lifted his head and loosed a howl that turned my blood cold. But I didn't give up. I emptied another syringe into his shoulder just as he swatted me across the room.

It felt like I'd been kicked in the chest by a horse. I slammed into the opposite wall, dazed as Henri took a step toward me, and then another, Ludovico frozen in horror at his back.

Too late, I realized, my head throbbing from where I'd struck the wall. It was too late.

Then Henri stumbled. He grunted and collapsed, and I saw that his feet had shifted back, shrinking in upon themselves, as had his hands. His hair began to retreat back into his skin as I let out a sigh of relief and allowed myself to close my eyes.

THIRTY-ONE

"Wake *up*."

I groaned and lifted an eyelid, wincing at the fingers digging into my arm. Then I noticed a hand at the ready to strike me.

"Whoa!" I sat up and scrambled back as Annette brightened.

"You're up," she sighed. "Thank goodness."

I rubbed my cheek, which stung as if I'd been slapped several times, and I realized that was exactly what had happened. I felt the back of my head, where a sizable lump had appeared. "I was already beat up. You didn't have to do more damage."

"Apparently I did." Annette shrugged. "You were out cold."

"And you're here. I didn't know what had become of you."

I suddenly realized that I was alive, and I straightened, looking around as the world came into sharp focus.

My eyes found Henri, pale and shaking nearby. "What? You didn't eat me."

Henri rolled his eyes. "Of course I didn't eat you. You would be far too gamey for my tastes." He touched my back gently. "You're making a habit of saving me."

"Very touching." Annette interrupted, helping me to my feet. "But we mustn't tarry; we're in a hurry."

"Hurry where?"

Ludovico held a shiny object up in front of my face. It was a key, large and gold, with a skull etched into the top.

"What is that?" I asked, reaching out to touch the skull.

"A skeleton key. For the castle." Ludovico's eyes twinkled as he yanked the key out of reach. "Don't ask how it came into my possession. I found it in my bedchamber, along with one of your notes. I immediately went to retrieve the antidote from the laboratory, and found Annette and Blanche locked in the dungeon."

"My sister is well?" Henri asked, leaning against Ludovico as he shivered.

"Henri, are you alright?" I asked.

"It's the poison," Henri waved my concern off. "It will wear off soon." He glanced back at the window, where I glimpsed a dark sky beginning to lighten.

"Your sister is fine," Annette said. "She's just very weak right now, like you. I saw to her injections through the night. She sent Ludovico to save you, and this morning, she wanted me to fetch you before daybreak had fully arrived so we might evade Montoni. She thought she would only slow me down if she came with."

"So the door is open?" I asked, almost not daring to believe it. "We can leave?"

"We can leave," Annette said, grinning. "But we should make haste. Blanche is waiting for us."

"Right," I nodded, following her down the winding staircase. I sighed as I stepped out through the tower door, as if a portal had returned me to the real world, the nightmare behind me.

I turned back to survey the place that had been my prison for this past week, freezing when that horrid pike inevitably drew my eye. I swallowed hard but was startled to find no head upon the pike. I blinked, as if my eyes were malfunctioning, but it remained empty. "Where is it?" I asked, imagining for a moment that it had rotted so completely that it had tumbled from the pike, and even now was being feasted upon by worms and rats. I shuddered, but wasn't given time to linger in my grief, as Annette hauled me across the ramparts to a side door into the castle. "What now?" I asked.

"We fetch my sister," Henri said, sending me a look that told me the answer should have been obvious. And I supposed it should have been.

"What about my aunt?"

Henri hesitated, then nodded. "Right. I'll see to her. She's likely in the west wing, close to my uncle's room." He pushed away from Ludovico, grunting as he leaned against the wall.

Annette sighed. "Ludovico, go with him."

Ludovico nodded, helping to steady Henri, who still looked too sick to move quickly.

I winced. "Are you sure we shouldn't collect our friends together? Henri doesn't look too good."

"We haven't the luxury of time," Henri said. He sent me a grin. "But it's nice that you care."

"Of course I care." I grabbed his hand and offered it a squeeze before Ludovico pulled him along the hallway and out of sight.

I glanced around to get my bearings and realized that we were in the east wing, near my bedchamber. The dungeon was nearby, at least. "How was Bram in the end?" I dared ask Annette.

Annette hesitated. "He was brave until the last, my lord. He was protective of you, and of me. You would have been proud to see it."

I nodded, emotion pulsing through my chest, but we'd lingered for too long already. We rushed along the hallway until we came to the stairs up to my room. I bypassed that, making for the door beneath it, which was closer to the recess that led to the hidden passage. A few minutes more, and we were in the laboratory.

Annette tapped a test tube as she passed. "It's so strange that this has been hidden here all these years. I always thought Monseigneur Schedoni made it with the other monks, his brotherhood, the Order of the Dragon. It's hard to believe that the family owes their humanity to a bunch of leeches." She shuddered.

"And don't forget that Montoni and Schedoni have been murdering people in the dungeons of this castle," I reminded her.

Annette nodded solemnly. "So much evil in this castle. I'd always felt something wrong with the place. I just never could have guessed how deep that horror went."

We pushed through to the adjoining room, which held the dungeon. Blanche sat on the floor, pale and breathing through her pain. Her normally flawless skin was lined with dirt, as were her clothes, but she didn't seem harmed aside from the effects of the antidote.

"Fancy meeting you here," Blanche greeted, trying for a smile that was more of a grimace.

"It's good to see you again," I told her, helping her to her feet. "I honestly wasn't sure I ever would." I winced as I took in her short hair anew. "I take it Annette wasn't able to do much about that?"

Annette huffed. "We've been otherwise distracted, my lord."

"I would have been more distracted by that hair."

Blanche sent me a look. "I'm sure the hair can wait."

"I was just pointing it out," I said, giving Lady Morano a hug. "Although it does make you look more intimidating."

"Ah, perfect," Blanche murmured into my shoulder. "Just what my suitors are looking for, I'm sure."

I pulled back and looked her over. "You'd still be the belle of the ball."

Blanche slapped my chest playfully. "Stop flirting or I'll tell my brother."

I bowed to her in reply. "Let's fetch him and leave this accursed place forever, shall we?"

"Please."

Annette led us to the laboratory and stopped short after stepping inside.

"Annette?" Blanche asked.

Suddenly, Annette was yanked from the doorway, and I heard her cry out as I pushed my way into the lab. I blinked in surprise to find Father Schedoni standing over the lady's maid. He sneered at me. There was something in his hand that I couldn't quite make out.

"You," Blanche snarled behind me. "You're the one who's been feeding me leech food and killing men. You're as bad as my uncle."

"As bad as your uncle?" Schedoni chuckled. His eyes watched as Annette braced herself against the wall to help herself up, before kicking her in the stomach, forcing her back to the ground with a sharp gasp. "I am much worse than your uncle."

Blanche held up a hand, and I watched with fascination as her hand began to lengthen, talons jutting from her nails. Even with the antidote running through her veins, if she wasn't actively holding the monster back, she could let it out and, hopefully, control it.

Schedoni tossed two small bags at our feet, and we suddenly found ourselves blinded by dust. I coughed as it invaded my nose and mouth, tickling my lungs. It had a terrible smell to it, like burning metal.

Silver, I realized, as I wheeled to find Blanche on the floor, curled into a ball, her skin sizzling as if she was being boiled alive, foam pouring from her mouth.

I acted quickly, undoing my cloak and tossing it over Blanche in one fluid motion, then shoving her back into the dungeon and closing the door on her to keep any more of the silver dust from harming her.

"That will be your last mistake," Schedoni promised, pulling a dagger from his robes and advancing on me.

Annette threw a leg out and tripped the monk, sending him sprawling.

Cursing, Schedoni climbed to his feet, and I searched the room for something to use against him. I had no idea what was in any of the beakers and tubes on the table, but I grabbed them at random and began to throw them at the monk.

Schedoni grunted under each blow as glass shattered against his habit. He held his arms up to protect his face, but even that didn't protect him when something began to eat away at the cloth covering his arms, like an acid, making it smoke.

"Enough!" Schedoni bellowed, rushing me, knife raised overhead, as if he meant to deliver a death blow upon reaching me.

I spun out of the way, and the monk sliced the dagger into the table, whereupon it became embedded in the wood. He took a moment to try to free it, but I swung at him with a fist, and he danced out of my way before he could resecure his weapon.

Schedoni hissed but drew something else from the folds of his robe. It looked like a tape measure, but when he opened it, I saw that it was outfitted with a metal wire. A garrote. I wondered what else Schedoni had in his arsenal. These were tools of an assassin, not some simple monk. That explained a lot, actually.

I moved in for another punch, but Schedoni sidestepped me and sent me spinning as he rushed at my side. I grunted as the edge of the lab table knocked the wind out of me, but I still had the presence of mind to reach for a weapon. My fingers wrapped around a glass beaker, but it slipped out of my hand when Schedoni grabbed the back of my shirt and yanked me back toward him. If he pulled me any closer, he would slip that wire around my neck and that would be the end of me. My hands scrambled for purchase, grazing the beaker. I fought against Schedoni's grip on my shirt and the fabric gave a little. It was just enough to allow me to reach forward and grab ahold of the beaker, but as I was pulled back with renewed force, I smashed the beaker against the top of the counter, shattering most of it into useless shards.

I felt Schedoni slip the garrote wire over my neck and draw it taut against my throat. It dug into my skin and my eyes bulged as I took what was left in my hand and thrust it back into Schedoni's face, hoping it would be enough to get him to release me.

It was.

I gasped as the garrote slackened, and I pushed myself away from Schedoni, leaning back against the counter to assess my adversary and plan my next move. But there was no need.

I had shoved a large shard of glass into his right eye. As I watched in horror, Schedoni ran his fingers over the shard, as if to pry it loose, slicing the flesh of his fingers to ribbons in the process before he stumbled back into a wall and slid to the floor.

I swallowed hard as I watched him tumble onto his side and lay still. He faced the wall, so I didn't have to gaze upon that terrible glass in his eye, the blow that I had dealt him, sealing his fate.

I peered down at my hands. I was a murderer now. And I had blood on my hands. Actual blood, from where the glass shard had also sliced my hand. Now that I noticed it, it stung terribly, and I pulled a kerchief from my coat pocket and wrapped it carefully.

"Are you alright?" Annette asked as she shuffled into the room with Blanche, who had recovered, but bore bloodshot eyes and raw-looking skin from her exposure to the silver.

"I'll live," I said.

Blanche's jaw clenched as she gazed down at Schedoni's still form. "Good riddance." She looked up and nodded to me, as if thanking me for ending his life, even if it had been an accident.

I nodded back.

THIRTY-TWO

T he castle was eerily quiet as we pushed through dark hallway after dark hallway on our way to the west wing.

"Udolpho truly feels haunted now," Blanche observed, as if reading my mind. We encountered no resistance as we stepped into the front hall, and I grew uneasy as we slipped into the halls that led toward the dungeon beneath Montoni's room, where I hoped Henri had already succeeded in liberating my aunt. With all that had happened in the past week, including Bram's head raised on a pike, I doubted many servants, save for the most faithful to Montoni, had decided to stay at the castle. Bertolino, at the very least, should be attending the front room, yet the man was nowhere to be seen. I couldn't imagine the butler had vacated the premises, given his devotion to the count, especially as he had been trusted with the care of the castle in his master's absence, a castle that held many of Montoni's secrets.

"This doesn't feel right," I whispered to Blanche.

Blanche sent me a sideways glance. "I know." She held my gaze for a moment before her resolve settled on the halls we navigated.

It was only a few more minutes before we found ourselves in the secret passage beneath the apartments in the west wing. I was anxious to see Henri again, but we had to be cautious, and so I followed Blanche's example, slowly creeping up the hall to the dungeon. Once it opened up and I caught sight of the bars, I felt a moment's relief, and pushed ahead.

Aunt Cheron stood on the other side, eyes wide when she saw me. "Emile? Is that you?"

"It is," I agreed, stepping up to the bars. She looked like she hadn't had much sleep but was otherwise in fine condition. "Is Henri with you?"

"Henri?" she echoed, confused.

I glanced back and met Blanche's eyes. She pursed her lips in concern. He should have been here with Ludovico by now.

Annette grabbed a key dangling from a nail on the wall nearby and unlocked the dungeon door, throwing it open wide.

Aunt Cheron swallowed as she exited the dungeon and looked me over. "I'm . . . I'm glad you're alright, Emile." Her eyes filled with tears. "I've been so very wrong about so many things." She surprised me by reaching out to hug me. "But you came back for me, you darling boy. Your parents would be so proud if they could see you right now."

I blinked and returned the embrace, thrown by her behavior toward me, but then again, I supposed that being tossed into a dungeon by her husband and having some time to think about her past transgressions had caused her change of heart. Either way, I was glad for it.

"I'm happy to see you aren't covered in leeches," I joked, and Aunt Cheron pulled back, chuckling. She wiped at her eyes. "Yes, well, don't think that monster didn't threaten me with them. I think it was only a matter of time before he followed through." She paused. "Did he hurt you, Emile? I don't know if I could live with myself if he did."

I looked down into her concerned face with bewilderment. I was so used to seeing cold regard that this warmth I found in her was unsettling.

"I'm fine, I assure you," I said.

"Come, we can't linger here," Blanche said, glancing around the dingy, dark room. "Let's find my brother and leave this god-forsaken place."

"Where could they be?" I asked, staring through the bars as if they might appear if I looked long enough. "Is there another dungeon?"

Blanche stared into the room, chewing on her lower lip thoughtfully. "I'm not sure. Henri may have seen Ludovico to safety first, especially if Montoni was near this dungeon when they tried to make for it." She shrugged helplessly. "Maybe the courtyard?"

I nodded slowly. "Then that's where we go."

"Um, miss? My lord?" Annette's voice held a tremor that quickly rose to hysteria.

We all turned at once to find the lady's maid staring down at a ball that was rattling against the bars of the dungeon, as if it were trying to climb inside.

"What in the world?" Aunt Cheron breathed.

I stepped cautiously toward the ball. In the gloom of the dungeon, it was difficult to make it out, but it seemed to be covered with hair. Was it an animal of some sort?

I nudged it with my foot, and Annette squeaked, leaping back as the ball dislodged itself from the bars, then tumbled toward the open door to the cell. I watched with wide eyes as I realized that it had a nose, and a face, rotten and crisscrossed with slashes, its neck a mess of torn skin.

A moan escaped my mouth as I stumbled back into the women, the head continuing into the cell, where it seemed pulled toward a pile of clothing. Not clothing, I realized with renewed terror, a body. A headless corpse.

As if drawn together like magnets, the head fit itself into the exposed pulp of the body's neck, and a squelching sound filled the air.

"What is going on?" I asked, my voice shaking.

But no one answered. We continued to watch, until the corpse suddenly sat up and climbed to its feet. It had no shirt, so I could clearly see the planes of muscle and dark flesh. The head was on backward, but it began to right itself, shifting very slowly along the neck as a shaft of light from a window illuminated the creature more thoroughly for us.

The skin at its neck began to sew itself together, as if the flesh was merely melding into one another, the bloating of the face subsiding and the dark complexion beginning to match the body's. Maggots were pushed out from the pores, dripping to the ground like squirming raindrops, as eyes expanded to fill gaping eye sockets. The jaw, hanging askew, swung back up into place as the man before us suddenly drew in a deep breath and blinked his eyes at us in disbelief.

"Oh my God," I whispered.

Bram stared down at his hands. "Oh my God," he echoed.

"Am I dead? Am I a ghost?"

"A werewolf," Blanche said, recovering faster than the rest of us, and stepping forward to meet him. "You're very much alive, I assure you." She paused. "You were just dead for a few days."

"A week," I helped, feeling detached, like I was witnessing a dream. "Your head was . . . um . . ."

Bram closed his eyes as Blanche placed a hand on his shoulder. "I remember dying. Montoni was ripping my head . . . and then I felt my neck tingling and . . ." He let out a breath, meeting Blanche's eyes. "You're a family of werewolves."

"We are," Blanche agreed.

"But how . . . ?"

"You must have been bitten by my uncle before he killed you."

Bram nodded slowly, looking down at his hand, where I recalled he'd been scratched by Montoni through the door. Scratched not by Montoni's claws, it would seem, but his teeth.

"The curse can be transferred through an alpha's bite," Blanche said. "Either Montoni didn't realize he bit you, or he didn't think the curse would take hold so soon before he killed you. My parents were probably right that the curse is stronger near Udolpho, so it likely set in sooner than usual." She tilted her head. "But during a full moon, a body will heal itself from any wounds sustained since the previous full moon, so long as it wasn't a lethal blow from silver."

"Any wounds." Bram swallowed hard. "That's . . . something." I noticed his hands shaking slightly as he looked up to meet my eyes.

"It's okay," I assured him, crossing the distance between us, caught between wonder and horror, relief, and disgust. I grabbed his hands, then hesitated only briefly before burying myself in his chest. "You're okay. Thank God."

Bram relaxed into me. "I think I'm in shock. I should be more disturbed by this."

Annette raised her hand from the corner of the dungeon. "I'm still quite disturbed."

I chuckled and looked up to find Bram laughing, tears in his eyes. "I'm alive," he said.

"You're alive," I agreed.

Blanche glanced back at us from the window she had walked to. "And it looks like your body healed itself just in time to miss turning into a mindless monster. The sun is up."

"And you look better as well," I observed, looking her over. She stood steady, the poison finally driven from her system.

Blanche nodded, lifting a hand and flexing it. "I feel better."

"Then Montoni might be starting to recover as well," I said. "We need to escape this infernal castle and regroup."

"After we find Ludovico," Annette added, then ducked her head. "And Henri, of course."

We made our way back to the front hall, where Blanche stopped us. "I'll go ahead to make sure the gates can be opened. If they can, you all leave. I'll go back for Henri and Ludovico once you're safe, if they're not already waiting for us."

"No way," I protested. "I'm coming with you."

Blanche hesitated. "Emile, my uncle won't hurt me or Henri. We're family. Plus, we're far more durable than a puny human." She paused. "No offense."

"None taken." I crossed my arms and stuck out my jaw. "But I'm coming. If Henri's in trouble, I need to be there. He would do the same for me."

Blanche sighed but nodded. She pointed to Bram. "You, protect Annette and Madame Montoni. You're probably more of a liability than anything, being newly turned, but just slash and bite if someone comes for them. Think you can manage that?"

Bram's eyes were wide as he nodded.

Blanche let out a breath. "Good." She glanced at me sideways. "You ready?"

"Ready."

We slipped out into the courtyard beyond, my eyes darting every which way for signs of trouble. We walked in the direction of the castle gates, sticking as close to the shadows of the buildings as possible, hoping to escape detection. All we had to do was find a way to open the gates, then our friends could simply disappear into the surrounding forest. After that, we could focus on finding Henri and Ludovico. I knew from personal experience how relentless Montoni was. If we did all manage to escape, would Montoni ever stop hunting us? Perhaps this was but a prelude to what awaited us on the other side of those castle walls.

As we drew closer to the gates, I saw three carts waiting, horses yet to be hitched to them, and I paused. Perhaps Montoni was waiting for us, standing guard before the only exit from this terrible place, but I heard Blanche's sharp intake of breath beside me and knew that something was wrong.

Blanche rushed forward, throwing caution to the wind, and I followed uneasily. I threw glances all around us, wondering where Henri was, but he was nowhere to be seen.

"Blanche," I whisper-shouted, "Wait. We have to think about this."

But even as I said it, I could make out Henri in the back of one of the carts. He was covered in a net and as it shifted and grazed his skin, steam burst from his flesh. Silver. He was trapped in a silver net.

Henri saw us coming and began to struggle more adamantly, his agonized cries echoing across the courtyard as the silver net chafed against his naked chest, burning him with its brutal poison.

I faltered briefly, as I realized what I was looking at. He was bait.

"Blanche, we have to stop," I insisted, trying to keep pace with her. "Montoni is clearly . . ."

My voice trailed off as something suddenly sang through the air, and I looked up to find an object hurtling in our direction. I opened my mouth to gasp out a warning, but it was already too late. A large silver bolt slammed into Blanche's leg and out through the other side, digging into the stone ground at her feet and pinning her to the spot. Blanche roared as blood oozed from her leg, which continued to steam as if burning her. In a flash of blonde fur, she suddenly stood in her half-wolf form, growling as she yanked on the bolt, to no affect.

"You weren't simply going to leave without saying goodbye, were you?"

I felt a shudder pass through my body as I tilted my head up to find Montoni standing on the rooftop, grinning down at us triumphantly, a harpoon canon mounted beside him.

He'd been waiting for this. And now Blanche, our only real chance of facing off against him, was indisposed, pinned down like a butterfly.

Montoni shook his head with a chuckle. "And just when things were starting to get good."

THIRTY-THREE

Montoni climbed down from the rooftop with practiced ease, while I frantically tried to pull at the bolt in the stone at Blanche's feet. It was like trying to draw Excalibur from rock.

"I should have listened to you," Blanche said, voice garbled in her half-wolf form. She whimpered deep in her chest as her leg continued to steam from the silver.

I swallowed hard, unsure of what to do. I looked up at Henri, still several yards away, thrashing against the silver net with futile gestures that only served to inflict more pain. Next to him, in one of the other carts, I saw Ludovico, bound and gagged. Standing over him, Bertolino grinned—the smug bastard.

I cursed silently. This was a doomed escape attempt from the start.

"That leg doesn't look good, niece," Montoni mocked as he landed on solid ground. His eyes found mine and his grin spread. He was enjoying this, dropping all civility and punishing us, hurting us. This was the true Montoni: vicious, ruthless, cruel.

There was nothing I could do to help Blanche. But if I could free Henri . . .

I sprinted for the carts, and Montoni chuckled behind me. "What does our little hero expect he'll be able to do?"

I ignored him and propelled myself forward, toward Henri, who looked up with wide eyes, pained and hopeless.

"That's quite enough," Montoni's stern voice commanded, and I stopped short as he leaped into my path, his body still transitioning to a man-wolf, black fur thickening across his body. "I have no need of your insolence. I will—"

He was cut off as a blur of gray fur slammed into him, sending him into a nearby wall, where he grunted and dropped to a knee, eyes glittering dangerously. I blinked as a new man-wolf bared its teeth at him, claws clenching and unclenching at its sides. Who was *that?*

I realized that my way was now unimpeded and raced for the carts, only hesitating when Bertolino dropped to the ground, brandishing a dagger. But I'd just taken down Schedoni. I wasn't afraid of this pathetic underling. I screamed as I launched myself at him, barreling into his stomach as he shrank back in surprise. I thudded his arm into the ground until he dropped the dagger before I landed a solid punch across his face.

It only took the one hit to knock him out.

Ludovico grunted in the cart above, and I sent a quick look back at Montoni and the gray wolf, to find them grappling in a blur of fur and teeth, their maws snarling and their claws raking.

I quickly untied Ludovico. "Join the others in the front hall," I ordered him, leaving no room for objections. I turned to the cart with Henri and met his eyes, green and blazing.

"Henri," I whispered, rushing to his side. I assessed the net, pinned to the base of the cart by a dozen silver rings. I would have to cut the net loose from each of them, and as I grabbed a length of net, I realized that it was tough material. It would take some time to saw through it. Although I didn't necessarily need to cut through them all. Three, maybe four, would be enough to free him.

Henri gasped, and I looked up to find the net taut against his arms. I released my grip on the net and he sighed with relief.

"Sorry," I murmured.

"You have nothing to be sorry for," Henri told me. "You came for me."

"Of course I did." I met his eyes. "I will always come for you."

His lips quivered. "Emile . . . I've put you in danger once more. I—"

"Later," I silenced him. I dropped from the cart to procure Bertolino's dagger, before kneeling at Henri's side and beginning to saw at the net where it attached to one ring. Luckily, the dagger was made of solid silver and was up to the challenge. "There'll be plenty of time for that later."

"Please, save yourself. Montoni . . . he's so much stronger than we are. We won't be able to last long against him. At least if you all run, you might escape. At least some of you."

I stood and reached through the net to grasp one of his hands. I squeezed it, looking into his face with a smile. "Henri, I am not leaving you. We haven't been through all we have just for me to run away now."

"You're a fool." Henri's lips pressed into a thin line to hold back his emotions as I dropped his hand and returned to the task at hand.

A squeal pierced the air and my head shot up to find the gray wolf lying in a heap at the bottom of a nearby wall, blood coating one of its shoulders. Montoni heaved as he stood over the other wolf, eyes promising death.

"Mother!" Henri cried.

"Mother?" I asked, turning to him with wide eyes. "That's . . . ?"

"I'd recognize her anywhere, in any form," Henri confirmed.

I turned to watch Montoni's wary eyes travel over the gray wolf, then growl deep in his chest, a warning of intention. I swallowed hard, wondering if I could watch what was about to happen.

But the gray wolf wasn't finished. She was up in a flash, darting between Montoni's legs. Before he could turn to face his opponent, she was on his back, shifting into full animal form. She clamped her jaws down into Montoni's neck, earning a scream of rage from the count.

"Emile." Henri gestured to the ring I'd been sawing at. "Hurry, so I can help."

I nodded, resuming my work. A moment later, one ring was free of the net. I sighed with relief. My arms were already burning from the effort of the first ring, but I didn't hesitate before moving on to the next. And then the next. I did my utmost to ignore the snarls and cries behind me, focusing my energies on the knife slicing over and over again.

When three rings were free, Henri tried to climb out from under the net, but the gap still wasn't wide enough. I needed to cut through at least one more.

"You've performed admirably for a human."

Montoni's voice was right behind me. I sawed faster, but I

couldn't escape his grip on the back of my neck as he yanked me from the wagon. He tossed me to the ground like a rag doll, and I grunted upon impact, biting my lip and drawing blood. I swiped at it, grimacing as Montoni stood over me, back in human form.

"You've been far more trouble than you're worth." Montoni scowled.

My eyes darted past Montoni to the gray wolf, unconscious and covered in bloody wounds.

"Yes, I'll take care of her later," Montoni sneered, running a hand over his neck, where he still bled from deep teeth marks.

I swallowed hard and glanced behind me, past Bertolino's prone form, to the carriage where Ludovico had been tied up. Hopefully, the others had been smart enough to make their own escape.

"They won't get far either," Montoni promised, as if reading my thoughts. His lips curved into a smile. "Right now, it's just you and me."

He reached down and I tried to scramble back, but he was too fast. His hands gripped my throat and yanked me to my feet, and then up into the air, my feet dangling beneath me uselessly. I gasped for air and clawed at his hands, trying to break his grip. He was too strong. I was helpless as his hands squeezed my neck, red dots beginning to dance in my vision. My lungs screamed for air while my head grew fuzzy and light.

My eyes found Montoni's, dark and full of violent delight. He wanted to watch the life drain from my eyes, and I wasn't going to be able to stop him.

I heard Henri screaming behind me, begging for his uncle to stop, but Montoni's eyes were sadistic, beyond reason. He would not loosen his grip unless it was to drop my lifeless corpse to the ground.

Movement beyond Montoni drew my eyes, and I saw a blur of blonde fur before Blanche's jaw buried into Montoni's side. Dark blood immediately oozed from Montoni's flesh, but Montoni merely grunted and held firm to my neck.

I blinked, vision hazy as I noted the flesh missing from Blanche's leg, leaking heavily into a pool at her feet. She had freed herself from the bolt. I'd read of wolves biting off their own legs to free themselves from traps. Blanche had done that, chewing through her own flesh and muscle to free herself. For me and Henri.

But it was for naught.

Even as I watched, Blanche grew weaker from blood loss. Her grip on Montoni's side was loosening, her eyes becoming unfocused. My own eyes were becoming unfocused.

Montoni released me suddenly.

I gasped as I fell to the ground. My lungs ached as they drew in heaving breaths of air. I coughed, lifting my head to find Montoni standing before me, arm still outstretched, as if still gripping my neck, but missing a majority of his arm, his bicep hanging uselessly from the bone. Blood was spraying everywhere, including over me, hot and sticky, and I pushed myself away from him until my back hit the wagon.

My eyes darted to Blanche, weakly holding fast to Montoni, although this new development had given her more fight. And on Montoni's right was yet another wolf, this one a deeper black than Montoni's wolf form, like that of obsidian. I stared at the new wolf, large and powerful with murder in its eyes. Montoni's missing arm was between its jaws, still leaking blood, the fingers twitching as if trying to understand what had happened to it.

Montoni shook off his shock and pulled his injured arm

against himself. With his free arm, he shoved Blanche off him. Blanche grunted but managed to seize a leg in her jaws, earning a cry from Montoni as his eyes found the obsidian wolf. "Who the hell are you?" he demanded.

In response, the wolf spit out the arm and licked its lips slowly, as if promising to taste more of Montoni's flesh.

The wagon shifted behind me, and Annette was suddenly at my side, helping me to my feet. I glanced back to find Ludovico and my aunt sawing through more of the net covering Henri.

"You should have run," I croaked, voice hoarse.

"Not bloody likely," Annette snorted, clinging to my arm as the new wolf lunged at Montoni.

I watched, mesmerized, as the wolf sank its teeth into Montoni's exposed side, Blanche anchoring him to the spot so he was unable to dart out of the way. "Is that . . . ?"

"Bram," Annette confirmed.

The gray wolf had recovered and stood behind Bram, eyes on the wagon behind me, expectant. And then Henri strode out from the wagon, skin blackened across his arms and face from being exposed to silver.

I swallowed hard as I watched Henri step up to his uncle, held in place by the two wolves gripping him with their teeth. He held Bertolino's silver dagger in his hand.

"You always were a ruthless prick," Henri spat, gazing hard into Montoni's eyes.

Then the silver dagger was buried in his uncle's chest.

Montoni's eyes bulged, his face screwing up with pain and disbelief. The veins across his chest suddenly stood out, turning black, as if with rot. They grew thicker and kept expanding across his body until it began to sink in upon itself like moldering fruit. After a minute, he fell to the ground with a splat, Bram and Blanche letting go and stepping back.

Montoni's skin softened until it fell from his bones, black blood oozing out beneath him.

And he was no more.

THIRTY-FOUR

A nnette and Aunt Cheron were making a tourniquet for Blanche. When she'd shifted back to her human form, she'd been pale from blood loss, her leg a mangled mess and still leaking.

"She needs a physician," Annette said, looking drawn and pale herself.

Henri reached down to grasp his sister's hand. "She's a fighter. Obstinate, actually. And the whole supernatural wolf thing helps."

Blanche chuckled and then coughed. "Don't make me laugh. It hurts."

"And if she bleeds out, she'll just revive again on the next full moon," I agreed. "Right, Bram?"

"I wouldn't recommend it," Bram said dryly before smiling at me with those damn dimples of his standing out.

Henri watched Bram warily. "You're lucky that Montoni

didn't realize the curse had set in. If he had, he would have lanced your head or heart with silver. As it was, your head didn't look particularly good on that pike."

"Yes, lucky," Bram echoed, tilting his head. "A pike, you say?"

"It's probably best not to think about that." Henri held out his hand to Bram. "Thank you, Valancourt. You saved us all today."

Bram ducked his head, embarrassed, but accepted his hand with a shake. "I guess I did, didn't I?"

"We owe you a great debt."

Bram hesitated but shook his hand. He winked at me. "What are friends for, right?"

"Friends could keep friends from losing more blood," Blanche told him, grunting as Annette tightened the tourniquet over her thigh.

"Right," Bram agreed, kneeling down between Annette and Aunt Cheron to help.

Henri walked over and settled a hand on Bram's shoulder, causing the other man to stiffen and look up. "I hope we can be friends, Valancourt. Truly."

"I would like that."

The gray wolf trotted over and licked Blanche's face. I stared for a moment, while Blanche smiled at it.

Henri returned to my side and gazed down at me, his green eyes conveying an array of emotions. "I'm so happy you're alright." He swallowed hard. "I don't know what I would have done if . . ."

"You don't have to worry about that now," I told him, putting a hand to his chest. "We're okay now."

He nodded, then leaned forward, resting his forehead against mine and closing his eyes. "Thank you for saving my family."

"I will always fight for you and Blanche," I told him, finding his lips with mine. "You're my family now too, whether you like it or not."

The next day, we sat in the front room of Udolpho Castle, Annette having just made tea. Blanche was still pale and weak, but she already showed great progress according to Bram, and whatever hadn't healed completely by the next full moon would heal then. Until that time, we decided to remain at Udolpho Castle. We had plenty of decisions to make anyway, about where we wanted to go from there.

"I won't take that antidote anymore," Blanche insisted, sipping daintily at her tea. "Not now that I know where it comes from. And with Schedoni out of the picture, I'm not sure it could be replicated even if we wanted to."

"Wherever he is," Ludovico added, as the monk's body had gone missing. He likely had survived my attack. If his wounds hadn't been as terrible as we had at first thought, he may have even made it to the village before his injuries killed him.

"So, what will you do?" Aunt Cheron asked, meeting my eyes briefly before looking expectantly at Henri, the new head of the family.

Henri sighed, leaning back into the sofa beside me. "We'll have to use the dungeons of the castle for now, until we find an alternate way to keep us in check. Perhaps some of the scientists Schedoni has reached out to for a cure will come through. If not, I don't see another option aside from confinement on the night of the full moon."

Bram bristled on my other side, and I patted his knee. He

would have to become accustomed to life as a werewolf alongside the Morano family. I was sure he was up to the task, but he would clearly have a lot to learn. "It won't be all that bad, I'm sure," I told him. "I'll make sure you all behave."

He rolled his eyes and smiled.

"And we'll clean the dungeons up," Annette said, smiling at Blanche. "Maybe some nice potted flowers and rugs will make them a little more comfortable."

Ludovico snorted but didn't say anything when Annette sent him a dirty look.

"I think it's a wise choice," a woman in her early forties said. She lifted a teacup to her mouth, long blonde hair so much like Blanche's before she'd cut it that I couldn't help but stare. Her kind green eyes sparkled as she gazed around the room. "I think this family has denied their legacy for too long. Perhaps a reckoning for cheating the curse was always going to find us."

The woman, of course, was the same from the portraits I'd seen of her, an amalgam of her two children. Countess Helena Morano, alive after all these years.

Blanche set down her tea and cleared her throat. "Mother, we know how you've been kept in that horrible turret the past five years, but . . . I have to know more about what happened to you. How did you become Montoni's prisoner?"

"And how are you not dead?" Annette added, nodding.

"You left the skeleton key for Ludovico," I said, to confirm what I'd already pieced together.

"I did," Helena confirmed. "I stole it from Bertolino weeks ago." She shifted, then looked thoughtfully around before finding my eyes. "We've met before, you realize?"

I blinked, then frowned at her. "Have we?"

Helena nodded. "I was emaciated and sickly, practically a living skeleton, in the gallery. I think I scared you half to death."

I tried to reconcile the beautiful woman before me with the creature I had mistaken for a corpse, eyes sunken and emaciated beyond possibility. "That was *you*?" I asked, incredulous.

"Yes. I was still taking the antidote during that full moon because I couldn't chance losing control. It wasn't until last night that the full moon renewed my body to peak health." She ran a hand back through her hair. "The first full moon, after I fell from the cliff, my brother, Count Montoni, refused me the antidote, and my body healed from the fall. Then I was locked in the turret and the antidote was forced on me, keeping me weak and complacent, a wilted shadow of my former self. I watched from the window all these years as my children visited the castle, unable to speak or call out to them. I was wretched, the curse keeping me alive even as I let myself wither away."

Blanche walked over and placed a comforting hand on her shoulder. "What changed?"

Helena considered. "Your arrival was different this time. Probably due to Emile and Madame Montoni's presence. The castle was distracted and one of the newer guards brought me my meals, expecting me to be as weak as ever. Knowing that I would be forced to watch helplessly yet again, I drew on strength deep within to overpower him. I escaped and hid in the secret passages, then managed to steal Bertolino's skeleton key while he slept that first night. I've kept tabs on you children, but I needed to know how I could help. Until then, I had to constantly avoid Montoni's men."

My head was spinning with the revelations. I realized that Montoni had been searching for Helena the first night we'd arrived at Udolpho, and she'd likely been who had unfastened the bolt on the second door in my room, as well as the figure I'd seen enter my bedchamber, whom I'd mistaken for a specter.

"It's fantastic," I said breathlessly. I glanced at Henri briefly before looking once more to Helena. "And your husband? Victor? Is he . . . ?"

Helena swallowed hard. "He is dead, I'm afraid. He was more thorough than I."

"Silver bullet," Blanche supplied.

I grabbed Henri's hand, squeezing it, and he sent me a soft smile. He looked happy. Of course he was—he'd gotten his mother back. But it was also bittersweet, given not only Victor's death at his own hands, from which he could never return, but also the circumstances surrounding his mother's return to him. The events of the past month at Udolpho Castle had been traumatizing.

"I can never thank you enough for helping my children," Helena said, suddenly addressing me. She smiled and took in the room at large. "All of you. You're the reason we're here today and my brother's rule is at an end."

"We also couldn't have done it without your help apparently," I told her, lifting a teacup in her direction, as if in a toast. "You're a brave woman."

"I don't feel brave. The things I've done to this family . . ." She pursed her lips and Blanche reached down to hug her.

"We're just happy to have you back," Blanche assured her. "That's what matters."

Helena nodded, tears glistening in her eyes as she patted her daughter's arm in thanks for her words.

There was a lot of catching up to do amongst the family that night, and I smiled, listening to stories shared, imagining a younger Henri performing the antics that Blanche described through laughter. It made me admire him even more. I held his hand beneath the table for much of the evening. Bram seemed just as interested, asking questions pertaining to the curse as they were referenced in conversation.

When Helena and Madame Montoni retired for the evening, along with Annette and Ludovico, I knew the time had come to discuss our future, and specifically, what had been on my mind the previous day.

"How does it feel to be the alpha?" I asked Henri, who looked happier than I could ever recall.

Henri grinned. "It feels amazing not having to answer to Montoni. I feel like a great weight has been lifted, like I can finally start *living*."

I nodded. "And you have your mother back."

He shook his head. "I can't even . . . I never imagined. It still boggles my mind. It upsets me that she was in that turret the entire time, unable to reach out to us, but we're together now."

Blanche nodded. "We'll just have to move forward with the time we have."

I straightened, clearing my throat. "Speaking of time, I wanted to discuss our eventual return to society, whether it be to La Vallée or the château."

Bram's chair scraped back. "I should excuse myself."

"This concerns you too, Bram," I said, stopping him. I hesitated, looking at Henri. "You know how I feel about you. Both of you. Just tonight, we fought for each other's lives, and it felt . . . right."

Bram and Henri exchanged looks.

I swept a hand nervously over my brow before continuing. "When Bram died, it hurt deeply. I never . . . I don't want to feel that loss again. And when he was revived, it was like a second chance had materialized before me. Before *us*."

Henri pursed his lips. "Emile. If you . . . if your heart has . . ." He let out a breath and leaned back in his chair. "I will respect whatever you decide, Emile. You know that I will never force your hand in anything again."

Blanche looked uncomfortable. "Emile, should I . . . ?"

"Please stay," I told her. "You are a part of this. You see, Montoni's plan was sound."

Blanche's eyes widened. "You mean *marriage*?"

"To keep up pretenses, yes. The thing is, I want us *all* to be a family. And I don't want to have to choose between the two people who have my heart. And there's no reason I should. I say we decide for ourselves. Today. And I want more than anything to be with both you, Bram, and you, Henri. The thought of losing either one of you makes me ill, and if you'll have it, I would like to see where that takes us. Together."

Henri hesitated, eyes lifting to Bram. Bram, likewise, watched Henri, as if searching him for signs of disapproval or perhaps, something else.

"You were in each other's lives once," I said. "I know you each felt something for one another then. Can you open yourselves to the possibility that you both could love me, and perhaps come to love one another as well?"

"It's very unconventional," Bram said slowly, eyes flickering between me and Henri. "I won't say that I'm not *surprised* by this idea. Two men in love is just as strange to this world."

Henri nodded thoughtfully. "I . . . have felt like I've needed to hide myself for a long time. I've felt ashamed of what I've wanted my entire life. But I won't be ashamed anymore. If this is how we can be happy together, then I am willing to give this a try." He sent Bram a sideways look. "And I won't pretend that I never desired something more with Valancourt in the past. I just didn't know if he returned my affection. I'd hoped, but I ruined that experiment."

Bram swallowed hard. "Your blossoming affection, Count, was indeed returned. I never expected anything to happen, but . . . through Emile, perhaps we truly can all find happiness. We've found our way back to one another, at the very least."

Blanche clapped, grinning from ear to ear. "It's all so wonderful. You shall all be happy together. I can feel it."

Henri felt for my hand under the table and squeezed it. Then I felt Bram's shoe knock into mine from across the table, and he looked at me shyly.

I let out a relieved breath. "I'm glad you're so willing. I wasn't sure how either of you would respond, but I truly cannot choose between the two of you. You each have my heart."

Henri grinned. "I certainly can't turn down the two dashing men who came to my rescue. Why settle for one?"

"Oh? Dashing?" Bram teased.

"Very dashing." Henri winked at Bram and kissed me on the cheek. Bram looked uncomfortable at the gesture, and I knew it would take some time for them to get used to the idea of all of us being with one another, but I had faith that our feelings would grow, and it would work out for us in the end.

"It won't be too strange for you, Lady Morano?" I asked, looking to Blanche. "You're going to be a part of the household, and I want you to be okay with this. I'm afraid it might be necessary, as a marquis, to be off the market and off people's minds. I know that asking for marriage is a lot."

Blanche snorted. "Surely you're jesting. I'd already warmed to the idea of marrying my good friend. And I could never leave Henri. Plus, I think I would make for a good marchioness, wouldn't you agree?"

"We could find another way to satisfy society," I offered. "You need not sacrifice yourself for our happiness . . . but something tells me that this arrangement will suit you as well? Unless I'm reading things incorrectly."

Blanche raised an eyebrow. "Oh, don't be such a bore, Emile. Do speak plainly."

I shifted in my seat. "I know that you've been corresponding with Carmilla. It seems to me that you two might have a connection? Unless I'm completely misreading the situation."

Blanche lifted an eyebrow. "Annette is sharing my secrets with you now, is she?"

"Not at all," I said, ducking my head. "I chanced upon you talking about her letters."

"He was spying on us," Henri supplied.

I elbowed him and he grinned back at me.

Blanche straightened in her seat. "To answer your question, Emile, yes. I have been speaking with Carmilla. It seems that we have a great deal in common." Her eyes flicked to Henri briefly. "And I believe your assumption is correct. Our marriage would be advantageous to me and my circumstances as well."

"My sweet, innocent sister," Henri shook his head, an even wider smile stretching across his face. "Full of surprises."

"Now, we just need to find you a wife to complete the charade."

Henri rolled his eyes. "I think people will find it very likely that I'm the sort of man who ends up a lifelong bachelor." He glanced at Bram. "Maybe a sickly bachelor who requires frequent attention from the local doctor."

Bram flushed in response.

Henri lifted his glass in a toast. "To living in sin in plain sight of everyone."

Blanche snorted, lifting her own glass. "To a bright future. For all of us."

"For all of us," I echoed as we all toasted.

As Henri and Blanche talked over Carmilla's attentions, Bram came to sit on my other side, his hand finding mine. I twined my fingers with his.

"Are you sure about this?" he asked softly.

"I am. So long as you are."

Bram eyed Henri. "I can share my love for you, so long as I have the chance to express it with you."

"We can sort out the details as this progresses," I said, lifting his hand to my lips and offering it a gentle kiss. "But this makes me very happy. Both of you make me very happy."

Bram kissed me gently on the lips in response.

The door closed as Blanche discreetly slipped from the room, leaving us to navigate this new relationship in its infancy.

"We can take this slow as we figure it out," Bram offered, his hand grazing my cheek, and then hesitantly trailing down over Henri's.

Henri sighed in response, before he grinned. "But what would be the fun in that?"

I laughed.

We would be happy, the three of us, no matter what lay ahead. So long as we were together.

ACKNOWLEDGMENTS

This book would not have been possible without Ann Radcliffe's ingenuity. This novel is a love letter to not only Ann Radcliffe and the brilliant novel this book is based on, *The Mysteries of Udolpho*, but to all the brilliant pioneers of gothic literature.

Of course, a book takes more than inspiration to come alive, and it truly took a group of special people to make this what it is today. I would like to thank my agent, Eva Scalzo, for seeing something in my writing—I would be nowhere without her advice and thoughtfulness. My deepest gratitude goes to my insightful editor, Tamara Grasty, who took a chance on this novel and was instrumental in polishing these words. Thank you, as well, to Madeline Greenhalgh, Shannon Dolley, Alexandra Murphy, Cassandra Jones, Lauren Knowles, Rosie Stewart, Hayley Gundlach, Emma Hardy, Molly Young, Lizzy Mason, Lauren Cepero, and the rest of the team at Page Street. I would also like to thank my copyeditor Juli Barbato for making the process so painless, C.J. Merwild for that amazing cover, as well as Alice Speilburg and Saint Gibson.

ABOUT THE AUTHOR

David Ferraro grew up in Minnesota, where he was raised on a steady diet of comic books, horror movies, and YA novels. He graduated with a BA in English and creative writing from St. Cloud State University and currently resides in Milwaukee, Wisconsin, with his partner and a very spoiled tortoise.